A Wild Land
of the ...

LILLY. The beauty whose life would be one of secrets and discoveries...and whose future would hold both glamour and pain.

CHASE. The cavalry soldier who captured Lilly's very soul...but lost her to a conspiracy of lies.

ZEB. The patient farmer who married Lilly...but found that keeping her was no more possible than capturing the wind.

GARTH. The gambling man who wanted to seduce Lilly...and planned to break her heart in the cruelest way.

JOEY. The son who adored Lilly...and never suspected the lies she hid about their past.

**The First Time Was Only For The Moment,
But Now She Promised...**

Also by F. Rosanne Bittner

Destiny's Dawn
Frontier Fires
Savage Horizons
Texas Bride
Tennessee Bride

Published by
POPULAR LIBRARY

This Time Forever

F. Rosanne Bittner

POPULAR LIBRARY

An Imprint of Warner Books, Inc.

A Warner Communications Company

POPULAR LIBRARY EDITION

Popular Library® and the fanciful P design are registered
trademarks of Warner Books, Inc.

Cover illustration by Tom Galasinski

Popular Library books are published by
Warner Books, Inc.
666 Fifth Avenue
New York, N.Y. 10103

 A Warner Communications Company

Printed in the United States of America

First Printing: May, 1989

10 9 8 7 6 5 4 3 2 1

This book is dedicated to Beth Lieberman, my editor, who has worked so patiently with me on this and the several other books I have written for Warner. A special thank you also goes to Jeanne Tiedge, for forcing me to expect nothing less than the best from myself. *This Time Forever* has been my most difficult and challenging project; yet, in many ways, it has been the most rewarding.

From the Author:

This Time Forever is based, in part, on the true story of a woman who came to America from Scotland and traveled west with the Mormons. Lyrics in this novel are from actual Mormon hymns. Although many of the historical events in this story are true, including the hardships encountered by the Mormons on their journey west, all characters in this novel, and the details involving their lives, are a product of the author's imagination.

As to locations mentioned in this story: the Mormon city of Nauvoo was located in western Illinois; the temporary Mormon settlement established on the journey west, called Winter Quarters, was located in what is now Florence, Nebraska, a suburb of Omaha; and the Mormon migration westward basically followed what is now called the Oregon Trail and the Hastings Cutoff into Utah. Actually, the Mormons are the ones who opened this road—cutting trees, building bridges, and in general, making it more passable for the thousands who followed on their way to Oregon.

The use of the word *Gentile* in this novel was used by Mormons to refer to anyone who was not Jewish or Mormon. The Mormon practice of referring to themselves as *Saints* comes not from thinking of themselves as heavenly beings who are above other humans, but rather as followers of Christ, who were called saints. The term simply refers, in their faith, to anyone who is a believer in the Church of Jesus Christ of Latter-day Saints.

It was in the springtime of her life that he came,
Most unexpectedly...
His promises were sweet, as was the summer
    love they shared.

But then came winter, and he was gone.
Her heart was as cold as the winter snows.
And in the spring, it did not warm.

It was the autumn of her life that he returned,
Most unexpectedly...

This time forever....

PART I

Chapter One

March 1845

Sixteen-year-old Lilly Brannigan shivered against the cold, damp wind, and wrestled with the terror she felt at the sight and sound of her mother's coffin splashing into the gray Atlantic waters. Lilly wanted desperately to cry, but the events of the past several weeks seemed so unreal to her that it was difficult to grasp the reality of this moment. Instead, she clung to the railing of the massive cargo ship, watching the spot where her mother's coffin was slowly sinking.

And should we die before our journey's through,
Happy day! All is well!

Nearby, the small group of newly converted Latter-day Saints sang their hymn of joy in death and of sacrifice and toil for their cause. Lilly hardly heard the words. She blamed these people for her mother's death, for if her mother had not embraced the Mormon religion, she would never have left Scotland.

We then are free from toil and sorrow, too;
With the just we shall dwell!

The ship rose and fell in gentle sways while the crew went about their duties. They were hard men, to whom death at sea was common. None had any particular interest in Lilly's loss, although all of them did have an interest in her beauty. There was not a man on board who had not noticed the fair young woman from Scotland, whose wide-set green eyes defied her innocence, and whose auburn hair fell in thick, gentle waves over slender shoulders, leading to full breasts

3

and a tiny waist. The plain gray dress and brown, frayed cape Lilly wore did little to detract from her natural beauty.

Hiram Williams, a Latter-day Saint missionary, read to the little gathering of mourners from the Book of Mormon. Hiram was a gentle but stern man, short and rather portly, with blue eyes that could be coldly critical, but usually sparkled with kindness. The lovely passages about life after death that Hiram read were no comfort to Lilly. Nothing could soothe the agony she now felt.

"Sister Frances Brannigan is with God now," Hiram was saying. "May her joy be boundless. One day all of us will be with her again. God bless her soul."

The eulogy and hymn singing were finished, and the little gathering broke up. Someone touched Lilly's shoulder. "Do you want to go below, child?"

The voice belonged to Frieda Dutch, another convert from Scotland, who had first befriended Lilly's mother and brought her into the religious sect headed for the Mormon city of Nauvoo in America.

Lilly continued to watch the spot where her mother's coffin had disappeared. "I just want to go back to Scotland," she answered, her voice sounding strangely distant.

"Life will be much better for you in America, Sister Lilly —you'll see. We will all look after you when we get to Nauvoo."

"I'm not a Mormon, Mrs. Dutch, and now I never will be," Lilly told her in a quivering voice. "This is *their* fault!"

Frieda smoothed the girl's hair. "You're wrong, Sister Lilly. Your mother is happier now than she ever would have been slaving away in that textile mill back in Glasgow. This is what she wanted for both of you." The woman sighed deeply. "She wanted to get you away from all that ugliness and start a new life in America. Oh, I'll miss her very much." Her voice broke on the words. "She was a good, good friend."

Lilly stared at the water. Frieda was a kind and loving woman with three children of her own, but her presence did little to ease Lilly's sorrow. She had left Scotland, probably forever, because her mother had wanted to live among these Latter-day Saints. Her mother was not the only one who had

died from the strange sickness. Several others had been lost
during the long voyage.

Frieda patted her shoulder. "I'll leave you alone for a
while, dear."

As Lilly watched Frieda's retreating figure, tears began to
stream down her face. She stood at the railing, alone. The
realization that her mother was dead clawed at her stomach
and brought an unfamiliar tightness to her chest. She leaned
her head on her arm, and began to sob like a little girl.

Lilly suddenly realized that her mother would never see
her new home. She decided she would never join the Mormons, no matter how kind they might be to her. She wanted
desperately to go back to Scotland—to open her eyes and
discover that none of this had happened. There she would
be, back at Paisley, in the little cottage where they had lived
before her father's death—before she and her mother had
left to work in the textile mills. She would not miss the
smell of Glasgow and the dirty skies above it. But she would
miss the Lowlands, and the secret place in the foothills behind the cottage, where she had gone when she wanted to be
alone.

There Lilly would sing. Her mother had often told her she
would be a famous singer someday. At her secret place in
the foothills, she used to sing to an imaginary audience,
opening her arms and letting her voice pour through the
meadows. She would pretend she was the greatest singer in
all the world, and that her audience was enraptured by her
performance.

Lilly was sure she would never see her secret place again.
She missed the Grampian Mountains and Ben Nevis, the
high mountain peak she used to be able to see from her
hideaway. But the Mormon missionaries from America had
told her that soon after arriving at Nauvoo, the entire city of
Latter-day Saints would set out for lands farther west, where
they hoped to find a place to call their own—a place they
called their "Zion." There were supposedly mountains where
they were going—maybe even higher than Ben Nevis.

Lilly was confused about why thousands of Mormons
would need or want to pick up and move into a supposedly
unsettled land, where wild Indians even roamed. There was

some kind of trouble at Nauvoo, she had heard, but no one had told her exactly what had happened. "All of you must be brave and ready for ridicule from our Gentile neighbors," Hiram Williams had told the converts. "Until we find our Zion, life will be dangerous for you at Nauvoo. But we believe God is with us and will sustain us. We take care of our own, and all our needs are provided by our own hands."

Lilly wondered what kind of people lived in the land called America, where there was supposed to be religious freedom. She reasoned there must be something bad about the Mormons—something she didn't know yet.

Salty ocean water lightly sprayed her face, mixing with her tears.

"Please come below, Sister Lilly," came a man's voice. "You should rest."

Lilly turned to face Hiram Williams. His blue eyes studied her with almost fatherly affection. Hiram was the self-appointed leader of the group of Mormon missionaries bringing the new converts home with them.

"I'm so sorry about your mother, Sister Lilly."

It was not without a sense of guilt that Lilly refused to acknowledge the apology. She wanted Hiram to feel bad. Blaming someone for her mother's death somehow made her feel better.

"She wouldn't have died if we had stayed in Scotland," she pouted.

"You can't know that for certain, child. God thought it best to take her now, and might have done so even if you were still in Scotland. And then what would you have done? At least she died a happy woman, Lilly, knowing she had gotten you away from Glasgow and the mills."

The air was beginning to cool. Lilly pulled her cape closer as the ship rose gently again. She looked up at the billowing sails of the mainmast.

"But, I don't want to go to America—not without my mother. Can't I please go back to Scotland, Mr. Williams?" Lilly's pleading eyes met Hiram's.

"And what is there to go back to, Sister Lilly—the mills? You're a young woman alone now, and Glasgow is no place for you. It wasn't, even when your mother was alive. You have no money to get you back, and no family to turn to when you get there. We are your family now." He put a hand on her arm. "I have a daughter nearly the same age as you. I want you to know you have a home with me and my family. I would like you to stay with us when we get to Nauvoo. I feel responsible for you."

Lilly studied his eyes. She liked and trusted Hiram, but took note of his stern countenance. What would it be like living under the same roof with him? In her confusion and ignorance of the details of the Mormon faith, she wondered if Hiram meant that he wanted her for a second wife. She knew some Mormon men took more than one, but she didn't know why—nor did she personally believe it was right. She drew in her breath and quickly wiped her red, puffy eyes.

"I'll not be a second wife to any man," she announced proudly.

Hiram smiled, his eyes sparkling with amusement. "I wasn't asking that of you, Sister Lilly. You would be more like a daughter—a companion for my Laura. She's fifteen."

Lilly reddened deeply. She wanted to cry all over again for her stupidity. She turned to look out over the waters again. "I . . . I don't like being indebted to anyone," she told Hiram. "I'll earn my keep, Mr. Williams."

"You don't have to worry about that, Sister Lilly. And I do wish you would call me Brother Hiram."

Lilly took a handkerchief from her pocket and blew her nose. "I can't get used to saying *sister* and *brother*. And I'm not Mormon, Mr. Williams—I'm Presbyterian. I . . . I have a right to believe however I want."

"Of course you do. But there is little difference in our faiths, Lilly. There are many things you don't understand yet, but there is plenty of time for all that. I'm only here to tell you that you are welcome in our home. I own a little shoe factory at Nauvoo, and we have a fine brick home with lots of rooms. Of course, we'll be leaving Nauvoo within a year or so to find our Zion, but I promise you that wherever we settle, we'll build an even bigger and more beautiful city. And no matter what happens, we'll protect you and provide for you."

Lilly knew she had little choice. No one was going to turn

back the ship. And even if she could go back to Scotland,
there was nothing there for her now.

"Thank you, Mr. Williams. I'll try not to be a bother to
anyone."

"You would never be that." He took hold of her arm.
"Come below now and rest. The air up here is chilly and
damp."

Lilly turned reluctantly. The coffin had long since disappeared from sight. Her mother was gone forever, and so was
Scotland. She walked with Hiram to the wooden steps that
led to the cargo hold below, where forty-five people—Mormon missionaries and their new converts—had been quar-
tered during the long voyage. They were good, kind people,
but all the kindness in the world would not change the fact
that her mother was dead.

Lilly hated being dependent on these people, who she felt
were the cause of her predicament. She vowed inwardly that
one day soon, she would be independent of these Mormons
and make a new life for herself in the land called America.
As she reached the hold below, Lilly pressed her lips tightly
together and nodded to the others. Nothing could ease the
helpless feeling that overwhelmed her. She crawled over
several piles of cloth to the little cubbyhole she had fash-
ioned for herself amid the cargo and she buried her face in
her blankets. Then, pulling them over herself for warmth,
she cried herself to sleep.

The ability to adjust that comes with youth, as well as the
kindness of the people around her, helped ease Lilly's grief.
Two weeks after her mother's death, their ship entered the
bustling harbor of Lake Pontchartrain at New Orleans. The
activities in the harbor captured Lilly's natural curiosity, and
the excitement of seeing a new land for the first time helped
keep her mind in the present, rather than the past.

Hundreds of windjammers peppered the harbor, most of
them with sails furled. As the ship neared it mooring, Lilly
stared at Negro slaves, some carrying cargo, others scrub-
bing the decks of ships already docked. The dark-skinned
workers were a curiosity to Lilly, and a source of pity.

"Do the Saints have slaves?" she asked Hiram.

"No, child, we think slavery is wrong. No man can own another."

Lilly felt relieved. It seemed ironic to her that a land that boasted freedom would allow the practice of slavery. She tried to ignore the poor souls, turning her eyes to the brick warehouses lining the harbor. New Orleans appeared even bigger than Glasgow. She noticed that there were no mountains on the skyline, and wondered whether there really were some farther west, or if it had all been a lie to make her feel better.

The few trees she could see were still leafless, but their branches were covered with new buds. Although it was still cold and the skies were gray, there was a smell of spring in the air. Lilly tied her bonnet tighter over her ears and pulled her wool cape over her hands to keep them warm. As the ship maneuvered closer to the docks and prepared to drop anchor, Lilly's heart pounded with a mixture of dread and anticipation. She reminded herself she was not the only foreigner in a new land here. Most of the Mormon converts who stood at the railing watching the coastline were Scottish, English, German, or Norwegian.

"Are you sure you have everything, Lilly?" Hiram asked her.

Lilly looked down at her burlap sack of clothes, all she had left to her name. "There isn't very much for me to look after," she answered.

"Well, I will make sure you have new clothes when we reach Nauvoo," the man told her. "My wife and daughter will gladly work with you to help you put together a new wardrobe."

"It's all right, Mr. Williams."

"No, no. They'll take great pleasure in it."

Hiram turned to the others in their group and raised his hands. "We are finally coming to our homeland. I think we should sing God's praises for bringing us here safely." They began a hymn of hope and joy, one Lilly had heard often. She joined in, softly at first. It had been a long, long time since she had sung. It felt good. Gradually, she raised her voice to its full potential, and all eyes turned to her. The voices of the others dimmed, but their smiles encouraged the girl to keep going alone.

Suddenly, she had an audience. Lilly found a secret joy in her performance.

"Sister Lilly!" Frieda Dutch exclaimed. "You have a *beautiful* voice. Has anyone ever told you that?"

Lilly felt the color rising in her cheeks. "My mother thought so, too. She used to say that one day I would be a great singer." A lump rose in her throat at the memory. "But, I haven't felt much like singing for a long time."

"Oh, but you must *never* stop singing, sister. God has blessed you with a voice far superior to any I have ever heard." Frieda turned to Hiram. "Brother Hiram, she is surely a special gift from God." She looked back at Lilly. "As close as your mother and I had become, I never knew about this."

Lilly reddened more at the words, but she felt a sweet satisfaction inside. For the first time in a long while, she could envision a great sea of faces before her, all enraptured by her voice.

"Well, I certainly agree about her voice, Sister Frieda," Hiram answered. He turned to Lilly with a smile, pride shining in his eyes. "Lilly, I never knew you could sing like that. Surely God led you to us."

The ship's bells clanged, and a plank was lowered for its few passengers. There was no more time to talk. Hiram picked up his baggage and urged Lilly to hurry in front of him. As they walked down to the docks together, Lilly sensed that people were staring at them.

"There's some of them Mormons," she heard one man comment in a scathing tone. She stayed close to Hiram as they hurried through the crowds on the docks. The docks were packed with people and animals, and she had enough of a job keeping Hiram in sight. They ducked around black slaves carrying heavy loads of cargo on their heads, and Lilly had to force herself not to stare at them. A young boy scurried past them, chasing some chickens that had gotten loose from a cage. Lilly glanced at the comical sight for only a moment, keeping her eyes on Hiram's nearly white hair, using it like a kind of beacon. As they passed a group of young men in military uniform, Lilly heard the word *Mexico*. She remembered hearing Hiram mention problems between that country and America, down in a place called Texas.

But there was no time to ask questions. Lilly soon found herself boarding a steamboat that would carry them north along the Mississippi to Illinois and Nauvoo. As a few of the Mormons climbed to an upper deck for a better view, Lilly hurried to the railing. She watched people boarding the riverboat. Some farther below even herded horses and cattle onto the boat, and a few rolled heavily packed wagons on board.

"Those people will be heading west from St. Louis," Hiram explained when he leaned over to see what Lilly was watching. "We'll be doing the same in another year or so. We might even go all the way to California."

The thought both frightened and fascinated Lilly. Clear back in Scotland people had talked about California. They talked about America as though it was some magical place of enchantment.

"Won't it be dangerous going into the desert?" Lilly asked.

"Oh, we'll all be together. We'll manage. And it isn't all desert, Lilly. There is some beautiful country in the west, or so I'm told. You'll even see some of those mountains you've been missing."

The steamboat was soon noisy with conversation and laughter as more and more people came aboard. Lilly could hear a cow bawling below and, somewhere in the distance, a man began playing a banjo. She jumped when the boat's steam whistle blasted its long, deep alert. A bell clanged, and a few more people hurried aboard before men pulled away the gangplank. Lilly was certain the boat would sink, but it was soon underway, smoke billowing from its tall stacks.

As she turned to drink in the sights and sounds of the big riverboat, she spotted another group of men in uniform. One of them glanced at her. He was tall and broad-shouldered, with dark-brown hair and vivid blue eyes. Their eyes held for a moment. Then, he flashed a quick smile of approval at what his eyes beheld. Lilly felt suddenly conspicuous in her old brown cape. Some of the other women on the boat wore lovely dresses of bright colors, with matching hats and parasols.

Lilly dropped her eyes, embarrassed that the young man had caught her watching him. She wished she was dressed in a pretty, bright dress, then chided herself for caring about what a perfect stranger thought of her appearance.

"We had better find a place in the cargo area where we can all stay together," Hiram told her then. "Follow me, Lilly."

Lilly picked up her bag. Unable to control the impulse, she glanced at the group of soldiers again. The one with the blue eyes was still watching her. He grinned again, nodding slightly. Lilly could not help smiling back at him. She followed Hiram then, wondering if the young man thought her too bold.

"Better keep your eyes off those women, Chase," someone said to the young man who was watching Lilly walk away. "They're Mormons. Every woman there is probably some man's second or third wife."

Chase Mitchell frowned, his blue eyes studying the long, flowing hair that hung nearly to the waist of the pretty young woman who had smiled at him. He felt a sudden, keen disappointment. "What a waste," he muttered.

The night air was alive with banjo music and laughter. Lilly lay wide awake on the sacks of feed she was using for a bed. Hiram was being as thrifty as possible, since money for missionary work came from communal donations.

"We must not waste money that others have given us through great sacrifice," Hiram often repeated. "Once we get to Nauvoo, life will be much better, and the discomfort of our trip will be over."

"If not for the Gentiles ruining our crops and constantly giving us trouble, there would be more money to go around," one of the others had grumbled that night.

"In another year we'll leave the Gentiles behind us," Hiram had answered. "We have to remember that there are many more good Gentiles than bad ones. It's our own apostates who cause the most trouble."

Lilly had asked what an *apostate* was.

"It's one of our own who, for personal reasons, deserts his faith and turns against us. They are often our worst enemies."

Lilly lay staring at the damp wooden beams overhead, lit dimly by a lantern. She wondered about apostates, about Nauvoo and what it would be like, and about the troubles the Mormons seemed to have. She could not see why outsiders would give them so much trouble. They did no one any harm, even in their practice of taking more than one wife. They had their own city, where they stayed together and kept to themselves. Perhaps if the Gentiles, as the Mormons called outsiders, better understood these people, they would leave them alone.

She sat up, frowning. She realized that she was herself a Gentile, since she had not formally declared herself a Saint. Yet, they were all being so kind to her. She still harbored a resentment toward them for her mother's death, but the hate she once felt for them had dissolved. She reasoned that she might even consider becoming a Mormon, if it were not for the polygamy. She would never, never be any man's second wife, nor could she ever share a man if she were his first wife.

The thought suddenly brought to mind the vision of the young soldier she had seen earlier. She wondered if he was one of those laughing on the deck above; if he had thought about her at all since that one glance. She sighed deeply. She would never share a handsome man like that with another woman. If such a man were her husband, she would want to keep him all to herself, to be loved by him totally, with his full attention and devotion.

She drew up her knees and chided herself for the silly thought she had just had. It was getting late, and she felt wide awake. To stay awake half the night meant she would think about her mother being dead, or about what awaited her at Nauvoo. She decided that perhaps a brisk walk would help her sleep.

She quietly moved off the feed sacks. Hiram lay snoring nearby. She moved past him and lifted her dress and slips so they wouldn't rustle as loudly, then quietly tiptoed past the others to the stairway that led above. She wondered how wrinkled she looked. There was no privacy in the cargo deck and most slept in their clothes. Lilly was anxious to have a real home where she could live like a normal human being again.

She stopped at the base of the ladder to the deck above, smoothing her dress as best she could. She climbed above, where a few people walked about. Most seemed to be at the other end of the boat, where the music could be heard. Lilly walked toward the sound, keeping to the shadows as much as possible. Several men, most of them drinking, were gathered around a man playing a banjo. Lilly realized she should not be there, but at that moment she wanted to hear the songs.

She moved up behind a pillar and watched. Several men with whiskey bottles in hand gathered in a circle then and began singing about *Home, Sweet Home*. Some of them were soldiers, dressed like the man she had seen earlier in the day. She wondered where they were from, how far they were from their own homes.

An exile from home splendor dazzles in vain;
Oh, give me my lowly thatch'd cottage again!

The words struck Lilly's heart. She thought about the little cottage near Paisley, and tears came to her eyes.

The birds singing gaily that came at my call;
Give me them with the peace of mind dearer than all.
Home, home! Sweet, sweet home!
There's no place like home! There's no place like home!

Would she ever call America home? She listened to a few more songs, and quietly hummed them to herself, concentrating on the tunes and the words. Two men walked by her, laughing and drinking, and Lilly ducked deeper into the shadows. She turned to go back to the sleeping immigrants when someone suddenly moved in front of her, his tall frame blocking her way. Lilly gasped and stepped back slightly.

"Hello," came a man's voice. "I waited a long time to see if you would come out of that hole down there."

Lilly started to dart around him, but he grabbed her arm.

"Hey, it's all right. It's me—the man you saw earlier, remember?" He pulled her into the light of a lantern, and Lilly looked up into the face of the young man with the blue eyes. He smiled for her again, and some of her fear left her.

"I . . . I shouldn't be here," she told him. "Please let me go!"

"Why? You some old codger's second or third wife or something? My friends said you're with Mormons. You a Mormon?"

"No!" She felt almost guilty at answering so quickly, for feeling embarrassed that he would think she was Mormon. Poor Hiram would be hurt if he knew. "My . . . my mother was Mormon. She decided to come to America with them, but she died on the trip here."

A look of true sympathy passed through the young man's eyes. "I'm sorry." He let go of her arm.

"What kind of accent is that, anyway?" he asked. "Kind of like singing, without singing at all. It's pretty."

"I'm from Scotland."

His blue eyes studied her intently. "What's your name?" he asked.

"I don't think it's your business, sir."

He grinned, feeling a sudden urge to kiss her slightly pouting lips. Her clothes were worn, but they were clean. She was the most beautiful creature he had ever met.

"Suit yourself," he told her. "I don't mind telling you *my* name. It's Chase Mitchell."

Lilly folded her arms and stepped back, studying the high

collar of his blue-gray uniform. "Are you going to war or something?"

He gave her a teasing look. "Would it make you feel sorry for me?"

She shrugged. "Why should it? I don't even know you."

He shook his head and laughed. "No, I'm not going to war—not yet, at least. But it looks like there *will* be a war between us and Mexico, eventually. The Mexicans just can't get it through their heads that Texas belongs to the Union now."

"I wouldn't know about those things. I've just set foot in America. I'm on my way to Nauvoo with the Mormons."

"I know where Nauvoo is. I'm from Illinois, myself."

"Really?" The remark stirred her interest. "What is it like? Are there mountains there?"

He laughed lightly. "Hardly. A few high hills."

"We have mountains in Scotland. It's very beautiful."

"You must miss it. Will you go back?"

She dropped her eyes. "There is nothing left there for me. I'll be staying on with the Mormons until I decide what I should do."

"I've heard of Nauvoo. People talk about it—about the Mormons. I don't pay much attention to most of the rumors. As industrious as the Mormons are, I figure they can't be all bad, except for the men being able to have more than one wife. That's got people riled." He frowned, bending a little closer. "You never answered my question earlier. You aren't some old man's second or third wife, are you?"

Lilly stiffened. "I'd not be second or third wife to *any* man! I think it's wrong. Right now I'm *no* man's wife!"

His eyes moved over her again. "That so?" He shook his head. "I sure am sorry that I'll be getting off this boat tomorrow—and that you'll be going on to Nauvoo. I don't suppose I'll ever see you again."

Their eyes held for a moment. To Lilly's amazement, she realized his remark made her sad. "I suppose not," she answered, holding up her chin to show she didn't care. "It makes little difference. I'll be going below now, where I belong."

"Mmmm-hmmm," he answered, his blue eyes sparkling.

"Won't you at least tell me your name? What would it matter that I know it?"

Lilly pushed a piece of hair behind her ear, thinking about how ragged she must look to him. "It's Lilly Brannigan."

He breathed deeply, as though to digest the name. "Lilly Brannigan. It has a nice ring to it. Sounds like a name that should be on a theater bill, don't you think? Someone famous. Lilly Brannigan."

Lilly realized only then that he had been drinking. He put out his arm when he spoke the name, as though to announce her, and he swaggered slightly when he did so.

"I have to get back," she told him.

He bowed slightly. "Goodbye then, Lilly Brannigan. I will remember you always, as I go off to war, and throughout my life."

She smiled slightly, thinking he was only exaggerating because of the whiskey. "Goodbye, Mr. Mitchell."

"Chase. Call me Chase."

"It makes little difference. As you said, I'll not see you again. And a young woman does not call a man by his first name when she hardly knows him."

"Oh, certainly not!" Lilly felt embarrassed, realizing she had been much too forward. She hurried away, refusing to look back at him. Yet in her mind, his face was as clear as if he stood before her. She hurried below, walking quickly back to her makeshift bed, wishing inwardly that she had been wearing a lovely dress, and that her hair had been done up in a beautiful coif when Chase Mitchell had spotted her. He was a man who probably had many women interested in him. She chastised herself then for caring.

She glanced at Hiram cautiously. He was still asleep. Lilly breathed a sigh of relief, then climbed back up on the feed bags, realizing that now she would have trouble dozing off. Her heart was pounding so hard that she could feel it without putting a hand to her chest. The encounter with Chase Mitchell seemed like a strange dream, and she wondered why it saddened her to realize that he would be getting off the boat tomorrow, and she would not see him again. She suddenly felt guilty for not wishing him good luck, should he have to go to war.

Chapter Two

On the journey north, Lilly began to learn just how big America was. They had been traveling over ten days, winding through rugged, tree-lined country, passing through several states on the banks of the Mississippi River—Louisiana, Mississippi, Arkansas, Missouri, Tennessee, Illinois. Lilly wondered if she would ever remember them all. She knew there was a great controversy brewing over the issue of slavery, and was glad that the farther north their riverboat traveled, the fewer slaves she saw.

In Louisiana, the trees had looked ready to leaf out, but in Illinois, most of them didn't even have buds yet, and snow lay in little frozen patches scattered throughout vast, open prairie land.

Small towns sprawled lazily along the river, all seemingly on the edge of civilization. Beyond the western riverbank lay a land still mostly wild and unsettled—a land of Indians and bears and mountain men. This much Lilly had learned by listening to passengers talk—especially men dressed in clothes Hiram told her were made from deerskin.

It seemed that at nearly every stop along the way such men either boarded or disembarked the riverboat. One particularly fascinating character had been all the way to California and back. Lilly wanted desperately to ask him about the mountains—how high they were, and how wide. But she was afraid to talk to the wild-looking stranger. At night she lay awake, full of anticipation and terror, wondering if the Mormons would really go west, and if she might be wise to find a way to get away from them before they began such a dangerous journey.

After three more days the riverboat finally reached Nauvoo. Its whistle blew long and loud as the captain maneuvered the vessel against a dock. Lilly could see a city not far from the river's edge, gleaming in the morning sunlight. She could already tell it was better kept than other cities she had seen along the way. On a distant hill she noticed the beginnings of a great stone building.

"That will be our temple!" Hiram told her, ecstatic himself at finally being home. "All of us have sacrificed goods and money toward the building of the temple. It will be finished in another few months. It's made almost entirely of limestone." He breathed deeply, as though suddenly revitalized. "Thank God we're home at last!"

Lilly realized this new land would have to be her home, too. The green hills of Scotland were gone forever, and a sudden pang of desperate homesickness stabbed at her heart.

Hiram led her from the boat, sweeping one hand in the direction of Nauvoo. "There is your new home, Lilly. We build our temple even though we are persecuted and are being forced to vacate Nauvoo. The temple is sacred to us—a place where men and women are united in marriage for all eternity, where baptisms and other sacred ceremonies are performed. If the Gentiles want to run us out of Nauvoo, we will leave behind a city far grander than any they have built. Already Nauvoo rivals Chicago in size, and far surpasses any other American city I have seen in beauty. We are nearly eleven thousand people strong now, and every week new immigrants land on these shores. Nauvoo is a living example of how we prosper without the help of the Gentiles."

Lilly took a deep breath for courage. People and wagons were coming toward the dock. In minutes, people from town began to greet the immigrants warmly as they disembarked the riverboat. There were many smiles, and some tears, as some of the missionaries were greeted by family members. Lilly realized with greater clarity how much their religion must mean to these Latter-day Saints, for Hiram and the men with him had been away from home and family for months. It had been a hardship for the missionaries, and for those left behind; and, according to Hiram, Mormon missionaries were scattered throughout several other countries. Greeting immigrants was a common and joyful experience for those who approached them now.

Lilly searched the crowd, wondering if any of them were part of Hiram's family.

"Here's our ride," Hiram told her then, indicating a waiting flatbed wagon. He threw his baggage and Lilly's into the back of it and helped her board, then climbed up onto the seat with the driver.

"This is Brother Zebulah Adams, Lilly," he said, nodding toward a gaunt, rather homely young man sitting in the driver's seat.

Zebulah turned and Lilly nodded to him. He smiled softly, but reddened and said nothing.

"Zeb will take us to my home," Hiram explained. "Brother Zeb, this is Lilly Brannigan, from Scotland. She lost her mother on the trip over, and she'll be living with me and my family for the time being."

Zeb tipped his hat slightly. "Sorry about your mother, Miss Brannigan. But you'll have a fine home with Brother Hiram." Zeb's face reddened even more at having to speak to the pretty young woman from Scotland. He turned his attention immediately to his team of horses, deciding it wouldn't be wise to let his gaze linger, even though Lilly Brannigan was the prettiest thing he had ever seen. After all, perhaps Hiram Williams meant her to be a second wife.

As Zeb snapped his team into motion, Lilly settled into the soft hay of the wagon bed. The wagon bounced over still-frozen ground. At times it slowed, when coming to a section of road that was thawing. The land bordering the river was especially soft and swampy, but as they neared the city, Lilly paid no attention to the mud. Nauvoo lay in tidy, blocked streets, some bricked, some made more passable by buried timbers. Most of the buildings were also made of brick. Hiram pointed out various businesses, including a building that had WILLIAMS BOOTERY painted on the front window.

"That's my factory," he told Lilly. "My brother has been taking care of it for me. And you should know that nearly all the bricks you see here, in the street and the buildings, were made by Mormons. We are almost entirely self-sufficient, Lilly."

Lilly stared at the loveliest city she had ever seen. Vacant lots were dormant for the moment, but it was obvious they had been plowed that past autumn.

"Later this spring Nauvoo will look to you like a garden paradise," Hiram explained. "We have no ugly areas between buildings. We grow vegetables and flowers wherever there is room, and later this summer, the fields beyond the city will be alive with corn and grain. Some call us the City of Gardens."

"I wish Mother could have lived to see this," she told Hiram. "She would have loved it here."

"Yes, and we love it, too. But, I'm sorry to say, we won't enjoy it for much longer." He turned to Zeb. "How have things been, Brother Zeb?"

Zebulah shook his head. "Bad. The apostates and Gentiles print so many lies about us. People think we're all crazy troublemakers, and that we're too powerful here. Brother Tod Miller's farm was raided just last week—they killed a lot of his stock and burned a barn that was full of feed. We've been pooling what we can to get him restocked."

Lilly shivered at the words, finding it amazing that anyone would want to harm such peaceful, generous people.

"Brigham Young already has men building wagons," Zeb continued, "and this year, we're suppposed to put up extra food when the crops come in. I don't think there's any doubt we'll be heading west, maybe as early as next spring."

Hiram pointed then. "Up ahead there, against the hill, Lilly, is my home."

In spite of Zeb's bad news, Hiram's face was rosy red with excitement. It made his hair seem even whiter. He was pointing to a pleasant, two-story brick home surrounded by a low picket fence. Lilly's stomach churned with a mixture of dread and anticipation. She would be an outsider in his home, but it was a beautiful house—much finer than any she had ever lived in.

As they gradually came closer, a woman and four children ran outside. Hiram climbed down from the wagon before it came to a full stop, and Lilly watched longingly as all four

children and the woman hugged him. The woman was crying. Lilly wanted to cry, too. How she wished she had a
mother to hold her, a father to run to.

Zeb Adams came to the back of the wagon and offered his
hand to help Lilly down; when Lilly grasped hold, she
thought how surprisingly big and strong his hand seemed for
his thin frame.

"Welcome to Nauvoo, Sister Brannigan," the man told
her.

"Thank you, Mr. Adams."

Zeb reddened again and turned to unload the baggage. He
tipped his hat to her, then climbed back into the wagon and
drove off. Lilly stood awkwardly, waiting until Hiram and
his family acknowledged her. He dragged his wife forward.
"Mary, this is Sister Lilly Brannigan, from Scotland."

The woman's smile instantly left her, and her dark eyes
turned suddenly cold.

"How do you do, Sister Brannigan?"

"Hello, Mrs. Williams."

Hiram turned back to his children, too engrossed in them
to notice his wife's reaction. He exclaimed over how they
had grown as he hustled them toward the house.

"Come inside!" he told them all. "I'll explain more about
Lilly and we'll get her settled in." As the man whisked
everyone into the house, Lilly struggled against tears and an
urge to turn and run. She felt even worse when she caught a
cold stare from Hiram's eldest daughter, whose dark eyes
showed the same disappointment and seeming animosity as
her mother. This was surely the young woman to whom
Hiram meant Lilly to be a companion, but Lilly saw no
friendship in the way the girl looked at her now.

Lilly could not imagine why mother and daughter seemed
so cold, when they hardly knew her. Hiram led them all into
the parlor. Lilly found herself wishing she could melt between the cracks of the polished hardwood floor.

Mary Williams was a short, dark woman, slightly plump,
but solid. Lilly supposed that if the woman were smiling at
the moment, she would be attractive; at the same time, her
nearly black eyes could be almost frightening when penetrating deeply as they were now.

All four Williams children looked like their mother, with the same dark eyes and hair, the same facial features, and skin that looked too white against such dark hair. The girls were not especially pretty, and the boys were not what one would call handsome. They were all simply pleasantly plain, and for the moment, uncomfortably discerning.

"Lilly, this, of course, is my wife Mary," Hiram spoke up.

Mary finally gave her a grudging and obviously forced smile that was stiff and meaningless. Hiram moved on to the rest of him family. "And this is Laura, my fifteen-year-old. Her sister Beth is eleven; Gerald, here, is ten; and our baby, Henry, is seven."

Henry fidgeted, scratching his head. Beth just blinked and stared, and Gerald smiled.

"How do you do," Lilly said, nodding to them.

"You're very . . . beautiful, Sister Brannigan," Mary Williams spoke up, almost sadly. The woman looked at her husband.

Hiram frowned, finally noticing the look of near anger and disappointment in his wife's eyes. Her reaction surprised him, for Mary Williams was normally a loving, gracious woman.

"Lilly's mother accepted our faith back in Scotland," he explained to all of them. "On the trip here, she died and was buried at sea. I told Lilly she could have a home here with us."

Mary seemed to soften, and Laura gasped. "Your mother died coming over?"

Lilly nodded, struggling now not to cry. The memory would not have hit her so hard, if not for the cold reaction she had felt from all of them.

"I . . . I can go live with someone else if you prefer."

"No, no!" Mary spoke up, looking suddenly ashamed. "Hiram already offered you a home here." The woman looked at her husband. "Do you really think it's proper, Hiram? Several of the others . . . keep two homes."

Hiram frowned. "Two homes? Whatever are you talking about, Mary?"

The woman began to redden. "Well, I . . . she's a young

woman, Hiram, and homeless. She traveled clear across the ocean with you. I supposed . . ."

"I don't want you to have another wife, Father," Laura blurted out, her eyes brimming with tears. "I know Brother Smith made it a law, and Brother Young already has several wives, but—"

"Hush, Laura!" Mary put in. "You have no right to speak to your father that way."

Hiram stiffened.

"You think I intend to *marry* Lilly?" Hiram asked, his blue eyes wide with surprise.

Beth covered her mouth and snickered.

"Mary! If it were true, do you think after all these months apart I would have just brought home a second wife without speaking to you first?"

The woman looked at the floor. "I'm sorry, Hiram. Others have taken second and third wives. I just thought . . ."

"Well, you all thought wrong. I brought Lilly here because she is homeless, and since her mother had converted to our faith, I felt responsible for her daughter. Lilly has not even decided yet if she wants to join our faith. She is a Gentile, but she is a sweet young woman, and I look upon her as a daughter, as I hoped you would do." He turned his attention to Laura. "And I thought she would be a good companion for you, Laura. You can teach each other about your different countries, and you can help Lilly feel welcome here at Nauvoo."

Mary smiled sheepishly at Lilly. "Forgive us, Sister Brannigan, I mean, Lilly," the woman spoke up. "Even if Hiram had brought you here as a second wife, we should have welcomed you fully into our household."

Lilly held her chin proudly. "I would never be a second wife to any man. And as I said, if you would rather I went to live someplace else—"

"Oh, no!" Laura stepped forward. "I'm sorry, too, Lilly. You're most welcome here."

The smiles on Mary and Laura's faces seemed to completely change their appearance. Now their dark eyes sparkled. Beth giggled more and the two boys grinned, young Henry not even sure what was so funny. Laura took hold of

Lilly's arm. "Come upstairs with me and I'll show you my room. Bring your bag."

"You all have chores to do. Don't be too long, Laura," her mother told her.

Lilly and Laura went upstairs, and the other three children, full of excited curiosity, followed. Mary turned to Hiram.

"Your brother kept the shoe factory running smoothly, but raiders burned out the Millers two days ago. They killed several of his cattle. Things have only gotten worse since Brother Smith was murdered." Her eyes teared. "Oh, Hiram, the Gentiles say the most terrible things about us!"

He grasped her arms. "Zeb Adams already told me about the Millers, but it's to be expected. You know that, Mary." His eyes shone with love. "I am so happy to be home. How could you think I would bring along a second wife when I have missed you so?"

She dropped her eyes again. "Several others are doing it. It's almost expected of you, Hiram. Brother Smith declared it a divine requirement."

"In accordance with ancient biblical teachings. But he also stressed it must be done out of love, not lust; and out of necessity. It's a way of taking care of our own, Mary—you know that—so that there are no homeless widows and no children without the leadership of a father. And no man shall take another wife without being able to provide for her and for their children. And with all that is happening at Nauvoo, the possibility of leaving here and heading into an unknown land, I am not going to take on any more than what I have right now—nor do I have any desire to do so." He kissed her forehead. "Now, we'll talk no more about it. Let's concentrate on making Lilly feel at home here. I'm sure that, inside, she's afraid and confused and feeling quite lonely."

Mary smiled faintly, wiping at tears. "I was so sure . . . she's so beautiful, Hiram. We'll have young men knocking at the door constantly."

"And I'll turn them all away. Lilly has some adjusting to do first, and besides that, she's still too young to be serious about a man. And she's a Gentile, Mary. A Mormon man should marry a Mormon woman. It's only right."

"Yes, Hiram." The woman straightened. "I'll see to lunch."

He caught her hand. "And tonight we will retire early," he added.

The woman reddened deeply and hurried off to the kitchen.

"Oh, Mary," Hiram spoke up.

She stopped and turned. "Yes?"

"Wait until you hear Lilly sing. I don't think there is anyone in all of Nauvoo who can match her. Later this evening, I want you to play the piano for her, and we'll get her to sing for us. I'm going to ask special permission from the council for her to sing at our services. Gentile or not, her voice is truly a gift from God and should not be denied us. I am convinced that that is why God directed her to Nauvoo."

The woman smiled. "Then, I look forward to hearing her. Right now, we need our hearts lifted by song." She hesitated a moment. "Brigham Young still says we will have to leave, Hiram. How I hate the thought of moving, and starting all over again."

"I know, Mary. But we'll find Zion this time. You'll see."

The Williams household was run by stern leadership combined with love. Everyone had duties to perform. Every night after dinner, Hiram read to the family from the Book of Mormon. It quickly became obvious to Lilly that within the Mormon family, the man had the first and last word, and the woman was usually expected to remain silent.

Out of respect, Lilly sat patiently through the nightly worship, still determined she would not herself become a Latter-day Saint.

The Williams children were fascinated by Lilly's lilting accent, and every night after worship they begged her to sing Scottish folk songs for them. Lilly loved it. She sang hymns in church, along with everyone else, until several people asked Hiram if he would allow her to sing solo, even though she had not yet accepted the Mormon faith for herself.

Although she was beginning to feel more at home at Nauvoo, Lilly sometimes felt almost imprisoned—cut off from a world outside that she knew nothing about. Not all Gentiles were their enemy. In fact, outsiders were a common sight in Nauvoo. They came there sometimes to trade, sometimes just to get a look at the "strange Mormons."

But, for the most part, the world beyond Nauvoo seemed hostile and dangerous. Much of the trouble was caused by disgruntled apostates. Lies led to increased misunderstandings. People feared the huge voting bloc the Mormons represented, loathed their practice of polygamy, and spread stories about alleged sinful doings within the sect. Raids continued to be staged frequently on outlying Mormon homes and farms.

Amid the havoc that surrounded Nauvoo, Lilly settled into the Williams household. She was given chores and duties, the same as the other children, and she worked hard on her studies. Together, Lilly, Laura, and Mary created a complete new wardrobe for her—lovely but simple and prim dresses.

Still, no matter how plain her clothing, Lilly's beauty brought stares and frequent visits from young men. Hiram always turned away gentlemen callers. Lilly found herself resenting the fact that Hiram made such decisions for her, but she felt obligated to abide by his rules as long as she was dependent on him.

She had dared to complain once to Mary, to no avail. Mormon women did not defy their husbands' decisions. Mary was a kind and generous woman, who cared for Lilly as well as any mother, but she was rather distant, and Lilly could not quite warm to her. She liked schedules, worried about proper behavior, and insisted on an immaculate home. Lilly often thought she seemed to be more concerned about dust than about her rights as a woman and wife.

There were nights when Lilly lay awake thinking about Scotland and her mother. She wondered if she would ever be free of Hiram's stern hand, but dreaded the thought of leaving Nauvoo. Her only comfort was Laura—a totally sweet, giving, friendly girl who seemed to all but worship Lilly. There were many nights when the girl kept her awake with a barrage of questions about Scotland and what it was like working in the textile mills, how she felt when her mother had died at sea, what it was like to sail across the ocean.

"You're the bravest person I've ever known," she told

Lilly one winter night. It was January 1846, and Lilly had been at Nauvoo for ten months.

"That's silly," Lilly answered. "Many of the people right here in Nauvoo are much braver. And you'll have to be brave yourself, Laura, if we go west."

Winter winds howled outside.

"Brigham Young has sent scouts into the west to find the best place to go," Laura answered.

The room was dark, the house quiet.

"I don't like to think about leaving," Lilly said softly. "I still get homesick for Scotland. Now, this is becoming home to me. I don't want to leave again. I haven't had a real home since my mother and I had to leave Paisley."

"At least we would all be together. And Father says we'll build a city even bigger and more beautiful than Nauvoo."

"But they have only just finished the temple. It's so beautiful. What a shame to have to leave it."

"I know. But you must understand how important it is to us, to find a place where people will leave us alone. Down in Missouri we had terrible trouble, too. I remember the awful attack at Haun's Mill, just before Henry was born. Some men and women, and even children were killed. It was a terrible thing. And then Gentiles captured and killed Brother Joseph Smith."

"I don't understand why people behave that way. Back in Glasgow there were ruffians who picked on me and my mother for no reason—just because we were helpless and poor, I suppose. Someday I am going to be wealthy and independent, Laura, and no one will take advantage of me."

"Won't you ever become a Saint, Lilly? We so want you to be one of us."

"Never. That would mean that when I marry, my husband could take another wife. I'll never share a man."

"I would, if he thought it was God's will and a necessary thing." Laura sat up, wide awake even though it was late. "Do you think much about men, Lilly? You're so beautiful. A lot of young men ask me about you, and I think Zeb Adams has a crush on you. He's not much for looks, is he? But he's a good man."

"I could never be interested in a Mormon man." Lilly got up and moved onto Laura's bed, beside her. "There is one man, though, who I've never forgotten—the only one who made me feel all funny inside."

"Oh, tell me who, Lilly!" Laura grasped Lilly's hand.

"I met him only once, and I'll probably never see him again," Lilly said. "It was on the riverboat. His name was Chase Mitchell, and he was the most handsome young man! He was a soldier. With all this talk about a possible war with Mexico, he could already be down in Texas now, for all I know."

"Oh, Lilly, however did you meet him?"

"I saw him standing with some others when we boarded the riverboat. And later that night, while everyone else was asleep, I sneaked up to the deck to hear the banjo playing. I remember one song, called *Home, Sweet Home*. When I turned to go back, he was there. He stepped right out in front of me, took hold of my arm, and insisted on introducing himself!" Lilly sighed deeply. "He had the most beautiful eyes I have ever seen. I have never forgotten his face."

"Lilly! Weren't you afraid?"

"I was at first, but he had such a lovely smile. I found myself feeling sorry for him because he was a soldier, and might be going far away to fight a war. I never saw him again after that night, and it has always made me kind of sad."

Laura sighed. "I would have been frightened to death." She moved to scoot under her covers; her feet were cold. "You shouldn't think about him now, Lilly. You'll never see him again."

"I know. But it was all so strange, as though it had some meaning. I got such a wonderful feeling the first time our eyes met—kind of weak and happy and excited and afraid, all at the same time. He said he liked my name—said it sounded like the name of someone famous. I would like to be famous someday, Laura—perhaps as a singer. I would like to sing in an opera house."

"You probably could. I've never heard a voice like yours,

Lilly. When you sing for the people here, it gets so quiet you could hear a feather fall."

"I'm happy when I sing. It's a kind of comfort to me." Lilly's eyes teared. "After my father died and my mother and I went to Glasgow, I didn't feel like singing for a long time. And I didn't realize how much I actually *needed* to sing, until the day our ship landed at New Orleans and I sang with Hiram and the others. It's like . . . I don't know . . . like I *have* to sing in order to feel good inside. I love singing for others. Do you think that sounds selfish?"

"Goodness, no! It would be selfish *not* to sing—to deny the rest of us the pleasure of listening to you."

Lilly laughed lightly, embarrassed. She wiped a sudden tear from her cheek. "Sometimes, I wonder how singing will fit into my life. I'm so mixed up, Laura. I don't want to live forever with the Mormons, but I have no place else to go, and no money to support myself."

"Don't you like it here with us? I thought we were best friends."

Lilly looked at the girl, whose dark eyes shone like marbles in the moonlight. "We are, and I do like it here, but I don't really belong. Since leaving Paisley, I've never felt I belonged anywhere. It frightens me sometimes. When they dropped my mother's coffin into the ocean, I felt myself drifting away with her, like a person lost forever at sea."

"But, you'll never really be lost as long as you stay with us, Lilly. We all love you." Laura moved closer and hugged Lilly. "I hope you'll always stay." She released her hold. "Mother and Father are so stern sometimes, and when I talk to you, it's kind of like being free, doing things I will never really do, through you—like talking to that Gentile soldier. What a bold thing to do! And just think—in another month, you will sing for our first temple service! Oh, the temple is so beautiful! And you've been practicing so long. Next month, you will have the biggest audience you have ever had. Are you nervous, Lilly?"

Excitement and anticipation swept through her, leaving goose bumps on her skin. "Yes. But it will be exciting."

Lilly smiled and squeezed Laura's hand. "We had better get some sleep."

Lilly moved to her own bed and crawled under the covers. She closed her eyes, thinking about Chase Mitchell.

"Do you think that soldier you met ever thinks about you, Lilly?" Laura whispered.

To Lilly's surprise, her heart leaped at the thought. Telling Laura about him had made the memory so vivid again. "No," she answered, "I don't think so."

The day had finally come. Lilly had practiced her songs daily for two months, and now she would be a part of the dedication of the new temple of the Latter-day Saints. The grand, gleaming limestone building meant everything to these people who had given her a home, and she wanted to sing her best for them.

She walked to the building with Hiram and his family, breathing deeply to calm her nerves. The building's white-painted spire seemed to reach for the heavens. The temple was the most noticeable and dominant building in all of Nauvoo. Even Gentiles from outside came to the city to view the magnificent structure.

They walked inside, and Lilly took her seat at the front of the building, near the choir. The organist was already filling the temple to the top of its vaulted ceiling with inspiring music. For the next twenty minutes Lilly watched as people crowded into the sanctuary, while hundreds more faithful Latter-day Saints still stood outside in the cold, ignoring a brisk wind and frozen toes in order to participate in the dedication.

It seemed so ironic to Lilly that while they all stood celebrating the completion of this magnificent house of worship, Brigham Young and others were already scouring western lands, looking for yet another place to settle.

A priest came to the pulpit and directed everyone to stand for a hymn. The temple seemed to almost vibrate with the sound of organ music and human voices. Lilly stood in front with the choir, waiting her turn to solo. She was able to spot many friendly faces among those in the pews, including Frieda Dutch, who was standing several rows back with her husband and three children. Frieda was crying, and Lilly knew she was thinking of her mother. It was that thought that gave Lilly courage.

When they finished the hymn, everyone sat down to listen to a few words of dedication from the priest. Then, it was Lilly's turn to sing her first song. She rose, and the organist began to play, filling the sanctuary with rich, harmonic chords that thrilled Lilly to her very soul, and gave her the remaining courage she needed.

Now she was being carried into the world she loved best —a world that was all her own. She raised her eyes to the vaulted ceiling, putting aside all sad and lonely thoughts. She was at her secret place again, singing to Ben Nevis— only this time, it was real. The audience was not wild flowers and rocks.

> *Come, come ye Saints, no toil or labor fear,*
> *But with joy wend your way.*
> *Though hard to you this journey may appear,*
> *Grace shall be as your day.*
> *'Tis better far for us to strive*
> *Our useless cares from us to drive;*
> *Do this, and joy your hearts will swell*
> *All is well! All is well!*

How she hated the thought of leaving Nauvoo for another long and dangerous journey, but she knew that, for now, she would have no choice.

> *And should we die before our journey's through,*
> *Happy day! All is well!*

How fitting were the words! Mother! If only she could see her once more.

> *We then are free from toil and sorrow, too;*
> *With the just we shall dwell!*

The words spilled forth with little effort, but with a power that defied her slender, youthful form. Lilly Brannigan now had her captive audience. Especially in one Zebulah Adams, who watched her with near worship, looking upon the beautiful Lilly Brannigan as someone a man could adore from afar, but could never really possess.

Chapter Three

Early April 1846

Chase stood on the hillside, looking down on the city of Nauvoo. This was the first time in his twenty-four years he had visited the Mormon city since it was founded. He first had heard about it in his teens, and he remembered his mother telling him not to judge the Mormons by hearsay.

His mother had suffered terribly before she died. He hoped the little pine tree he had planted at her headstone would survive. It would be a long time before he could go back and visit the grave.

Chase couldn't help resenting his father for not being with his mother when she had died. The man had never been present for anything important—the army had seen to that. Now, here he was, an army man himself. It had always seemed the right thing to do—something he had never questioned—until he had met Lilly almost a year ago on the riverboat.

He felt foolish about coming here to find the pretty, auburn-haired Scottish girl. He had never quite gotten her off his mind, and now it suddenly seemed important to locate her before he headed for Texas. He could only hope that she hadn't already been married off to some Mormon man, or he would be double the fool.

Nauvoo lay almost glittering in the morning sun. Chase was impressed by its clean and sturdy-looking buildings, and the neat pattern of its streets. On a nearby hill stood the temple, like some great, protective bastion, its white spire seeming to stand for everything holy and pure.

Standing in this peaceful place, it hardly seemed possible to Chase that war could break out at any time along the Rio Grande, or that he would soon find himself involved in it. His father was waiting for Chase to join him at Matamoros, where Brigadier General Zachary Taylor waited with thousands of volunteers. Trouble was expected, and although war had not yet been declared against Mexico, Chase suspected it was only a matter of time.

He mounted his horse and rode in closer to town. If not for his mother's death, he wouldn't even be back in Illinois. He would already be on his way to Texas with the rest of his unit. But as long as he had been forced to come back, he could not resist steering his course through Nauvoo. The memory of Lilly Brannigan and that night on the riverboat had teased him long enough.

His ears picked up the sound of organ music drifting over the soft wind. He dismounted, standing quietly to listen, hearing the lovely voice of a woman. The music came from the direction of the temple. He walked in that general direction, leading his horse and watching for mucky spots caused by the spring thaw.

A few birds daring to come north a little too early sang in soft, peaceful chirps, seeming to try to harmonize with the lovely music coming from the temple. Chase removed his hat and wiped the sweat off his brow. It had been a cold spring, so far, but a sudden wind had swept up from the south, warming what had been a cold morning.

He made his way over bricked streets and up the hill to the temple. Several hundred people stood outside, and a few turned to stare at him, but Chase hardly noticed. He was too curious about the singing that came from inside. Never had he heard anything quite so beautiful. He felt drawn to it.

When it finally stopped, Chase realized he was standing right in the middle of a crowd of Mormons. He self-consciously brushed himself off and wondered if he was presentable in plain cotton pants, riding boots, and a buckskin jacket. He told himself it didn't really matter. He was no Mormon, and he had a right to dress however he chose.

The service was apparently over, and people were beginning to exit the temple. Chase felt suddenly awkward, almost as though he was in a foreign land.

"Good morning," came a voice behind him.

Chase turned to see a little old lady staring up at him. "Good morning," he answered.

"Are you a Gentile?"

Chase frowned. "A what?"

"You are not a Mormon?"

"No, ma'am."

"Then, you are a Gentile. We refer to anyone who is not a Mormon as a Gentile—except for Jewish people, of course. You are welcome in Nauvoo, as long as you mean no harm, and as long as you do not go into the sanctuary. Only those of our faith are allowed inside."

"Yes, ma'am." Chase removed his hat and fidgeted with it between his hands. "I, uh, I wonder if you could tell me if you know of a young lady living in this town called Lilly Brannigan."

The old woman's eyebrows arched, and she looked at him warily.

"And why would you be wanting to know?"

"I, uh, I met her once. My name is Chase Mitchell—Charles Mitchell, that is. Most call me Chase. I've come from Burlington."

"Well, if you want to speak to Miss Brannigan, you will have to get permission first from Hiram Williams. She is his ward. And, if you didn't know, she sang the last song you heard coming from the temple. Doesn't she have a beautiful voice?"

Chase smiled, surprised and pleased. "Yes, ma'am, she surely does! And thank you for your help." He hurried away, standing off to the side and watching as more people came out of the temple.

He could hardly believe it was Lilly he had heard singing. How could such a small and delicate woman have such a strong, compelling voice? He waited, wondering if Lilly would ever come outside, or if perhaps he had missed her while he was talking to the old woman.

Finally, she appeared at the doorway, surrounded by peo-

ple complimenting her singing. Chase wondered if Miss
Lilly Brannigan had decided to join the Latter-day Saints
after all. She had quickly denied being a Mormon that night
on the riverboat, but the old woman had said no Gentiles
could go into the temple.

Lilly started to move. He watched her walk down the temple steps with the white-haired man from the riverboat and
what appeared to be his wife and children.

Chase's heart tightened at the sight of her auburn hair,
hanging in thick, radiant waves, just as he remembered. She
filled out her mint-green dress in tempting curves, and when
she turned her face in his direction, he could see he had not
been wrong about her exquisite looks. For months he had
wondered if it could have been the whiskey and the darkness
that had made her look so pretty to him that night, but the
girl he watched now was prettier than he even remembered.

He put on his hat, wondering how he should approach her,
or if he should approach her at all. She and the family with
her began walking, and Chase followed, leading his horse
behind him and keeping his distance. He wondered if he was
crazy to be here. He supposed Lilly Brannigan must be some
kind of witch to have such a hold on him. In his whole life
he had never gone looking for a woman, but something
about Lilly had captured his imagination, and the memory of
her face and exotic green eyes would not leave him.

They entered an attractive brick home several blocks
down the road. Chase sat down in some shade. He told himself it would be stupid to have come all this way to find Lilly
Brannigan, only to turn around and leave without speaking
to her. He stood up and took a deep breath for courage, then
approached the house, and knocked. After a few seconds a
dark-haired, dark-eyed woman opened it.

"Yes?"

Chase removed the hat again. "Afternoon, ma'am. My
name is Chase Mitchell, and I'm with Company H, Second
Regiment, of the Illinois Foot Volunteers." He gave her his
best smile. "I'm on my way to St. Louis to meet some other
men headed for Texas. I, uh, was wondering if you folks
know when a riverboat might come by next that would be
headed for St. Louis? I'd like to rest a bit, but I wouldn't

want to miss it, and I know they don't always stop." He hoped it was a good enough excuse. The woman frowned.

"Wait here a moment," she told him.

Lilly took down some dishes to set the table for dinner, but she almost dropped them when she heard Mary and Hiram talking in the hallway.

"There is a young man at the door who claims to be an Illinois volunteer headed for Texas. He says his name is Chase Mitchell, and he wants to know when the next river-boat for St. Louis might be by," she said.

Lilly felt her cheeks begin to burn. Chase Mitchell! Could it be the same one? Had he come looking for her? It didn't seem possible! Her dress suddenly felt too warm, and when she picked up a gravy ladle to hand it to Laura, she dropped it. She kept her ears open to Hiram and Mary's conversation as she picked it up and wiped it off.

"He could be a Gentile spy," Hiram was saying.

"He could, but he has such kind eyes and a nice smile. I hate refusing our hospitality to anyone, Hiram."

"Lilly, where is the gravy bowl?" Laura asked as she stirred the sauce from the roast that had cooked in the wood-burning stove while they were at services.

"Shhhh!" Lilly put up her hand. Immediately, Laura's eyes widened and a smile of excitement passed her lips.

"What is it, Lilly?"

"All right," Hiram was saying. "Let me talk to him. If he seems all right, maybe we should see if he would like to eat with us."

Lilly laid the gravy ladle on the table. "I'll be right back!" she told Laura, dashing out of the room without explanation. She pulled up her skirts and hurried upstairs to a window to cautiously peer out. From her vantage point she could see the front door below. She stared down at the top of a man's head. His hair was thick and dark, and he wore a buckskin shirt.

". . . Chase Mitchell." She caught the words being repeated to Hiram. "All I want is to know if a steamer will be by here today, headed for St. Louis."

"Yes, there will be one in, oh, about three hours. You told my wife you were with the Illinois Foot Soldiers?"

"Yes, sir."

"Why aren't there other men with you?" Hiram asked.

"I was sent home on special leave from Fort Leavenworth. My mother died about three weeks ago. Since my father is already in Texas—he's a career man in the army—someone had to come home and take care of things. Now that everything is squared up, I'm on my way to Texas to join my father and General Taylor on the Rio Grande."

Lilly recognized the deep voice. Her heart pounded wildly. Had Chase Mitchell found Hiram's place deliberately? Did he know she lived here?

"That so? Well, I'm sorry about your mother, Brother Mitchell. If you're on your way to join up with General Taylor, the time is coming soon enough when you won't be enjoying any home-cooked meals. Since you have to wait for the riverboat, perhaps you would like to eat with us? My wife and daughters are just getting some food on the table—a roast and biscuits, some vegetables, and I believe there is a pie or two in the kitchen."

Lilly didn't wait for the young man's reply. She hurried to a mirror and ran a brush through her hair. She was glad she had on her green dress. The color suited her. But she was so nervous she felt damp all over and much too warm. She had no doubt the young man at the door would accept Hiram's offer, nor did she doubt who he was. She could only pray that if he had come here deliberately, he wouldn't look too surprised when he saw her. She had never told Hiram about that night on the riverboat. If Chase Mitchell acted as though he already knew her, there would be some explaining to do.

She hurried back down the rear stairs to the kitchen, where Laura was pouring gravy into a bowl.

"Lilly, where have you been?"

Lilly glanced at the kitchen door. She could hear voices out in the hallway now. She rushed up to Laura and pulled her aside. "Laura, a young man is at the door asking about the riverboats. I heard your mother tell your father he calls himself Chase Mitchell, and your father just asked him to stay for lunch!"

"So?" Laura blinked in wide-eyed innocence. "My father has opened his home to Gentiles before."

"This is different! He's the young man I saw on the riverboat!"

Laura's mouth fell open. "Lilly!"

Lilly put a hand to the girl's mouth. "Don't say anything, please, Laura. Your father doesn't know. I just hope Mr. Mitchell doesn't say anything about meeting me on the riverboat."

"Oh, Lilly, do you think he came here *looking* for you?"

"I don't know." Lilly rolled her eyes. "Oh, Laura, I don't know what to do—how to act."

Laura squeezed her eyes shut and grinned. "Oh, this is so exciting!"

Suddenly Mary and Beth walked into the kitchen. "Girls, I want you to set an extra place. We have a guest for dinner. He's a Gentile, but he is a young man on his way to war, and he has just lost his mother. We have offered to let him eat here with us."

Lilly and Laura both struggled to hide their giddy excitement. "Yes, Mother," Laura answered.

"Lilly, go set the extra plate, please," Mary told her.

Lilly's ears were ringing, and she felt removed from her body. Had Chase actually come looking for her? It was so romantic. Surely he wouldn't have looked her up unless he had never been able to forget her—just as she had never been able to forget him.

She clung tightly to the extra plate as she carried it into the dining room, afraid she would drop it, as she had the gravy ladle. Just as she set it down, Hiram and Chase Mitchell walked past the arched entrance to the dining room. Chase glanced into the room and met Lilly's eyes, and for a second they held like magnets. Lilly felt as though lightning had just bolted through her body, and it took all her effort to tear her eyes away.

"We can sit here in the parlor until the food is on the table," she heard Hiram saying.

"Thank you, sir." She heard Chase's heavy footsteps as he walked on. "This is very kind of you, Mr. Williams. I'll pay you for the meal."

"Nonsense." Their voices faded, and Lilly breathed a sigh of relief that Chase had not shown that he recognized her. She went back into the kitchen to finish the food preparations, refusing to look at Laura for fear of laughing and appearing too excited.

From then on every movement became a struggle for Lilly—a deliberate effort to remain calm. The table was set and the women and boys took their proper places at the table. Mary called for Hiram, and Lilly finally glanced at Laura. The girl's lips were pressed together, her dark eyes sparkling, her hands gripping the back of her chair as tightly as were Lilly's.

As Chase entered the room, Lilly could not bring herself to meet his eyes again. But when Hiram introduced him, she had no choice. Hiram would not want her to appear rude.

"Brother Mitchell, this is my family," Hiram said as he led Chase to a chair between Gerald and Henry. "You've met my wife, Mary. Beside her is my daughter, Laura, her sister, Beth, and a young lady who is living with us for a while—Lilly Brannigan. Lilly is from Scotland. Her mother was a convert and wanted to come to America, but the poor woman died coming over, leaving Lilly homeless."

Lilly raised her eyes to meet Chase Mitchell's. Her heart almost ached with gratitude when she saw his handsome, sweet smile. He nodded to her, telling her with his eyes that he would say nothing. "Nice to meet all of you," he said, making sure to scan all the women, and not pay too much attention to Lilly.

Laura reminded herself not to gape at her father's guest. Chase Mitchell was more handsome than any young man in Nauvoo. Her heart pounded with such excitement for Lilly that she worried someone could hear it beating.

"Beside you are my two sons—Henry, the youngest one there, and Gerald," Hiram was telling Chase.

"I'm eleven!" Gerald boasted.

"Well, then, you're coming close to being a man," Chase told him.

"How old are you, Brother Mitchell?"

"I'm twenty-four."

"Now, you needn't be asking personal questions, Gerald," Mary spoke up.

"And I haven't finished," Hiram told all of them. "Family, this is Charles Mitchell, from Burlington. He's on his way to Texas to join General Zachary Taylor in a march on Mexico—or, at least, that is what is rumored will take place. Brother Mitchell's father is an army man, already down on the Rio Grande, waiting for his son." Hiram frowned. "I'm sorry to say Brother Mitchell has recently lost his mother, and is on special leave to take care of family affairs. His father is not aware yet of the death. Brother Mitchell feels the kindest thing to do is to wait until he gets to Texas, so he can tell his father in person."

"Oh, I'm so sorry, Brother Mitchell," Mary told him. "Sister Lilly would understand how you feel."

Lilly met Chase's eyes again, and she felt a new closeness to him, something akin to pity pulling at her heart. Yet it was more than that—a feeling she didn't quite understand yet.

Mary directed everyone to be seated and food was passed around. Lilly ate little. She wanted desperately to ask Chase Mitchell what had brought him to Nauvoo—to find out if he had come by chance, or deliberately to see her. Her heart raced when he mentioned that he would be leaving again that very day. She had to find a way to catch him alone, if only for a moment. She couldn't let him move on and out of her life in minutes again, like on the riverboat. Occasionally Chase would steal a glance her way, and she was certain he was thinking the same thoughts. Surely he *had* come deliberately to find her.

The meal seemed to take forever. Hiram and Chase talked about Mexico and possible war. Lilly's heart went out to Chase when he talked about having to arrange his mother's funeral. He had rented out her home, since he would not be going back there himself for months.

Months, Lilly thought. *Once he leaves here, he'll be gone for months.*

"I've hardly had time to mourn her death," Chase was saying. "In a way, it hardly seems real to me yet."

"When we lose a loved one, sometimes the hurt of it

doesn't set in until later," Mary told him. "That's how it was for me when my mother died."

Lilly's stomach grew even tighter.

The conversation turned back to Mexico. "I'll head to St. Louis from here," Chase said. "More men will be waiting down at New Orleans. We'll march west into Texas from there."

"Lilly and I took that very route along the Mississippi just a year ago," Hiram answered. "Landed at New Orleans and took a riverboat to Nauvoo."

Chase glanced at Lilly again. *Yes*, he wanted to say. *I know. That's where I met her.*

Mary asked Lilly and Laura to get the pies. Lilly gladly left. As soon as she got through the kitchen door she leaned against the wall and breathed deeply, feeling a sudden urge to cry.

Laura hurried in behind her. "Oh, Lilly, he's the most beautiful man I've ever seen!" she whispered.

"He is, isn't he?" Lilly answered. "Oh, Laura, he came here looking just for me, I'm sure of it. I have to find a way to talk to him before he goes. What should I do? Hiram is so strict about letting young men call on me, and this man is not only a stranger, he's also a Gentile. Hiram would never let me speak with him alone."

Laura glanced at the kitchen door, then grasped Lilly's wrists. "I'll tell Mother we want to walk to Rebecca Martin's house as soon as Brother Mitchell is ready to leave. I could go on to Rebecca's, and you could flag down Brother Mitchell and talk with him."

Lilly studied the girl's dark, dancing eyes. "Oh, Laura, do you think it would work?"

"Of course it would!" Laura giggled. "We'd better get back out there with the pies."

Lilly got a pie server while Laura picked up the pies and they hurried back to the dining room, where everyone still sat at the long mahogany table that was Mary Williams's pride and joy. It was one of the finest pieces of furniture she owned, but one Hiram had already said would have to be left behind when they headed west. Chase Mitchell was going to Mexico, and soon she would have to go west with the Mormons! Once that happened, she would surely never see Chase Mitchell again. It seemed pointless to bother trying to see him today, and yet here he was, apparently wanting to talk to her as much as she wanted to talk to him.

As Lilly began to carve one of the pies, she finally found her voice. "This one is apple," she said, looking straight at Chase. "The one Laura is cutting is peach. Which would you like, Mr. Mitchell?"

"Apple is fine," he answered. Their eyes held, and Lilly barely heard the other requests.

"I want apple, too," Gerald chimed in.

Lilly cut the pie and everyone began to eat. Chase asked questions about troubles the Mormons had been having, and Hiram gladly explained his side of the story. Lilly studied the way Chase's lips moved when he spoke, and took note of his strong hands as he cut into his pie. They were rugged hands—the hands of a man who knew hard work. His dark hair hung in beautiful, symmetrical waves through the crown, over his ears and past his collar. His laugh was deep and genuine.

"So, Lilly, you're from Scotland."

Lilly reddened when she realized Chase had suddenly turned his attention to her. "Yes," she answered, cutting a piece of pie with her fork.

"Well, don't leave it at that. I know nothing of this place called Scotland, except that I think it is on the same little island as England, isn't it?"

Lilly swallowed and cleared her throat. "Great Britain is not such a little island. Scotland makes up about one-third of it—the northern section. We are governed by the queen of England." She struggled to keep her voice from cracking from nervousness.

"Kind of like our states belonging to the whole United States, I suppose," he was saying. *How I love your lovely accent*, he thought, *the beautiful way you speak*.

"Yes. Kind of like that. We can govern ourselves in most matters."

"Here, we call that states' rights." He cut into more pie. "So, what is Scotland like? Is it anything like Illinois?" Lilly wondered if he could tell her voice was shaking. She felt

Laura looking at her, wanting to laugh, and it made her more nervous. She refused to look back at the girl.

"It's greener, and in Scotland we have many beautiful mountains. There are no mountains here. I miss them very much."

She wondered if she had already told him these things that night on the riverboat. She couldn't remember now.

"You'll see your share of mountains when we go into the western desert to find our Zion," Hiram told her.

"You'll really leave this beautiful city?" Chase asked.

"I am afraid we have no choice, with all the raiding going on. Outsiders won't let us live in peace, Brother Mitchell. Brigham Young is firmly convinced that we will find our haven somewhere west, perhaps in an area called the Great Basin. Some have gone on ahead to explore the idea. Messengers from that group should be coming back to Nauvoo soon. I am glad to say that in the meantime, we have many non-Mormon friends, some in high places, who are helping in our fight to get some compensation from the federal government for our losses here. We are leaving some fine buildings and farms behind."

"Our enemies will swarm in here and take over Nauvoo, paying nothing for all that we have worked so hard to build," Mary put in, bitterness in her voice.

"We've had to rebuild more than once, Mary," Hiram told her. "We'll just have to do it again. Maybe this time, Brother Young will find the place we are truly meant to call our own." He looked at Chase again, smiling. "We will not be defeated, Brother Mitchell. We will go on, as God would have us do."

Lilly glanced at Mary, feeling sorry for the woman. Journeying west would not be easy for someone like Mary, who would have to leave so much behind. She was sure she detected tears in the woman's eyes, and she wondered if Hiram realized how much his wife was dreading the trip. She knew Mary Williams would voice no objections.

"Well, you've shown me nothing but generosity and kindness, Mr. Williams," Chase was saying. "I appreciate it, and I wish you luck in your own long journey."

The meal was finished, and Lilly was expected to help

clean up. She was relieved to hear Hiram telling Chase
Mitchell to feel free to rest in the parlor, since it would be a
while before the riverboat came by. That would give her
time to finish the dishes before Chase left the house. She
hurried Laura and Beth. Laura kept giggling, but she
scrubbed the dishes as fast as she could. Beth pouted, realizing Laura and Lilly were sharing some kind of secret that
they wouldn't tell her.

When they were nearly through, Mary came into the
kitchen, and Beth whined to her to make Laura and Lilly tell
what they were laughing about.

Mary arched her eyebrows. "The handsome Gentile man
sitting in the parlor, I don't doubt," the woman answered.

Lilly and Laura both reddened and glanced at each other.
Mary folded her arms. "I will remind both of you that
Brother Mitchell is not only a stranger and a Gentile, but he
is leaving Nauvoo this very day. I have a feeling it's a good
thing. You two just remember you aren't even allowed to see
young *Mormon* men."

Laura sobered deliberately. "Oh, Mother, we know that.
But we can't help noticing how handsome he is. Anyway,
we want to go over to Rebecca's. Can we, please?"

"I want to go, too," Beth pouted.

"No. Lilly and I want to go by ourselves," Laura scowled.

"I don't know," Mary said thoughtfully. "You'll have to
be back in time for scripture reading."

"Oh, we will be," Laura insisted. "Please, Mother?"

Mary folded her apron. "All right. You and Lilly can go
alone—but stay together."

Beth made a face at them and stomped up the back stairs
to her room, while Laura grabbed Lilly's arm and pulled her
out of the kitchen and through the dining room, to tell her
father, in front of Chase Mitchell, that she and Lilly were
leaving.

Lilly's face reddened as Laura made the announcement.
She was almost too obvious. Lilly tried to tell Chase with
her eyes that this was their chance, but she wasn't sure if he
understood. She went to the hall to get her bonnet and cape,
and she and Laura hurried out the door and through the front
gate. They walked as slowly as they could, hoping Chase

would come out of the house. When they reached an old shed farther up the road, Laura darted around the side of it.

"He'll have to come by here when he leaves," she told Lilly. "Wait inside where nobody will see you. Watch through the cracks. Father can't see this shed from the house because of the bushes."

Lilly looked around. "Oh, Laura, I'm scared. Maybe he doesn't want to talk to me at all."

"Of course he does! Didn't you see it in his eyes?"

Lilly shivered. "Thank you, Laura. If I get caught, I'll tell Hiram it was all my idea."

"It doesn't matter. I just hope it works. Oh, Lilly, life was never this exciting before you came!" The girl laughed lightly and darted away, and Lilly opened the shed door and stepped inside.

Minutes seemed like hours. The shed grew stuffy, and smelled of old dust. Lilly hoped spiders weren't crawling over her dress. Finally, she spotted Chase Mitchell, walking with his horse, looking around as though trying to find something.

Me, she thought. *He's trying to find me!* She swallowed for courage and opened the shed door. Chase heard its squeak and turned to see her standing there.

"Lilly!" he said softly.

Chapter Four

Lilly felt her legs go numb as Chase approached. She wondered if she would be wiser to turn and run back to the house, but she knew that even if she wanted to run, her legs would not move. As Chase removed his hat, his dark hair blew softly in the wind. His eyes, surrounded by dark lashes, looked as blue as the sky. In the sunlight his facial features were even more distinct—high cheekbones; a straight, handsome nose; nicely formed lips. She noticed the shadow of a beard fighting a morning shave.

"I was hoping I'd find you waiting for me," he told her, smiling. "I never forgot you, Lilly Brannigan." He led his horse past the bushes, so it couldn't be seen. Lilly followed, all the while struggling to find her voice. He then tied the buckskin-colored gelding to an old post and turned back to her, his steady gaze moving over her in a way that made her insides flutter. "When I had to come home because of my mother, I couldn't resist coming through Nauvoo on my way back to see if you were here."

Lilly swallowed. "I can hardly believe you actually came here looking for me! Why?"

He shrugged. "I don't know. It's like I said—I just never forgot you." He patted his horse's neck. "I hope you aren't upset about my being here. I figured you didn't want Mr. Williams to know we talked that night on the riverboat, so I didn't say anything." He moved away from the horse and leaned against the shed wall. "But all during that meal I just wanted a chance to talk to you alone, to say hello again, to ask how you are. Did you ever think about me after that night on the riverboat?"

She turned away, wondering how bold she should be. Did she dare tell him she never forgot that night? "I . . . I thought about you a few times."

She didn't see him grin with discerning satisfaction. He wanted so badly to reach out and touch her hair. "I'm glad," he told her. He breathed deeply for courage, then stood straighter and walked behind her. "Would you walk with me, Lilly?"

She turned to face him, her big, green eyes widening with surprise and innocence. She glanced around nervously. "I'm obligated to Hiram to obey his rules. He'd be angry if he knew."

"So, don't tell him. We can walk along that ravine over there. Nobody will see us."

Lilly looked toward the ravine, wringing her hands. She felt torn with indecision. She reasoned finally that she was not a Mormon, and Hiram really had no right to direct her personal life. And, after all, Chase Mitchell was on his way to a possible war. He would only be here this one precious day, and only another hour or so, at that.

"All right," she answered, a bashful smile on her face.

Joy shone in Chase's eyes. He lightly touched her arm to lead her toward the brush-hidden ravine. Lilly felt warm at his touch, and the whole world seemed suddenly unreal.

"You must think I'm crazy," he told her.

"A little, I suppose, but it's nice having someone look for me like this. It's—I don't know—good that someone from the world outside Nauvoo knows I exist. It's lonely, being in a new country and all. How did you find me so easily?"

"I heard someone singing at the temple, and stood outside to listen. An old woman told me it was you. I waited for you to come out of the temple and followed you to Hiram's place." He shook his head. "I have to tell you, I almost changed my mind. But then I figured, what the heck—I had come this far; I might as well go through with it. I wasn't sure what to expect, or if Hiram would believe my excuse for coming to the door." He stopped and looked down at her, frowning slightly. "By the way, Lilly, I have never heard a voice like yours. It's absolutely amazing."

Lilly reddened. "Thank you."

"Where did you learn to sing like that?"

She still felt flustered from his touch on her arm, and wondered if he realized how hard her heart was beating. "It comes naturally, I guess. I've never had lessons or anything."

"Well, I was right about your name sounding famous. I bet it will be someday if you keep singing like that."

She shook her head. "You remembered saying that? I didn't think you would."

She glanced up at him and felt her heart quicken at the look that came into his eyes. Even in her innocence, she knew what that look meant. She felt suddenly on fire.

"I remember everything about that night, Lilly," he told her. "Call it fate, or whatever you want, but I felt almost compelled to come here and find you. And now, I'm almost sorry. You're prettier than I remembered, and I have to leave soon, so I won't get a chance to know you better."

Lilly tore her eyes from his, and started to walk again. "You . . . could always write me," she said, surprised she had made the bold statement.

She removed her cape and wrapped it over her arm. Chase studied her slender form beneath the mint-green dress as she walked ahead of him. "You wouldn't mind?" he asked.

"No. I wouldn't mind at all."

"Would you write back?"

"Of course I would, if you'll be someplace where letters can get to you."

How I'd love to kiss your mouth before I go, he thought. *How I'd love to crush you against me, feel every curve, touch your hair.* "They'd find me eventually," he said aloud.

He hurried to her side and took her arm, leading her down to a creek. They walked along its edge. "Are you a Mormon now, Lilly?"

"No." She picked her way over the grassiest spots to avoid the spring mud. "They're good people, but I'll never become a Mormon myself. I would never risk having to share a husband. And I guess I haven't quite been able to stop blaming the Mormons for having to leave Scotland, and for my mother's death. Not that things were so good in Scotland. My mother and I worked hard there, and life was pretty miserable in Glasgow, but it's still my homeland. I haven't gotten used to calling America home yet."

Her comment about sharing a husband stirred deep, painful desires in Chase. The man who bedded Lilly Brannigan would be lucky, indeed. "But you sing in the temple," he said aloud. "I thought only Mormons were allowed inside."

"By special request. Hiram says I was led here by God, to gladden the hearts of the Saints with my songs." She laughed lightly, shrugging her shoulders. "I don't know about being led here by God. I don't even want to *be* here. I hope to be on my own someday. But right now, I know nothing about the Gentile world, and I have no money. It's hard when you're in a new country and don't even know all their ways yet."

Chase grinned at the musical way she had of speaking. "I'm sure it is, but you seem to be living well here. Hiram takes good care of you."

"Yes, but soon they'll be heading west. It frightens me."
She stopped and looked up at him again. "Aren't you afraid
to go to that place called Texas? Hiram has talked about
possible war with Mexico. I've heard him say how hot and
dry it is down there, with snakes and thorny plants and no
water. I can't imagine a place like that. There is no country
like that in Scotland."

Chase studied her beautiful face, and felt something akin
to love at her sweet concern. "I'm not crazy about going, but
I have an obligation to fill now. My father is a strict army
man. If I didn't go, according to him, I'd be a deserter, and I
couldn't personally live with that label." He slipped his hand
naturally into hers. They walked a little farther, breathing in
the sweet smells of coming spring. "My father is waiting for
me. I can't turn him down—especially now that my mother
has died. I thought it would be best to tell him about her
death in person. I couldn't bring myself to tell him in a
letter."

Lilly trembled at the feel of his big hand around her own.
She knew she should pull away, but she couldn't bring herself to do so, and she didn't want to let go. There was something comforting about his touch. "It's thoughtful of you to
want to be with him when he finds out. At least you do still
have your father."

"I suppose. He's never really been much of a father—he
was always gone." He threw her a sideways glance. Lilly
thought she detected a sad loneliness and a hint of bitterness
in his words. "I still respect him, although I can't help blaming him for not being there when Mother died."

"Were you close to your mother?"

He sighed deeply, taking several seconds to answer. "I
guess you could say we were—when I was younger, anyway. I had an older brother who died when I was about five.
My father was always gone because of the army, so it was
mostly just me and my mother. But I had kind of a wild
streak in me, and was always off on one adventure or another after I turned sixteen. I guess I always knew my father
would expect me to join the army eventually, and follow in
his illustrious footsteps, so I thought I would sow a few oats
before getting into such a regimented life. I regret it a little,

though, because of my mother being so alone all the time. That's what hurt most about her dying. These last few years I could have been with her more, but it's really my father who had that responsibility."

"She's happy now. She's with your brother."

He grinned and squeezed her hand, appreciating the comforting remark.

When Lilly glanced up at him, she saw tears in his eyes. "What does that mean—sowing oats?" she asked, hoping to change the subject.

Chase laughed, stopping again and looking down at her. "It's an American term meaning—oh, I guess it means spreading yourself around, experimenting with different things you'd like to do before you take on a lot of responsibility.

"What kind of things?"

He studied her curious green eyes, and broke into a teasing grin. "Oh, like gambling, racing horses, trying different jobs." He gave her a wink. "Womanizing."

Her eyebrows arched. "Womanizing?"

He grinned more as Lilly's face reddened. She looked quickly away, surprised at the sudden jealousy she felt. "Oh."

He wanted to laugh at her faint reply. "I'm sorry," he told her, squeezing her hand. "I didn't mean to embarrass you. That wasn't very nice of me."

Lilly felt the defensive anger that often plagued her rising inside. She cast him a cautious look, her lips slightly pouted, and pulled her hand away. "Is that what you're doing now, Mr. Chase Mitchell? Womanizing?"

Their eyes held. Chase sobered, and Lilly saw nothing but sincerity in his blue eyes when he spoke. "No. You're too nice and too sweet. I've never had a woman pester my thoughts the way you have, Lilly. I just wanted to see you again—find out more about you before I go away. I'm sorry if I offended you."

She turned away, angry now with herself for making the remark. "I have no right even being offended." She began to run ahead of him, breathing deeply, wanting the awkward moment to be over with. She then turned to face him from a short distance. "Do you really want to be in the army? It seems to me you're just doing it for your father," she asked in a louder, stiffer voice.

Chase was walking quickly to catch up, and he shook his head. "You read people pretty well for one so young," he told her. *Now that I've met you, I'm not sure what I want anymore*, he wanted to tell her. Lilly waited for him as he approached. "I suppose it's mostly for him, but maybe I'll find out I like it. At any rate, I'm committed now for at least two years. I'll have to decide after that if I want to make a career of it."

She wondered why her heart fell at the words. Two years! "Well, it seems we will each be taking long and dangerous journeys," she said. "I hope our letters find each other."

Their eyes held. Lilly thought for a moment that he might try to kiss her. To her surprise, she almost wished that he would. She felt suddenly dwarfed by his tall, broad frame, and she quickly turned away, walking ahead of him again.

"What about you?" he asked. "I've told you about my own background. All I know about you is that you're from Scotland and your mother died on the voyage here. No father?"

"He died about three years ago." It was easier to talk about it with someone who had just lost a parent. "We used to live in a little cottage in the Scottish lowlands. That's where I did most of my singing." She turned to face him again, her eyes dancing. "I had a secret place I used to go, where I'd pretend hundreds of people were listening to me sing." She blushed. "That must sound silly to you."

Chase shook his head. "No, it doesn't."

She smiled shyly and watched a winter bird across the creek. "After my father died, there were debts to pay. My mother had to sell the cottage and we went to Glasgow to work in the textile mills." She shuddered. "It was long hours—hard work. It took its toll on my mother." She paused, remembering those dreaded two years. "I hated Glasgow. I still have callouses from the mill. See?" She held out her hands and Chase took them in his own.

"Someone as pretty and delicate as you shouldn't work like that," he said softly.

Lilly raised her eyes to meet his and wondered if she might faint. She had never met a man quite so good-looking, or been with a near stranger who made her feel so comfortable. The touch of his hands sent a tingle through her body, and she experienced desires new to her. She pulled her hands away, her heart pounding so wildly she was afraid he could hear it. As she hurried ahead of him again, Chase thought she seemed like a butterfly, colorful and flighty.

"My mother met Frieda Dutch," she continued, talking louder so he could hear. "Frieda was a Mormon convert. She introduced my mother to Hiram, and before long, my mother had embraced the Mormon faith, too. Then she reasoned that life would be better for us here at Nauvoo, so she decided to come to America. You know the rest."

"No friends left behind in Scotland? No lovers?"

Lilly felt the flush returning to her cheeks, and she refused to face him. "I had some friends in Paisley. In Glasgow, there was no time to make friends—it was all work and sleep. And I was too young for lovers."

"And how old are you now?"

Do you want to be my lover? she wondered. "I'm seventeen. I'll be eighteen this fall."

"Some women are married by that age."

Lilly was confused about what he wanted of her. Was he actually thinking seriously about her? After all, he wanted to write to her. She had never been in such a situation, and she felt suddenly awkward and ignorant. She wished she understood men better. "You'll miss your riverboat if you don't get down to the docks soon," she told him, again dodging the topic of conversation. She turned and waited for him to come closer again.

"There's always tomorrow," he told her, catching up to her and grasping her hand again. "A day or two won't matter much."

Her heart pounded harder. He wanted to stay longer! "You wouldn't get into trouble?"

"I have until the end of the week to get to St. Louis.

That's only two or three days from here. I intended to go right away, but . . ." He squeezed her hand gently. "Lilly, do you think Hiram would let me see you, walk with you, the next couple of days? I wasn't sure I'd find you at all, but now that I have, I hate the thought of leaving right away."

Lilly could hardly believe her ears. "I . . . I don't know what to say. I never expected to see you again, Chase." She realized she was using his first name as easily as if she had always known him. She remembered telling him that night on the riverboat that it was improper to call a stranger by his first name, yet somehow, this stranger had done more to relieve her loneliness in the two hours he had been here than Hiram and his whole family had been able to in the whole year she had lived with them.

"I think I should tell Mr. Williams the truth, Lilly—that we've already met and I came here deliberately to find you. I don't want to go off to war without seeing more of you first. Hiram doesn't own you. He can't keep us from seeing each other. If . . . if things work out, we can write each other while I'm gone. I know it all seems pretty crazy, but—"

There was no time to finish. They both turned at the sound of horses, approaching at a fast gallop. Chase frowned, unsure at first who it could be. He then realized how far he and Lilly had walked—several hundred yards beyond the outskirts of Nauvoo. Instinct told him that whoever was coming, they meant no good. Why else would they be galloping through underbrush along the creek?

"Come on!" he told Lilly.

"What is it?" she asked as he grabbed her arm and started running with her.

"Trouble!" he answered, half dragging her. "We've got to get back closer to the house!"

Someone yelled then, not far behind him. "Look there, Denny! There's some of that mother-lovin' Mormon trash!"

"Ya-hoo!" another shouted. "One of them Mormon wives! Out here sportin' with some other woman's husband, I'll bet!"

"Murderers! Adulterers!" came a third voice. "Get the hell out of Illinois!"

The horses came close enough to make the ground shake, and Chase felt Lilly being torn from his grasp. Something hit him hard between the shoulders and he fell face forward. He scrambled back to his feet to see three men circling him, one of them hanging on to a struggling, screaming Lilly.

"Let her go!" Chase shouted.

One of the men laughed.

Chase lunged at the man's horse, grabbing Lilly. She screamed in pain and terror as the man holding her pulled her hair while Chase pulled the rest of her. "Let go of her, you sonofabitch!" Chase yelled.

The man pulled a handgun and bludgeoned him about the head with it, but Chase would not let go. Lilly reached up and scratched wildly at her abductor's eyes until he dropped his pistol and was forced to release her. Both Chase and Lilly tumbled to the ground.

"Get him, boys," the one who had been holding Lilly ordered. "I want that pretty little Mormon bitch."

Chase got to his feet again. He took hold of Lilly's arm and tried to push her out of the way. Lilly ducked around the scrambling legs of the three horses, while one of the attackers pulled his musket from its boot and began hitting Chase with the butt end of it.

Chase's fury knew no bounds. He grabbed the musket out of the man's hands and pointed it back at him, while Lilly looked for something she might use for self-defense. Sure Chase was going to fire the musket at his friend, one of the others pulled a pistol and shot first.

Lilly screamed as Chase went down, a bloody hole in his right thigh. He kept his grip on the musket, rolling to his knees in a split second and firing back. His shot clipped the man across the ear and he screamed, putting his hand to the side of his face to feel warm blood.

"He shot me!" the man yelled.

Chase hoped he could keep from passing out from pain. He spotted the pistol dropped by the first man and pointed it at all three men. "Don't make me kill one of you!" he told them. "I'll do it if I have to!"

"Goddamn murderin' Mormon!" the wounded man yelled, almost in tears.

"Come on, let's get out of here," Lilly's abductor grumbled. "We'll be back, you bastard," he threatened Chase.

"I look forward to it!" Chase growled, panting. He forced himself to stay alert and hold the pistol on the men until they reluctantly turned their horses and rode off. Chase stared after them, still gripping the pistol, until they were well out of sight.

"Oh, Chase!" Lilly exclaimed, her face stained with tears and her hair in disarray. Her dress was torn at the waist from Chase tugging at it, and she shivered at the feel of her abductor's flesh under her fingernails. "Chase, you're bleeding badly! They shot you!"

Chase's breath was coming in shorter gasps. He still clung to the pistol but put his other arm around Lilly's shoulders. "Got to get back to my horse . . . get help."

"Oh, Chase, I'm so sorry about this!" Lilly wept. "If you hadn't come here, it wouldn't have happened!" She felt faint herself from the shock of the violence. She knew instinctively what the raiders would have done to her if Chase had not intervened with such skill and bravery. He could have let them take her, but instead, he had risked his life for her. His leg was badly wounded, and his face was bloody and battered from the pistol-whipping.

Chase leaned on her for support as they headed back toward his horse. His leg was becoming more useless with each step.

"Hiram and Mary will help you," Lilly told him.

"Hiram will be pretty angry when he finds out we went off alone," Chase answered, struggling now to keep from passing out.

"I don't care what he thinks. I just want you to be all right," Lilly answered, her voice shaking. She kept looking back to be sure the raiders weren't following. The distance to Chase's horse suddenly seemed like miles, and Chase began to crumble. It was impossible for Lilly to hang on to his big frame, and she screamed his name.

"Get . . . help . . ." he mumbled.

"Oh, dear God!" Lilly wept. She ripped away a piece of

her petticoat and tied it tightly around his wounded leg, then removed one slip completely and rolled it up to make a pillow under his head. "I'll be right back, Chase. Hang on," she told him. "Please hang on!" She leaned down and kissed his forehead, placing the pistol beside him. "The gun is right here, Chase, in case you need it."

She rose, struggling against an urge to scream and panic. She had to keep her head clear. Chase needed her help. She lifted her skirts and began running then, as fast as she could. By the time she spotted Hiram's house, her lungs were burning fiercely and her head was spinning.

"Hiram!" she screamed. "Hiram!" She charged through the front door. Mary came into the hallway and Lilly practically fell into her arms. "Chase!" she panted. "He's hurt bad! You've got to help him!"

"Lilly!" the woman exclaimed.

"What in God's name is going on?" Hiram hurried out from the parlor to see Lilly covered with sweat and tears. A scratch on the side of her face was still bleeding, and her torn dress hung limply. She pulled away from Mary.

"Charles Mitchell—he's lying along the creek," Lilly sobbed. "Farther up . . . out of town. He's been shot! Please help him, Hiram!"

A mixture of anger and concern moved through Hiram's blue eyes. "Mary, get the girl settled. I'll go see about this." He glared at Lilly. "And I'll be wanting an explanation when I get back!" The man turned to leave and nearly ran into Laura, who was just then returning. He charged past her, and Laura stared at Lilly, her dark eyes wide with fright and shock.

"Lilly!" she almost whispered. "What happened!"

Mary's dark, discerning eyes drilled into her daughter. "What do you know about this, Laura Williams?"

Laura swallowed. She had never been a good liar, and now she had been caught off guard.

Lilly burst into tears, sitting down on a chair in the hall. "Nothing," she wept. "Laura doesn't know anything. It's all . . . my fault. All mine!"

Outside, Hiram hitched a flatbed wagon to a draft horse and headed for the creek.

Chapter Five

Laura sat on her bed, head hanging, eyes puffy. She felt responsible for all the turmoil in her father's house. Lilly lay weeping on her own bed. When Hiram had brought the man back, Chase was pale, and so still that at first, Lilly thought he might be dead.

Lilly and Laura could both hear Chase groaning. The other three Williams children had crouched in the hallway, listening to Hiram and Mary in one room, peeking around the doorway at Laura and Lilly in the other.

"Lilly, what if he dies?" Laura sobbed. "It was all my idea."

Lilly sat up, wiping at her eyes. "No. I wanted to go with him. You didn't do anything, Laura. You shouldn't have told your mother it was partly your idea. I would have taken the blame."

"I couldn't let you. You're my friend."

Mary shooed away the other children and walked into the bedroom. The front of her dress was spotted with blood. Hiram followed her.

"The doctor has done all he can," Mary said, looking at Lilly. "He'll live. The biggest problem was loss of blood. That shot went all the way through his leg, so there was nothing to dig out." The woman sighed. "I suppose we owe him something for saving you, Lilly. He mumbled enough while the doctor worked on him for us to gather what happened and to know he apparently risked his life for you. If it matters to you, he kept asking about you, wanted to know if you were all right. What we need now, dear, is an explanation as to what you were doing so far from Nauvoo, walking with a stranger. People are going to ask questions."

Lilly wiped her eyes and breathed deeply for control. She spilled out her story—about the riverboat, about why Chase Mitchell really came to Nauvoo. Hiram paced the whole time, his anger evident.

"You should have told us," he grumbled.

"We were going to. That was what we were coming back to do when we were attacked. Chase is an honest man, Hiram. He wanted to come and talk to you, and ask you if he could see more of me over the next couple of days." She sniffed. "He was going to prolong his trip, but first, he just wanted to find out if I remembered him—if I *wanted* him to stay."

Hiram stopped and glared at her, his hands behind his back. "How do you know he's honest? How do you know anything about him after a total of perhaps one hour with him? He might have come here just to try to take advantage of you, Lilly, before going off to war. You don't know anything about men!"

Lilly rose, fists clenched. "And I never will if you don't let me see any!" she answered. "I'm going on eighteen years old, Hiram. I'm not a member of this family, or even a Mormon! I have a right to see whoever I want. I appreciate the home you've given me, but you can't tell me what to do with my life! It isn't right!"

Hiram sucked in his breath and jerked back, as though he'd been hit. He stared at her for a long, quiet moment. "No, I suppose it isn't," he answered. "But I feel responsible for you, Lilly, and I want only what is best for you. Chase Mitchell is a Gentile."

"And so am *I*!" Lilly answered.

Laura began to sob and Mary turned away. Hiram only nodded. "Yes, you are. I guess I keep forgetting that." He folded his arms. "Well, apparently your Mr. Mitchell will be in this house for several days, maybe a couple of weeks. You'll have your chance to get to know him better. If that's so important to you, then so be it. We'll send a messenger to St. Louis to tell his unit what happened to him." He dropped his arms and stepped closer. "I can't let you sing in the temple anymore, Lilly—not after this embarrassment."

Lilly felt her heart fall. Singing in the temple was her

main source of happiness here in Nauvoo. She pressed her lips together and swallowed. "Fine," she answered. "May I please go and see Chase?"

Hiram frowned at her use of his first name. He sighed deeply and ran a hand through his hair. "I suppose. Don't take too long—he needs to rest. I'm not even sure he'll be conscious enough to know you're there."

"It doesn't matter." She blinked back more tears. "Thank you, Hiram." She hurried past him and into Hiram and Mary's bedroom, where Chase lay still. She leaned over him and spoke his name softly. He groaned, moved his head, and opened his eyes. Lilly's heart went out to him at the sight of his battered face.

"Lilly," he murmured. "You . . . all right?"

"I'm fine. Oh, Chase, I'm so sorry this happened. Please don't die!"

He managed a faint smile. "Can't . . . got to see more of you, first."

To Lilly he was a hero—*her* hero. And she knew that what she felt right now was surely love, even though she still barely knew him. But she knew all she had to. Chase Mitchell was the bravest, strongest, most handsome man she would ever meet the rest of her life. She reached down and grasped one of his hands.

"You'll be all right, Chase—the doctor said so. You just have to get your strength back from losing so much blood."

"Got to . . . get to my unit."

"Don't worry about that. Hiram will see that they know you can't come right now."

His blue eyes stared at her intently. "Lilly," he repeated almost lovingly. "Maybe tomorrow, you can sing for me," he told her, his voice barely audible. "I'd like that . . . make me feel better."

"Yes, Chase." She leaned closer. "I'll sing for you all you want." His eyes closed as she answered him, and she wasn't sure he even heard her.

Lilly carried a tray of food upstairs. She forced back the hurt of the cold stare she had received from Hiram when she had passed him in the hallway. He had very reluctantly agreed to let her talk to Chase and take food to him in the bedroom, but had told her she must always be properly dressed, and should never let him see her in her robe.

Lilly never felt more an outsider than now. Something had changed since the incident with Chase. Mary had softened somewhat over the three days it had taken Chase to be well enough to sit up and eat, but Hiram's anger was still evident, and suddenly, life in the Williams household no longer brought Lilly the feeling of security it had once held for her. What hurt most was being told she could not sing in the temple again. Singing for the Saints had helped her feel as though she belonged and was accepted. And singing was her greatest joy. Hiram had added that not only could she not sing, but since she was so adamant about refusing to convert, she would no longer even be allowed inside the temple.

"You should have considered it a privilege," he had told her. "Now, you've thrown it all in my face. I pray someday you will change your mind, Lilly."

Lilly tried to understand what was so terrible about what she had done. After all, she had not let Chase kiss her. She had had no wicked plans when she had gone for the walk with him, and it wasn't her fault the raiders had attacked them. If anyone was at fault, she decided, it was the Mormons themselves. Good and kind as they were, they had a way of attracting trouble, and Chase could have been killed, just because the raiders thought he was a Mormon.

She was more determined than ever that she would never embrace the Mormon religion. She would merely tolerate it until she found a way to be free.

"Good morning," she told Chase as she entered the room.

He smiled his handsome smile. The swelling on his face had gone down enough so that Mary had been able to shave him, and his hair was combed. He grimaced with pain as he adjusted himself in the bed to sit up straighter.

"Am I proper?" he asked her. "Mrs. Williams made a real fuss about how I should put on a shirt and keep it buttoned. She told me to keep myself covered."

Lilly reddened as she smiled. "You're proper, Mr. Mitchell," she answered formally.

"Well, I'll do whatever it takes for you to be allowed to bring me my food."

Lilly set the bed tray over his lap, being careful not to bump his wounded leg. "Do you need any help?"

"Oh, I think I can manage, but you stay right here."

She smiled bashfully, feeling a little bold being in a bedroom with him, now that he was so much more alert. But she felt she had to take advantage of every moment he was here, and she thanked God he was better.

"These last three days, I haven't been sure you even knew I was around when I came in to see you," she told him.

He tucked a napkin into his shirt. "Oh, I knew you were around, all right." He looked at her, and she could read the adoration in his blue eyes. "That's what got me through, Lilly Brannigan. That, and the way you stood here and sang those hymns of hope to me the first couple of nights."

She blushed and smiled. "I wanted to do whatever I could to make you feel better, and singing makes me happy. It made me feel better, too. I'm just so glad to see you sitting up and looking so alert." She sobered. "I was so scared, Chase, and I'm so sorry about all of it."

"Well, I suppose I should have said something to Hiram in the beginning. I've apologized for that, but he still seems pretty upset." He frowned with concern. "How about you? I imagine it's been hard for you, not being a part of the family and all."

Lilly's heart tightened at the memory of Hiram's words to Laura. *I don't want you thinking about men the way Lilly is, Laura. I know you are good friends now, but you're my daughter, and you're still too young for such things. I'm very disappointed that you helped Lilly deceive me.*

Poor Laura, Lilly thought, feeling responsible. The girl was confined to her sister Beth's room for a full week. Lilly slept alone now, kept away from Laura as though she were somehow tainted. She missed Laura's company and friendship, but she refused to unload all the hurt on Chase, or to tell him she could no longer sing at the temple. She smiled as she pulled over a chair and sat down next to the bed.

"It will work out," she answered him. "Hiram will get over it. And right now, I don't care. I'm not a Mormon,

Chase, and I'm old enough to see whoever I want. Hiram can't stop me, and he knows it. He said I can talk to you all I want before you go away. I just hope there's no permanent damage to your leg." *I'm so scared and lonely,* she wanted to tell him. *I'm a stranger in this house now. All I have is you.*

"That's yet to be discovered," he told her, sipping some milk. "Hiram said he would have a carpenter friend make me some crutches, and I'll start testing the leg out tomorrow." He gave her a grin. "Will you walk with me?"

Lilly laughed lightly. "You know I will."

Their eyes held. "I'm so sorry, Lilly," he said then, sobering. "I shouldn't have walked so far with you. When I think of what could have happened to you . . . I guess I didn't realize how bad things are around here. No wonder the Mormons are leaving."

She looked at her lap. "This is all their fault," she pouted.

"You can't really blame them, Lilly."

"Yes, I can!" She met his eyes again. "Hiram acts like I did something wrong, but I didn't! And if it weren't for all the trouble around here, we never would have been attacked. You should hate all of us."

She was surprised then to see something that bordered on love move through his eyes. "Not you, Lilly—I could never hate you. Nothing has changed. I still want to see you all I can before I go away, and I want to write to you."

She smiled faintly again.

"We'll talk all you want," she answered him. "And we'll go for walks."

Chase bit into a biscuit and swallowed a bite. "I'm almost glad for the injury," he told her. "Gives me more time to get to know you. Now I have a legitimate excuse not to go back right away."

Her eyes teared. "I don't think I ever really thanked you for what you did. You could have let them take me."

His blue eyes were suddenly icy. "Like hell! They would have had to kill me first."

Lilly felt a surge of desire and adoration. Surely he cared very much for her, and he was so brave.

"Sorry for the cuss word," he told her. He sighed deeply

and nodded toward the tray. "I'm afraid I can't eat it. I don't have much of an appetite yet." He ran a hand through his thick hair. "The last three weeks sure have been crazy— burying my mother, heading for Mexico, being haunted by a pretty Scottish woman I met only once. . . ." He met her eyes and smiled softly. "We're quite a pair, aren't we? Our lives have been turned kind of upside down in different ways. We're both a little lost."

His words could not have struck her with more meaning. It felt so good to know someone understood.

"Yes," she answered. "That's just how I feel."

He put out his hand and she hesitantly took it. "I didn't mean to cause you all this trouble, Lilly, but I couldn't resist trying to find you. I'll get out of this bed as fast as I can so we can take some walks, find a place to be alone. I feel like this house is all ears and eyes."

Lilly smiled. "I know." She felt suddenly hot and flustered. Her whole body seemed to ache for him. She could think of nothing more comforting at this moment than to be held tightly in Chase Mitchell's arms. The thought embarrassed her, and she drew her hand away, then stood to pick up his tray. He put his hand around her neck and pulled her face toward him.

Lilly stiffened, at first. She knew she could easily get away from him in his condition, and yet, she did not fully resist. Her heart pounded and her mind raced with indecision as he leaned up and gently forced her mouth against his own. His soft, gentle lips covered her mouth then in an exquisite kiss that made her feel lightheaded. His tongue lightly traced the edges of her lips, startling her. She had never been kissed that way. She pulled away and he let her go, but their eyes held for a lingering moment, and Lilly felt as though fire was surging through her, instead of blood.

She put her fingers to her lips. "I . . . shouldn't have let you do that," she said in a near whisper, looking ready to cry.

"I needed to do it, and so did you, Lilly. It was very nice." *I've never wanted a woman so badly in my whole life,* he wanted to tell her. Every nerve end in his body tingled with desire, and a dull ache moved through his groin. He had no doubt she had never been touched by a man, and suddenly, the thought of any man but himself touching her brought a surge of jealousy and possessiveness to his soul.

"I'd better go," she said quietly, taking the tray.

"I didn't mean to offend you, Lilly."

She was sure she was red all over. "You didn't." She turned with the tray. "It was very nice." She hurried out of the room, and Chase grinned. He decided he would damned well get a lot more kisses out of her before he headed for Mexico. He wanted to make sure Miss Lilly Brannigan would wait for him until he got his duty finished and could come back to her.

Lilly felt someone shaking her lightly. She jerked awake and sat up. "Lilly? It's me, Laura," came a whisper. "Oh, Lilly, I've missed you."

They reached out for each other and hugged. "I've missed you, too," Lilly answered. "I only see you at the table, and even then, we can't talk. Oh, I'm so sorry, Laura. I didn't want you to get into trouble."

"It's all right. I don't care, as long as you got to be with him. Is he all right, Lilly?"

"He's going to try walking tomorrow."

They spoke in low whispers. Laura pulled away and sat down on the bed beside Lilly. "I closed the door. Besides, Mother and Father have been sleeping downstairs because Chase is in their room." She grasped Lilly's hands. "Oh, Lilly, are you in love?"

Lilly frowned. She had never really allowed herself to dwell on it.

"I don't now. I think I might be, Laura. I know it's sudden, and maybe even wrong, but the feelings I have for him . . . and the way he looks at me . . ." She leaned closer to Laura's ear. "He kissed me today," she whispered.

Laura gasped and squeezed her hands. "Oh, Lilly, this is *worth* staying in my room! What was it like? I've never been kissed by a man. Did he kiss you on the lips?"

It felt good to be able to tell someone. "Yes. It was so beautiful, Laura. So . . . so soft and sweet. He isn't even angry about what happened. He said he's glad he has an excuse to stay around and get to know me better."

"Lilly, he's so handsome and brave. Look what he did for you! Oh, I hope it turns out all right. I'm so sorry about Father telling you you can't sing in the temple anymore, but don't hate him, Lilly. He's only going by our rules. And he does care about you—very much."

Lilly pulled her hands away. "He only cares about me as a possible convert. Now that he knows I won't join, he doesn't want me around anymore."

"That isn't true, Lilly. Mother and Father are very generous, loving people. Father only got angry because he *does* care. He's letting you see Chase because he doesn't want you to hate him."

Lilly drew up her knees and hugged them. "He lets me see Chase because he knows he can't stop me. He acts like I've done something bad, Laura, but I haven't. It hurts. I don't feel like I belong here anymore. I feel so lonely, except for Chase."

Laura put an arm around her shoulders. "You have me, Lilly. Even if we can't talk for the next few days, you know I care about you."

Lilly smiled through tears. "I know. Thank you, Laura, for not hating me."

"Why should I hate you? Besides, things have never been so exciting around here. Father will calm down in another few days—you'll see. And once Brother Mitchell leaves for Mexico, everything will be like it was."

Lilly's throat ached with a need to cry. "I don't think it will be exactly the same, Laura. And when Chase goes away, he won't go out of my life. We're going to write each other. He already asked me, and I told him he could." She sighed deeply. "Oh, Laura, I've never felt like this before—shaky and scared, and happy and sad, all mixed together. I don't want to go against Hiram, but it seems like when I'm near Chase, I can't even think straight." She put her knees down and faced Laura. "We didn't do anything wrong, Laura, I swear it. We couldn't help what happened."

"I know, Lilly. I just wanted you to know I'm still on your side. And I miss talking to you. Maybe we can—"

The door opened suddenly, and Laura jumped up from the bed. Hiram stood in the doorway, holding an oil lamp. "Laura!" he barked. "I thought I heard the floor squeak up here. You get back to Beth's room. You know you aren't supposed to be in here!"

Laura touched Lilly's arm and squeezed it. "'Bye, Lilly." She kissed Lilly's cheek and turned, facing her father. "Lilly didn't do anything wrong, Father."

"She knew I wouldn't have approved, and so did you. What you did was the same as lying to me, Laura. Making you stay in Beth's room for a week is almost too light a punishment for such a thing. Now I'll have to add three extra days. Go on with you now."

Laura darted past him and Hiram stood there, facing Lilly. He stepped closer, concern showing in his eyes. "I just want her to understand I'll not tolerate lying, Lilly, but I want you to know I'm not angry with either of you any longer. I've prayed about this. Our faith is a joyful one, and we don't linger on the past. We learn from our mistakes and go forward."

Lilly rose, facing him squarely. "But, I didn't do anything wrong. You act like I'm a terrible person."

"Lilly, I don't think that at all."

"Then, why can't I sing in the temple?"

Hiram sighed deeply. "Because you have made it very clear that you do not intend to join our faith. I had prayed it would be otherwise, and perhaps someday it will. But it doesn't change how we feel about you, Lilly. We care very much about what happens to you."

"But, you won't let Laura even talk to me."

"That's just a temporary punishment—and I've allowed you to visit Brother Charles, haven't I?"

Lilly again felt like a prisoner. "That's just it, Hiram. I appreciate the home you've given me, but who I see or don't see shouldn't be up to you. I'm not Laura. I'm Lilly Brannigan, and I have rights of my own. I'll gladly earn my keep by helping Mary, and doing anything else you want me to. But you make me feel like I'm in prison here."

An odd disappointment moved through Hiram's eyes. "Lilly, please understand that I still think highly of you.

You're beautiful and extremely talented, and I know you're a good-hearted young woman, but you have a streak of independence that just doesn't fit in this household. It isn't good for Laura. A Mormon woman accepts what must be accepted. She has a certain place within the home and the community—highly honored and respected, but always within her place. Your personality seems to go against everything I'm trying to teach Laura."

Lilly felt the dread of rejection creeping through her. "What are you saying, Hiram?"

There were tears in his eyes as he said, "I'm sorry, Lilly, but Laura has changed since you came. I wanted you to be good friends, but she becomes more independent and obstinate every day. As God is my witness, I don't want to send you away, but I think you should stay with someone else for a while."

Lilly felt as though something was pinching at her heart. *Send you away . . . send you away.* The words seared through her insides. She could see her mother's coffin again, floating into nothingness.

She stiffened, refusing to cry or beg. This had been her only home since she had come to America, but if she was not wanted here, then she didn't want to stay. She held up her chin, pretending not to care. "Where would I go?"

Hiram ran a hand through his white hair. "I talked to Catheryn Jules this morning. You know who she is, don't you?"

"Yes," Lilly answered firmly. "She's the widow woman four houses from here—the one with all the children. Her brother Zeb provides for her."

"Yes. Catheryn can't quite get over losing her husband, and she hadn't had much interest in going to another man yet. She's struggling with depression, and the five little ones are difficult for her to handle. She could use some help. When I mentioned you, her face lit up. She loves your singing. It might be good for her to have you around. You would earn your keep by helping with the children."

"Fine," Lilly said curtly. "When do you want me to go?"

"Lilly, don't be that way. I feel terrible about this."

"No, you don't. You're glad to be rid of me."

"That isn't true, Lilly. And you can stay until Brother Mitchell leaves. That way, you'll be able to see him as much as you want until he's gone."

Lilly turned away and sat down on her bed. "Thank you."

Hiram came closer and knelt in front of her. "Please understand, Lilly. We're here for you anytime you need us. And if things don't work out with Catheryn, you can come back with us. We *aren't* abandoning you, Lilly. I'll even help Zeb and Catheryn with expenses. But for now, I have to think about Laura. I have my own way of running this home and caring for my family. That's *my* right, just like you have a right to live your life however you want. I'm not saying you did anything so terribly wrong, but if you insist on my having no say in anything you do, then it's best if you live someplace where you *can* be more independent. Catheryn and Zeb will have no say in your personal life." He reached out and patted her arm. "We all love you, Lilly."

Hiram rose and left, taking the oil lamp with him. Lilly curled under her covers, fighting tears. Again she was abandoned and alone. The only person who really mattered to her now was Chase Mitchell.

Chapter Six

Lilly watched Chase with love and pity as he clung to the railing on his way down the stairs. Mary followed behind, carrying newly carved crutches.

A cot had been prepared in the parlor for Chase. He would spend the rest of his nights there until he was healed. Hiram, standing at the bottom of the stairway, suggested he go and lie down on it as soon as he reached the last step, but Chase refused. "I want to get some fresh air," he protested.

"Brother Charles, this is your first walk. You're still weak," Mary reminded him.

"I can make it for a while yet." Chase glanced at Lilly, who seemed to look prettier every day. She stood in the hallway watching him, her hair brushed out long and beautiful, her lovely form adorned in a pink dress. "I'll walk outside with Lilly for a bit," he told Hiram, "if that's all right."

"It's Lilly's decision, not mine," Hiram answered rather grudgingly. He took the crutches from Mary and handed them to Chase, giving him a warning look. Chase put the crutches under his arms and tested them.

"Pretty good fit." He looked at Lilly and smiled. "Will you walk outside with me? Somebody has to run for help if I fall on my face."

He seemed taller than Lilly remembered, his shoulders broader. She glanced at Hiram, who raised his chin, his blue eyes challenging her to defy what she knew he considered proper.

"I would be glad to walk with you," she answered Chase, keeping her eyes on Hiram when she spoke.

She then turned to look at Chase. "You mustn't do too much this first day."

His eyes met hers with a steady gaze. Lilly realized she felt more and more as though she belonged to him. She took her bonnet from a hook in the hallway and tied it under her chin, then wrapped a shawl around her shoulders. "It's a littly chilly today," she warned Chase. "I took your jacket from your gear. I knew you'd want to go outside for a bit." She picked up the fringed buckskin jacket and handed it to him. He slipped one arm into it, then leaned on his left crutch while Mary helped him slip into the other sleeve. Chase limped to the door and Lilly opened it. They stepped outside into sunshine, the air cool and crisp. Chase breathed deeply.

"This feels good," he told her. "Let's walk out to the gate."

Lilly walked slowly beside him, her heart aching at the perspiration that beaded on his forehead in spite of the cold. She knew he was in a great deal of pain, and she felt as though she was the cause of it.

"Are you all right, Chase?"

"I'll make it. I'm going to get this leg working, no matter what."

Lilly grasped his arm, pointing to a huge tree in Hiram's front lawn that had a wooden bench built around it. "Can you get to that tree? We can sit down on the other side of it. The trunk is so big no one at the house would see us."

"Sounds like a good idea to me."

Lilly stayed close beside him until they reached the bench, where Chase slowly lowered himself to a sitting position. He set the crutches aside, leaned his head back, and gave out a long sigh. "Well, I made it." He was breathing heavily.

"Maybe you should go back inside. The air is chilly."

"No. It feels good. Besides, I'm sitting now. I'll be all right in a couple of minutes."

Lilly sat down beside him and he turned his head, his blue eyes gently drinking in her beauty. Again Lilly felt surges of desire that frightened her. She turned her attention to the trunk of the massive oak under which they sat. Tiny buds were appearing on its limbs, but no leaves had opened yet.

"Isn't this the biggest tree you've ever seen?" she asked Chase.

Chase looked up into the sprawling branches. "I believe it is." His eyes dropped to the milky-white skin of her face, the long lashes framing her exotic eyes, and he wondered if it was possible to fall in love in such a short time. How he wished he never had to leave her.

Lilly shifted away from him slightly, self-conscious in the bright daylight. "What will you do when you come back from Mexico?" she asked him. "I mean, what do you do for a living?"

"Oh, I've had a lot of odd jobs, but I never got serious about any of them, because I knew I'd be joining my father in the army. I kind of put it off for my mother's sake, but now that she's gone . . ."

Lilly could tell the loss was still fresh and painful for him. "What was she like, Chase?"

He looked at the sky as he spoke. "Quiet. She never complained to my father about his being gone so much. Sometimes I wished she would speak up more, show a little more spirit. He didn't have to be gone that much." He sighed deeply. "My mother was pretty—she was tiny and had honey-colored hair. I take after my father—he has dark hair and a big build—but I have my mother's eyes."

Lilly smiled. "She must have had beautiful eyes, then."

Chase looked at her, his own eyes watery. "It must be the same for your mother—or was it your father who had green eyes?"

Lilly blushed and looked down at her skirt. "My mother." She smiled and laughed lightly. "She was never quiet. She was pretty independent, and a hard worker. Sometimes I wonder if she really could have survived here, where men have so much control. It might not have worked out for her."

Chase reached out and took her hand. "Lilly, I heard Hiram talking to you last night. It isn't right, him making you go live someplace else. I felt like telling him so myself, but he and his wife have done so much for me, putting me up like they have. I guess I can't be telling the man his business in his own house, but it makes me really angry. I'm damned sorry about it. It must hurt and frighten you to have to go and live with someone else."

She studied the big, strong hand, his skin darkened by sun. "It's all right. I've met Catheryn Jules. She's very nice. And I'll have more freedom there."

"What about the brother she lives with? What is he like? Is he single?"

Lilly smiled, meeting his eyes. "Yes, he's single. His name is Zeb Adams. But he's not a man I would ever be interested in."

Their eyes held and he squeezed her hand. "And me?"

She felt lightheaded, and her stomach felt as though a bird was flying around inside of it. "I let you kiss me, didn't I?"

His eyes suddenly glittered with desire, and he leaned closer. Lilly sat nervous and rigid as his mouth once again touched her lips. He pushed slightly, parting her lips with his tongue. She was sure that allowing him to do so was much too bold and she pulled away, her cheeks crimson. Taking the opportunity to stand, Lilly moved quickly to a spot a few feet away from him.

"We're a lot alike, Lilly, you and me. And we both had

trouble forgetting that night on the riverboat. That has to mean something. I know this is sudden and all, but I already asked you to write to me. Now I'm asking you to do more than that. I want you to promise to wait for me."

Lilly wondered how she should interpret such a request. "It could be a long time."

"I know. I hate pressing you this way, but I don't have a lot of time, especially for social niceties and courting you for weeks or months. I guess I'll have to court you through my letters. I just want to know you won't go and marry someone else before I've had a chance to spend more time with you. I want to know you'll wait for me, Lilly, and I want to get all of that out of the way right now so every minute we spend together will be important and genuine, not bashful and proper. I admit we still have a lot to learn about each other, but we both know we're attracted to each other and would see a lot more of each other if I didn't have to go away. Tell me you'll wait for me, Lilly."

Lilly put a hand to her forehead, confused, wishing she knew more about men. She folded her shawl closer around her arms. "That's a big request."

"If there was any way to get out of leaving, I'd do it, Lilly. You understand why I can't, don't you?"

She nodded. "You're a man of your word, a man of pride." She turned to face him. "And I *will* wait for you."

His eyes filled with gratitude. "You don't know how glad that makes me, Lilly. I hate the thought of you going west. But at least you'll be with people who will look after you. It's better than worrying about you being left behind, alone."

"It will be worse for you. You're the one who'll be in real danger, Chase. I'll pray for you night and day." She came closer. "I don't know why this is happening—why I never forgot you. It must mean something special, yet I can't decide if it's right or wrong. And I worry what you think of me."

He grabbed the crutches and struggled to his feet, limping closer to her. "I think the world of you, Lilly. Why else would I ask you to wait for me? And this *is* right. Some force stronger than we are wants us to be together. We owe it to each other to say what needs to be said. I've never felt like this before. I swear you cast some kind of spell on me that night on the riverboat, because you've been gnawing at me ever since, and I don't have time to dance around the facts."

Chase wondered if he could actually be in love with her, and he saw by her eyes that she was wondering the same thing about him.

She blinked and looked away, then walked around the tree toward the house. "We'd better go back," she told him, without turning. She waited, listening to his slow struggle to reach her.

"Don't be afraid of it, Lilly. It's all right to tell me everything you're thinking and feeling."

"But . . . how do I know it's real? I mean, this is all so new to me. And how do I know you aren't lying to me about wanting me to wait for you? How do I know you'll come back at all?" She whirled, meeting his eyes. "Please don't lie to me, Chase."

His eyes held only love and sincerity. "I would never lie to you, Lilly. You said just a moment ago I was a man of my word, and I am. I meant everything I said."

She put a hand to her chest, sure she was walking in some kind of dream. As a buggy clattered past the house, two women riding in the back of it turned their heads to stare at Lilly. Lilly glanced at them, noticing how they leaned together and whispered. The gesture brought up her stubborn pride and she met Chase's eyes again, holding her chin proudly. "I believe you," she told him. "And I want to be with you every day until you have to go."

He gave her a melting smile. "Whether Hiram approves or not?"

"It's as Hiram told you earlier—*my* decision."

He loved the way she looked when she was being stubborn and independent. He almost laughed out loud, but she was serious, and he felt sorry for her, knowing she was not being treated as well now as she had been before he had interrupted her life.

"You had better get back inside," she told him.

His eyes moved over her, making her shiver with desires she was sure were forbidden. "Thank you, Lilly."

She smiled, her heart feeling suddenly lighter. For some reason it didn't matter so much anymore that she would have to leave Hiram's house. Chase Mitchell cared so much about her that he wanted her to wait for him! Knowing he would come back to her would make putting up with a new household bearable, and it would give her hope on the dreaded long journey west. She would not think about those things now—only about Chase Mitchell and the present. Somehow, it seemed unreal that he would ever really go away.

Three days turned into ten, and Lilly did not let one of them pass without spending most of her spare waking hours with Chase. Hiram's cold silence did not deter her; nor did the fact that Laura was not allowed to be alone with her. Lilly knew Laura understood. She was determined that nothing would stop her from being with Chase.

By the middle of April, the buds on the maple trees had begun to burst open, and yellow daffodils and purple and white hyacinths had pushed their way through the freshly thawed earth. It seemed to Lilly that her heart was like the buds—ready to burst with love. She felt as colorful and alive as the flowers.

Chase had not told Lilly that he loved her, but she knew he did, and that any day she would hear the beautiful words. She ignored the way some people stared at her in town. She told herself that not being able to sing in the temple was not the end of the world, nor was not being asked anymore by Hiram and Mary to sing for the family. There was still a song in her heart—it was there for Chase Mitchell, and no one else.

The hours Lilly and Chase spent together were happy ones. Lilly often sang for him softly when they walked outside alone. She taught him Scottish songs, and Chase taught her American songs, like *Drink to Me Only with Thine Eyes* and *Aura Lee*.

When the weather turned warmer, Lilly planned a picnic for herself and Chase. As she stood in the kitchen packing lunch into a basket, she felt Mary's unspoken disapproval of her decision to walk off alone with Chase. She closed the basket and glanced at Laura, who sat at the table frosting a

cake. The girl was struggling not to giggle. Lilly picked up
the basket and walked into the hall, where she grabbed a
blanket she had left folded on a bench. She carried both
outside, where Chase waited for her.

"Are you ready?" she asked.

"Yes, ma'am. Want me to carry the basket?"

"No. You're still favoring that leg. You've got to get used
to walking without the crutches. Take the blanket." She
handed it to him. "The creek across the road winds behind
the house. There's a nice place there where we can be
alone."

She no longer felt awkward and bashful with him. If he
never became anything more, Chase Mitchell had become a
good friend. But Lilly wanted more than that from him, and
she was sure he wanted more, too. They walked together
slowly down to the creek, where Lilly spread out the blanket.

"The ground might still be cool, but the blanket should be
enough of a barrier." She set down the basket of food, then
took hold of one of his arms. "Hang on to me until you get
yourself down."

Lilly could feel firm muscles through the sleeve of
Chase's shirt as he eased himself down. She sat down beside
him and opened the basket.

"I brought a pie."

Chase smiled, studying the way her hair glowed in the
sunshine. "You think of everything, don't you?"

"Well, I try." She set out a bowl of chicken and a loaf of
fresh-baked bread. "I'll fix you a plate." She met his eyes,
smiling. "I'm so happy it turned out to be a nice day. Hiram
says that this time of year in Illinois, you can't be sure of the
weather. Sometimes, it can even snow in the spring."

"Well, he's right there. How about Scotland? Does it ever
snow there?"

"Oh, yes, in the Highlands."

Chase tried to picture the land this beautiful creature had
come from. "Tell me more."

Lilly smiled. "Well, Scotland is very, very green, but
there are not many trees. Most of the farming is done in the
Lowlands. But then, Glasgow is there, too. It's a big indus-

trial city surrounded by farms. Everything must come through Glasgow—farm products, manufactured goods— because of the Clyde River. It flows into a bay there, which opens into the Firth of Clyde."

"What's a firth?"

"It's just another name for a bay." She turned her attention back to the food. "Have you ever heard of the Loch Ness monster?"

He laughed as he watched her prepare his plate. "That's a fairy tale."

"Is it, now?" She gave him a teasing grin. "There have been many reports of a great monster in Loch Ness—per- haps a prehistoric animal that never died. What do you think of that?"

"I think somebody has a wild imagination," he answered.

Lilly laughed and handed him his plate. "Listen to me, talking about Scotland as though I'm going back there—as though I were just a visitor here."

"Maybe someday you *will* get to go back."

She smiled longingly as she sliced the bread. "It would be nice, but I really don't have anything to go back to now." She spread jam on the bread, then began fixing a plate for herself. "How long do you think you'll be in Texas, Chase? Will you be there the whole two years?"

"I'm not sure. Depends on what's happening when I get there, I guess—what my father is involved in, how things stand with Mexico. I'm hoping war can be avoided. If it can, I figure I can come back in maybe a year or less."

"A year! That's much better than two, but it still sounds like a long time."

Their eyes held. Chase wondered if he could wait that long to claim Lilly for himself. "It does to me, too, but I'll write, like I promised. And I *will* come back."

"But, if I go west with the Mormons, how will you find me?"

"I'll find you—don't worry about that. The Mormons have a way of attracting attention, you know. Plenty of peo- ple will know where you are."

She sighed deeply, biting into her chicken, but suddenly not feeling hungry. A year. And what if there *was* a war, and he got caught in it? It could be even longer before he came back. All kinds of things could happen to him. She swallowed the chicken, but her stomach felt tight. She glanced at Chase, who was chewing his own meat. She watched his jaw muscles work, studied his high cheekbones, the lovely line of his lips. There had been more than one burning kiss in stolen moments, and she never failed to be surprised at the way she felt on fire when his sweet lips tasted her mouth. But they had been quickly stolen kisses, and he still had not embraced her fully. She didn't know how to let him know it was all right—that she wanted and needed to feel his strong arms around her.

Chase swallowed the meat and gave her a soft, reassuring smile. "Don't worry about going west, Lilly. 'If God be for me, who can be against me?' Isn't that some kind of Bible passage? Surely you Mormons believe that. If we're meant to be together, we'll be together."

"Chase Mitchell, you know I'm not a Mormon, but I suppose you're right about the other."

He wiped his hands on a linen napkin. "What faith are you, then?"

"Presbyterian. That's the faith my mother taught me. And what about you?" she asked. "You actually quoted a little scripture."

He laughed. "That's just a little bit of Bible learning I remembered from when I was a boy and my mother used to take me to church—Methodist. I haven't been inside a church in a long time. Not that I'm proud about it, or refuse to go. Things like that just have a way of slipping away from you, I guess."

"Well, what matters is how you conduct your life, Chase. I'm sure God knows you're a very fine man."

He grinned. "I hope so. I wouldn't want to be on the wrong side of Him, especially when I might be going off to a war."

Her smile faded. She poured him a cup of apple juice and handed it to him. A current of feeling coursed through her when his fingers touched hers. They finished eating quietly.

"Want to learn another song?" he asked her when they were both done. "I know one that fits us."

She smiled, setting the basket she was refilling aside and tucking her skirt under her feet. "Oh, do sing it, then. I love learning new songs."

"Just don't make fun of my voice," he answered, clearing his throat.

"You know I wouldn't. You have a very fine voice."

He laughed lightly, then drew in his breath and sang. "My Bonnie lies over the ocean. My Bonnie lies over the sea . . ."

Lilly smiled and listened intently, concentrating on the tune and the words. Chase moved closer, and their eyes held as he softly repeated the song, using the name Lilly instead of Bonnie.

"Bring back, bring back, oh, bring back my Lilly to me," he finished.

Neither of them spoke for a moment. "Lilly," he finally whispered softly.

Lilly wondered how one word could open up such an array of emotions and make her suddenly so weak and on fire. His face came closer. She knew he would do more than kiss her this time. His lips touched her own, tenderly parting her mouth. He pressed harder, his tongue floating along her lips as the kiss turned into a hot branding. His lips never left her own as his arms came around her and he laid her back. He pressed close, his chest crushing her breasts, his kiss drawn out, demanding, hot with passion.

When he finally left her mouth they were both breathing heavily, and intense, almost painful urges surged through Lilly. She moved her arms around his neck and hugged him tightly as he kissed her cheek, her neck. He whispered her name, and one strong hand pressed against her ribs, moved up toward her breast.

She told herself to stop him, but desire and curiosity and a terrible need to know she had pleased him left her speechless. His lips covered her mouth again, and she relaxed at the touch of his big, strong hand covering her breast, grasping at it tenderly.

"God, Lilly, you're so beautiful," he whispered then, leaving her mouth and kissing her neck again. "I think I love you, Lilly."

She was astonished that he actually seemed to be trembling as much as she. Her heart pounded so wildly and her chest was so tight, she wondered if she would lose her breath altogether. He had finally said it! He loved her!

"I love you, too, Chase. I love you so!"

She returned his kisses, and they lay entwined for several minutes, kissing, whispering, reveling in each other's touches.

His hand moved down and she felt it run along her leg, pushing up her dress. He moved farther on top of her, resting on his good leg, ignoring the pain in the wounded one. Lilly felt a hardness against her thigh as he pressed against her, and his hand moved even farther up her leg. Instinct told her what she felt, and for a moment right and wrong became blurred in her mind. Passion and desire consumed her so that for a moment she considered letting him do whatever he wanted. But inexperience and a fear of the unknown finally overcame the other feelings, and she grasped his arm.

"No, Chase, don't."

She felt him stiffen slightly. He sighed deeply, kissing her mouth once more, tenderly, this time not quite so searching and demanding. "I'm sorry," he whispered. He raised up on one elbow, petting her hair and kissing her cheeks, her eyes. "I'm sorry," he repeated.

She felt wilted. It was difficult for her to look into his eyes. She curled against him, burying her face in his neck. He held her there, kissing her hair.

"Forgive me, Lilly."

"It's all right," she answered, her voice sounding tiny. "I . . . wanted you to touch me." She breathed in his masculine scent, relished in the feel of his strong arms around her. It was the most glorious moment, the most beautiful feeling she had ever experienced. There was no doubt in her mind that it was love. "Did you mean it, Chase—that you love me?"

"I do love you, and I want you to wait for me, Lilly."

She finally met his eyes and reached up to touch his face. "I love you, too, Chase. You're the first man who's ever kissed me—the first man I've ever *wanted* to kiss me.

Maybe I'm young and you're the first, but love only comes once, doesn't it?"

He studied her beautiful green eyes. "That's the way I always thought of it. I've never felt like this about any woman either, Lilly. I've never found one I wanted to be with for the rest of my life—one that I hated the thought of leaving."

"Some people might say it's too soon, but I know in my heart that I love you. And you know that I'll wait for you, Chase. God meant us to be together—I just know it."

He grasped her wrist, turning his face to kiss her palm. "We had better go back before I..." He didn't finish the sentence. He suddenly sat up, as though startled. "We'd better go back, Lilly," he repeated.

Lilly frowned. "Are you all right?"

He gave out a little laugh, glancing back at her and away again. "You're such an innocent. Yes, I'm all right. Just a little too tempted, that's all."

Lilly reddened, suddenly feeling awkward. She sat up, shaking out her hair and brushing herself off, then picked up the basket and set it aside. "I'll help you up and shake out the blanket."

He looked up at her with an oddly bashful smile on his face. He reached up and she hung on to him as best she could to help him stand up. Then she shook out the blanket and folded it, laying it on top of the basket and turning to him.

"God, Lilly, I wish I could just stay here forever," he told her. "But I can't—I just can't. Please say you understand."

"You know I do."

Their eyes held, each of them wanting what was most forbidden. He pulled her into his arms and met her lips again. She was lost in him, relishing his powerful, comforting embrace.

"I'll be back, Lilly. That's a promise," he told her.

"I know you will," she answered softly. "You aren't the kind of man who would go back on a promise—just like you can't go back on your promise to your father. That's part of what I love about you."

Chase reluctantly pulled back. "It's settled, then. We'll talk about it more tonight, tomorrow." His eyes actually teared. "I'll have to get going in two or three days, Lilly."

In that one, quick moment, they both suddenly realized the gravity of the statement. He really was going away.

"Oh, Chase," she whispered.

Chapter Seven

The night was nearly sleepless for both of them. Never had Chase wanted a woman more than he wanted Lilly Brannigan. It didn't seem fair to marry her before going off to war, yet he wondered how he was supposed to bear the agony of not being able to claim her before he left Nauvoo. Somehow, he had to ensure that she belonged only to him. And he couldn't bear the thought of any other man being the first to make a woman of her.

Lilly's own thoughts were filled with the shuddering ecstasy of imagining Chase Mitchell lying in her bed with her, touching her again, the way he had touched her when they picnicked at the creek. Ever since then, her body had felt on fire and her heart ached with love for him. She could hardly wait for the sun to rise so that they could go walking again. When morning light finally penetrated her bedroom window, she was up and dressed, brushing her hair over and over until it shined. She hurried through morning chores and felt nervous and flushed at breakfast. Wonderful desires moved through her every time Chase looked at her. She hurried to help with breakfast cleanup and sat impatiently through morning worship.

Finally, the free time she had been waiting for arrived— time Hiram had told her she could spend with Chase, if that was what she wanted.

"Don't stray too far," he warned.

"We won't. We'll walk down by the creek," she answered, not even sure what they would do. She hurried to the shed out back, where Chase was currying his horse. She could tell from his eyes when he looked at her that he was happy she was there.

"You finally get away?"

"Yes!" Their eyes held. "Let's walk down by the creek out back again," she told him.

Chase gave her a wink and turned to throw some oats into a trough for his horse. Then he took her hand and led her down the hill. "Let's walk farther," he said aloud. "We'll take the back streets to the river."

Lilly said nothing. Hiram had said not to go too far, but if Chase wanted to go to the river, she would. She wanted to be alone with him. When they arrived at the river, Chase flagged down two young boys with a raft.

"I'll give each of you two pennies if you'll let me use that raft," he told them.

"Sure, mister!" The boys eagerly handed Chase their paddles. He paid them, then turned to Lilly.

"Would you like to take a little pleasure cruise downriver on my elegant riverboat, Miss Brannigan?" He extended his arm toward the wooden raft, which floated on four barrels.

Lilly smiled. "Why, of course, Mr. Mitchell." She pulled up the hem of her dress and lightly stepped onto the raft. Chase climbed on, still favoring his injured leg. He used an oar to push the raft farther out into the river, then sat down on one side of it, using a paddle to maneuver the awkward "riverboat."

"Sit down across from me and use this other paddle," he told Lilly.

Lilly obeyed, finding sweet relief and joy in the adventure. It felt good to get away from the somber Williams household and Hiram's intense looks. In the past week the dinner table had become like a morgue, with Laura ordered not to speak and Hiram cool to both Chase and Lilly. She was glad now she would be going to live with Catheryn

Jules. Anything would be better than the loneliness of living in the Williams household.

Poor Laura. She was the only reason that Lilly hated to leave, but she was left with no choice, and she vowed to find ways to visit with her only real friend.

They floated downriver until Nauvoo was no longer in sight. As Lilly drank in the sights and smells of spring, Chase kept glancing at her. She wore yellow today—a long-sleeved, high-necked dress that fit her bodice perfectly.

"There's a pretty meadow," he said aloud, pointing. "Look at all the wild flowers."

"Oh, it's beautiful!" Lilly exclaimed. "Let's push the raft up to the edge and get off, Chase."

He laughed lightly at her almost girlish reaction. They paddled the raft to shore and Lilly jumped off.

"Hang on to the raft while I get off," Chase told her, wincing as he got up himself. His leg was still stiff, but the wound looked completely healed. Chase suspected that he would be plagued with painful problems from it all his life. His only consolation was that every time it gave him trouble, he would think of Lilly. He knew now that it was Lilly's chastity for which he had fought that day—that deep inside, even then, he had been willing to risk his life to make sure no other man touched her. He had saved Lilly for himself.

Chase grabbed the blanket and stepped gingerly from the raft, then pulled it farther onto shore. "Hiram would be pretty upset if he knew we were doing this," he commented.

"I don't care anymore," Lilly declared. "He's sending me away anyway."

Chase put an arm around her waist, giving her a light squeeze. "I sure am sorry about how it all worked out. But I'm not sorry about having all this time alone with you."

"And neither am I," she replied before she darted away to pick wild flowers. Soon, she had a huge bouquet of them.

"It won't do you any good," Chase warned. "Nothing wilts faster than wild flowers."

"I don't care. They're so pretty," she answered, running farther ahead. "Oh, Chase, look! There's an old abandoned cabin, partly fallen. Let's go and look at it!"

Chase shook his head, walking as fast as his leg would

allow, but still unable to keep up with her. "Wait up!" he shouted. "And be careful! You might get hurt."

Lilly turned and waited, smiling. When he finally caught up, she pushed open the wooden door of the cabin, still holding the bouquet of wild flowers in her other hand. She peeked inside.

"Look, Chase! There are some old animal skins in here!"

Chase followed her inside and looked around. Rays of sunlight filtered through cracks in the roof, lighting up the inside of the cabin. One wall was partly caved in. Shelves on another wall displayed a couple of abandoned pans and a few tin plates and cups. Aged beaverskins lay in one corner, and a deerskin hung on the wall.

"Must have belonged to some old trapper, before whites took over the area," he commented.

"I wonder what could have happened to him—why he left and apparently just never came back."

"Probably died."

Lilly looked at him. It struck her full force that that very thing could happen to Chase. He could go away and be killed and never come back. Chase read her thoughts and wondered the same.

In the next moment Lilly ran to his arms. He dropped the blanket and embraced her fully, his mouth covering her own in a searing kiss that spoke of his own desperate fear of not returning. He released the kiss, and she buried her face against his chest.

"Lilly, I want very much to marry you, but it would be wrong right now. You know that, don't you? We have to wait until I come back."

"But, I don't want to wait." She could hardly believe she was saying the words. "I don't want to wait to belong to you. You might get killed, Chase, and never come back." Suddenly, the tears came. "Oh, Chase, what if you don't come back? That means someday—someday—after a very long time of getting over losing you, I might marry someone else. Then he would—he would be the first. I don't *want* him to be. I want it to be you, Chase."

"Lilly," he said softly, tangling his fingers in her hair. "Do you realize what you're saying?"

"I don't care. If you go away and die, I'll never have known you that way." She looked up at him, tears spilling from her eyes, breaking his heart. "I'm not afraid with you, Chase. And if we can . . . share each other before you go, you'll remember me more. You'll try harder to come back."

He kissed her hair. "I'd come back anyway, Lilly."

"But, it's not the same."

Their eyes held, and fire ripped through him with uncontrollable force. He knew in that moment what had to be, right or wrong.

"Lilly, I—I've thought the same thing, but I didn't want to hurt you, or want you to think I might just be using you." He crushed her close. "Oh, Lilly, I want you so badly I feel like a crazy man."

"Then . . . you can have me," she answered, wondering who had said the words.

Lilly closed her eyes as his mouth met hers. She cast the wild flowers aside and flung her arms around his neck as he pulled her tight against him, lifting her feet off the ground. His tongue searched deep, drawing out her own raging fires.

Lilly wasn't even positive exactly what would happen. She only knew she wanted Chase Mitchell to be the one to make a woman out of her. She was terrified, excited, in love, curious—filled with wonderful desires that made her insides ache.

Chase released the kiss, moving his lips to her neck, and whispering her name. He then let her go and looked down at her with such obvious love and worship that Lilly lost all remaining doubt about whether this was right. Chase leaned down and picked up the blanket, opening it and spreading it over the soft dirt floor of the old cabin.

"I don't think anybody comes around here much, from the looks of things," he told Lilly.

Their eyes held as he sat down, then reached up and pulled Lilly down beside him. Somewhere in the distance they both heard the rumble of thunder, but neither cared about it. There was a bigger storm in their souls—a violent energy that had to be released.

The moment Chase met her mouth, Lilly was his, totally. In his wild need, Chase's every move was designed to bring out the womanly needs in the sweet innocent he touched. Lilly lay almost helpless, unsure what to do herself, but knowing Chase would show her. She merely closed her eyes, telling herself not to be afraid. This was Chase— sweet, handsome, virile, brave Chase. He was going away, maybe for two whole years—maybe even forever!

His hot kisses left her almost breathless, and Lilly realized with utter ecstasy that his gentle hands were opening her prim dress, then reaching inside to grasp her breasts. Chase's thumb moved over a nipple, making it almost hurt with a need to be touched more.

She was lost in him—totally, willingly, happily. He raised her up slightly and pulled her dress and cotton lace undergarment to her waist, laying her back again and kissing her everywhere—tasting, feeling, kissing her belly, making her whimper with glorious pleasure. Then he was taking off his own jacket and shirt.

He came down gently on top of her, his hot skin touching her breasts. He met her mouth again as he reached down and pulled up the skirts of her dress. "Don't be afraid," he whispered.

There was no time to be afraid. His hands, reaching inside her bloomers, grasped at her bare hips. Lilly had trouble breathing, her heart pounded so wildly. She kept her eyes closed as she felt him pulling down the bloomers. She knew her face was crimson as he pulled them over her knee-high stockings and shoes, and she wondered if he was pleased with what he saw.

"My God, Lilly, you're so beautiful," he almost groaned.

She had her answer, and she was thrilled at the thought of Chase looking upon her nakedness for the first time. He lay down beside her, moving a hand over her bare thigh, up to that secret place she never dreamed she would be able to let any man touch.

His mouth covered hers again, while his fingers moved deep into her private nest, making her groan and whimper. He seemed to have touched some magic spot that made her lose whatever resistance she might have had left. She felt totally free. The more he touched her, the more she wanted him to touch her, until she felt her legs opening so that he could touch her even more.

"Lilly, my Lilly," he groaned. He felt her warm moistness and knew she was nearly ready for him. Suddenly she began panting and arched against his hand.

Lilly had no idea just what had happened to her. Chase had worked some kind of magic on her with his strong but gentle fingers. A wonderful explosion ripped through her insides, and all remaining sense of reality left her. She was floating now. Chase was on his knees, unbuttoning his trousers.

"It might hurt, Lilly."

"I don't care," she answered, surprised at her own boldness.

He pushed her dress to her waist, then lay on top of her. She felt strangely helpless at the way her legs were parted. Something pressed against her private place, and Lilly felt a sharp pain deep inside, so stinging that she cried out. Thunder from the overhead storm drowned out her virgin awakening.

Suddenly she wanted to stop him, but she knew instinctively that was impossible. He lay on top of her, moving rhythmically, his strong arms under her, his lips and tongue searching her mouth so wildly that she was soon caught up in the glory of the act. The initial pain had lessened, but was still there, yet it didn't seem to matter.

She arched up to him, meeting his rhythmic thrusts, surprised at how easily she responded, how wonderful and beautiful it was to be a woman. It was like entering a whole new world, and she knew she was changed forever.

They remained tangled together as it began to rain, sharing bodies in glorious abandon. Lilly Brannigan was a woman now, and it was Chase Mitchell who had made her one. She would have had it no other way, no matter what the future held for them both.

Wearing only his pants, Chase ducked outside the cabin with an old tin pan. Thunder seemed to literally shake the ground, as the rain continued to pour down. He let it fill the pan, then came back inside.

"This looks as if it could last all day," he told Lilly, setting the pan filled with rainwater down beside her. "If it keeps up we're either going to get mighty wet going back, or we'll get back too late. Either way, Hiram won't forgive this one."

Lilly lay curled on the blanket, completely naked, she covered herself with her dress. "I don't care if he does or not," she answered. She looked at him with wide, sad eyes. "I just want to stay here with you—forever."

Chase took a handkerchief from his pants pocket and dipped it into the water. "I want the same thing, Lilly." He leaned closer, kissing her lips lightly. "But I think the best thing to do is go back in the rain, rather than spend any more time here. At least now we can still say we were just walking and got caught in this."

He sighed deeply, pulling back again. "I'm afraid this old pan of water will have to do if you want to wash. It's better than nothing."

Lilly blinked back tears, sitting up and dropping the dress to her waist. Chase felt a burning ache at the sight of her full, white, soft breasts. He had made love to her four times, yet he couldn't seem to get enough of her.

"I feel funny washing in front of you," she said, her cheeks reddening.

Chase grinned, amused at her bashfulness after the almost wanton way she had given herself to him. "I won't look." He went to the door and opened it, watching the downpour.

Lilly had no idea how long they had been here. She only knew that Chase Mitchell had made love to her over and over, and the initial pain had turned to glorious satisfaction. She was no longer the same Lilly Brannigan, and nothing in her life was as important now as this man.

She washed quickly, and also reluctantly. This meant she would not lie in his arms anymore today. They might not get any other chance. This could be all she would ever have of Chase Mitchell. She fought tears as she pulled on her bloomers. Every part of her body still tingled from his caresses. He had been so gentle, yet so virile. She put on her dress, watching him all the while. She studied every hard muscle, his slim hips, remembered that part of him she had never seen before on any man. At first it had frightened her.

Now, she thought it was beautiful. Everything about Chase Mitchell was beautiful.

"I'm finished," she announced.

Chase turned, and their eyes held in a new awareness, a love far deeper than either of them realized they could share. "You belong to me now, Lilly," he told her, his eyes misty. "Always remember that."

"I'll remember it forever." Her lower lip quivered and he came closer, embracing her. She wept against his chest.

"It's going to be all right, Lilly—you'll see."

"Nothing will be all right until you're back, Chase, and we can be together always."

He stroked her hair. "I'd marry you right now, Lilly—you know that. But it wouldn't be fair to you, not knowing what will happen once I leave here."

"It's all right. We're the same as married now anyway, aren't we?" She looked up at him.

"I suppose we are," he answered, wiping her tears away with his fingers. "But if I don't get back, Lilly, you'll be free to marry another, and he doesn't have to know. No one has to know about this."

"I don't *care* who knows," she sobbed.

"You *should* care. I love you, Lilly. I don't want people thinking things about you that aren't true. You're sweet and good and full of love, and in so many ways, you're just as innocent now as before I made love to you." He kissed her forehead. "You've got to promise me, Lilly, that you'll take care of yourself as you head west, and that you won't argue about anything that has to do with your safety."

"But I could stay here, Chase, get some kind of work. You could find me easier."

"No! It's too dangerous. I don't want you staying behind. The best thing for you now is to stay with the Mormons. They're all you've got, Lilly, and they're good people, in spite of your problems with Hiram. Being alone in a strange land would be more dangerous than going into a wilderness with people who will help you and watch out for you. I'll find you, Lilly. Don't you worry about that for one minute." He wrapped strong arms around her. "I *will* find you!"

She hugged him around the waist. "Tell me again you love me, Chase. I love you so much."

"I do love you. Someday we'll be together again, Lilly. You've got to believe in that. I'll write as often as I can." His voice choked, and Lilly continued to cry. "Come on, Lilly," he finally told her. "Where's the strong, fiesty girl I met on the riverboat? One thing that struck me was how brave you must be. Now you've got to be extra brave. We've got to go back, honey, and I think it's best that I leave tomorrow."

"No! No, not that soon!"

"Lilly, the sooner, the better. Why drag this out? It's going to hurt just as much if I leave later as it will if I go tomorrow. We'll find some way to be together once more first."

"Oh, Chase, I don't think I can be as brave as you think."

"Sure you can." He reluctantly let go of her, grasping her arms. As he looked her over lovingly, Lilly noticed that his eyes had tears in them. "You're the most beautiful woman in Illinois, Lilly, and the bravest. Hold your head up and make me proud of you."

She sniffed and wiped at her eyes. "I will." She smoothed her hair down.

He turned to finish dressing, then walked over and picked up the blanket. "This thing is a mess," he said, shaking it out. "We'll let it get good and wet in the rain so no one notices." He walked to the door and turned to her. "You ready?"

"I'll never be ready."

"Neither will I, so let's just get this over with."

She breathed deeply and walked up beside him. He kissed her once more and they both darted out into the rain.

Chapter Eight

"We only went walking. The time got away from us, and the next thing we knew, it was raining," Chase explained to Hiram. They both stood in the hallway, Lilly holding a fresh, dry blanket around her wet dress.

"Lilly could get sick from this!" Hiram fumed.

"I'm all right, Hiram," Lilly insisted.

"I'm perfectly aware it was risky," Chase argued, meeting Hiram's eyes squarely. "But I knew you'd react this way, and we decided to go ahead and get wet in order to get back before sundown. We waited for a long time in someone's barn, but the rain just wouldn't let up."

Hiram eyed him warily. "I'm sorry, Brother Charles, but I think you'd better get a room someplace else until you feel ready to leave. I deeply appreciate what you did for Lilly when you were wounded, but Lilly is obviously infatuated with you, and I don't think it's wise—"

"I'm leaving tomorrow," Chase interrupted.

Hiram looked surprised. "Tomorrow?"

"Well, I think my leg is healed enough to travel. I can't put things off any longer. The sooner I get to Texas, the sooner I can come back. And I want you to know right now that I *am* coming back—for Lilly. I'm going to marry her. I'd do it right now if my future wasn't so unpredictable."

Lilly looked up the stairs to see Laura standing on the landing, watching and listening. The girl's mouth hung open. Lilly wished she could share with Laura what had happened to her this day, but even if she could, the girl would never understand the fulfilled, satisfied, glowing feeling Lilly had at this moment, or the horrible ache of knowing the man she loved was going away, and she would not be held in his arms for a year or more. "It is easy to speak of marriage when you're going a thousand or more miles away for no one knows how long," Hiram answered Chase.

Chase stiffened. "Are you accusing me of making false promises?"

Their eyes held, challengingly. "I'm saying a healthy young man like yourself who is going off to war would be sorely tempted by a woman as sweet and beautiful as Lilly. Right now, it would have to be difficult for both you and Lilly to predict what will happen. You've just lost your mother, and now you're headed for God knows what, and Lilly is a young woman alone in a new land, still getting over the loss of her own mother. I'm only glad you *are* wise enough to put off marrying now, but it isn't fair of you to ask Lilly to wait upwards of two years, only to find you aren't coming for her at all."

"He *will* come!" Lilly spoke up defiantly. "He *will*!" She couldn't hold back the tears that stung her eyes. "You have no right to talk to Chase like that!"

Hiram frowned with genuine concern. "Lilly, I just don't want to see you get hurt."

Chase kept his eyes on Hiram as he spoke. "Hiram has a right to his opinion, Lilly. You can't blame him for worrying." He put an arm around Lilly's shoulders. "I'm telling you right now, Hiram, that I *will* come back, unless a bullet prevents it. I love Lilly."

Hiram sighed and shook his head. "Well, you both will have a great deal of time to think about it."

"I deeply appreciate everything you've done for me," Chase added. "I'll go get a room someplace else for tonight, and I'll pay you for all you've done before I leave."

Hiram frowned. "Payment is not necessary. We helped you because you were a man in need, and because of what you did for Lilly. I hold no grudges against you, Brother Mitchell. It's simply a matter of putting Lilly first. I feel totally responsible for her welfare. I would hate to see her get hurt."

"I *won't* get hurt," Lilly sniffed.

Hiram studied her sadly, wishing he understood and knew how to handle her stubborn nature. He looked up at Chase.

"If you're only staying one more night, you needn't bother getting a room. We'll see that you get a good breakfast in the morning, and Mary will pack some food for you to take along."

"It really isn't necessary."

"Yes, it is. I insist," Hiram concluded gruffly.

Lilly could see the hurt in Hiram's eyes, but she refused to soften. Hiram had all but accused Chase of lying, of using her, but she knew better. Hiram didn't know that she was a woman now. He hadn't heard Chase's whispered words of love, or seen the tears in Chase's eyes when he talked of leaving. She knew Chase Mitchell loved her beyond his own life, and she loved him in return—as much as any woman could ever love and worship a man. Hiram's doubts would never become her own.

"I want to know you'll look out for Lilly when the Mormons head west," Chase told Hiram then.

Hiram looked back up at him. "Of course we will. She'll have us, plus Catheryn Jules and her family. Catheryn's brother is a strong, able man. We'll all take good care of Lilly."

Thunder rumbled outside, and Lilly felt a storm in her heart. He was leaving tomorrow! There wasn't much time left now!

"Lilly, you had better get into some dry clothes," Mary said.

"Mary's right," Chase told her, giving her a light squeeze. "Go get out of those wet clothes."

She looked up at him, the same intense urges rushing through both of them at the comment. She had already been out of these clothes once, and she wanted to be out of them again and in Chase's arms before he went away. Her throat ached fiercely. She wanted to scream and cry and hold him close, but his eyes told her not to give away too much. She turned reluctantly and went up the stairs, stopping partway up to look down at Hiram.

"I'll pack my things tonight," she told him. "I'll be leaving tomorrow, too. Catheryn Jules has waited long enough for my help."

Hiram watched after her sadly as she went the rest of the

way upstairs, and Chase took off his hat and hung it on a hook. "I'm going to get out of my own wet clothes." He walked off to the parlor, which had become his own temporary private room. Hiram turned to Mary.

"I just want to do what's right, Mary. I wish Lilly understood that. The girl hates me. Even if I told her she could stay now, she wouldn't."

Mary patted his arm. "It will all work out, Hiram, and she doesn't hate you. She's just so much in love that she doesn't know how she feels about anything or anyone else right now. Once he's gone, time will take care of a lot of things."

Upstairs, Lilly began flinging clothes into the old cloth bag she had used on her trip from Scotland.

"Will you really go tomorrow?"

Lilly turned to see Laura standing just inside the door. "Yes."

Their eyes held. "I'll miss you terribly, Lilly. It will be lonely and boring around here without you."

Lilly swallowed to keep from crying. "I'll miss you, too, Laura, but we'll still find a way to see each other, and you can come visit me." She put out her arms and the two young women embraced. "I love him so much, Laura," Lilly sobbed. "I wish I could make Hiram understand how good Chase is—how much we love each other. He'll come back, Laura. I know he'll come back."

Lilly rode in front of Chase on his horse. She thought how beautiful the morning would seem if he could stay and she could lie in his arms every night, from this day forward. The sun shone bright, and birds sang. Trees were bursting with life and grass was greening.

But he was going away. The reality of it hung over her like a weight, so that her back and shoulders actually ached. All they had left was this one last chance to be alone together.

Breakfast had been quiet and strained. Lilly's clothes were packed to go to Catheryn Jules's as soon as Chase was gone. Chase had asked if he could take Lilly riding before he left, the mere thought of which brought a smile to Lilly's lips, for

there had been a bold look of determination in Chase's eyes
when he had looked at Hiram.

The family said a round of goodbyes and thank yous, and
Mary kindly packed Chase a potato sack full of food. Laura
had cried, and Beth, who was the artistic one in the family,
had given Chase a penciled drawing of Lilly. The likeness
was so good that several minutes were spent exclaiming over
it, and Lilly's heart was warmed when Chase said he would
treasure the picture and keep it with him while he was in
Mexico. Gerald and Henry shook Chase's hand like little
men, and Lilly was glad that, in spite of their father's disapproval of Lilly's feelings for the Gentile man, all the children liked Chase very much and hated to see him leave.
Even Mary seemed sorry he was going. She had quickly
embraced him, telling him they would pray for him.

Lilly closed her eyes and leaned her head against Chase's
chest. She told herself not to think about the agony this day
would bring. For now, she would live for each moment,
relish this last rendezvous with the man she would love for
the rest of her life.

Chase rode along the riverbank until he spotted the familiar meadow, then he headed for the cabin. As he dismounted
and helped Lilly down, she wondered at the irony that such a
dilapidated structure could seem so beautiful. It had become
a special place to her, where she had found love and discovered the joy of being a woman. She knew now that when
one was in love, everything was beautiful. Nothing mattered—not how much money someone had, or where they
lived. She had no money, and she would never see Scotland
again, but her heart soared with joy, for she was with Chase,
and soon she would again lie in his arms.

Chase took a blanket from his gear and they went inside.
He spread it out on the dirt floor, and then turned to her. He
began to remove her clothes gently. Lilly watched him with
trusting eyes, feeling wild and bold as he stripped her and
caressed her body with strong hands, his blue eyes drinking
in her beauty. Part of her wanted to pull something over
herself, but there was no time for modesty. She wanted
Chase to enjoy every moment, every touch; to drink in the
sight of her fully, so that he would never forget her.

She stood and watched as he undressed, before he turned to embrace her, pressing her naked breasts against the soft hairs and hard muscle of his chest. No words had been spoken. She reached up and wrapped her arms around his neck. He covered her mouth with his own, and she wrapped her bare legs around his hips.

Chase lowered her to the blanket, his kisses hot and wild, his hands strong as they reached under her hips, grasping at her bottom as he suddenly and almost violently entered her. He moved in hard thrusts, and she answered them by arching up to him in total abandon. The birds and rabbits outside must have heard her cries of ecstasy and agony, his groans of pleasure and heartbreak.

It seemed only moments before their first wave of need was finished, but Chase remained inside of her. Soon she felt his glorious manhood again filling her with virile force. He moved more slowly the second time, deliberately drawing out the pleasure for both of them, waiting for her to experience the lovely, pulsating release deep inside that told him she had reached her climax. He moved in circular, teasing thrusts, wanting her to enjoy every last moment of being together.

When he finished, words of loved spilled out, and both of them wept.

They stood arm-in-arm on the river bank, watching the steamboat approach, its huge paddle wheels churning lazily. Lilly looked up at Chase and they embraced, caring little if anyone saw them.

"You be careful walking back," he told her.

"I'll go right through town. I'll be all right."

Their eyes held. Lilly was fighting back the tears that wanted to fall. He had asked her to be brave for him. She knew that leaving was hard for him, too, and there was no sense in making it even worse by carrying on at this last moment.

"I love you, Lilly Brannigan."

"And I love you, Chase. I'll love you forever."

He forced himself to smile the smile that she loved. "Don't ever stop singing, Lilly. Remember the songs I taught you, and that your voice is something that belongs just to you. It's a gift you should share with those around you. Singing can help you through bad times. Don't let our parting take the music from your heart."

"I'll keep singing—just for you."

The steamboat was docking then. Chase and Lilly stood arm in arm, watching Mormons load goods they had made to be sold elsewhere. Other supplies were unloaded. A few disgruntled apostates boarded, headed out of Nauvoo; and lumber from farther north was unloaded, to be used to build more wagons for the overland journey to Zion. A load of canvas for wagon tops was also unloaded.

"We both have a long journey ahead of us," Chase commented.

Lilly put a hand to her stomach, fighting the terror of it. She wondered if this was how it would be for her the rest of her life—never really belonging anywhere, having no special place to call home, always moving on, losing those she loved most.

A steam whistle sounded the call that the riverboat was preparing to leave.

"This is it, Lilly," Chase told her. "I've got to board."

She clung to him. *Just one more moment! One more second!* "I love you, Chase. Please don't ever, ever forget that I love you and I'll be waiting for you! I'll pray for you every night and every day."

He pressed her close, wanting to weep again himself. "And I love you, sweet Lilly. Someday we'll be together again. And it will be forever—I promise."

They kissed hungrily, neither of them noticing that Zeb Adams was watching from a wagon onto which he was loading some canvas. Zeb had to look away, for his cheeks flushed at what he saw. He envied the Gentile man for capturing Lilly Brannigan's heart.

Chase let go of Lilly reluctantly. "It's got to be done." His voice choked. "Goodbye."

He grasped the reins of his horse and led it away, walking quickly then to the river bank.

"Chase," Lilly whimpered. She wanted to run after him,

but it would do no good. She watched him board the river-boat. He led his horse to a deck below where animals were kept. Moments later he reappeared as the boat headed out into the middle of the river. Lilly spotted the buckskin jacket and familiar floppy hat. He waved.

Great sobs of aching loneliness and sorrow welled up inside of her as she kept waving back, barely able to see him for her tears. She watched until the riverboat disappeared around a tree-lined bend in the river. He was gone. She leaned against a tree and wept.

Lilly waited nervously at the door after knocking. She thought she must look terrible after so much weeping. She had considered waiting one more day before going to Catheryn's, but when she had returned to Hiram's house that morning, she could feel Chase's presence in every room, and she half expected to see him emerge from the parlor. She had lain and cried in her room until she was sure there were no more tears left inside, then said her goodbyes. Laura was the hardest to leave, but Lilly detected a distant sadness in Mary's eyes, as well. There were times when Lilly wondered if Mary Williams longed to be more independent.

Surprisingly, Hiram had looked ready to weep himself when Lilly told him goodbye at the door, but Lilly could not stop the bitterness she felt.

"I'm sorry for making trouble, Hiram," she had told him.

"Lilly, I wish you would try to understand. We do love you, child."

"I'm not a child. I'm a woman," she had replied.

The door opened. "Good afternoon, Sister Brannigan." Catheryn Jules was a thin woman, plain-faced and flat-chested, her blond hair worn in a tight bun. Lilly noticed that even her lips were thin, and her chin came to a point. She was not homely, like her brother Zeb. In fact, Lilly was sure the woman could be considered pretty, if she would not dress so plainly and would do up her hair in a prettier style.

"Good afternoon, Mrs. Jules. I—I've come to stay, beginning today."

Catheryn smiled. "I know. Mary came to tell me this morning. Did your Gentile friend catch his riverboat, then?"

The lump returned to Lilly's throat, and she struggled to keep her composure. "Yes. He's gone."

Catheryn frowned. "I'm sorry. Mary said you cared very much for him—that he intends to return and marry you. I sincerely hope he'll be all right." Lilly liked Catheryn already. There was nothing pretentious about her, and she seemed to understand how Lilly must feel. She had always noticed what a quiet, gracious woman Catheryn was, and sometimes she wondered if the woman had ever raised her voice in her entire life. "Come in," she told Lilly, stepping aside.

Lilly entered the modest frame house. It was not nearly as elaborate as the Williams home. Since Zeb had built this for himself, it was not too comfortable for the large family it housed after Catheryn had moved in with her five children.

Lilly knew Catheryn Jules and Zeb Adams only by casual acquaintance. She knew that Catheryn had been widowed for over a year now, her husband having died before her last child was even born. Lilly thought it quite tragic. He had been killed by a simple fall from his horse—a freak accident that people just don't expect to happen. Now that she was in love herself, Lilly could not imagine what it must be like to have a husband or a lover die in the prime of life, yet she knew it could happen to Chase.

"You'll have to share a room with my girls, Myra and Ella," Catheryn was telling her. The woman led her to a small, stuffy room at the back of the house. "Our house isn't nearly as grand as Brother Hiram's, as you can see, but it really doesn't matter. Before long we'll all be in wagons heading west."

"Yes." Lilly patted the sides of her hair, wondering if anyone could tell she had made love that very day. She had trouble paying attention to what Catheryn was saying. Her mind and heart were still with Chase.

"Sister Brannigan, you look so tired," Catheryn was saying then. "Are you all right?"

Lilly fought back the tears, forcing a smile. "Oh, yes, I'm fine. I . . . I didn't sleep well last night—the thought of coming someplace new, I guess, and knowing Chase was going away."

"Oh, of course, but you shouldn't worry about coming here to live. I only need some help. I don't intend to work you like a servant. And Zeb and I so enjoy your singing. I do hope you'll bless us with song in the evenings."

Lilly nodded awkwardly, wondering if she would ever feel like singing again. But she would, because Chase had told her she should.

"You'll have to tell the children all about Scotland when they get back from school," Catheryn continued, leading Lilly into the hallway.

Lilly wondered how old Catheryn was. She had few lines on her face, and no gray hairs. Surely, if her eldest child was only nine, the woman could be barely thirty. But losing her husband must have put an incredible strain on her, for she had the look of a woman who was carrying some great weight on her shoulders.

"This is Zeb's room," Catheryn told Lilly, stopping at a small, plain room with wood floors. The room seemed packed, with two full-size, homemade beds, a dresser, and two trunks. "It didn't used to be so crowded until I moved here. The boys sleep in here with him." She led Lilly to a third small bedroom. "This used to be Zeb's study, but he had to give it up so the baby and I could have a room. My baby girl is a year old now. She's the only one who doesn't go to school, but today she's at Sister Ann Brady's house. I didn't feel well when I woke up, so Zeb took her over there for me."

"I'm sorry. Did I come at a bad time?" Lilly asked her.

"Oh, no. I'm all right now."

She led Lilly into the main room of the house, which served as kitchen, parlor, main living area, dining area—everything but bedrooms. Lilly tried to concentrate as Catheryn showed her where the dishes were kept, where potatoes were stored, where the bread pans were stacked.

"Zeb always eats promptly at five-thirty a.m. every morning and goes right to work," the woman was telling Lilly. "It's just a short walk out back to his fields. He takes care of all the farm equipment, the horses and such. I suppose I could handle all the washing and mending and teaching and discipline that goes with five children, if I wasn't plagued by terrible headaches. I never had them before my husband died." The woman's dull, gray eyes met Lilly's green ones.

"I'm sorry about your husband," Lilly told her. "I'm sure he was a fine man."

Catheryn turned away. "He was."

The front door opened then, and Zeb Adams entered, looking taller and more homely inside the small house than he did outside. His blond hair was windblown, and his eyes seemed the same dull gray as Catheryn's. Everything about him seemed bony and sharp, and as he removed his hat, Lilly noticed again that his hands looked huge—too big and strong-looking for the rest of him. He reddened deeply as his eyes fell on Lilly in surprise. He nodded to her. "Sister Brannigan," he spoke up.

"Hello, Mr. Adams." Lilly looked from him to Catheryn. "I do wish both of you would call me Lilly."

Catheryn smiled. "Then you must call us Katy and Zeb."

"All right." Lilly untied her bonnet.

"Lilly has come to stay now, Zeb," Catheryn explained.

Zeb barely looked at Lilly, afraid she would see the admiration in his eyes. "Good to have you," he managed to mumble. He looked at his sister. "I just came in to get my other boots. It was real muddy where we unloaded the canvas, and I don't feel like wearing wet boots all afternoon out in the fields. There's time left to get some planting done."

"Why do any planting at all, now?" Catheryn asked him. "We'll likely be heading west before the summer is out."

"Maybe so, maybe not. Can't stop everything on maybes. I'm not much for going west, but God knows we can't stay here forever. Meantime, maybe I can get in a few beans and such before we go." He sat down in a chair and removed his boots. "Brigham Young says we should plant. The groups that leave last can get in some of the harvest and use it for more supplies.

His eyes darted Lilly's way again, as though he had to steal a chance to look at her. He quickly looked back at his boots. "You can see we don't live quite as fine as Brother Hiram, but you'll be well taken care of," he told her.

"I'll be just fine, Zeb."

He walked to a corner and picked up a different pair of boots, setting his wet, muddy ones near the cookstove. "Sorry for the mud, Katy," he told his sister.

"It's all right, Zeb. It's your house, not mine."

"And not a very clean one, till you moved in." A faint smile passed over his lips. Lilly was relieved to see he apparently had some kind of a sense of humor buried behind that shy countenance. He put on the boots and nodded to her once more before opening the door and going back out.

"You're welcome to lie down in the girls' room for a while, Lilly," Catheryn told her then. "You do look very tired. I'll go and get my Marian while you rest. Then, the two of you can get to know each other."

"Yes, I would like to lie down," Lilly told the woman. "Thank you." She turned and walked down the short hallway to the girls' room, where she gladly closed the door and lay down on a bed.

Again the tears came. She couldn't help worrying that Chase might die and never come back to her, or perhaps be unable to find her once she went west. Oh, but surely he would. Chase Mitchell could do anything, and he would let nothing stop him. And God would never let him be killed. He was gone, but he would come back. He *would* come back! Until then, he had promised to write. Already she was anxious to get that first, wonderful letter. She would cherish every word, hold each letter to her heart. And she would faithfully wait for him.

But this was only the first day. The agony of that realization pierced her heart like a sword. *Only the first day.* There were many long, lonely days to go before he held her again.

Chapter Nine

Hours turned into days, days into weeks. Mormons were already beginning to leave Nauvoo in groups of up to fifty wagons, headed for a location Brigham Young and his scouts were calling Winter Quarters. It was a settlement on the western bank of the Missouri River in Omaha Indian Territory, a halfway point where those who left Nauvoo this summer would camp for the winter, waiting to discover just where their final Zion would be.

Lilly literally shivered at the foreboding sound of *Indian Territory*, but Zeb Adams assured her that the Mormons had always gotten along with Indians. They believed the Indians were descendants of the Lamanites—one of the lost tribes of Israel. Lilly had yet to meet Brigham Young, but it was obvious that these people thought of him as only slightly less important than God. She guessed him to be an extremely intelligent and charismatic man, to have so many thousands of people follow his leadership in such an organized and willing manner.

But there was only one man Lilly cared about. Every day was filled with an aching loneliness for Chase Mitchell. She had thought she knew the meaning of loneliness when she first came to Nauvoo, but this was worse, and she didn't even have the comfort of being able to see Laura. Hiram and Mary always seemed to find a reason why Laura couldn't come and visit. Occasionally they would come themselves to make sure Lilly was all right, and Lilly managed to reinstate a civil friendship with Mary, but Lilly could not find any friendly feelings for Hiram.

Catheryn and Zeb were kind and friendly, but Catheryn's prim, distant nature sometimes made Lilly feel even more isolated. Zeb was seldom in the house, but it wouldn't have mattered. He was quiet and shy, not someone with whom Lilly could share her feelings, although at times she sensed he could be a very understanding man, considering all he had done for his sister.

In spite of his shyness and homely appearance, Lilly had come to respect Zeb. He was a hard-working man who seemed to think only of others. He worked diligently on his field of vegetables, wanting to be sure there was plenty of food for Katy and the other women to put up in storage for the coming journey west. He had opened his home to Katy, and was patient and fatherly to all five of his nieces and nephews. And he had a good sense of humor, which came out in the most unexpected moments.

Zeb was a good man, but Lilly feared he was too bashful to ever find a wife. He was twenty-six years old but looked older from years of hard work. Catheryn was twenty-seven, but she also looked older, not so much from hard work as from too much worrying and from mourning her husband. Sometimes it seemed to Lilly that the plain, thin woman was trying to literally melt into the walls, and it was obvious the only thing that kept her going was her children. Lilly sang often for both brother and sister, since they seemed to take exquisite joy in her songs. But in her heart, Lilly was singing only for Chase. How she wished he was sitting right there in the house with Zeb and Katy, his blue eyes alive with love.

The nights were the worst. Lilly ached to be held by Chase, and longed for the sweet satisfaction of having him make love to her again. Her heart ached so badly sometimes that it caused her physical pain. Lilly found some joy in helping care for Catheryn's five children, who were inquisitive but obedient. They eagerly listened to Lilly's tales of Scotland, and she sang for all of them every night before bedtime.

Nine-year-old Myra and four-year-old Ella shared a room with Lilly, but often Jeffrey, eight, and Herbert, six, would sneak out of the room they shared with Zeb and hurry on bare feet to Lilly's room to listen to the stories Lilly told their sisters to help them fall asleep. More than once Lilly had to wake the boys up and guide them back into their own room. When she did, she always hoped Zeb would stay asleep, for she felt awkward coming into his bedroom.

But Zeb Adams was well aware that the beautiful Lilly Brannigan had come into his room, and he had caught more than one glimpse of her in her robe. He had wondered many times if Chase Mitchell had been sincere about coming back for Lilly, or if he had simply been a deceiving Gentile who had taken advantage of her, perhaps had stolen some kisses with no intention of making any real commitment. After all, he had been a man going off to war, and he was a hero in Lilly's eyes. He could easily have taken advantage of the situation. Zeb all but worshipped Lilly and wished that just once, she would look at him the way he had seen her look at Chase Mitchell. The way her beautiful green eyes lit up when she talked about Chase brought intensely envious feelings to Zeb's heart—feelings he daily prayed would go away, for they made him feel guilty.

Zeb had no idea that Lilly herself was getting worried about Chase's sincerity. The promised letters did not come. She told herself that it would take time—that she had to be patient. She refused to listen to a tiny voice that tried to tell her Chase might just have used her after all. Not Chase! His love was real, and she refused to believe otherwise. He had told her he might have to wait until he was settled in camp along the Rio Grande before he could write her, that it would be difficult to find a regular letter carrier on the long march to Texas.

Ten weeks passed. July brought hot, muggy weather that only depressed Lilly more. She was not accustomed to such temperatures and humidity. Every day became a battle to stay cool, and to keep from crying over hearing nothing from Chase. Lilly was sure that by now he must have reached his destination. She could only wonder if he had arrived all right, if his leg had given him any trouble. And her worry was only enhanced by the fact that she felt constantly sick of late, which she was sure was caused by the hot weather and her concern over Chase.

Soon the distance between them would be even greater. The day when Zeb and Catheryn would join one of the wagon trains headed for Winter Quarters was not far off. Every day the air echoed with pounding hammers and scraping saws as more wagons were built. Thousands had already left Nauvoo; Zeb and Hiram and their families would be among the last to go. Messengers from Winter Quarters had arrived to help them prepare and to show them the way. One of those messengers was Henry Guest, a widower who, Lilly learned, had been a good friend of Catheryn's husband.

"You people leaving late like this, you're luckier than those who went earlier this spring. You'll miss the mud," Henry told them one night as he sat at their dinner table. "Some we passed on our way back here were buried to the axles. Their poor animals couldn't pull those wagons another inch."

"What is it like at Winter Quarters, Henry?" Zeb asked. "Is Brother Young going to stay there?"

Henry put down his fork. "No. Brother Young says we haven't yet found our Zion. Winter Quarters is just a halfway point—a place to stop and regroup, replenish supplies and so forth. Brother Young has already started a mill there, and those who stayed behind have already planted crops, so food can be put up to be taken on the rest of our journey."

"Think we'll go all the way to California?" Zeb asked.

Lilly listened intently so she would know what to tell Chase when she was finally able to write him. She watched Henry talk. He was a big-boned, good-looking man of about thirty-five who was already balding and who wore his sideburns very thick.

"I don't think so," Henry answered. "Brother Young says there are too many people headed there. Our goal is to have a place all our own, where there will be no more worry about outsiders."

Lilly remembered the day she and Chase had been attacked by "outsiders"—people who lived in that mysterious world beyond Nauvoo. Her heart beat faster at the memory of how valiantly Chase had fought for her.

"Brother Young wants to find a place where we'll be isolated from the Gentiles as much as possible," Henry continued. "Some say it's Oregon we should go to, but Brother Young said he's had a dream about where it should be, and that when he saw it, he would know. He thinks it's some-where in the Great Basin."

"What is the Great Basin?" Lilly asked.

Henry looked at her curiously, not accustomed to a woman speaking up when men were talking. He had heard many rumors about the Gentile woman from Scotland. No one seemed to be quite sure why she had left Hiram Williams's house and had come to live with Catheryn, but she seemed to be getting along well with them.

He moved his eyes from Lilly to Catheryn, who sat with little Marian on her lap. She had said nothing during the entire meal. She was a quiet, obedient woman about whom Henry had romantic thoughts. He greatly admired her.

He turned his eyes back to Zeb. "The Great Basin is a big stretch of land on the other side of the Rockies, but this side of California. They say that once there was an enormous lake there. There still is one, but it's smaller now. And it's a salt lake—just like the Dead Sea in the Book of Mormon."

Lilly stopped eating, trying to picture the place Henry spoke about. "They say the land all around is as barren as Palestine. The climate and the lay of the land are unlike anything we've ever seen. That pathfinder, John Frémont, explored the area, and Brother Young has a copy of his report. Brother Young thinks that might be the place for our brothers and sisters to settle. Nobody else wants to settle there, so there would be no one to interfere with our lives. We could set our own rules, be free at last. Brother Young intends to set out for the Great Basin next spring. If he finds our Zion, we will all go there. We will be home at last."

"Hmmm." Zeb swallowed a piece of potato. "I'm not so sure I'd *want* to go there. If nobody else wants to settle there, kind of makes you wonder why, doesn't it? Barren land? A lake that's no good for watering crops? Sometimes I can't help wondering about Brother Young's idea of Zion."

Lilly tried to stifle a snicker, but did not fully succeed. Zeb glanced at her and grinned. Henry only scowled.

"We mustn't question Brother Young," he told Zeb, to-tally missing the humor in Zeb's remark. "If God wants us to settle there, that is where we will be. He'll give us a sign. You'll see."

"Maybe so," Zeb answered, pushing some of his food together on his plate. "One real nice sign would be to change that salt lake to fresh water."

Lilly struggled to swallow some food without laughing again. She felt good again tonight, and it puzzled her, since she was miserable nearly every morning. She had not had her time of month for over two months now, and she wondered if she had developed some kind of disease. But in the evenings, when she felt so much better, she gave it less thought.

When they finished eating, Zeb and Henry walked outside. The children followed them out the door to play, and little Marian, who had only been walking for a month, toddled around after her mother as Catheryn and Lilly cleared the table.

"What do you think of Brother Guest, Lilly?" Catheryn asked, after saying next to nothing for several minutes.

"Oh, I don't know. He's awfully serious most of the time, but he seems very nice."

Catheryn faced her, her cheeks crimson. "Zeb has told me Brother Guest wishes to call on me." She looked down at the floor. "Do you think it's wrong to allow the best friend of your dead husband to come calling, Lilly?"

"I don't see what's wrong with it. If you are fond of Henry Guest, then you should let him call on you. I think it would be good for you to be interested in Brother Guest. You're still young, Catheryn, and you have five children to raise."

Catheryn nodded. "I feel bad about putting so much on Zeb's shoulders, him being unmarried and all. I mean, it's one thing to take in a woman and her children when you love the woman and want to marry her, but it's another thing to have to take in your widowed sister."

"Zeb doesn't seem to mind."

"He would never say if he did. He's that way." She met Lilly's eyes. "Zeb is a good man, Lilly, and I've seen how he looks at you. I know you were fond of the Gentile man, and promised to wait for him, but . . . I thought you should know that Zeb—Zeb thinks the world of you. Oh, he would never tell you, and he would be angry with me if he knew *I* had told you."

Lilly turned away, speechless. She had never dreamed that Zeb Adams noticed women in any special way, and he was certainly not the kind of man a woman noticed in return.

"I love Chase," she told Catheryn, wishing she could tell the woman all that had happened.

Catheryn wiped her hands on her apron. "You told me that when you first came here. I suppose it was foolish of me to mention Zeb. I just . . . well, in case your Mr. Mitchell should not come back—"

"He will!" Lilly interrupted, tears of frantic doubt coming to her eyes.

Catheryn frowned with concern. "I'm sorry. Of course he will. I had no right saying such a thing."

Lilly sighed. "It's all right. I'm the one who's sorry. I know you're just concerned." She was tempted to tell Catheryn about the peculiar sickness she had been having, but she decided not to say anything yet. After all, she still felt good tonight. Perhaps it wouldn't come back anymore. And if she had her time of month soon, she would know nothing was wrong with her. "I'm glad you confided in me, Katy. I hope we can talk more. You should feel free to tell me anything. I'll try to understand."

Catheryn smiled. "And you should feel the same way about talking to me, Lilly. I do hope for your sake that Brother Mitchell will be all right, and that there will be no war."

"Yes. So do I," Lilly answered, feeling the aching loneliness all over again. "I hope you can find another man to love, Catheryn. Maybe it will be Henry Guest."

The woman laughed lightly, her red face making her look like a young girl in love for the first time. "Maybe," she answered.

Lilly turned and put away some plates, wondering suddenly what would happen to her if Henry Guest really did end up marrying Catheryn. Where would that leave her? Catheryn would go to live with Henry, and Lilly certainly couldn't stay on alone with Zeb. Perhaps she would have to go back to Hiram, but that was the last thing she wanted now.

All of those problems seemed suddenly unimportant when Zeb came rushing inside minutes later. He approached Lilly, his gray eyes full of genuine concern as he removed his hat.

"Lilly?"

Lilly hung two cups on hooks and turned to face him. "Yes, Zeb?" She reddened a little at the thought of what Catheryn had just told her, but the knowledge of Zeb's feelings for her mattered little when she saw his eyes. Her chest tightened as he nervously fidgeted with his hat.

"I just thought I'd tell you . . . Brother Bailey just came back from delivering some lumber to a family of Gentiles who trades with him. He . . . uh—" His eyes moved over her as though somehow he felt sorry for her.

"What is it, Zeb?" she asked, wondering why on earth it mattered that Stu Bailey had delivered some lumber.

"Well, I know you had a liking for that Gentile man— Charles Mitchell—so I thought you'd want to know. Brother Bailey says the man he delivered the lumber to told him President Polk has declared war on Mexico."

Lilly paled visibly.

"Oh, my!" Catheryn gasped.

Zeb took Lilly's arm and led her to a chair. "You don't look so good, Lilly. I'm sorry if I upset you."

Lilly could not find her voice. She merely shook her head, looking at her lap and struggling against tears. Chase would go to Mexico now! He could be killed! How was she going to know what was happening? The awful ache returned to her chest, and her stomach churned. She wondered again if she had some terrible sickness of her own and would die before Chase was ever able to come back to her.

"*All plants here have thorns,*" Chase wrote. "*In fact, everything is thorny, prickly, or dry. The deserts of Texas are like hell, and I can only pray, Lilly, that your journey west won't be like this.*"

Chase stopped writing for a moment to lick the stinging cuts on his fingers from his encounters with thorny plants and prickly weeds. How he wished he could run those fingers through Lilly's soft hair.

"*I don't know when you'll get this letter, Lilly, as I can't even send it till I get to my pa's camp, where messengers take and deliver mail from us to our loved ones. We should arrive in just a few more days. I wrote you when I got to St. Louis, but our lieutenant hurried us up before I could get the letter to anybody to bring it to you. He took it from me, and I have a feeling he never posted it. I sure hope you get this one, so you won't worry and wonder.*

"*My heart is so heavy, Lilly. A rider came in yesterday, telling us President Polk has declared war. I don't see how I can avoid having to go into Mexico, and I don't know how long it will take, or if I'll come out of it alive. All I can ask is that you will wait for me until this war is over. I will get letters to you any way I can, but this might be my last one for a long time.*"

He decided not to tell her just how bad his journey had been. He had sold his horse in St. Louis and now walked with the rest of the men in his unit. Every day he choked on burning alkaline dust. When it rained, it poured, and they marched nearly to their knees in mud. Once they passed the Nueces River, water fit to drink was scarce. Some of the men who marched with him had collapsed from dehydration and exhaustion, and they would stagger into camp, either alone or in pairs, throughout the night.

"*So often only the thought of you keeps me going,*" he continued. "*I love you, Lilly. I can't tell you enough, and I can only hope that after I left, you didn't start hating me for taking advantage of the sweet love you offered me. I suppose I should have been able to resist my need of you, but I will never regret what we did, and neither should you. You're in my thoughts night and day. I can see you as clearly sometimes as if you were standing in front of me, and when I close my eyes, I can remember what you feel like, the way you smell, the sound of your singing.*

"*I'll worry about you, Lilly. When you go west, stay close to others so none of those wild Indians get you, and keep yourself warm. I've met a man who's been out there, and he says it gets mighty cold in the mountains. Also, keep your*

*bonnet on so the sun doesn't burn your pretty skin. Some-
times I picture you standing in the great open desert and
singing, and your voice carries over the whole land.*

*"God meant for us to be together, and until we can be
again, I love you. I can't say it enough. I'll love you forever,
and that's how long we'll be together when I come back.
Keep that in your heart always . . . and wait for me. Chase."*

He put his head back and folded the letter. His body ached
from head to toe, and though his leg seemed to have healed
by the time he reached St. Louis, it had been a source of
considerable pain at the end of each long march. The pain
was gradually easing, but he wasn't sure whether that meant
his leg was getting better, or if he was just becoming numb
to it. He thought how nice it would be to be lying in a cool
bed with Lilly. They had never shared a real bed.

He shoved the letter into his shirt pocket, then closed his
eyes and pictured Lilly singing, "All is well! All is well!"
He could only pray that was how it would be for them.

Chapter Ten

"At ease, Private Mitchell." Major Howard Mitchell
smiled and lowered his arm. "Son! I've been so worried
about you."

"Hello, Pa."

The elder Mitchell walked closer and they embraced.
Even though they were father and son, they were strangers
in many ways. Chase had been separated from his father
twelve of his twenty-four years. He had grown up with a
vision of the man as the greatest soldier ever born, but he
really didn't know him.

"A messenger told me you had been injured," Major
Mitchell said, stepping back from Chase and looking him
over.

"It's a long story, Pa, but I'm all right now. My leg gets awful sore after a long march, though."

His father moved around behind a makeshift desk. The air hung still and hot inside the tent. "Sit down, Chase. I want to hear about what happened, but first, tell me about your mother. How is Claire?"

Chase's chest tightened. He sat down on an upended barrel, and faced his father. The major could see the troubled look on his son's face.

"What is it, Chase?"

Chase sighed deeply. "Mother is dead, Pa."

Howard Mitchell's smile faded. "What!"

Chase rested his elbows on his knees. "It happened before I even left. I decided not to send you a letter—I didn't want you to be alone when you found out. I figured since I was coming anyway..." His own eyes teared. "I'm sorry, Pa. She had some kind of cancer. I was with her right to the end. When my unit heard she was ill, they gave me leave to be with her. I sold everything off, rented out the house, made sure she had a nice headstone and all. I've got the money with me from what I sold. The neighbors—Jack and Henrietta Hannapel—will collect the rent and watch the house. They were always good people—good to Mother."

The major hung his head.

"Her last words were to ask me to tell you she loved you, Pa."

Mitchell nodded. "God knows I wasn't much of a husband, or much of a father. I loved her, Chase, but...we were two very different people. I suppose if I had been home a lot, we might not have gotten along so well. Some marriages are mistakes, Chase." He met his son's eyes, his own wet with tears. "And sometimes, we love people we have no business loving. That's part of the reason I chose to stay in the army, and I regret to say it meant I couldn't be the kind of father I should have been."

He sighed deeply, rose, and turned away.

"You want me to leave you alone for a while, Pa?"

"Not just yet. And I do thank you for waiting until you got here to tell me." He cleared his throat and swallowed.

"Your mother did well—you're a fine son. I'm glad you're here, Chase. We'll fight the Mexicans together."

Chase wasn't sure how he felt about that. All he wanted was to get this war over with and get back to Lilly. "How bad is it, Pa?"

The man took out a handkerchief and blew his nose, then turned to face Chase. "The country we have to go through will be hell, Chase, but we'll make it. You realize, of course, that I can't show you any favor, but I'll be close by if you need me, and I'll be keeping an eye on you. We're in this until we win it, Chase—even if we have to follow Taylor all the way to Mexico City!"

Chase realized with dismay that his father was more devoted to the army than he had ever been to Claire Mitchell. He wondered if his father would be disappointed when he found out Chase had no such loyalties. Once this war was over, he would never put the army before Lilly. He felt a sudden cloud of resentment toward this man he had always admired, but he told himself that perhaps there were things he just didn't understand. The major moved behind his desk and sat down again.

"You're all I have left now, Chase. I hardly knew your younger brother, but he was always sickly, like your mother. You were always the strong one. I know you'll make me proud, Chase. I don't doubt you'll move up in rank when this war is finished."

Chase fidgeted with his hat, studying a stain on it as he spoke. "I'm not so sure it matters that much to me, Pa."

His father's eyes showed immediate alarm. "What are you talking about? You told me a long time ago you were going to make a career out of the army."

Chase held his gaze. "That was before I met Lilly—Lilly Brannigan."

The man's eyebrows arched and he leaned forward on his desk, which was no more than a board stretched over two barrels. "And who is Lilly Brannigan?"

Chase spilled out the story of how he had met Lilly, and how his leg had been injured. He noticed an odd look on his father's face when he mentioned that Lilly lived with Mormons. He couldn't quite read the look, except that it seemed

almost angry. Chase hastened to explain that Lilly was not a
Mormon herself. He told his father about how beautiful she
was, and the way she sang. "I'm in love with her, Pa. When
we're through here, I'm going back to marry her. When you
meet her, you'll understand why I feel like I do."

The man shook his head. "You don't want to get mixed up
with Mormons, Chase."

Chase felt a hint of alarm. "I won't be. When we get
married, I'll take her back to Illinois, or wherever I can find
work."

"I've heard a lot about the Mormons. Once they get you
in their web, you're caught forever, Chase. They'll have you
converted before you know what hit you. You'll go running
off into the desert to live in some Godforsaken place removed from the rest of the world, and turn into a polygamist
who goes around chanting prayers and betraying his country."

The words were not spoken loudly, but firmly. Chase realized his father must believe every bad thing he had ever
heard about the Mormons.

"They aren't like that at all, Pa. They love their country.
They're good people—no different from the rest of us."

"You see? You're already defending them."

"That doesn't mean I'm going to *be* one myself!"

"Doesn't it? A woman can make a man do some pretty
strange things, Chase."

"Well, in Lilly's case, it doesn't matter. Lilly doesn't *want*
to be a Mormon. She stays with them because they're her
only friends right now. She's in a new country and doesn't
know anybody."

"Which makes her not only a Mormon, but a foreigner.
And if she's as beautiful and sweet as you say, one of those
Mormon men will sweep her up for a second or third wife in
no time. Do you really think someone her age is going to
wait two or three years for you, Chase? This war could take
that long, you know."

Chase frowned with anger. First it was Hiram saying they
were not right for each other because Chase was a Gentile.
Now his father was saying they were not right for each other
because Lilly was a Mormon.

"If you knew Lilly, you'd know she'll wait for me, Pa," he answered, rising. "And even if she turns to the Mormon religion, I'd marry her anyway when I get out of here. I love her. You must know—" He didn't finish the sentence. The woman his father had loved was dead. "I'm sorry, but I'm not going to spend half my life away from the woman I love because of the army, and I'm not going to let religion stand between us, either. Lilly *will* wait for me. All she needs is to keep getting my letters so she knows I'm all right. And when you meet her, you'll change your mind—I can promise you that. I'm sorry if you don't like the idea of me not staying in the army, but I never promised I would. I promised I'd join up, and that I'd come down here to fight the Mexicans. I'm here. I'm no coward and no deserter. I just don't want to be in the army my whole life. Leaving Lilly behind was the hardest thing I've ever done, and I don't intend to go through that more than once."

Major Mitchell nodded, a little anger still showing in his eyes. "Give me some time to think about it, son. You've hit me with an awful lot of surprises this evening, and right now, I've got the weight of your mother's death on my mind."

The man rose, and Chase faced him squarely. "I'm sorry, Pa. But right now, you should understand more than ever how I feel about Lilly."

The major sighed deeply. "I'll try, but I've got no use for Mormons, Chase. I can't picture my son walking around with a meek smile on his face and flowers in his hand, turning his cheek when another man strikes him."

Chase shook his head. "Mormon men aren't like that at all. Some of them even got in a fistfight back in Illinois when some local citizens tried to keep them from voting. Besides, I told you, Lilly's not a Mormon."

Chase's father waved him off. "We'll talk about it another time. Go report back to your unit. I'll talk to you in the morning. We'll be heading for Mexico in just a few days." He came closer and put a hand on Chase's shoulder. "For now, it will be easier on you if you try real hard to forget about this Lilly, Chase. What's ahead of you will require all your skill and concentration. You have to prepare to fight

Mexicans, and to head into some miserable country to do it. I'm damned proud of you, son."

Chase stared at him. He was actually excited about going to war. Chase was disappointed in his father. "Good night, Pa," he said, so quietly the man barely heard the words.

"Good night, Chase. Rest well, son. Thank God you're here, safe and sound. Thank you for waiting to tell me about your mother." As his father stepped back, Chase straightened and saluted him, his jaw rigid with repressed anger. Mitchell saluted in return, wearing a proud smile. Chase turned and left. He knew that if someone had come to tell him Lilly was dead, he wouldn't care about anything but dying himself.

Howard Mitchell moved to the tent entrance to watch his son walk back to his own unit. He then called over a sergeant, beckoning him to come inside. The sergeant obeyed, saluting Mitchell before being ordered at ease.

"You're in charge of mail call, are you not, Sergeant Handy?"

"Yes, sir," the young man answered.

"The young man who just left me—his name is Charles Mitchell. He's my son."

The sergeant grinned and nodded. "It must be very nice for you, sir, to have your son here."

"It is. But I'm giving you an order now, Sergeant, and I expect it to be obeyed. If it is, I'll see what I can do about getting you a promotion."

The young man's eyebrows arched and he nodded. "Yes, sir. What is it, sir?"

"I want you to bring any letters sent out by Charles Mitchell, and any letters coming in to him, directly to me. Understand? I don't want any of his correspondence to be given to the messengers. Go through the mail every day and pull anything with his name on it, or the name Lilly Brannigan."

The sergeant frowned. He was full of questions, but he knew better than to ask them. "Yes, sir. Charles Mitchell— Lilly Brannigan. No letters to or from either one." All kinds of explanations came to the sergeant's mind. Lilly Brannigan must be some girl Mitchell loved. Apparently she was a no-good—somebody his father didn't want him involved with.

"Don't forget those names."

"No, sir, I won't."

"Good. You can go now."

After the sergeant saluted and left, Howard Mitchell sat on the barrel that served as his chair. "A Mormon!" he muttered. "They'll not get their pious, polygamist hands on my Chase! He's all I have left!"

He rested his head in his hands, trying to picture Claire—how she looked, how her voice had sounded—but he couldn't. They had been apart a long time. He realized that to make a career of the army, it was better not to get too serious over any woman. There were plenty to be had for free if a man needed one. His son would forget about Lilly Brannigan soon enough, when he realized the girl was never going to answer his letters. In the meantime, he would make sure she never wrote him at all. He took out some parchment and a quill pen, then took a letter from his supplies that Chase had written him the year before. He studied the handwriting, then began to compose a letter to Miss Lilly Brannigan.

"Dear Lilly," he wrote. *"I have had considerable time to think about us since I left Nauvoo, and I realize that what we felt for each other was too sudden, and only because of my injury. You are so beautiful that I forgot all my senses. Now that I am here on the Rio Grande, I realize how deeply the army life runs in my blood. Lilly, I'm so sorry, but we can't be married. I want to make a career of the army, and I don't want to be an absent husband, like my father was all his life. He has lived with too many regrets. When I saw how he wept over my mother's death, I knew that to marry you would simply be too cruel to both of us.*

"I love you, Lilly, but not the way a man should love a wife. My career has to come first, and it is not a career for a married man. I love you enough to want you to be happy— to be married to someone who can be a real husband to you, a real father to your children. So, with this letter, I free you of all promises you made to wait for me, and with great regret, I disavow my own promises. It isn't that I don't love

you enough, Lilly. It's that I love you too much to force this life on you. I will be fighting in Mexico for a long time, which will give both of us time to heal. I hope that by the time I am through here, you will have found someone who will love you as much as you deserve to be loved. Time and distance has helped me think more clearly.

"I won't be back, Lilly, but you will always hold the dearest place in my heart. Love always, Chase."

Mitchell folded the letter, just as the sergeant reentered the tent. He saluted, then stepped closer. "Private Quinton just gave me the night's bundle of letters, sir. I found this one among them." He handed the letter to Major Mitchell. It was addressed to a Lilly Brannigan at Nauvoo, Illinois. Mitchell nodded.

"Thank you, Sergeant. Wait just a minute." He folded his own letter and addressed it to Lilly. "Send this one, instead."

"Yes, sir."

Mitchell reached into his supply bag and took out a plug of tobacco. "Here's some extra tobacco for you, Sergeant. It's hard to come by."

The young man's eyes lit up. "Thank you, sir!"

"You just keep an eye on those letters."

"Yes, sir." Once Mitchell was alone again, he took Chase's letter outside and threw it into a campfire. He watched the paper burn, then walked slowly back into his tent.

As August came, hot and heavy, the remaining Mormons at Nauvoo prepared to leave for Winter Quarters. While Lilly helped Catheryn pack dishes, she wondered what was happening at the Williams household. Lilly had seen women weep at meetings held to instruct them in how to pack for their journey west, and she knew many would have to leave many beautiful things behind. This was no short journey. Mules and oxen would have enough trouble pulling their necessities. Beds, dressers, clocks, and all other heavy objects would have to be left behind. That meant that some women would have to part with family heirlooms—furniture handed down to them from mothers and grandmothers, precious items brought all the way across the ocean. They had made it over water, but they could not make it over the land they would be crossing.

"Too much mud," was one explanation.

"The rivers are too deep and too dangerous."

"They say in some of the mountain passes, wagons have to be lowered on ropes."

"The weight can cause accidents on steep hills."

"Axles and wheels can break if you're too loaded up."

"Only necessities—food and water and the right tools are the most important."

"The prairie sun is mighty hot. Can't overwork the animals making them pull too great a load."

The warnings went on and on, until Lilly thought she might go crazy with the thought of how terrible the trip was going to be. What made her dread it more was the dawning realization that she must be pregnant.

She still had not heard from Chase. He was surely well on his way into Mexico now, and maybe injured or dead already. Certainly he would have tried to get a letter to her before he marched out of Texas; she prayed it would arrive at Nauvoo before they left.

"It's so hard to decide what to take and what to leave," Catheryn was saying. "But it's much harder for some of the others. I don't have so many extra nice things as some. Zeb and I were orphaned at a young age. An aunt raised us, and she gave us nothing when she turned us out on our own. It was the Mormons who helped us get on our feet. That's when I met my husband."

Lilly packed a china plate into some straw. "I had nothing but a gunny sack of clothes, myself, when I got here. I feel sorry for those who have to make decisions about what to leave behind," she answered. "Sometimes I think I'll never have such nice things to even be concerned about."

"Oh, you will someday, Lilly. Chase Mitchell will come back for you, and you'll have a fine life together."

"I'm so worried about him." Lilly suddenly felt weak and sweaty. She sat down in a kitchen chair, unbuttoned the top buttons of her dress, and fanned herself with a towel. "I . . . I don't feel well. I haven't for over three months now, Katy. I kept hoping it would go away, but now that we're getting ready to go on this journey, it frightens me, the way I feel."

"Oh, Lilly." Catheryn came over to her and put a hand on her shoulder. "Zeb and I have both noticed—you haven't looked well for a long time, but you never said anything. What's wrong?"

"I didn't want to bother anyone with it, but I feel sick to my stomach a lot, Katy. It's always worse in the morning. Sometimes in the evening I feel better, but certain smells make me feel sick again—smells that never used to bother me. And I'm so tired all the time. And . . . I don't mean to embarrass you, Katy, but you've had five children. You must know about . . . about woman things."

Catheryn frowned. "What do you mean, Lilly?" She knelt in front of her, truly concerned. Lilly fought back tears of dread. She couldn't put off telling Katy her problem any longer. She could only pray the woman would come up with a better explanation than Lilly had. She looked at her lap and spoke so softly Catheryn could barely hear. "I . . . I haven't had my time for over three months now," she told the woman, reddening at the words.

Catheryn looked at her strangely, saying nothing. She slowly rose. "Dear God," she finally whispered.

Lilly looked at her in alarm. "What is it, Katy! Am I dying?"

Catheryn studied her, shaking her head, a mixture of shock and sorrow in her gray eyes. "You feel sick mostly in the morning? You're tired? Certain smells make you feel ill? And you haven't . . . you haven't had your time for over three months?"

Lilly nodded in reply to every question, terror in her eyes. Catheryn turned away. "It couldn't be. Unless . . . unless I don't know you as I thought I did, Lilly."

She turned. "Lilly, you must be very, very honest with me." She swallowed, reddening. "The Gentile—Chase Mitchell—did you . . . did the two of you . . . did that man make love to you, Lilly?"

There was a long silence. Lilly began to tremble.

"Oh, Lilly," Catheryn said, terrible disappointment in her voice. "Lilly, I have borne five children. If anyone knows something about being with child, it's me. The morning sickness, feeling tired . . . and there is seldom any other reason for a healthy young woman to miss her time of month. If you . . . if you were so foolish as to let your love for Chase Mitchell get out of hand, then you must be . . . carrying his child."

Lilly just stared at her, dumbfounded. The horror of it began to creep through her blood—pregnant and unmarried, like some kind of harlot! Chase! Oh, if only he knew! If only she could tell him, he would get leave and come right away, she was sure. But she didn't even know where he was. There had been no letter. And if he didn't show up for a year or two, she would give birth to a child everyone would call illegitimate—or that other name that was so much worse! She couldn't let that happen to her baby—not to Chase's child!

But what was she to do? She would rather have been told she was dying. If Chase were here—if they could be married—having his baby would be the most wonderful thing that ever happened to her.

Lilly covered her face and burst into frantic tears, feeling the weight of being doomed to the worst in life. Nothing had gone right since she had left the little cottage in the mountains. Nothing. She seemed destined to be homeless and lost, a wanderer in a foreign land, and now, an outcast among the only people she had been able to call friends.

She felt a gentle hand on her shoulder. "In our faith, we believe that we learn by our mistakes, Lilly, and that we must always move forward. God does not stop loving us because of our feeble errors. Try not to cry," Catheryn soothed. "You will just get sick again. Go and lie down. I'll get Zeb."

"No! No! Don't tell Zeb!"

"Lilly, I have to tell him."

Lilly only wept harder, never feeling more desperate and ashamed and desolate than she did now.

"Please wait . . . just a couple more days," she begged through tears. "Maybe something . . . will happen. Maybe I'll get my time, or I'll hear from Chase. Either way . . . I have to think, Katy. I want to be calmer before you tell

Zeb." She raised tearful green eyes to Catheryn. "Please, Katy. Please wait, just a few days. And . . . whatever you do, don't tell Hiram. Don't ever tell Hiram!"

Catheryn closed her eyes and sighed. "I'll try to avoid it, Lilly, but it's really up to Zeb. Perhaps you should go and lie down now. And have faith, Lilly. No matter what happens, God has chosen for you to have this child. You must never blame the child. Children are such sweet, innocent beings. Go and rest now. I will pray for you."

Lilly rose and walked to the bedroom. Catheryn could hear her crying. She could not help feeling sorry for Lilly. Their impending journey would be difficult enough without this new burden.

Chapter Eleven

Lilly stayed in bed almost three days after telling Catheryn about her "sickness." Now she wished she truly was dying. She felt guilty for not being more help with the packing, but depression had settled into her soul, like a great rock floating to the bottom of a river, and it was made worse by the fact that she had still not heard from Chase.

At the end of the third day, Catheryn came into the bedroom where Lilly lay, and Zeb walked in behind her. Lilly pulled the covers over herself and turned away from them.

"Lilly, Zeb was concerned about how sick you have been. I had to tell him," Catheryn said. "He wants to talk alone with you."

Lilly lay still, saying nothing. She heard Catheryn go out and close the door, but felt Zeb's presence in the room. She heard him move, then heard Myra's bed squeak as he sat down on it across from her.

"I'm not usually one to interfere in someone's personal

business, Lilly," he said calmly. "And I, uh, I'm not much of a talker, as you well know. But this has to be talked about." He sighed deeply before continuing. "Personally, I am of the opinion that Chase Mitchell used you in the worst way a man can use a young girl. He never meant to come back."

"That's not true," Lilly cried, turning to face him. "Chase would never have done that—never! He wanted to marry me when he came back. He just thought it wasn't right to marry me before going off to war."

"But he thought it was right to use you like a wife?"

Lilly reddened, her eyes tearing. "You don't understand. How could you understand when you've never been in love?"

She didn't notice the hurt in Zeb's eyes. He didn't hold the remark against her though—he realized she was lost in her own misery, for the moment.

He leaned forward, resting his elbows on his knees. "I might know more about love than you think," he told her. *And I love you, Lilly Brannigan*, he added to himself. He wished he had the courage to say it aloud. "Whether Chase Mitchell truly loved you or not, the fact remains that he is *not* here, Lilly, and you can't be having a baby without a husband—not just because of how it looks for you, but for the sake of the baby. You don't want him or her to be born without a father—without a man to give it a last name, do you?"

"I don't know what I want." Lilly's words were more subdued now, as though she had resigned herself to the worst. "What choices do I have? I won't go back to Hiram, no matter what else you make me do. He'd only tell me how foolish I was, how I should have listened to him." She met Zeb's eyes. "I don't regret loving Chase, and I *still* love him! And I'm not ashamed to be carrying his baby. If Chase knew, he'd be here."

Zeb decided it was useless to try to convince her that Chase Mitchell had no intention of coming back.

"I know what you must think of me," Lilly said then, sitting up and wiping at her eyes. She looked down at her lap. "And now you're wondering what to do with me. I'll just have to make it alone, Zeb. If you provide me with a wagon and driver, I'll find a way to work and pay you back. I'll go to Winter Quarters and have my baby, and people can just think what they want."

He smiled a little at her attempt to pretend it didn't matter what happened to her.

"We can't just let you have a baby without a husband, Lilly. For one thing, some might think it's mine. If you tell everyone who really fathered the baby, it would make you look... well, like the kind of girl I know in my heart you aren't. I don't want you to be shamed, Lilly, and I don't want your baby to be born without a father. I've come to tell you that if you'll have me, I'll marry you—right away, before we leave Nauvoo."

Lilly's eyes widened with surprise. "*Marry* me!"

He nodded, some color coming to his cheeks. "I know I'm no prize as far as looks go, Lilly, but I work hard, and I can provide for you."

Lilly closed her eyes and turned away. Marry Zebulah Adams? What about Chase! "Your offer is very kind, Zeb," she said quietly. "But I can't marry a man I don't love. And... what if I married you because of the baby, and then Chase came back? He *is* coming back, you know."

Zeb rose. "Lilly, I give you my word I wouldn't expect you to be a a a wife in every way. Nobody needs to know but us. If Chase doesn't come for you or write you, we'll decide later what to do about it. Even if you divorced me, the child would still have been born with a father and a last name. We'll let folks think I really am the father. They'll think you and I... that we committed a sin before we married. But if we at least marry, it won't be so bad. The gossip will die down after a while. Besides, we believe in a person's goodness, and we don't rant and rave about sin. Our religion teaches forgiveness and going forward, not living in the past and pointing fingers. If Chase does come back, you can go to him if you want. I can bear the scandal. I have big shoulders."

Lilly looked up at him, studying his soft gray eyes. Yes, he truly did have big shoulders, for what he was offering was a way out of her shame—at his expense.

"Why are you doing this, Zeb?"

He smiled softly, a rare smile Lilly felt honored to have been allowed to see. "I . . . care about you. The first day I heard you sing in the temple, I knew you were special. You're too pretty and too nice to be suffering like this."

She almost wished she could find some of the feelings for him that she felt for Chase. She remembered Catheryn telling her how Zeb felt about her, but she had ignored the remark. She didn't realize until now just how deep his love must run.

"How do I know you would keep your promise . . . about not expecting . . . certain things from me? And how do I know that when Chase comes for me, you will release me from the marriage?"

"Because you have my word. That's all you need."

Their eyes held. "Yes. I suppose so." Her throat tightened with a desperate need to cry. "I seem to be a bother for whoever takes me in. If I marry you, I promise someday Chase will come and relieve you of your burden. If he doesn't come, I'll . . . I'll find a way to be independent of you. I'm sorry you even have to consider doing this."

He put his hand on the doorknob. "You'll be no burden, Lilly. The fact is, if things were different, I would have wanted to call on you and do things the right way, and I would have been honored if you had accepted." His face got so red Lilly wondered if he would pass out.

"Thank you, Zeb. I think . . . I'm the one who would have been honored."

He wished he could go to her and hold her. "You think on it, Lilly. Nobody needs to know but you, me, and Katy. She'll never say anything—not even to Henry. If some people want to think it's Chase Mitchell's baby, let them wonder. I'll swear it's mine. If you decide to marry me, we'll start talking right now like the baby is mine."

"I can't make you take all the blame, Zeb. You're too good a man."

"It's better than you walking around all swelled up with child and no husband. And you don't want your son or daughter to carry the ugly brand babies like that usually carry."

She wiped at a tear that slipped down the side of her face. "Thank you for not kicking me out of your house, Zeb."

The faint grin returned. "The only thing I'd kick out of my house would be a skunk, and you sure don't smell like any skunk."

She smiled through her tears.

"You think about it tonight and we'll talk in the morning," he added. "And, I want you to start eating tomorrow. You can't make your baby suffer because of your own problems. It's not his or her fault, you know. You starve yourself, and you starve your baby, too. What if Chase Mitchell *does* come back? You want to have a nice healthy baby for him, don't you?"

"Yes," she answered in a near whisper.

Their eyes held a moment longer, and Zeb finally turned and left. Lilly stared at the door once he was gone, feeling numb, exhausted, and strangely resigned to her condition now.

She thought how cruel fate could be. If she married Zeb, she would be going against her vow never to marry a Mormon man, and would be marrying a man she didn't even love. And if she did leave Zeb later on, she would have to get a full divorce—an annulment would be impossible. No one would believe that a woman who had gotten herself pregnant before marriage had lived with a healthy young man without sharing his bed. A divorce would leave another brand on her, but it would not be quite as shameful as having a baby without any husband at all.

She had to think about how Chase would feel when he returned. Would he still want her? Would he understand that she had only married Zeb for the sake of the baby, and believe that she had not shared his bed? There was little time to decide, and only one logical decision to make anyway.

She lay back down, aching for Chase, wondering if he was in some terrible battle somewhere, perhaps hurt and calling for her.

"Oh, Chase," she whispered, wondering if the awful ache would ever, ever go away. She put a hand to her belly and tried to put him out of her mind, for the moment. She had to think about Zeb's offer.

Zebulah Adams was the last man she would have picked to marry, but the choice was being made for her, and she knew already that he was right. Marrying him was the only logical thing to do. If only she had received a letter from Chase, she would know he was all right. She could write to him and explain.

It was a quick and simple wedding at the Adams house, performed by a friend of Zeb's who was a Mormon priest. Lilly still refused to embrace the Mormon faith, and decided it was just as well that this was not a temple marriage, for she understood the sacredness of such a union. Considering the circumstances, she felt guilty enough pledging her love to Zeb Adams, without doing it in the temple.

Hiram and his family, Frieda Dutch, Henry, Catheryn, and her brood of children were the only witnesses. Lilly had not wanted Hiram and Mary there, but Zeb had said it was only right. The joy in Hiram's eyes only made Lilly resent him more. She almost wished she could tell him to his face that she was pregnant by Chase Mitchell. Hiram was glad that she had decided to marry a Mormon man; it hurt Lilly that he had never understood how much she loved Chase.

Laura, on the other hand, showed a mixture of joy and confusion. Lilly wished she could explain.

To Lilly's surprise, she felt comforted by the feel of Zeb's hand around her own as he spoke his vows with what seemed sincere conviction. She felt overwhelmed with guilt for making promises she did not intend to keep, and for the lies Zeb would have to tell and live with. She wondered what God was thinking. She had been brought up believing nearly everything was a sin, and to sin could mean damnation in the pits of hell. But the Mormons believed that God was a warm, loving Being who forgave anyone whose heart was good. She could only hope He would forgive this.

The ceremony was quickly over. There was no kiss. Witnesses supposed Zeb was too bashful. Frieda Dutch congratulated Lilly and wished her happiness. When she got the chance, Laura pulled Lilly aside and hugged her.

"Oh, Lilly, I didn't think you would get over Chase Mitchell so quickly. Father was surprised, too, but he and

Mother are very happy for you. They always feared Brother Mitchell would never come back and he'd break your heart, but now you have Zeb. Father is so happy you've married a Mormon. He has even said I can come and visit you now."

For Laura's sake, Lilly struggled to hide her bitterness over Hiram's attitude. She didn't care whether Hiram was happy or not.

"Zeb is a good man," was her only reply.

Laura frowned, thinking Lilly didn't seem nearly as excited and flushed as she had over Chase Mitchell. She didn't quite understand how Lilly could have forgotten him so quickly, but Hiram had said she would forget him soon enough, and apparently, that was what had happened.

"It's too bad your first home has to be a covered wagon," Laura told Lilly, "but at least you'll be heading west with a man to take care of you properly. Father is so glad of that."

Lilly glanced at Zeb, who stood on the other side of the room now with Henry. She wondered how he could take the entire incident so calmly. In the nearly four months she had lived with Zeb and Catheryn, she had come to realize that Zeb Adams had incredible inner strength. He thought things through logically, worked hard, and put everyone else ahead of himself. She felt terribly sorry that she could not be a real wife to him.

Catheryn cut a cake and served it with milk and a little tea. That was unusual—the Mormons seldom drank the beverage. Coffee was even rarer, and liquor was unheard of. Catheryn's children devoured most of the cake, and Zeb accepted a hand-carved mantel clock from Henry who had made it himself. It was a beautiful gift. Lilly was overwhelmed by everyone's kindness. Even Hiram and Mary gave them a gift—a set of expensive china.

"You'll have to pack this very carefully," Mary told Lilly, tears of joy in her eyes. "It belonged to Hiram's mother, and it's quite valuable."

"Mary, you shouldn't—"

"We want you to have it."

Lilly wondered how these people would treat her when they found out she had already been carrying a child when she had married Zeb.

Hiram approached hesitantly. "Lilly, we couldn't be happier about this."

Lilly just stared at him. Hiram, confused by the unhappiness he was sure he saw in her face, wanted to ask what had changed her mind, but she had a way of warning him with her eyes that certain things were none of his business. He wondered how poor Zeb was going to handle a woman as independent as she was, and how he had convinced her to marry him in the first place.

"Lilly," he said aloud, "people have asked me to ask you if . . . well, if you would consider singing once more for us in the temple tomorrow. It's our last worship service there before we leave Nauvoo. It's going to be very sad, leaving that beautiful building to people who will probably destroy it. I know how you feel—about not being allowed to sing there these last few months. But now that you've married Zeb, and, considering how important this service is to us—"

"Please, Lilly," Laura put in. "It will mean so much to everyone. The journey is going to be so hard, and we all need hope in our hearts. If you sang *All Is Well* for us, it would help so much." Laura looked over at Zeb. "Brother Zeb, please make Lilly sing for us tomorrow. It's our last service."

Zeb walked a little closer, holding Lilly's eyes. "God gave Lilly the voice, not me. It's her decision."

All Lilly could think about was Chase's parting words. *"Don't ever stop singing, Lilly. Don't let our parting take the music from your heart."*

She looked up at Zeb, and he leaned down and whispered in her ear. "Everything is going to be all right, Lilly." He kissed her cheek, and Lilly felt comforted. She realized that the better she got to know Zeb Adams, the less homely he looked to her. And she knew that he would keep his promise not to touch her as a husband unless she was willing. She had never felt more grateful, or guiltier that her heart still cried out for Chase. She turned her eyes to Hiram.

"I'll sing at the temple," she told him. *But only for Chase —not for you,* she wanted to add.

* * *

The temple resounded with voices. The Mormons sang with more emotion and zeal than they had ever felt before. For most of them this was their last service at Nauvoo.

Zeb had been quiet all that morning. As Lilly stood with the choir and watched him now, she was almost certain there were tears in his eyes. Behind her, Mary Williams had to stop singing because her voice choked up.

Lilly waited for her turn to solo. She knew all eyes would suddenly be on her. People would whisper and wonder about her sudden marriage to Zeb. They would surely think her the happy bride this morning, but none of them would know she had not slept with her husband on their wedding night. It would be harder to hide their separate lives on the trip west, she knew; Lilly did not doubt that the journey would leave little opportunity for privacy. At least no one would think much about Lilly sleeping inside the wagon and Zeb sleeping under it.

But the burden of her secret felt like a weight in the middle of her back. She knew she might carry that weight the rest of her life, if Chase were killed and never came back to her. The weight would be doubled when the baby was born, for if Chase did not return, there was no sense in telling the child about his real father at all. He would only suffer shame, and wonder about Chase—perhaps even question his mother's morality. Lilly could not bear the thought of seeing shame in her child's eyes.

Now it was her turn. She prayed she could get through the hymn without weeping. There were so many things to cry about. Instead, she stepped forward and sang:

Come, come ye Saints, no toil or labor fear;
But with joy wend your way,
Why should we mourn or think our lot is hard;
'Tis not so; all is right . . .

She glanced at Zeb, and held his gaze.

Our God will never us forsake;
And soon we'll have this tale to tell—
All is well! All is well!

Lilly rose above her sorrows when she sang. She realized she could make up for any wrong she had done by praising God with song, and by bringing hope and courage to those who listened. She was going to have a baby, and that was something else that no one could take from her. A baby would be a constant in her life—something that would be all hers to love and to love her back.

> *We'll find the place which God for us prepared.*
> *Far away in the West,*
> *Where none shall come to hurt or make afraid;*
> *There the Saints will be blessed.*
> *We'll make the air with music ring.*
> *Shout praises to our God and King;*
> *Above the rest these words we'll tell—*
> *All is well! All is well!*

Together the choir and the congregation sang the last verse of the hymn, some smiling, some crying, a few women breaking down completely. Lilly knew that as long as she kept singing, she would not cry.

The service ended, and people came up to congratulate her on her marriage to Zeb. She greeted more people on her way out. As she accepted their praises, she began to feel more loved again. She realized that, in spite of how she felt about Hiram, most of these people had been kind and generous to her.

She finally got outside, and spotted Zeb standing a distance away. He held up his hand. Something was in it—it looked like a letter.

Lilly hurried past everyone, ignoring their praises. She hardly noticed the disappointed look on Zeb's face as she raced up to him. Everyone else thought she was simply running to be near her new husband, but all Lilly could think about was Chase.

"Zeb, what is it!"

He held out the letter. "When I came out of the temple, a stranger was waiting—a man who makes his living carrying messages for people. He brought this for you."

He handed out the letter, and Lilly saw Chase's name on

it. "Finally!" she exclaimed. "Oh, thank God!" She tore the letter from Zeb's hand and walked away. Zeb watched her as she read it over and over, withering a little more each time. Finally, she wadded it up and threw it down. Keeping her back to him, she hurried off into a stand of trees. Zeb walked over and picked up the letter, unwrinkled it, and read it.

"Oh, dear God," he muttered. He walked over to where someone was burning trash, tossed the letter into the fire, and went to find Lilly. He moved through underbrush, calling for her, until he found her sitting on a rock, surrounded by wild lilacs. The scent of the now-withering flowers still hung in the air.

"Lilly?" he spoke up softly. "I . . . read the letter. I burned it."

"Good," she answered, her voice strangely cold.

"You all right?"

She rose, turning. Zeb almost gasped at how much older she suddenly looked—still beautiful, but without the wide-eyed innocence. "I'm fine," she answered. "We had better get home. We have a lot to do to get ready."

He walked a little closer. "I'm sorry, Lilly."

She looked away. "I know you are. So am I, Zeb." She met his eyes then. "I want to know if you intend to be a real father to my child—if you could love it like your own."

He searched her beautiful green eyes. "Of course I could. The main reason I married you is because of the child."

"And you would always keep the secret? You would raise the child like your own, and let him believe you are the real father?"

"I would."

"Then, I will stay married to you," she told him bluntly, her voice cool. "Don't expect too much from me for now, Zeb, but I will not be a divorced woman, and I will not visit the shame of the truth upon my child." She walked past him. "Let's go, please. We have to be ready to leave in the morning."

He followed Lilly. She seemed like a stranger. A minute's reading, one short letter, had changed her.

PART II

Chapter Twelve

August 1846

Lilly walked beside the wagon, her aching back and feet overtaking the pain in her heart. For nearly a month an oppressive heat spell had enveloped the emigrants with sweltering cruelty. Lilly didn't know which was worse—walking in the hot sun, or sitting inside the canvas wagon, where the heat was even more intense.

A heavy, cold rain had pelted them for nearly a week straight before the intense heat set in, and Lilly had spent that week inside the wagon with three of Catheryn's children, while Catheryn rode in Henry Guest's wagon with the two youngest children, baby Marian and four-year-old Ella.

Henry and Catheryn had married just before they set out for Winter Quarters. Lilly could not imagine a worse way to spend a honeymoon. It mattered little to her, for she did not think of Zeb in any romantic sense, but she felt sorry for Catheryn, making this agonizing journey at a time when she should be in a solid home, enjoying her new husband.

Although they were no comparison to a real house, Lilly was amazed at how much the canvas-topped wagons could hold. She and Catheryn had sewn pockets into the sides of the canvas to hold small items such as combs and scissors. Small barrels and boxes of dried beans, flour, sugar, and other provisions had been carefully placed in such a way as to utilize every available space inside and outside the wagon. Feather mattresses were rolled up during the day and unrolled at night for sleeping.

Catheryn's dishes were packed in straw, as was the china Mary had given Lilly. Lilly had rolled up a handmade rag carpet and tied it on the inside of Zeb's wagon. Three small trunks held all the clothes Catheryn had been allowed to bring along for herself and the five children, and a favorite mirror and chest of drawers were stored in Henry's wagon.

All other available space was reserved for human bodies, as well as an array of tools, farm equipment, seeds, butter churns, buckets, pans, more bedding, drinking gourds, guns and ammunition, axes, axle grease, water barrels, and the like.

Henry and Zeb both slept outside under the wagons, but no one, inside or out, was able to escape the buzzing, pesky mosquitoes that seemed intent on keeping them awake after dark. Comfort was rare, if it could be found at all. It came up in the form of a shade tree or simply being able to put one's feet up at night after a long day of walking. But riding in the jolting, rocking wagons was worse than the endless walking. Lilly could barely go to sleep at night without the sensation that she was still rocking and swaying and bouncing over the uneven and endless hills of Iowa. The sickening movements made her dizzy and had only aggravated her morning sickness. Even some of Catheryn's children had gotten sick from the movement, and often leaned out over the back gate of the wagon to vomit.

Henry and Zeb and most of the other men had to walk no matter what the weather, for the oxen that pulled the wagons needed to be led. Only those who used mules could sit on the wagon and drive their animals with reins. Horses were not used at all, for they did not have the strength and stamina for the journey. They were either herded or tied to the backs of wagons, as were milk cows.

Lilly could not help pitying the men who walked, as they plodded onward through all kinds of weather, getting soaked until Lilly was sure they would be sick, then sweltering in the hot sun.

Last night it had rained, and in spite of today's sun, everything remained damp because of the almost unbearable humidity. Lilly could see steam rising from the ground, and she felt the thick air pressing on her like a weight.

She longed for Scotland, and the cool mountain cabin where she had spent her childhood. She occasionally wondered if the oppressive heat and the pain in her blistered feet were punishment for the sin she had committed with Chase

Mitchell. The terrible, unexpected letter had left an ugly ache in her soul, and she quietly suffered the humiliation of being spurned. Chase's statement that he really did love her did little to help her wounded heart. She was sure it meant nothing—that it was only an excuse to get out of a commitment he never meant to keep.

Only Zeb knew about the letter. He had not mentioned it since he had thrown it into the fire that awful day. He had been kind and attentive since they had left Nauvoo, helping her with chores however he could, despite having his own to do. Lilly sensed it was more than just feeling sorry for her. She could not imagine that he could love a woman who had been so foolish and sinful as she—a woman who had so freely given herself, in the most intimate way, to a man who was not her husband. But it was love she was sure she saw in his eyes.

She didn't *want* Zeb to love her. It only made the marriage more unfair to him, for she was certain she could never love him back—not in the way a woman should love her husband. Lilly blamed Chase not only for leaving her in this humiliating position, but for making her hurt Zeb Adams, as she was surely going to end up doing.

She unbuttoned the top button of her dress, wishing she could strip it off completely. A shiver moved through her as she thought about the cruel, unbelievable words in Chase's letter. She could not recall ever feeling such agonizing hurt. It was different from the pain of losing her mother. She would almost rather have heard Chase was dead, than to know he was alive but didn't mean to keep his promises. She wanted to hate him, and sometimes she was sure she *did*.

She could not forget the sincerity she thought she had seen in his eyes, the feel of his arms around her, the tender ecstasy of his kiss, the beauty of being one with him. How could he think she could just forget him and find someone else. Surely, he knew how painful it would be for her to get his letter.

She put a hand to her stomach. What if Chase knew about the baby? Would it make him change his mind, to know she was carrying his child? Still, if she couldn't have Chase

Mitchell because he loved her and wanted to be with her, she didn't want him at all. She would keep her vow that he would never, ever know about the baby, and that her child would never know who its real father was.

"Lilly!"

Lilly turned to see Laura trying to catch up with her. She waited, as the wagons lumbered by. Everything seemed so quiet in the stifling heat, for no one felt like talking or laughing. Even the animals made little noise. She watched the two milk cows they had brought along, one tied to the back of each wagon. They lumbered along with their heads hanging low, their tails swishing at flies that kept trying to land by the hundreds on the poor animals' backsides. One flew at Lilly's cheek, and she brushed it away, then felt another one bite her on the neck. She slapped at it as Laura walked up to her.

"Oh, Lilly, I don't think I can bear another minute of this heat!" the girl exclaimed, looking close to tears.

"We don't have much choice, Laura." Lilly tried to hide her alarm as she saw her face. Laura's almost-black hair made her look even paler and her dark eyes looked wide and almost glazed. "Laura, are you sick?"

"I don't know. How can a person know if he or she is sick when it's this hot?"

"I know what you mean."

"Oh, Lilly, what a terrible way for you to spend your first weeks as a new wife. You should have married Zeb sooner, and had some time alone together before leaving Nauvoo. Or maybe you should have stayed behind with the group waiting for the new arrivals from Europe."

"I would rather get the trip over with, if it must be done," Lilly answered. "But right now, I wonder which would be worse—staying in Scotland and working at the mill, or this journey. Hiram never really explained it would be like this."

"I don't think Father knew himself what it would be like. He says it will be two months or better before we arrive at Winter Quarters. The word *winter* sounds nice, but I hardly think real winter will be here for a long time after that. I wonder what it will be like there."

"We'll live out of wagons and tents, I expect."

"Mother is already low on sugar. When it rained, a corner of the canvas on our wagon leaked, and it soaked one of our sacks. Some of it can still be used, but the rest dissolved. And mother is still distraught over leaving behind so many of her nice things, especially the dining table. She so loved it. It belonged to her own mother, and came here all the way from England, years ago."

"Yes, it was a lovely table. I have never had such fine possessions to worry about losing."

"Lilly." Laura stopped walking a moment. "Will you come around to our campfire tonight and be friendly to Mother and Father? They would feel so much better, I think. It hurts them that you have hardly spoken to them since Chase Mitchell left. Now that you're married to Zeb Adams, couldn't we all be friends again?"

Lilly felt sick at the fact that Hiram had been right about Chase. That made it even more important to her that he believe her baby belonged to Zeb. He must never know what she had done with Chase.

"I'll think about it, Laura," she said aloud. "But only for you."

"Oh, I'm glad!" The girl stooped to pick some wild flowers, which grew in sprawling abundance across the hills and plains of Iowa. "Oh, Lilly, did you ever see so many flowers? I pick them fresh every day and decorate our wagon with them."

Lilly stopped and looked around at the brilliant colors, realizing she had not once noticed the flowers during the entire journey. Had her heart really turned so bitter that she could no longer see the beauty in anything? "Yes, they are pretty," she answered, picking one herself and holding it to her nose, remembering another day she had picked wild flowers. She had been so happy that day . . . so in love. *Oh, Chase,* she thought, almost shuddering with remembered ecstasy. She would never love that way again—she was sure of it.

She put a hand to her thickening waist and threw down the flowers, angry with herself for having feelings for a man who had so cruelly used her.

"Lilly, why did you do that?" Laura asked.

Lilly reddened slightly. She had almost forgotten that Laura had been walking with her. "I . . . I'm just so tired, I don't even feel like carrying flowers," she answered.

Laura frowned, reaching into the pocket of her dress and pulling out a dried apple. "Do you want one, Lilly? I have another."

"No. I can't bear the thought of another apple. Zeb makes me eat one every day."

"Father makes me eat them, too. We have to do it, you know. You wouldn't want to get scurvy and lose all your teeth."

Lilly wondered at the moment what difference it would make. She had wanted to be beautiful for Chase. Now, she didn't care. It was only for the baby that she knew she had to stay healthy, yet in her heart, she still wasn't sure whether she would love it or hate it.

"The heat ruined most of Mother's canned fruits and vegetables—and after all that work growing them, picking everything and canning it," Laura said.

"I know. I feel sorry for Zeb. He even had to leave some of his crops in the field for others to harvest."

Laura's eyes teared as she swallowed a piece of apple. "I miss Nauvoo," she said then, her voice choking. "I didn't think it would be like this, Lilly. Mother is always so sad. I feel so sorry for her. I heard her crying one night after we sold the dining table."

Lilly's heart grew heavier, and she put an arm around Laura's waist. "Zeb and I will come and visit after we make camp tonight," she promised. "We'll bring Mary some sugar."

Laura brightened. "Thank you, Lilly." She wiped at a tear that trickled out of her eyes. "I just wish we could go back to our big house and I could sleep in my own room again. And I wish you could be there, too—like it used to be." She sighed. "Don't you ever think about Chase Mitchell any more? He was so handsome!" She stopped walking. "Lilly, you said you would wait for him. Why didn't you? He even said he would marry you."

Lilly met her eyes. She realized that soon she would be

showing enough that people would know she was carrying. She had to start right now with the lies.

"He told me when he left that . . . that maybe we should try to forget each other, because he was going off to war," she lied to Laura. *My life will be full of lies now,* she thought. "He told me I was too young to wait, and that he'd been wrong to ask me. After he left and I went to live with Zeb and Catheryn . . ." Lilly blinked back tears. "I don't know. Zeb was so kind and solid and dependable, and I was so lonely. Things just . . . just happened, I guess. Zeb soon told me he had loved me since the first day he met me. I wanted to belong somewhere, to someone. I just knew Zeb was a good, dependable man—and with this trip coming and all, I decided the wisest thing to do was to marry him."

Laura studied her eyes, digesting what Lilly had told her, but she could not forget the day Chase and Lilly had come in from the rain, and the love that was written all over their faces. "Deep inside, you'll always love Chase Mitchell, won't you?"

Lilly saw the romantic hope in Laura's eyes. "Yes, but don't ever tell that to your father or Mary or Zeb or anyone. It's just our secret. Promise?"

Laura's eyes lit up like an excited child. "I promise! Oh, Lilly, what an exciting life you've led—coming here from Scotland and already being loved by two men! You're so lucky!"

Lilly felt like crying at the words, but there was no explaining the truth to someone like Laura. She realized more clearly than ever that she would have to live with her shame and sorrow alone.

Laura ran ahead of her, picking more flowers, then suddenly hunched over. Lilly hurried to catch up with her. "Laura? Are you all right?"

The girl looked at her, perspiration all over her face. "I will be—in a minute," she answered, trying to smile. "Sometimes . . . I get the most awful cramps in my belly. Maybe it's the dried apples."

"You'd better go find your wagon and lie down."

Laura's breathing seemed labored. "Yes. I . . . I think I will."

Lilly walked with her most of the way. It was easy for Laura to find her own wagon, as everyone had an allocated spot within the wagon train, and no one was allowed to change positions. This helped the scouts and wagon master know who was where.

"I'll be all right now," Laura told Lilly. "You had better go and stay with Zeb until we camp tonight." The girl hugged Lilly, a strange, frightened look on her face. "Come and visit with us, please."

"We will." Lilly watched Laura hurry off to find Hiram's wagon. As she turned, a woman walking past her nodded and smiled to her. There was no mistaking the agony in her smile, or the limp in her walk from aching, swollen feet. Lilly knew she was not the only woman who had not wanted to make this journey. And although she didn't really want to be with these Mormons, she could not help admiring their stamina and perseverance, their incredible faith in God and Brigham Young, and the quiet suffering of their women. It was comforting to know she did not suffer the agonies of this journey alone, but she bore an added heartache none of them would ever know about.

Lilly searched for her small barrel of extra sugar, which had somehow gotten buried under other supplies. Outside, children played. Supper was over. A few men came riding in after rounding up some cattle that had strayed, and a man was shouting somewhere in the distance. Lilly supposed the commotion was caused by a balking team of mules, an almost daily problem.

Zeb came to the back of the wagon and climbed inside to retrieve his bedroll. Lilly could smell his perspiration, but she was not offended. She knew that under normal circumstances, Zeb bathed and shaved, but on this trip there was little time or opportunity for such luxuries. He was up at dawn getting animals ready, then spent the day walking with the oxen or helping others who had problems with wagons breaking down. There was endless harnessing and unharnessing of animals, and almost daily, someone's wagon had to be pushed out of mud. In the evenings, spare time was spent hunting for the group's constantly needed supply of meat and chasing down their own animals that strayed from the campsite. Water had been scarce, but they knew they would soon be following the Platte River through Nebraska Territory.

"That was a fine supper you made, Lilly," Zeb spoke up.

Lilly looked at him, hardly able to see him in the darkened wagon. "Are you all right, Zeb?"

He smiled, wondering how much she really cared about him, wishing that just once he would see the look in her eyes she had once had for Chase Mitchell. "I'll make it. What's more important is you. I don't like you having to walk so much in your condition. Maybe you should ride in the wagon tomorrow."

"No. That's even worse than walking. I hate it inside the wagon."

Zeb sighed. He was already aware that it was useless to give Lilly orders. He could only suggest and hope she would listen to him. "Suit yourself, but I'm going to talk to Hiram about making you some softer shoes, maybe from a good piece of deer hide. I hear that's what the Indians wear on their feet, and the Indians are pretty practical, seeing as how they do plenty of walking themselves."

"I don't need anything from Hiram."

He slung the bedroll over his shoulder. "Lilly, I know how you feel about the man, but that doesn't mean you have to ignore your own health. Wouldn't you like a pair of softer shoes?"

She sighed, running a hand through her damp hair. "I suppose. And I did promise Laura today we'd visit their camp tonight. Do you mind?"

"It's fine with me."

"Do you know where that extra sugar is? I told Laura I'd bring some to Mary. Some of theirs got ruined in the last rain. Can we spare some?"

She could feel him grin in the darkness. "Now, you know that if we had one cup left, we'd share half of it. I'll get a lantern so you can see better." He left for a moment, then returned with the lantern and a large tin can. "Put some sugar in this. It's over there in that corner."

As Zeb held up the lantern, his heart ached at the sight of

the haunting loneliness and disillusionment that showed in her tired eyes. He wanted to hold her, tell her he loved her and would never leave her, the way her baby's father had. But he knew her heart was still full of Chase Mitchell, even though at times she might think she hated the man.

Zeb had never hated anyone before, but he hated Mitchell for what he had done to Lilly. He could not imagine a man not wanting to come back to this woman. He sometimes had trouble thinking of her as his wife—she was always so distant, so untouchable. He ached for her, but he had made her a promise, and he intended to keep it.

In the first few weeks of travel four graves were dug— one for a man who had died an agonizing death from a tooth infection; one for a young boy who died of snakebite; and two elders, both men in their seventies, who had died from sheer exhaustion. Trail guides told them that four deaths was a very good record; that so far, they had been lucky. Lilly thought it ironic that they should almost feel like celebrating.

Laura came to walk with Lilly every day. Being with her was comforting. So far, Lilly had managed to hide her pregnancy. As many other women had begun doing, she wore skirts and blouses rather than a tight-fitted bodice, and left the blouse hanging outside the skirt. Such clothing was cooler. But she knew it would not be long before her condition would be discovered.

Lilly's concern over her pregnancy became suddenly overshadowed by a bigger concern for Laura, whose health seemed to be failing. In spite of the sunshine, the girl continued to look too pale, and she was growing noticeably thinner.

After they crossed the Thompson River, Laura collapsed beside her family's campfire. Within hours a strange sickness had swept through the entire wagon train. Silent, invisible hands grasped the throats and bellies of the travelers, debilitating half the people of the train.

Lilly wondered if the disease had been with them before they had crossed the river, or if the hideous plague had been visited upon them by something in the river water. The crossing had been harrowing, but Mormons from Winter Quarters met them on the banks, waiting to aid them with rafts and ropes. Already the Mormons were in the process of setting up a ferrying service, with the intention of leaving a few families at the site to help all people migrating west, including the Gentiles.

Lilly remembered smelling mud and fish as she sat in Zeb's wagon, clinging to Myra, Jeffrey, and Herbert while the wagon floated across the river on a flimsy raft. Cattle, oxen, and horses were herded across by Zeb and the other men, who got soaked. Henry Guest's wagon had slid sideways when the raft carrying it hit a rock, and it reached the opposite bank half submerged, but still intact. However, little Marian had slipped out of Catheryn's arms when the wagon lurched, and the baby had landed in the water that had flooded one whole side of the wagon. Lilly would never forget the chilling sound of Catheryn's screams.

That had been three days ago. Now little Marian lay very ill with a high fever. Many others were experiencing fevers, headaches, and sore throats; some were sick to their stomachs. Laura and little Marian seemed to be the worst. Both were suffering from life-threatening diarrhea.

Laura lay in the back of Hiram's wagon. Some suggested she had cholera, because of the diarrhea and vomiting. The entire wagon train was held up for five days. Those who were still well lived in fear of coming down with the dreaded fever, and everyone was haunted by the groans of agony from sick friends and family members.

Lilly paid no attention to anyone's warnings to stay away from Laura for fear of getting sick herself. Laura was her best friend, and Lilly insisted on staying right beside the girl through her illness. For four days she sat with her, sure she could never be so lucky as to die and be freed of her own burdened heart, and the agony of this journey. It seemed more her fate to live and watch others die, like her mother; watch others move in and out of her life, like Chase.

By the fourth day, one man had died. Lilly insisted the news be kept from Laura. While she sat reading to her friend, telling her stories, quietly knitting whenever Laura slept, she worried about little Marian, who also had not improved. Other women helped care for Catheryn's other four children, and Lilly wished she could be two people so that she could sit with Catheryn, too. But everyone told her it would do no good. Catheryn cradled her baby next to her breast and spoke to no one.

Laura moved from fevered delirium to moments of coherence, when she would beg Lilly to tell her stories about Scotland, and to tell her how it felt to be in love. Lilly made up stories about how happy she was. She helped bathe Laura to keep her cooled down, and told her she had to get well so she could marry, too, someday.

By the fourth night of Laura's illness it became obvious that life was slipping away from her. Her breathing was shallow, her voice barely discernible because her throat was swollen.

"Sing for me, Lilly," the girl asked, the words so raspy and spoken so weakly that Lilly had to bend closer to ask Laura to repeat them. Tears welled in Lilly's eyes. She could not imagine how she could get a song out when her best friend might be dying. As a matter of fact, she had not felt like singing since the day she had received the letter from Chase.

"Please sing," Mary asked her. "It would do all of us good, Lilly. We're more than halfway to Winter Quarters. I can't imagine anything more uplifting than hearing your sweet voice carry over the night air, telling us all is well, just like the hymn goes."

Lilly looked at the woman's stricken face, and realized the agony she must be suffering. She leaned down and kissed Laura's hot cheek.

"I'll sing, Laura, just for you." She swallowed back her own need to weep. Laura grasped her arm before she could leave the wagon, and Lilly leaned close again. "I really am your best friend, aren't I, Lilly?"

Lilly smoothed back the damp hair from the girl's face. "Yes, Laura. You know you are."

"You're so lucky you were loved by two men," Laura said, every word an effort.

Lilly felt the stabbing pain of remembering Chase.

"I'll never be loved by even one," Laura added.

"Of course you will, Laura," Lilly told her, forcing herself to sound confident.

"No. I'm . . . dying."

Lilly felt numb. A chilling dread moved down her spine. "Don't talk that way, Laura. You're going to be all right."

"I feel it, Lilly. Glad I got to know you first. Don't cry . . . or feel bad. I don't mind. We'll see each other . . . again someday . . . in heaven. I'm . . . not afraid."

Lilly looked at Mary. She was struggling to keep from breaking down in front of her daughter. Lilly squeezed Laura's hand. "You'll feel better after I sing for you," she assured the girl. "I love you, Laura." She climbed out of the wagon, feeling the agony of death hovering over her, just as she had felt it when her mother had died.

Outside, everything was quiet. Supper, for those well enough to eat, was done. It had consisted mostly of dried beans and hard biscuits, for game had been scarce recently, and there was no meat in camp. The sun had set, and crickets sang.

Lilly breathed deeply of the night air, forcing herself to think only about singing—to let it carry her away as it always did, once she allowed the music in her soul to take over all other emotions. She sang the favorite Mormon hymn, and this time the last verse had special meaning. Her heart pounded as she struggled to keep her voice from quivering.

And should we die before our journey's through,
Happy day! All is well!
We then are free from toil and sorrow, too;
With the just we shall dwell!
But if our lives are spared again
To see the Saints their rest obtain,
O how we'll make this chorus swell
All is well! All is well!

Lilly sang several more hymns. A few of the emigrants gathered around her, some bowing their heads in prayer as she sang, many taking new hope and joy in the songs. It was not until Lilly was through that she heard Mary weeping inside the wagon. She wondered which song she had been singing when Laura had died.

Chapter Thirteen

Chase forced himself to hold back. The rest of the men with whom he marched hurried to the muddy water hole they had found. Little heed was given to rank, and men and horses drank side by side. Chase had a small amount of water left in his canteen, and he drank one swallow, remembering how sick some of the men had become at the last water hole they had found. It took all his strength to keep from filling his own canteen with the muddy water in front of them. He capped the canteen and walked swiftly to help a fellow infantryman who lay frothing at the mouth and digging at the sand around him.

"Come on, Jake, there's water just a little way ahead." He helped the young man to his feet. Jake was mumbling words that made no sense. His eyes were wild, his face burned. Chase led him to the water, and he fell face down into it.

"Chase!" Howard Mitchell rode up to his son, leading a horse. "I wish you would change your mind about riding. I told you, I can get you a promotion any time you want it."

"I can't desert them, Father. I've marched this far with them—"

"It isn't desertion, Chase! You have a right to this horse."

"No, I don't. You said there would be no favors, and I want that more than you do. Please, go back where you belong, Father."

Mitchell scowled angrily. He did not like to see his son suffering, but he was proud of the young man's perseverance, and his loyalty to his friends.

Chase watched his father ride away. He wondered more and more why he had agreed to this hideous campaign. His father was actually enjoying this march into Mexico against Santa Anna, and he seemed to have little regard for men of lesser rank, except for his son.

At Matamoros, troops had been turned loose on the civilian population, allowed to loot and rape. Chase found that the Texas Rangers were hardest on the Mexican civilians. He was amazed and angered at the way the officers allowed their men to ravage and harass those who were innocent in this war. The Texas Rangers were made up of some of the roughest men on the Texas frontier border, more outlaws than respectable citizens—men with a natural hatred for the Mexicans.

They were marching into Camargo, headed southwest toward Buena Vista. Never had Chase known such heat—the temperature soared above 100 degrees daily. A man couldn't even sit on a rock to rest, for they were too hot. Dust covered and drifted inside everything—clothes, eyes, mouths, food. Snakes and tarantulas, as well as hordes of ants, invaded their tents and sleeping bags and food every night. Dysentery and yellow fever were beginning to take their toll, and men were dying by the hundreds. It seemed that more men were being carried on stretchers and in army ambulance wagons than were marching or riding.

Chase was sure the entire campaign would be more bearable if only he got a letter from Lilly. He had written her several times, hoping that somehow, he would hear from her. But he realized that no messenger in his right mind would come back down into Mexico after leaving it—certainly not to the hellhole in which they would make camp the next day. He had no way of knowing what she was doing, except that she had surely left Nauvoo and was somewhere in the American desert by now. He prayed the land there was not as Godforsaken and unbearable as it was here in Mexico. And he knew he could not survive himself, if not for thoughts of Lilly—her face, her hair, her lips; the feel of her body; the memory of her sweet voice, her beautiful eyes; her whispered promises to wait for him.

He began to wonder if his promise to his father was so important that he should have left Lilly alone to face her journey westward. If he had stayed, he could have married her and set up a home for the two of them, sparing her the journey. But now he was here, part of Taylor's campaign into Mexico—so much a part that there was no turning back now. At least he would not be known as a deserter. No matter what he thought of his father, or how much the man had disappointed him, he would not shame the Mitchell name.

He could foresee many more weeks, probably months, of fighting in Mexico. There had been no serious battles yet—only long marches—but it was rumored there would be fighting at Monterrey, and probably at Buena Vista. Chase almost welcomed battle. It would be a nice break in the monotony of the daily marches, and a diversion from the physical agony of the journey. Better yet, it would be an outlet to help him stop thinking about Lilly. He constantly compared her cool, green eyes to the hot desert sun; her sweet fragrance to the smell of sweat and dirt; and her soft voice to nothing but male companionship.

Orders were shouted to resume the march. Chase helped Jake to his feet, but the man took no more than two steps before he stopped to vomit.

"We'll make camp at Camargo tomorrow," Chase told him. "Hang on till then, Jake, and you can rest." He shoved the young man's cap onto his head. "Come on. You can make it." He led the young man toward the others, who were trying to stay in straight lines, but unable to because of the loose sand and gravel beneath their feet. Chase reached into his pants pocket again, checking to make sure his next letter to Lilly was still there, as well as the drawing Beth had made for him that helped remind him of Lilly's pretty face.

Sickness continued to sweep savagely through the Mormon camps. Those malaria and dysentery did not take, malnutrition, tuberculosis, whooping cough, and the common cold claimed. Besides diseases, strains and injuries, ax cuts, falls, and broken bones took their toll, as well as toothaches, pleurisy, and exhaustion.

Scouts who came to meet them from Winter Quarters informed them that matters there were no better. But there was no turning back. Lilly was haunted by Laura's death. It seemed that every new loss and disappointment was worse than the last. Three days after Laura's death little Marian had also died, leaving Catheryn grief-stricken. Lilly thought she could not bear any more death and sorrow, and she was terrified of having her baby in this wilderness. She could not help wondering if her child would also be buried in this lonely land, its little grave never to be visited once the wagon train rolled on. That was how it had been for Laura and Marian, and Lilly could well understand the agony both Catheryn and Mary suffered. She still suffered the ache of remembering her mother's watery grave, a grave she could not visit. She pictured Laura calling out to her, asking her to stay with her and be her friend.

Zeb seemed to understand her sorrow, even though he suffered his own over the loss of his little niece. He was so attentive and helpful that it frightened Lilly, for now she wondered what she would do if she lost him to the sicknesses that continued to plague the wagon train. She began to feel more attached to the child in her belly. Much as she resented and sometimes hated Chase for putting it there, she realized that the child might be all she ever had that was all her own. She prayed daily that God would forgive her for not wanting it at first and let her have a healthy baby.

Her pregnancy had become more evident over the past two weeks. Her stomach had mushroomed to the point that the bulge could not be mistaken under her blouse. A few people had stared and whispered, but so far, no one had been unkind. Lilly was sorry that Zeb had to bear the stares and gossip, for people would surely begin to realize that Lilly was much farther along than the nearly two months they had been married. But Lilly continued to walk the journey rather than ride inside the wagon, and she held her chin high, refusing to act ashamed.

What she dreaded most was Hiram and Mary's scrutiny. So far, they had been so lost in grief that they had either not noticed, or simply hadn't bothered to bring it up. But one night, after making camp, Hiram came to their campfire. His eyes fell on Lilly's belly as he told Zeb he wanted to talk with him alone. Lilly felt a chill of apprehension and dread as the two men walked off together. She tried to keep herself busy cleaning up, but she trembled with worry. Her only consolation was to smile at the thought of how Laura would have reacted if she had found out that Lilly had been pregnant before she was married. She imagined how shocked yet excited the girl would have been if Lilly had told her it was Chase's baby.

The thought of Chase always brought a mixture of passion and hate. She knew she would never again experience such exquisite joy and love, nor such cutting emotional pain. Zeb was steady and dependable, but her heart belonged to Chase Mitchell, which left her with nothing to give poor Zeb.

Zeb and Hiram finally returned. Lilly watched warily as Hiram approached her. Her heart softened toward him when she saw the sorrow and love in his eyes.

"Lilly," he said aloud. "I . . . Mary is having a bad time getting over Laura. I wondered if you would visit with her more."

Lilly had expected some kind of chastisement, condemnation, accusation. A lump rose in her throat. "If you want me. I came before . . . because of Laura."

Hiram swallowed and breathed deeply, as though searching for words. "That's just it. I think having you around . . . knowing how much Laura loved you . . . it would help. We love you, too, you know. You are like a daughter to us. I'm asking you now to put aside the words we have had in the past and spend more time with Mary. She, uh," His eyes dropped to her belly again, and Lilly reddened. "She's concerned about the fact that you're obviously with child. She'd like to help, and it would be good for her. She said to tell you not to be afraid. There are plenty of women here who have given birth, many times over. They know what to do."

Lilly put a hand to her stomach and looked over at Zeb with questioning eyes. "Hiram's no fool, Lilly. But he and Mary are the only ones who know how serious you were about Chase."

Lilly turned away, hunching over slightly.

"Lilly, I feel like part of this is my fault—" Hiram started to say.

"Don't say it!" She whirled, glaring at him. "Don't ever talk about it again!" she almost hissed. She stepped closer, keeping her voice to a near whisper. "This baby belongs to Zeb Adams, do you understand? I have Zeb and Catheryn's word that they will never mention Chase Mitchell's name to anyone, especially to the child I am carrying! I intend that he or she will grow up knowing Zeb and will never know the shame I might have brought upon him." She stood and stared at him.

Hiram nodded. "The subject is closed. All I want is for you to help Mary get over her grief. I know you're experiencing your own, Lilly, and I'm sorry for those weeks I kept you and Laura apart. Maybe it would help you and Mary both to be together more. I just want you to let her help with the baby—let her be a part of all this. She'll be happier." A tear formed at the corner of his eye. "I'll make sure she understands the baby is Zeb's." He smiled sadly. "I can't help wondering how Laura would have reacted. She would have had a hundred questions, wouldn't she?"

Lilly could not answer. She only nodded, turning away to cry quietly. Hiram patted her arm and left, and in the next moment, she felt Zeb's big hand on her shoulder.

"I tried, Lilly, but Hiram knew. Don't you worry. Everybody else thinks it's my fault. I've already had my share of remarks."

She turned and cried against his chest. "Oh, Zeb, I'm so sorry."

He smiled softly. "I told you, I have big shoulders. You let me know if anyone says something unkind to you. I don't believe in violence, but I will use my fists when I have to, and I wouldn't be averse to using mine in your defense, even against another Mormon."

She put her arms around his middle, and he enjoyed the feel of her breasts against his chest. But he could also feel her swollen stomach—the life of another man.

"Everything will be all right, Lilly. You get some rest now. I don't want you getting sick, like so many of the others. I wouldn't want to lose you now."

She looked up at him in the moonlight. "I don't want to lose you, either, Zeb."

He studied her lovely green eyes, even prettier in the fire-light. *And what would you do if Chase Mitchell came back?* he wanted to ask her. But he knew the answer. He leaned down and kissed her forehead, moving an arm around her shoulders. At least they had come to the point of touching more. Just that much felt wonderful to him. But he knew their closeness was due in part to her dependency on him during this terrible journey, and her personal sorrow over losing Laura.

"Let's go see Mary for a while before we turn in," he told her.

The wagon train straggled into Winter Quarters in early October of 1846. Lilly had hoped to arrive at a thriving town, but instead, she saw a cluster of hundreds of huts and crude cabins, wagons and tents, perched on both the Iowa side and the Indian-occupied west side of the Missouri River. She clung to the sideboard inside the wagon as it was taken across the river by ferry, and when she stepped out she set eyes on Indians for the first time in her life. She found them both frightening and fascinating. Zeb assured her the Mormons had made friends with the Omahas and that she had nothing to fear.

"It's the Pawnees that make the trouble, but we made it through Pawnee country without them bothering us at all. We're safe here."

Lilly did her best to convince herself she should believe Zeb, but the painted, half-naked warriors and their quiet, dark-eyed women gave her chills. They had been at their final camp only two days when a meeting was called, re-quiring the presence of all the men. Lilly waited at the wagon. She had spent the entire day washing clothes with Mary at the river and hanging them from every practical spot she could find. It was a time to clean out wagons, reevaluate supplies, and to regain strength that would be needed for their journey to a final Zion.

Zeb returned to the wagon well after dark. He sat down beside Lilly on a log before the campfire, poured himself some hot water, and dipped a cloth bag filled with tea leaves into it. Tea was a drink Hiram had always forbidden, but one Zeb was not against. He simply had never kept any in the house. But Lilly liked tea, and when Zeb had discovered that some was available in the meager supplies at Winter Quarters, he had spent what he could spare to get some for his wife.

"What happened at the meeting?" Lilly asked him.

Zeb sighed deeply, taking a sip of the hot brew. "I have to go away, Lilly."

Her heart tightened. "Where? For how long?"

"Brother Young can get some help—supplies and money —from the government, if some of us volunteer to go down to Fort Leavenworth and join a Colonel Kearny on a march into the southwest. Kearny is supposed to claim New Mexico and California for the United States—part of this war with Mexico."

Lilly fought madly not to cry. She had grown attached to Zeb, had developed a deep friendship with him, a gentle fondness for the good man that he was. And she had counted on his being around when the baby was born. Her eyes filled with tears and her throat ached fiercely. "I . . . don't want you to go away," she told him, her voice shaking.

Zeb looked at her, wishing that meant that she loved him. "Brother Young says it will only be for about a year. I'll probably be back before you leave to go farther west. I don't expect that will happen till next spring. You'll winter here. I'm awful sorry, Lilly, but it's my duty to go. Outsiders are saying that Mormons are unpatriotic—traitors. They're challenging us to prove our loyalty in exchange for the help we need. These people have got to have some money to buy more supplies, Lilly, as well as the medicine and provisions they'll send up from Fort Leavenworth. You know how much sickness there has been. We need to replace what we've used."

She nodded, unable to speak. Zeb set down his cup and turned to her, putting an arm around her shoulders. "You have nothing to fear here, Lilly, as long as you stay in camp and keep yourself warm and fed. Henry will see that you get everything you need. He's older, so he's being allowed to stay. Katy and Mary will help you when the baby is born. Nothing is going to happen—to you, or the baby, or to me."

Lilly rose, pacing quietly around the campfire, coming back to stand in front of Zeb.

"I'm sorry, Zeb, about our situation. If you want to divorce me, after the baby . . ."

"There will be no divorce unless you want one. I'm the baby's father, remember? What made you say such a thing?"

She knelt in front of him. "You're going away. And I can't even give you a proper send-off, like a real wife would do. You . . . you could take a second wife . . . one who would fulfill your needs."

"I don't want a second wife." He leaned closer. "I promised you I wouldn't do that. Besides, maybe . . . after a time . . ." He said nothing for a few seconds. He rose then, turning away and sighing deeply. Throughout the camp they could hear babies crying and hymns being sung here and there. "We'll see how things stand when I get back," he said then.

Lilly struggled against her terrible sorrow. She rose and walked up beside Zeb. "I'll be waiting for you," she said softly. "I promise to take care of myself." She fought tears. "And when you return, you'll have a new son or daughter."

He turned to meet her eyes in the light of the fire. Their eyes held, and crickets sang. In the next moment he was kissing her, an urge he could not resist, and one she did not have the heart to deny him. It was a somewhat awkward kiss, but sweet. It lacked the hot passion that Chase's kisses had always aroused in her, and she did not feel the wonderful sensations she had felt in Chase's arms. But she wondered now if perhaps love was not always that way. Maybe there were different kinds. She suspected not all women enjoyed the kind of love with their husbands that she had enjoyed with Chase.

Zeb suddenly pulled away, turned back to look at the fire, and picked up his cup of tea. "I'm sorry. I had no right."

"I'm your wife, Zeb."

He said nothing for several seconds. "I love you, Lilly," he said finally. "I hope you'll . . . you'll think about that while I'm gone. Maybe when I get back . . . after the baby and all . . ." He sipped some more tea. "I'd like to think maybe I have a chance of making you my wife in the real sense. I know it wouldn't be like with Chase Mitchell, but you can at least depend on me. I'll always take good care of you."

"I know you will." She put a hand on his shoulder. "I'll give it a lot of thought, Zeb, and I'll miss you. I mean that."

He turned his hand and gripped hers, squeezing it lightly. "Thank you for telling me that. I'll miss you, too—especially your singing." He set down the cup and rose. "I'd better see to the stock."

He walked off into the darkness, and Lilly shivered in the night air. She was not sure she could ever give that much of herself again.

The music floated over the Indian territory that lay on the west side of the Missouri and set the waters of the Missouri to dancing. The Mormons, gathered to say goodbye to the young men who would be leaving them, also danced. The Mormons certainly set an example that helped Lilly find more courage.

Their determination to find joy where none seemed to exist never failed to surprise Lilly. The journey had been agony. Many lives had been lost. Now, their best young men were going to war. Yet they celebrated the life of those who had survived, their safe arrival at Winter Quarters, the fact that supplies would be coming from Fort Leavenworth, and that they were on their way to their Zion.

Contrary to most religions, Mormons believed not only in singing, but in dancing. Even Catheryn danced, with Henry. Her little daughter's death had not spoiled the woman's faith. Lilly could read the distant loneliness in the woman's eyes. But like so many others who had suffered and who longed to go back to Nauvoo, Catheryn had carried on. The Mormons believed that God was great and good, and He wanted His people to be joyful in all things. They believed that those departed had simply gone to a new world—and that those left behind would join them gladly in their own deaths.

There were no earrings or rings, no fancy dresses, but

there were smiles, and even some laughter. Those who could play instruments did—fiddles, banjos, harmonicas, accordions. Full skirts swished over dirt packed hard from so many feet pounding on it, and men and women whirled to the Virginia reel, or to a Copenhagen jig. The many nationalities of the inhabitants of Winter Quarters each had their own particular dance; and showing them to others was a way for them to remember home.

"Come on. I'll teach you the reel," Zeb told Lilly.

"Oh, I can't."

"Sure you can." He grabbed her hand. "Do it for me, Lilly. I won't be seeing you for a long time."

Lilly had never seen Zeb smile so much, as when he held both her hands and swung her around. She knew he was putting on his best show of bravery and lightheartedness for her sake. The coming winter would be hard on both of them. The summer here at Winter Quarters had been very dry, and the crops were not doing well. There would not be a lot of food, but at least there would be some from Fort Leavenworth. A mill had been built, and some of the men who would stay behind had found work with settlers outside Winter Quarters. In the spring, Brigham Young and a chosen few would head farther west to seek the final "promised land," and there was hardly a soul among the Mormons who doubted such a place would be found.

Lilly felt a stabbing pain of grief, realizing how much Laura would have liked this dance. She would have been so excited—full of laughter and questions and gossip. She would have carried on about Lilly's expected baby, asking about it with those big, curious eyes that made Lilly sometimes feel so many years older. But Laura lay silent in a grave, far away now—a grave Lilly would never see again. Lilly wondered at the faith of these people. Even Mary and Hiram were dancing.

"People are staring at us, Zeb," she told him then. "Maybe a woman in my condition shouldn't dance."

He grinned as the dance ended. He put a hand to her waist and walked her over to a table, where apple juice was being served. "They just like watching a pretty woman, and you're the prettiest one at Winter Quarters—maybe anyplace in this country."

Lilly blushed.

A German man began to demonstrate a dance step. Everyone clapped in rhythm, and some tried to learn it. There was an amazing amount of laughter, considering what they had all just been through. They danced well into the night. Hours later, when everyone quieted, riddles and stories were told. Prayers were offered—for lost loved ones, for the empty places left in their hearts, for their young men, who would be leaving them in the morning. Hymns were sung, and again, several people pressed Lilly to sing for them. The old desire to sing for others, to have an audience, never failed to surface at such times. Yes, she would sing. She would always sing when asked, for singing was her only joy in life—the one love no one could take from her. Even her baby could be taken from her in death. But her voice, which belonged to her alone, could not die unless she did.

She stepped near a campfire and began to sing, accompanied by a fiddle and a harmonica. Her voice, floating over the clear night air, brought an awed silence to the crowd. She sang hymns of hope and joy, and of home and distant lands.

Lilly ended with the favorite, *All Is Well!* She thought of Chase—how she had sung it just for him because he was going off to war and might be killed. She choked on the last words, and quickly left for her wagon. Others thought she was weeping over the fact that her new husband would be leaving her so soon. No one considered she could be weeping over the young Gentile who had been with them such a short time. They didn't know that she had lain in his arms, given herself to him in total abandon and sweet love.

Zeb followed her and put a hand on her shoulder. "You all right, Lilly?"

She nodded. "I think I'll go to sleep now."

She climbed into the wagon. Zeb watched her, hoping she would invite him inside, but she did not. There would be no exotic farewell for him. But he was a patient man. He would wait. He hoped being away from her would help, much as he hated to leave.

Neither of them slept well that night. Zeb lay under the wagon, imagining what it would be like to be inside it. Lilly lay inside, hating herself for not being a decent wife, disgusted with herself for wishing Chase Mitchell would come back and tell her it was all a mistake, that he truly loved her and wanted to be with her forever. *Forever.* He had used that word. It had been as precious to her as *love*—a word not to be used lightly. But Chase had used it and her lightly. She turned over and wept into the feather mattress.

Morning brought Lilly and Zeb welcome relief from their restless thoughts. Zeb began to get his gear together. The air was alive with the sounds of people busy with chores and with the smell of fried beans and biscuits. Soon, breakfast was done. It was all happening too fast for Lilly.

Everyone gathered at the river one hour after breakfast. Lilly clung to Zeb's hand for a moment, then leaned up and kissed him on the lips. "Thank you, Lilly," he said quietly. "See you in a few months."

"Goodbye, Zeb," she answered, tears in her eyes.

He nodded, quickly turning to join the other men on the ferry that would take them across the river. They would walk to Fort Leavenworth. Lilly watched as the ferry landed on the Iowa side of the river, and the men disembarked. The tallest among them turned and waved. She knew it was Zeb. She waved back and kept her eyes on him until she could not see him anymore.

Chapter Fourteen

Winter hit hard with a new wave of deathly illnesses. The camp at Winter Quarters was mainly populated by women alone, as so many men had gone to march with Kearny, and most of those who were left had taken the livestock to the

Missouri bottom rushes, where they could find more to eat for the winter.

Catheryn was pregnant with her first child by Henry, and Lilly's belly had ballooned so large that she had difficulty getting around, and especially in and out of the wagon. She moved in with Hiram and Mary, who lived in a small sod house Hiram had built for the family.

Lilly busied herself helping Mary with mending, and they sat together and enjoyed the warmth of the stone fireplace Hiram had built at one end of the house. Lilly supposed that if they couldn't have their old brick home, this one was certainly better than a wagon or tent. Hiram had built the little house well, had cut the sod just so, burned off the grass so that there would be less shrinkage when it dried. He had even managed to put a window in one wall—an absolute luxury on the Omaha prairie.

Barrels and sacks of seed and flour served for furniture, but Lilly was given the one comfortable, handmade rocker Hiram had brought along. A trunk served as a table, and as winds howled outside, carrying stinging sleet and snow, Lilly and the Williams family played games, read, prayed, sang, and invented a hundred ways to cook beans and to garnish dried apples so that it was not such a tedious bore eating them.

Lilly fought to keep from thinking about the death that surrounded them. Graves were dug daily, hacked out of the frozen earth by weary men and sometimes women. More than one woman had died in childbirth, a fact that silently terrified Lilly.

In November Lilly turned eighteen, and two months later, on the fifth of January, 1847, she felt her first labor pain. When she told Mary, the woman quickly put her to bed and chased everyone else out of the small house. As Mary helped Lilly get out of her clothes and into a nightgown, Lilly thought she heard Hiram say he was going to fetch Catheryn.

"The pain isn't that bad," Lilly insisted.

"You have not gone into deep labor yet, child. Just remember to work with it, not against it."

Lilly lay down in the homemade bed, its mattress stuffed

with feathers and straw. She remembered listening to rising winds outside, but it was not long before she lost her concern for the apparent snowstorm that was brewing. The initial pain she had felt was apparently not all there was to having a baby. Long fingers of labor gripped at her insides like a horrible vise—squeezing, pulling, tearing. She became lost in the pain, and it took all her strength and reason to keep from crying out Chase's name.

How she hated him now for doing this to her! If only he had come back. Now here she lay in this awful pain because of him. She wished there were a way to tell him, to make him suffer the way she was suffering now. Oh, how she hated him! She had wanted to hate him all this time. Now she could. Now it was easy!

All around her were voices—Mary, Catheryn, Frieda Dutch. She heard them talking about the terrible storm outside, and Lilly thought how fitting it was that her child should be born in the middle of it, for her own soul was full of turmoil.

Poor Zeb, she thought. *Poor, poor Zeb.* She had been so mean to him. She knew she should be a better wife. She didn't know what to do about her situation with him. She called out his name.

"He'll be back before you know it," Mary was telling her. "And you'll present him with a fine, healthy child."

Yes. It would be Zeb's child. That's what everyone must believe. That was very important. Even Mary seemed to believe it. If anyone thought otherwise, they had never let on.

The pain consumed her like a monster trying to eat her alive. The hours dragged on, until Lilly thought perhaps she was dying. She lay drenched in perspiration, while the women with her kept banking the fire in an effort to keep the cabin warm. Heated stones were placed under the mattress on each side of her to help warm the bed. Someone told her to bear down. Someone else washed her face, smoothed her tangled hair away from her eyes.

"This snow is going to bury us," someone said.

Bury! Would something happen to her child? How would they bury it with so much snow on the ground? She began to cry, and someone tried to soothe her. Again she was told to bear down, and suddenly she had no choice. Her body was taking over—pushing, pulling, with the sensation that her insides were being ripped apart.

"It's coming!" someone said. "Keep pushing, Lilly. It will be over soon."

Lilly hoped the howling winds outside were drowning out her screams so no one beyond the cabin would know what a child she was being about having this baby. Her stomach muscles contracted and pushed without her conscious aid, and suddenly she felt a strange relief. The pain was over. She lay panting and sweating.

"A boy. It's a fine little boy!" she heard Catheryn saying.

"Is he . . . all right?" Lilly asked. She heard a smack, and a strong squall came from the baby's mouth. Lilly opened her eyes, looking through the lingering haze to see a small, red bit of life hanging upside down from Mary's hand, its cry building in anger at being brought out of the warm nest of its mother's womb into the cold, cruel world. Its little fists were clenched and it trembled.

"He's just fine," Mary said with a big smile. "And he's angry! I'll clean him up and you can put him to your breast. It always surprises me that a newborn child so quickly understands hunger."

The three women helping Lilly all laughed, and Lilly smiled. Suddenly, the pain did not seem so bad. She watched Mary's every move, her eyes never leaving her baby, while Catheryn and Frieda washed her and worked on the afterbirth.

"Oh, this one is strong and healthy, Lilly," Mary was telling her as she gently washed the screaming infant. "Everything is here—all the toes and fingers. And such a set of lungs I have never heard."

Lilly smiled, tears coming to her eyes. If only Chase could see his child! Surely then he would regret his decision. He would change his mind. But it was too late for any of that. He would never know.

"What will you name him?" Catheryn was asking her as she slipped a clean gown over Lilly's head.

Lilly lay back. "Joseph. Joseph Nephi—after your

founder, Joseph Smith, and the prophet Nephi in the Book of Mormon. Zeb would like that."

"Oh, that's a fine name," Mary told her, bringing the baby over to Lilly. She lay the still-squalling boy beside his mother, and Lilly raised up on one elbow, studying the beautiful, unblemished face that was still red and wrinkled.

So, this is the result of my love for Chase Mitchell. The hurt would never leave her—she understood that now. As long as this baby existed, the memory of his father would always be with her.

"Hello, Joseph," she said softly. She opened her gown and lay down beside her new son. Mary helped her with the techniques of breast-feeding, explaining the right position, what to expect, and how to know when the baby had had enough. As soon as her son began pulling from her breast, Lilly knew she would never hate him. She would love him —more than she had loved Chase, more than she had loved her own mother. Her son would be the most important human being in her life, and she would not allow any person, or even death, to take him away from her.

April of 1847 found Chase on the march again, moving now with a reorganized army that had been reinforced by more men brought in by ships to Lobos Island. Together, under the new leadership of General Winfield Scott, general-in-chief of the army, they had taken Veracruz and were now marching west from the gulf coast toward Cerro Gordo. Chase knew their final destination was Mexico City, but there would be other cities to secure on the way before finally cornering Santa Anna in his last stronghold.

Veracruz had been a fairly easy victory. But the men who had volunteered to continue with Scott, after a year of marching and fighting with Taylor in northern Mexico, were weary. Some had deserted; others, who had signed up for only a year of duty, would soon leave freely. Chase had often thought about going with them. He had not received one letter from Lilly, and he could not help worrying what had happened to her.

Army life in Mexico was unbearable—camps full of dysentery, malaria, a host of other diseases. There was a constant shortage of proper food and water. The men were short-tempered and constantly on edge. They were marching deep into foreign territory, surrounded by the enemy, and were vulnerable.

Chase realized it would all be so much more bearable if only he had heard from Lilly. Messengers traveled back and forth to the States constantly. Surely at least one of his letters had reached her. Perhaps she had simply been too difficult to find. After all, the Mormons had surely left Nauvoo by now. How far west had they gone? Chase didn't know whether to love Lilly or be angry with her.

The thought of her face, those big, green, sincere eyes— surely she had meant every word, every promise. He had to believe she had received one or more of his letters, that she was waiting faithfully for him, or he could not bear another moment of these stinking camps, the blood and sickness, the mosquitoes, the weariness of the constant marching. His leg seemed to be working normally now, but there was an ugly scar on his thigh that would be there forever.

The men were called to a halt. He unstrapped his gear and collapsed to the ground, resting his head against the pack. He watched with mixed emotions as Sergeant Handy approached him. There was something about the man that Chase didn't like, and he didn't even rise when Handy came closer.

"Major Mitchell wants to see you, Private Mitchell," Handy told him.

Chase sighed wearily, irritated that his father had interrupted this rare break.

"Right now?"

"Right now."

Chase rose and followed Sergeant Handy to a little knoll where the officers who led his company rested. At the moment, General Scott had a huge battalion of over ten thousand men, all moving west in stages. Chase and his father were with General Worth's 1st Division. They would wait at Perote for the rest of the troops. Major General Scott was waiting at Jalapa for more troops—about ten thousand reinforcements promised by the War Department. Chase had little confidence in that promise. President Polk had let this war progress much too slowly. Everyone was discouraged, impatient to go home.

As Chase approached his father, the major rose from where he sat on a barrel. Howard Mitchell stood tall and strong, like always. He was thinner, but seemed undaunted by the death and heat and hardship around him. Yes, Chase thought, his father was an army man through and through.

Chase saluted him.

"At ease, Private Mitchell. It could be lieutenant, you know."

"I told you I want no favors, Pa—I mean, Major Mitchell. All I want right now is to get the hell out of Mexico and back to Lilly Brannigan."

The elder Mitchell scowled and shook his head. "Come with me, Chase." He turned and walked some distance away so that others could not hear them, then turned and faced his son. "Chase, what happened to our plans? With my help you can be an officer in no time. You'd have easier jobs, better money, prestige—"

"Not even the officers' jobs are easy in a place like this," Chase interrupted. "And they weren't *our* plans, Pa—they were *your* plans. I always looked up to you, until I got here and realized Mother's death hardly affected you. The army is everything to you, Pa, but not to me. The people I love have to come first."

The man looked wounded. "Chase, it's been nearly a year since you first arrived. Have you heard from this Mormon girl?"

Chase felt the now-familiar pain in his heart at the thought. "No, but there could be a lot of reasons. The Mormons are on their way west by now. Maybe whoever is carrying our letters can't find her. We don't have any guarantee that any of our letters will reach their destinations. For all I know, none of mine have reached her. But she's a good woman. She'll understand. She'll wait."

Mitchell shook his head. "You told me how beautiful she is. Those men aren't going to let such a woman sit around waiting for an outsider. Mormons stick with Mormons, Chase. They'll keep after her, and I don't doubt she's already married to one of them. All they think about is producing babies, gathering as many wives as their dirty-minded old men can gather—"

"Pa, don't talk that way! I lived among them for a while. They're nothing like that. They can't make Lilly marry anybody, and she's not a Mormon herself. She'd have to marry of her own free will, and she won't do that because she loves me and she's waiting for me."

Mitchell sighed deeply, studying his son's eyes. He felt a little guilty about the letter he had written Lilly, but not really sorry. Chase would find out this woman was no longer waiting for him, then he'd come back. He would see where he belonged. "Think what you want, Chase. I'm only trying to give you good advice. Stay away from Mormons, and quit pining away for a girl who probably has forgotten you and turned to someone else by now. But no matter what your feelings about her or hers for you, I brought you over here to ask you one thing."

"What?" Chase spoke the word impatiently.

"Don't desert, Chase. Whatever you feel for me, you surely respect the fact that I am your father, and you're right —the army means everything to me. Don't bring me the awful shame of having a son—my only child—desert, especially in this time of our greatest need. I assure you, all deserters who can be found are going to be hanged. Don't let one of them be you. We'll be taking Mexico City in time. I hope you'll be there."

Chase's jaw flexed with repressed anger and impatience. "I'm no damned deserter, Pa. But when in hell are we going to get the extra men General Scott promised? Why can't we just get this damned war over with?"

"Soon, Chase, soon. And lack of reinforcements isn't General Scott's fault. There is always red tape involved when the President and Congress are involved. But the War Department has promised the men. We'll get them."

"In the meantime, we sit around waiting in this hellhole?"

Mitchell straightened. "We do what is asked of us, Chase. We follow orders." The man looked Chase over, noticing he, too, was thinner. "You all right? No physical problems?"

"I'm fine. But I'm sick of the death all around—the damned mosquitoes, and the puking and groaning. I don't dare make friends with anyone because the next day he might be dead."

"That's war, Chase."

"Maybe. But I'm not so sure we even belong here. This is Mexico. What are we doing here, anyway?"

"We're beating Santa Anna as far south as possible and making sure he understands he'd better leave us alone from now on. We're making the borders of Texas safe."

"And grabbing up more Mexican land while we're at it. Mexico wouldn't sell us the land, so we're taking it by force, right?"

"Chase!" Howard Mitchell's eyes flashed with rage. "We're helping expand our great country. You're a part of history. And how dare you question our President and our government? We are not an aggressive country—we're simply teaching Santa Anna a lesson. That man committed atrocities against Americans when Texas fought for independence, and now he's harassing us again. We're just making sure this is the last time!"

Chase nodded, bitterness showing in his eyes. He had learned a lot about the truth of this war with Mexico since he had gotten involved in it. He had seen some of the rougher men of their troops—men no better than outlaws—commit atrocities of their own against Mexican citizens. Few were punished for their crimes.

"Sure, Pa," he answered. "You believe what you want. I'll fight for my country as willingly as any man. I just like to be sure we're fighting for the right thing, and right now, I'm not too sure we are. All I'm saying is that as soon as this thing is over, I'm gone. I'm going to find Lilly, and I'm going to marry her, whether you like it or not."

"You're a fool to think she'll wait for you—and a fool to get mixed up with Mormons. You'll change your mind, Chase. You'll see I'm right."

"I'd like to go back and rest now, Major Mitchell," Chase answered. He saluted. Mitchell sighed, and returned the salute.

"Fine. You need your rest. Dismissed, *Private* Mitchell."

Chase turned to go.

"Chase." The young man looked back at his father. "I'm

here if you need me. You're my only son. I only want what's best for you. America is still growing. It's still building its armed forces. A young man like you could rise in rank right to the top—maybe even end up President."

"Nobody is going to elect a President who's married to a Mormon girl, as you insist on calling her."

Mitchell shook his head. "I won't tell you to forget her, Chase. You'll have to find out for yourself that I was right."

Chase turned and walked back to his own camp, where he immediately began another letter to Lilly. Several men among his company were volunteers who would soon head home. He would give this letter to one of them, instead of sending it through whatever circuit the army used. Maybe he would have better luck paying a private citizen to deliver it.

In the end of April, Brigham Young left Winter Quarters with 143 men, three women, and two children, headed for "Zion." Lilly and the others left behind prepared to follow their leader as soon as he returned to tell them where they would go.

Lilly guarded Joseph like a hawk—kept him warm when it was cold, cool when it was hot, and hung netting over him at night so that mosquitoes could not attack him. She held him often, enjoying the feel of her son taking nourishment from her breast. She vowed that if Zeb did not return, she would find a way to make a good life for her son.

Throughout the summer of 1847, Mormons who had remained the past winter at Nauvoo to wait for more converts from Europe began to arrive at Winter Quarters. They trickled in slowly, some in wagons, many walking the entire distance pulling handcarts because they could not afford oxen. The stories they told about attacks by Gentiles back at Nauvoo were horrifying. Many homes had been burned, and slovenly outsiders no better than outlaws lounged in the beautiful temple, defecating on its floors, urinating on its altar, painting slanderous words on its walls.

Lilly's heart ached upon hearing these stories. She was glad Laura had not lived to hear them. It was not so bad for her, for she had only spent a short time at Nauvoo, and had never felt as though she really belonged. But most of these people had had homes there, farms, shops. They had worked very hard to build their beautiful, clean city. Now it was being destroyed, and Lilly began to understand even more clearly why they wanted to find a place where outsiders could give them no more trouble.

Late one night, nearly a month after welcoming the first of the new arrivals, Lilly woke up to hear someone weeping outside the wagon she slept in with little Joseph. The wagon had been pulled close to the Williams house, as had Catheryn's, since Henry Guest had been among the men who had accompanied Brigham Young farther west.

Lilly moved to the back of the wagon and looked out. By the dim light of the moon she could see a lonely figure sitting on the wooden steps in front of Hiram's house, her head bowed, her weeping pitiful. Lilly climbed out of the wagon and walked closer. "Mary?"

The woman looked up, apparently startled. She quickly wiped her tears.

"It's all right to cry," Lilly told her.

Mary buried her face in her hands. "We're supposed to look to the future," the woman sobbed. "To find joy in all things. But there is no joy in my heart right now, Lilly. All I can think about is Laura's grave—my daughter, buried out there in the middle of nowhere—and Nauvoo." Her body jerked in a great, deep sob that seemed to come from the depths of her soul. "We're supposed to forgive, but sometimes I hate the people who did this to us. I know it's wrong, but I can't help it."

Lilly sat down beside Mary on the steps and put an arm around her shoulders. "You're just tired. You never even had time to grieve for Laura."

Mary wept bitterly, turning and resting her head on Lilly's shoulder. It felt strange to Lilly, who was only eighteen, to be comforting a woman old enough to be her mother.

"You're so strong, Lilly. I don't know how you endured leaving your homeland to come to a new country . . . burying your mother at sea . . . making this terrible journey. I'm so sorry we couldn't all have stayed at Nauvoo."

"We're going to a better place, Mary," Lilly assured her, struggling to make herself believe it.

"We're going into a barren desert, where you can't even drink the water."

"There will be fresh water, too. And beautiful mountains. You've never seen mountains, Mary, but I have. Wait until you see them. It will be much more beautiful than Nauvoo. I know that in my heart, without even seeing it."

The woman pulled away, and wiped her eyes with a handkerchief. "Oh, Lilly . . . you have a way of making people feel better. How I admire your independent spirit sometimes. I wish I could be that way." She sniffed. "What a blessing you are at times, especially when you sing for us. Sometimes, it seems you have more faith than we do."

Lilly pulled her flannel robe closer against the cool night air. "I don't know about that, Mary. I just try to make the best of things. That's all any of us can do. Joseph has given me a new purpose in life, made me more determined to survive and succeed."

Mary blew her nose. "And you have Zeb."

Lilly wished she could explain how it really was with her and Zeb.

"And you have Hiram," she said aloud. "You should be talking to him, Mary, not me."

The woman dabbed at her eyes again. "Sometimes men don't understand a woman's emotions. Hiram is a good man—a good husband. But he has so many worries of his own right now . . . to think my own faith had faltered wouldn't help him much."

"But you need him as much as he needs you, Mary."

"Yes. Yes, I suppose. But . . . right now . . ."

Lilly put an arm around her again. "Your faith hasn't faltered, Mary—you're just tired. We all are. Things will get better again."

"I know. It's just that . . . I was holding Ruth Perry's little girl in my arms today when she died. And suddenly, I wondered what all this was about. Do you think that was a terrible thing to think?"

"No. Probably every person here has wondered at times."

Mary rose, sniffing again. She brushed more tears from her cheeks. "Please don't tell Hiram, or anyone else about this weak moment."

Lilly rose to face her. "I won't."

Mary reached out and hugged her. "You had better get back in the wagon with your baby." She pulled away reluctantly. "I pray for you every day, Lilly—for you and little Joseph and Zeb."

"Thank you, Mary. And everything *will* be all right. You'll see."

The woman walked wearily back into the house. Lilly climbed back into the wagon, crawled under the mosquito netting, and pulled Joseph close beside her. She prayed again that when they headed farther west, there would be no little grave along the way with Joseph Nephi Adams's name on it. And suddenly, more than ever, she wished Zeb would return.

Chapter Fifteen

"Are we winning this war, Chase, or have we just walked into a nest of wasps? Seems to me we're a hell of a long way from help if we need it."

Chase lit a thin cigar and looked up at Toby Gates, a young man he had befriended after they took Veracruz. Chase's eyes were bloodshot, his beard was several days old, and he couldn't remember the last time he had had a bath.

Back at Cerro Gordo he had given a letter to a volunteer whose duty was finished, and who couldn't wait to get out of Mexico. For two gold pieces, the man had faithfully promised to deliver it.

"I don't know what to think anymore, Toby," Chase answered his friend. "They bring us here to Puebla, then our stupid general doesn't even declare martial law. He might as well announce that every damned Mexican in town has permission to murder us at will. I can't believe I'm in this useless mess. I should have stayed back in Illinois, married the woman I wanted to marry before I left."

Chase's morale had dipped low. His father was still back at Cerro Gordo. Chase and the rest of General Worth's 1st Division had marched toward Mexico City and had occupied Puebla. They waited for Chase's father and reinforcements to join them.

The men lived in constant danger of death if they left camp. General Worth, apparently trying to show some sort of kindness, had told the authorities at Puebla that Mexican courts there could retain authority over Mexicans who committed offenses against the Americans. Chase and the other men felt as though they bore the brunt of their leader's stupidity.

The Mexicans were taking full advantage of the situation. American soldiers foolish enough to stroll about the town drinking and womanizing were often robbed and knifed.

"This war shouldn't bother you none," a Texas volunteer spoke up, looking directly across the campfire at Chase. "You can always get help from your daddy if things get too rough."

Chase moved ice-blue, menacing eyes past the flames at the man who had made the remark.

"I haven't once asked my father for any help, you sonofabitch. I don't want it, and I don't need it."

The man shrugged. "If my pa was along, I'd take anything he wanted to hand me—even a promotion."

Chase leaped over the fire and landed on the man. Tension was high and tempers were short. Chase's anger at his father, his frustration with the war, and his worry over Lilly exploded out of him at the unwarranted remark, and the fight was on.

Men circled around them, cheering, enjoying the diversion. Chase and the Texan tumbled on the ground, kicking and punching. Chase was doing the most damage, for his fury knew no bounds.

The onlookers began to fight over who were the best fighters—Texans, the Illinois militia, or those from Missouri, or Tennessee. Push came to shove, and the camp came alive with fighting. Chase landed a final blow to his opponent, then turned to take on another.

Minutes later shots were fired, and officers moved in to break up the melee. Several men lay sprawled on the ground. Others stumbled to their feet, moaning. Chase turned to face the officers, his clothes and face covered with dust and blood.

"Any more fighting and those involved will feel the lash!" an officer told them.

The Texan Chase had clobbered groaned and rolled to his knees, spitting blood. Men pounded dirt from their clothes; some went to a nearby stone well to wash off blood. Chase found Toby, and they both smiled through bleeding lips. "Felt good, didn't it?" Chase told his friend.

"Real good," Toby answered. "I'm ready for Santa Anna."

"So am I," Chase answered. "I wish they'd get this damned war moving."

General Scott finally joined the other men at Puebla, and immediately instituted martial law. The troops were soon joined by 4,000 reinforcements, making them now 13,000 strong, but all knew the odds of taking Mexico City were great. The City's nearly 200,000 citizens had at least 30,000 Mexicans to defend them. Such ratios had become the norm for the Americans. They were not afraid. They had suffered tremendous losses and hardships to get this far; they were not about to be defeated now. As the troops marched forward on August 10, 1847, they came upon a rise that overlooked Mexico City. It lay only twenty miles away, far out in a great bowllike valley before them. Lovely white stucco buildings gleamed in the hot sun; domes and spires of churches hung against a deep blue sky; and smaller outlying villages, lakes, and marshes were scattered around its outer perimeter.

Chase cleaned and primed his breech-loading army rifle, as well as his own personal flintlock pistol— a gift from his father. He was ready. He had long since quit caring whether this war was right or wrong. He just wanted it to be over. He hadn't seen Lilly for seventeen months, nor had he heard a word from her. In four more months his two-year voluntary service would be over. He would head straight for Nauvoo, and if no one was there, he would keep going west until he found Lilly Brannigan and got some answers.

Why had she never answered his letters? It made no sense. Those two weeks at Nauvoo seemed like a distant dream, and he wondered if Lilly had been only a vision, after all. Of course not! He had tasted her lips, invaded her body. She belonged to him, and he would damned well find out why she had never written to him.

His anger and frustration spurred his reckless courage as he joined 900 men who swooped down on 8,000 Mexican infantrymen at Valencia, a small town outside Mexico City. The attack was a surprise, and the Mexican soldiers were in complete disarray. As Chase and the other American soldiers let out bloodcurdling yells and charged, bayonets ready, the Mexican troops scrambled for their horses and guns. Before they could position their cannon, the Americans were upon them, ripping and stabbing with bayonets, smashing with gun butts. Mexican soldiers screamed and collapsed, eyes wide with terror. Within a few minutes any Mexicans still able to walk or run did just that, leaving Valencia behind. Cheers went up in a near roar as the Americans salvaged weapons and ammunition and some of the cannon.

They marched on. Churubusco was next. Scott directed one division to storm the main stronghold of the small city —a massive walled convent called San Mateo. The rest of the men, including Chase's company, would take the bridge that was the only route across the Churubusco River into Mexico City. The bridge was heavily fortified, with three cannons and several thousand Mexican troops entrenched along the opposite river bank.

But Chase was not afraid. He would get the job done and find out what had happened to Lilly Brannigan. He stormed the bridge with Toby on one side, and, ironically, the Texan with whom he had fought earlier on the other. Chase knew his father was somewhere nearby, but his thoughts were only of Lilly—a mixture of anger and worry. Perhaps she had died on the journey west!

Suddenly the ground seemed to explode in front of him. He saw Toby's stomach open up into a bloody nothingness and heard the Texan scream. He then heard a roar near his left side—so loud that it deafened him instantly. From that moment on, everything took place in total silence. He felt an odd jolt near his left hip and side, and through a strange, silent haze, he wondered if perhaps he was supposed to be feeling pain, for surely something had hit him. He felt himself sprawl forward face first, and no matter how hard he tried, he could not move or hear. He could feel the vibrations of men moving past him, but he heard no yelling, no gunshots.

Then there was simply nothing at all—nothing but blackness and quiet. Except that he could hear Lilly singing, *All is well! All is well!*

Winter Quarters were alive with activity. The winter of 1847–48 had been long and cold. Lilly found herself thanking God every day that her son had been spared from illness. Joseph, now fifteen months old, toddled on fat legs, following his mother everywhere as she readied the wagon for what she hoped would be their last journey—from Winter Quarters to the Great Salt Lake.

Brigham Young had returned to Winter Quarters in December, telling his faithful followers that the Great Basin was indeed the chosen land. He described to them a grand valley, full of color and chilling beauty, surrounded by tremendous mountains—a literal Eden in beauty. He said temporary mud and adobe homes had already been built, as the only trees that could be used for lumber grew far up in the mountains. But men left behind at what was already being called Salt Lake City were building a mill in the distant foothills so they could begin making lumber for solid homes.

Brother Young spoke of a difficult journey that lay ahead —of high mountains, and of rivers and streams that would have to be forded. But he and the men who had gone before had built bridges and ferries along the way, and had done everything they could to make the journey for those to come more tolerable.

Henry Guest had been among those to return. He verified that the Great Basin was indeed beautiful, but he had doubts as to how such land was going to be farmed. Lilly remembered when Zeb had joked about it, back in Nauvoo. From his description, Lilly could not imagine how such a desertlike area could be fit to live in, but at least once they got there, they could settle for good—build homes and start living like normal people.

"The whole area is still a part of Mexico," Henry told them once over an evening campfire. "When this war is over, it will belong to America. We're free to claim as much land there as we want, and we don't have to pay for anything. The land might not be the easiest to till, but at least it will be ours—as much of it as we are able to farm."

They left in April. Whips snapped, and shouts of "gee" and "haw" filled the air, bringing back to Lilly chilling memories of the first part of their journey. She thought about Laura and wished the young woman were here to walk beside her again. Then she knelt to pick a wild daisy and waved it under Joseph's nose. She thought of how much Laura had loved wild flowers. Joseph then laughed. Such a sweet laugh it was! When he smiled—oh, when he smiled —there was Chase again. . . .

The first two weeks of the journey, the Mormon emigrants were plagued with a cold, cruel rain that blew in on chilly east winds almost daily. Gerald Williams, now thirteen but built more like an eighteen-year-old, drove the oxen that pulled Zeb's wagon. Lilly spent a great deal of time inside the wagon, trying to entertain a restless Joseph, who wanted to run in the tall grass and play in the mud.

There was plenty of mud—on shoes and skirts, splattering off wagon wheels, filling potholes created from the rain and thawing ground. The mushy earth sucked wagons down like quicksand. Lilly could not help pitying the poor men, who were constantly putting their shoulders to wagons that became mired in the hated slop.

It was not long before several of those men, as well as women and children, began to take serious colds. Three died of pneumonia in one day. Lilly did not doubt that if everyone were not already weakened from going so long without proper food, shelter, and medicine, they would not now die so easily. They simply did not have enough strength and health to fight off their sicknesses. Lilly squandered the little bit of tea she had left, using it sparingly, often giving some of the hot brew to Joseph. She let him chew on dried apples, some of which had been brought from Nauvoo the summer before by the last straggling emigrants from that now-destroyed city.

After a month on the trail, there was still no sign of the mountains Lilly so longed to see. The weather had warmed, but Joseph had taken a cold and was feverish, and Lilly's greatest fear began to overwhelm her—that something would happen to her little boy. She knew she could bear anything life threw at her, except to lose Joseph and have to bury him in this wild land, in a grave she could never come to visit.

She nursed her son day and night, never leaving his side, but her fear of his death sometimes almost overwhelmed her. She shook in the night and was constantly sick to her stomach. There seemed to be no comfort for her—nothing that would take away the awful dread and the sleepless nights.

Then, she took a fever of her own. As they rolled on, Lilly and Joseph both lay in the back of Zeb's wagon, coughing and sweating. Lilly could not get the rest she so sorely needed, for she was terrified that little Joseph would need her—maybe die—while she slept. There was no consoling her, and no amount of talking or prayers helped alleviate her fear of losing her son.

When they passed something called Chimney Rock, Catheryn told Lilly she should look out and see the interesting landmark that helped guide their way. Lilly did not bother. She moved in and out of an exhausted sleep. That evening as the wagons halted to make camp, Lilly thought she heard shouting outside, a few cheers, and laughter. She had no idea what was going on. Then she heard Mary Williams's voice just outside the wagon.

"She's just worn out from worrying over the boy. I think it will really help to know you're back, Zeb."

"I hope so."

In the next moment a man climbed into the back of the wagon, then knelt beside her.

"Lilly?"

She felt a big hand at the side of her flushed face. In her daze she thought first about Chase. But no—Chase was not coming back for her, ever. She opened her eyes to see Zeb Adams looking down at her. He looked thinner but well, and right now, to Lilly, he was far from homely.

"Zeb!" She never thought she would be so happy to see him. She sat up and threw her arms around his neck, surprising him with her reaction. He embraced her.

"Everything is going to be okay now, Lilly. I'm here. I'm here."

"Oh, Zeb, don't let him die!" she sobbed.

Zeb ran a hand over her back, relishing the feel of her long, red-gold hair in his fingers.

"Nobody is going to die. Mary says he's a strong, healthy boy and he's got a strong, healthy mother. The first thing you have to do is get yourself well, or you'll be no use to Joseph. You rest now. We're camped for the night. I'll stay right here by Joseph."

"Oh, Zeb, how did you find us? Are you through now? Are you here to stay?"

"Yes, I'm here to stay. We marched back with a government man named Fremont. California belongs to the United States now. Once we got as far as the Great Basin area, the rest of the Mormon men and I cut north to see if Brigham Young was there yet. We found a pretty little settlement. The folks there told us the rest of you were on your way from Winter Quarters, so we kept coming this way. I didn't want you to make the whole journey without me, Lilly."

"Oh, Zeb, I'm so glad you're here."

A faint smile moved over his face.

"You lie back and rest now," he told her. "I'll sit right here by both of you and get a good look at my new son. We've got some getting acquainted to do. Mary told me what a healthy, fine boy he is."

Lilly leaned back, studying his eyes through her tears. "He's beautiful, Zeb. And he's such a good boy. I love him so much. I don't know what I'd do if anything happened to him."

"Well, nothing is *going* to happen to him." Zeb turned and

looked down at the sleeping boy. He grinned. "He's big for fifteen months."

"He is." Lilly wiped at tears. "And he's so bright, Zeb. He has the most beautiful smile, and big, blue eyes. And he's so good—so sweet-tempered and loving."

He touched the boy, his own big hand dwarfing Joseph's. He looked at Lilly. "I'll be the best father I can be, Lilly. During the time I was gone, all I could think about was getting back to you—wondering how everything went with the baby. I'm sorry I couldn't be here when he was born."

"It doesn't matter. You're here now, and I feel better already."

He smiled, sadness showing in his eyes. "Well, I'm glad I have that much of an effect on you, at least." Their eyes held. "I missed you, Lilly. I missed you a lot."

She put a hand to his face. "I missed you, too, Zeb."

He grasped her hand and squeezed it. "Go back to sleep now. I mean it. I'll look after Joseph, and I'll wake you up if he needs you."

She nestled into the feather mattress, putting an arm around her son. Zeb's return soothed her anxiety; his quiet strength boosted her own.

Chapter Sixteen

June 1848

Billy Drake rode into Nauvoo, wondering at Chase Mitchell's description of the place. It was not the beautiful, clean, prospering town Chase had told him about. Several buildings had burned down; others were boarded up. On a distant hill stood a building Billy realized must have once been the temple, where Chase had first heard Lilly Brannigan sing. Billy could not imagine why anyone would want anything to do with a Mormon woman, but that was not his concern. He simply had a letter to deliver.

He headed toward the temple, which was no longer a grand, glowing place of worship. It looked sad and dingy. A few vagabonds who looked as though they had been drinking all night sat on the steps of the building, some still asleep. Billy rode up to the steps, noticing people inside. He realized the building had been overtaken by slovenly, homeless men who had made it their temporary shelter, and he decided not to dismount, for fear someone would grab his horse and gear and ride off with both.

"You, there!" he called out to a man who sat on the steps with his elbows on his knees, his head hanging. "Hey, mister, are there any Mormons left around here?"

The man looked up, his eyes bloodshot. Billy caught his scent from several feet away.

"Mormons?" The man chuckled. "Look to you like there are any Mormons around here, mister? Them whorin' bastards left here a year ago. Ain't nobody around here but a few poor folk who don't have nothin'—a few farmers."

Billy looked around, taking off his hat and wiping sweat from his brow. He had taken his time coming home, enjoying just being away from Mexico's murderous climate. Before coming to Illinois he had wandered through Louisiana and Mississippi, then gone home to Tennessee to stay with his family for a while. He hadn't wanted to leave home again, but he had promised to at least get Chase's letter as far as Nauvoo.

"You a Mormon, mister?" the drunk on the steps asked Billy.

Billy wondered what the people around here would do to him if he said yes. In spite of his own prejudice, he couldn't help feeling a little sorry for them, considering the way Chase had described Nauvoo. All their work here had been destroyed.

"I'm no Mormon. I'm just looking for somebody," he answered. He turned his horse and rode back down the deserted street, turning then onto a side street at the east end of town. He rode only a short distance when he spotted a woman beating a rug in front of a fine brick home. Behind the house he saw a man approaching with a team of horses that pulled a plow. From the looks of the house, Billy could see that it had once been well-kept, but it was already showing signs of neglect. The front gate bore the name *Hiram Williams* in peeling paint. He rode closer to the front gate and nodded to the woman outside, who had put down her broom and stared at him. Billy removed his hat again. "Ma'am?"

The woman straightened. "What is it, mister?"

Billy almost winced at her humorless, sour face. The woman was stout. Her lips were compressed into a thin line, and her hair was falling out of the bun she had attempted to keep it in. Her clothes were simple homespun, and she looked like she needed a bath. "You Mrs. Williams?" he asked.

"Nope. That's who *used* to live here."

"You know of any Mormons left around here?"

"None that I know of," the woman snipped.

"Were you acquainted with any? Know where I might find a Mormon?"

"They know better than to be seen around here, mister. If you want to find a Mormon, you'll have to go way out west. They were camped on the Missouri—maybe six hundred miles west of here, last we knew—but folks say they ain't even there anymore. They went on ever farther west—'least, some of them did. Why do you want to know? You one of them?"

Billy looked to the west. "No. I brought a letter for one of them, a Miss Lilly Brannigan. It's from a man down in Mexico. He's still down there, far as I know."

"Maybe he's back here by now. They say a treaty was signed a couple of months ago. Did you fight down there?"

"Yup. I'm from Tennessee. Left when my volunteer duty ended, about ten months ago."

"We sure enough got ourselves a lot more land, didn't we? Me and my husband have thought about heading for California—hear there's some beautiful farmland there. Oregon, too. I don't think the Mormons went that far west, though. Heard they settled somewhere in the desert."

Billy shook his head. He had not anticipated traveling into

hostile territory to deliver the letter, risking his life on a trip that would take months. Chase Mitchell had not paid him enough money for that.

"Well, thank you, ma'am. I reckon I'll just let my friend find the Mormons himself. Might be he's already on his way to join them."

"Might be. I sure wouldn't go out of my way for any Mormon, mister."

"I agree with you there. I only came this far because I thought maybe I could find somebody to carry the letter the rest of the way for me."

"You won't find any Mormons around here anymore. They know better."

"I expect so."

Billy turned his horse and rode out of Nauvoo, trying to picture what it must have once been like. He decided Chase Mitchell must be heading home himself now. There was no sense going out of his way to deliver a letter for a man he had hardly known. He rode through the woods to the south, unaware that just a few miles to the east, a new wave of Mormon immigrants from Europe were heading west for Salt Lake City. If he had arrived and left just an hour later, he would have come across them.

The Mormons pushed onward through high winds and summer storms. One man lost two oxen to lightning during a fierce storm that destroyed two wagons and sent livestock scattering. It took three days to repair damages, round up stray animals, and redistribute what was left of the belongings of those who had lost their own wagons.

Grassy plains turned to more hilly country, then to flat, gravelly land full of the stinging odor of sagebrush, which made good fires but became tiresome to smell. What water could be found was often poisoned with alkali, and there seemed to be no life except bunches of yellow grass here and there, and the ever-present mosquitoes. The Mormons moved anywhere from ten to fifteen miles a day, in spite of sickness, snakebites, and accidents.

Every day Lilly was grateful she did not have to add her husband or son to the death toll. She finally began to feel more like her old self, and Joseph regained his own energy. The boy had taken to Zeb as easily as a bee to honey, and Zeb often carried Joseph on his shoulders while he walked beside the oxen. The quick and easy closeness that developed between them was a great relief to Lilly, both emotionally and physically.

Lilly's spirits became even lighter when she finally spotted mountains in the distance. She quietly watched the dark line on the horizon, realizing before many of the others what she was seeing. She heard someone say something about dark clouds in the distance, and smiled. She remembered how the coastline of Scotland had looked from the ship sailing west across the Atlantic. For a moment she longed to see Ben Nevis again. How different this barren land was from the green hills of Scotland. But there, ahead of her, lay something that finally made her feel closer to home.

"You see what I see?" Zeb shouted to her then.

"Yes!" Lilly walked closer to him. "They're big, aren't they, Zeb?"

"I told you they were. Those up ahead aren't anything. Wait till we get near the basin, Lilly. The land might not be much good, but you've never seen prettier country. The mountains around there are so big it just gave me the shivers. I'm glad now that I've already been there. Brother Young has a mill started, so before long, I can build you a real house."

Joseph, on Zeb's shoulders, began bouncing up and down. "Giddap! Giddap!" the boy shouted, giggling as Zeb ran with him, then shouted at the oxen.

Lilly watched the mountains again, eager now to reach Fort Laramie for a well-earned rest. She ignored the little voice inside that asked what she would do about her marriage to Zeb once they were settled in a real home of their own.

The nurse let go of Chase's arm. He took a few faltering steps before reaching a doorpost and clinging to it.

"Very good, Mr. Mitchell," she told him with a smile.

Chase smiled in return. He had lain in a makeshift hospital in Mexico City for weeks before being brought to the hospital in New Orleans. The terrible wounds to his side and his leg had not been properly treated, and the specialist in New Orleans had operated on him four different times. Chase's pain had been indescribable. For a long time it had been impossible to communicate with him. The explosion that had wounded him had left him temporarily deaf, his mind disoriented.

After his life-threatening ailments had healed, he had been sent to a veterans' hospital for further rehabilitation, and it was April before his hearing finally began to return. At the same time his sense of balance also returned, and signs of his old physical strength began to show again. But he could not speak, except for the one word he repeated over and over all during his recovery—Lilly.

No one knew who she was. Chase's father had been killed in Mexico City. A partially written letter to a Lilly Brannigan at Nauvoo, Illinois, had been found in Chase's pocket, but since it was not finished, it had never been sent, and Chase had been unable to speak properly or coordinate his hands well enough to write more. Deep in his confused mind he felt frustrated, for he could see Lilly, could remember her, but he didn't know how to tell others around him about her, or how to ask them to write to her for him.

Chase's mind remained strangely removed from the real world until June of 1848, when his coordination returned and he began to walk again. He was able to talk, his words slow but clear, and he could hear. Recovery had taken months—months of lost time for him and Lilly. The drawing that had been in his gear was gone. It seemed sometimes that there had never been a Lilly Brannigan in his life. He wondered if Billy had ever delivered his last letter, written so many months ago now.

Chase felt lost and alone. He understood now that his father was dead. And he vividly remembered the day he had been wounded—realized Toby Gates was surely dead, too. There was no one and nothing left, except Lilly, who was somewhere out west. He had to find out what had happened to her, if there was any love left between them.

"I can . . . go home soon, can't I?" he asked the nurse slowly.

"Oh, I suppose so, Mr. Mitchell. You're doing so much better. You practice walking and get all your strength back, and I don't see why the doctor wouldn't let you go. And you've got some money coming from the government for serving in Mexico. We'll help get you all set up with a fine horse and everything you need, when the time comes. But I think you had better lie back down now for a while, don't you?"

"Yes. I . . . suppose."

It irritated Chase that the words came so slowly to him. He knew what he wanted to say, but it just wouldn't come out as fast as he wanted it to. The doctor had assured him that, in time, the spoken words would catch up with his thoughts, and he would be back to normal—except for the long, deep, puckered scar down his left thigh, an addition to the one he already had from the gunshot wound at Nauvoo. His left side bore a permanent indentation near the waist. He had been told more than once how lucky he was to be alive, let alone to be walking again. Nurses and doctors kept asking how he did it, what gave him the courage and determination to live.

"Lilly," he had answered. It was all he could manage to say for a long time. Now, at last, he had been able to explain who Lilly was, and the nurses hoped he would find the mysterious young Mormon woman who sounded so beautiful and precious. The story had sounded so romantic, and more than one nurse wished she were Lilly.

"I suppose the first thing you're going to do is find Miss Lilly Brannigan," the nurse was telling him now, as she helped him back to his bed.

"Yes. I hope . . . she's still . . . waiting for me." In his pain and sickness his memory of Lilly had become keener, his love for her deeper than he knew he should allow. There might not even be a Lilly to love, or she might belong to someone else by now.

"Oh, what young girl wouldn't wait for a handsome man like you, Mr. Mitchell?"

"I wrote to her. Couldn't . . . this past year. Think I'll just

... go to her now. Find her. No sense writing ... don't know for sure ... where she is."

"Well, then, you just get all well and you can go see her yourself. No more letters. Before you know it, you'll find Miss Brannigan and you can be married, like you planned. How long has it been?"

"Two years ... five months. She must be ... nineteen now. I'm ... twenty-six ... feel sixty sometimes."

The nurse laughed. "We all have times like that, Mr. Mitchell." She covered him and patted his shoulder. "I'll come around in the morning and you can walk as much as you want. Would you like to go outside?"

Chase smiled again. "Yes ... I'd like that."

"Fine. Then, that is what we will do. The weather has been beautiful." The woman sighed, studying him for a moment. "I must say, we'll miss you an awful lot, Mr. Mitchell, once you leave. You're our favorite patient, you know. But we know you'll be heading straight for Lilly Brannigan, and we all wish you our best. Just knowing you'll be with her and will be happy again makes the parting bearable."

"Thank you ... Mrs. Lyons."

The woman smiled and left, and Chase closed his eyes, his heart pounding harder at the realization that he was truly healing now—that soon he could leave this place and find Lilly. Lilly! Would she be waiting for him? Did she still love him?

Fort Laramie was a welcome relief from the hard, often monotonous journey. It was higher here, and cooler. There were fewer mosquitoes. Lilly was in better spirits than she had been in months, and she went to a dance given by the men at the trading post and the Mormons.

There was much laughter—more than Lilly had heard in a long time. She whirled around with Zeb, and because she was so young and unusually beautiful, several of the men at the fort asked her if she would honor them with a dance. Zeb allowed it. Lilly had not felt so young and gay since those few precious days when she had loved Chase and had been so sure he loved her in return.

She forced herself not to think about that now. Now there was Zeb, and her baby was healthy. They were well on their way to their destination, and no one else close to her had died. She whirled to the Virginia reel, laughed when someone called out a square dance that made no sense, joined in singing spiritual songs. She listened to talk of gold being discovered in California, and wondered how it looked when it was first dug from the earth. She ate from a side of beef roasted by the men at the fort, and stuffed herself with rhubarb and wild berry pie made by Mormon women. Joseph's face was purple from the berries. Lilly picked him up and held him in her arms, whirling around to another dance and making him laugh.

The boy was a hit with everyone at the fort, his big blue eyes and winning smile getting him a lot of "pony rides," and even a stick of peppermint candy. Joseph seemed to have no fear of strangers. He toddled around babbling to everyone, even burly-looking mountain men and their quiet, Indian wives. Indians were so prevalent everywhere that Lilly had lost her own fear of them; and Joseph seemed to fascinate the painted, half-naked natives, who always smiled and pointed when he came near them.

Everyone urged Lilly to sing for the trappers and traders at the fort, a couple of whom were Scottish themselves. Lilly gladly obliged.

When she finished, a dark, wild-looking Indian man approached her, saying something to her in his own halting tongue that Lilly did not understand. Then he turned to Zeb and said something more, pointing to Lilly, then to himself. He finished speaking and stepped back. A couple of the traders standing nearby chuckled, and one leaned close to Zeb.

"He says your wife sings prettier than the birds of the air," the man told Zeb. "He wants to know if you would consider selling her and the boy—says he'll pay many horses and robes for her."

"Sell her!"

Lilly stepped back a little, keeping Joseph beside her.

Several of the Mormon women gasped, while men stiffened, ready for a confrontation.

"I certainly will not!" Zeb told the trapper, turning defiant eyes to the Indian.

"Stay friendly, Mr. Adams," the trapper told him. "An offer to buy your wife is a great compliment. Put a smile on that face and I'll tell him you appreciate his offer, but that you don't want to sell anybody." The man turned and spoke to the Indian in a mixture of the Sioux tongue and sign language.

The big Indian nodded, disappointment showing in his eyes. He reached behind his neck then, removed the bear-claw necklace he was wearing, and handed it out to Lilly. He said something more to her, and the trader smiled.

"A gift, Mrs. Adams. You should know that a bear-claw necklace means good luck to these people—it's a sign of bravery and manhood. He probably killed the bear himself. You should consider it a great honor to be given the necklace."

Lilly took the necklace from the Indian and forced a smile, for she had not quite gotten over the fact that the man had wanted to buy her.

"Tell him it truly is an honor. I will treasure the necklace always."

The trapper interpreted for her and the Indian seemed satisfied. He grinned and nodded, then turned and walked away. Lilly breathed a sigh of relief and leaned against Zeb, as others gathered around, laughing and talking about the incident. Someone joked to Lilly that she missed her chance to be an Indian princess.

"No, thank you," Lilly answered, laughing herself then as she clutched the bear-claw necklace. She had Zeb tie it around her neck.

It was late by the time things finally quieted and Lilly put Joseph to bed. The boy was so stuffed and so worn out from toddling among the crowd all night that he was asleep on her shoulder before she even reached the wagon. Zeb walked with her, taking the boy from her and lifting him into bed. They both laughed at how Joseph flopped down onto the mattress, sleeping so hard he didn't even know he was being moved around. Zeb lit a lantern and they studied the sleeping infant. His eyes were closed tight, and his lips were slightly puckered.

"Oh, Zeb, he's such a good boy, but I'm afraid everyone inside the fort spoiled him terribly."

"He'll get over it."

Lilly grinned, feeling happier this night than she had felt in months.

"I like it here, Zeb. I feel invigorated, being closer to the mountains. The air seems cleaner here." She untied the necklace. "I can't believe that Indian wanted to buy me!"

Zeb watched her lovingly. "I can. What man wouldn't want you for his wife?"

She met his eyes as she set the necklace aside, her smile fading. "Maybe most. I've not been much of a wife to you, have I, Zeb?"

He smiled almost bashfully. "I'm a patient man."

She held his eyes. "More patient than I deserve. You're a good man, Zeb. You should have a real wife."

He frowned with confusion. His heart began to pound as she leaned forward to kiss him lightly. "Turn out the lamp," she told him softly.

He swallowed, hardly believing her words. "You sure?"

"I am when I see you and Joseph together."

He studied her beautiful eyes. "I don't want it to be for Joseph, Lilly. I want it to be for me." She could tell he was actually trembling. "I love you, Lilly—more than my own life."

She breathed deeply for courage of her own. "And I love you, Zeb," she said. She told herself it wasn't really a lie. She did love him. But she didn't love him the way she'd loved Chase Mitchell. She would probably never love another man that way. For now, this was her destiny.

Zeb turned down the lamp. In the darkness Lilly felt his lips on hers, and his trembling hands on her shoulders. He laid her back into the feather mattress as Joseph slept soundly beside them.

Chapter Seventeen

September 1848

The mountain country was so new to most of the travelers that its awesome beauty kept their spirits alive. There was more game in this region—bear, antelope, deer, elk, ducks, and geese—and fresh streams that carried trout and bass. But there was also more danger from Indians and bear attacks, and difficulty in keeping teams of oxen on the right path to avoid tumbling hundreds, sometimes thousands of feet into gaping canyons. Some roadways, if they could be called that, were so narrow that one wagon could barely squeeze through.

At some points wagons had to be lowered slowly with ropes. Lilly held Joseph and watched the first such venture with dread. Zeb led the oxen, whipping and yelling at them. Men at the top of the steep embankment held onto ropes, digging their heels into the soil and hanging on for dear life to keep the wagon from rolling out of control.

Wagon after wagon was lowered this way throughout the day, and once Zeb's was down, he climbed back to the top of the embankment to help lower the others. Women and children walked to the bottom. By the end of the day the men's hands were rubbed raw, and overused muscles twitched with pain. Lilly made Zeb lie down inside the wagon, and she rubbed hot liniment on his shoulders and back, while Joseph tried to help, rubbing his little hands over his father's sore arms.

"Poppy hurt?" he asked.

"He sure does," Zeb answered the boy. "Seems like you're asking me that just about every day, Joey. And I always answer the same, don't I?"

Lilly smiled, massaging his back with as much strength as she could muster. "Do you think it's true, Zeb—about the sea gulls saving the crops at Salt Lake?"

Just that day Mormon men had arrived at their camp, traveling east from Salt Lake to see if any of those along the trail needed help. They had told of a miracle at "Zion." The crops they had managed to plant that spring had been attacked by hordes of large locusts, and nothing the Mormons did could get rid of the hideous insects that chomped on leaves and stems and tender plants. The settlers had beaten them with wet blankets and pieces of wood, and had opened irrigation ditches, drowning some. But there were simply too many of the creatures, crawling under clothing, flying into people's eyes, and finding their way into homes.

"It was the most horrible thing I have ever seen," one of the Mormon men said, and Lilly still shivered at the thought. She hoped such a thing would not happen again.

"We all started praying," the man told them, "right there in the fields. And suddenly, in came a flock of sea gulls from the Great Salt Lake—so many the sky was black with them. We thought at first that we would suffer a second attack from the birds. But the gulls settled over the crops and ate the locusts, scooping up several at a time into their beaks. In no time at all, the gulls had eaten most of the locusts. The birds flew away, and we were able to salvage much of the crops. Now there will be a little something for those of you just arriving. I never saw anything like it, and I suppose I never will again."

"It was truly a miracle," Hiram had said, his voice trembling with faith and joy.

Everyone there had fallen silent as they listened to the story. Then someone began singing the hymn that gave them such strength—*All Is Well!*—and by the time they had finished, there was not a dry eye in camp.

Joseph's head began to nod as he rubbed his father's skin with the smelly ointment. Lilly carefully laid the boy back and covered him. A moment later he was asleep.

"Sure it's true," Zeb told Lilly quietly, referring to the story about the sea gulls. "You know a Mormon wouldn't lie about something like that."

She put the cork back into the bottle of ointment and placed it in a pocket on the inside of the canvas. "It gives me shivers to think of it."

"Does me, too. But it just goes to show you that Brother Young must have picked the right spot, for God to put in a helping hand like that."

"I don't know. Maybe it was just a natural thing. I mean, maybe the locusts come there every year, and the gulls feed on them."

"Maybe." He rose up on one elbow and looked at her, a sly smile on his face. "You want to go out there and tell them that?"

She laughed lightly. "I don't think so."

He laughed with her, reaching out and touching her hand. He sighed deeply. "Do you have any idea how beautiful you are?"

Lilly blushed a little and looked down at her lap. "Our looks are a gift from God. I can't take credit for them or boast about them."

He laughed again. "Well, God must love you a lot more than He loves me, considering this big nose and these narrow eyes and this straight hair that's already beginning to get thin on me."

She smiled, meeting his eyes again. "Looks don't mean much, anyway. It's what's inside that counts."

He nodded, frowning slightly. "I suppose. And God knows you're a good woman. You've got both, Lilly— you're beautiful inside and out."

Lilly looked down, again feeling the guilt of not loving him as she should. "I can't tell you what it means to me, Zeb—the way you've taken to Joseph."

He watched her quietly for a moment. "You still think about his pa, don't you?"

She felt the flush coming to her cheeks, and to her frustration, her eyes immediately teared. She took the pins from her hair. "Not anymore."

"Lilly, you're a poor liar."

She swallowed, a lump rising in her throat. "What does it matter?"

"It matters because the Mexican War is over. What if he changes his mind and decides to look you up?"

She met his eyes squarely. "It would simply be too late for him. Besides, it's been almost two and a half years since the treaty was signed with Mexico. I think that's plenty of time for a man to make up his mind about something like that. He either isn't coming, or he's—he's dead. Either way, I've forced myself to forget about him—to get over him. Even if he's dead, the fact remains that he deserted me, so there's nothing more to be said about it."

He watched her hair fall down past her shoulders. "I don't want to lose you now, Lilly. I have to be the luckiest man in the world to have you for a wife. I'm no Chase Mitchell, but nobody could love you more. I don't know what I'd do if . . . if he came back and you and Joey ran off with him. I love Joey like my own boy."

A tear slipped down her cheek and she quickly wiped it away. "I know, Zeb. And you should know me well enough by now to know I would never do that to you. I made a vow to you, and I intend to keep it. Besides, Joey loves you as his father. I would never take him away from you."

She began to brush her hair. "You'd better get some sleep now, Zeb. You'll probably be hurting so bad tomorrow it will be hard to drive the team." She met his eyes again. "Zeb, please don't ever bring up the subject of Chase Mitchell again. I have buried it, and I want you to do the same—for Joseph's sake."

He nodded. "All right. Just so you're telling the truth that you've done the same.

"I have. You're a hundred times the better man, Zeb Adams. And you're my husband." She leaned down and kissed his cheek. "Now, get some sleep. I left a pot soaking over the fire. I'd better scrub it before I go to bed."

He gave her a rather sad smile and stretched out on his stomach. Lilly covered him, then climbed out of the wagon and walked into the darkness, where she quietly wept alone.

During the last week of the journey, it seemed as if progress was judged by feet rather than miles, as men worked with shovels and hatchets to chop, dig, and pry their way through rugged canyons grown thick with willow. The Mormons who had come through the year before, as well as a Gentile wagon train, had already made a road through the area. But no sooner were the willows cut down than they grew back like weeds. Sometimes they hid dangerous holes and drop-offs.

The wagons creaked slowly through deep canyons, around boulders, and over freezing-cold creeks. Lilly supposed she could enjoy the undeniable beauty of the land if she were not so concerned that an accident would occur. She could not dismiss from her mind a horror story Zeb had told her about the Donner-Reed wagon train that had been through here the year before and had gone on to California, only to become stranded in the Sierras.

Lilly wondered if it was really true that some of the survivors had eaten the flesh of the others who had died while they were all buried in snow on top of the mountains. She realized that this time of year, prospects of a snowstorm increased. There was snow on the tops of the mountains they broke through now, and anyone who knew anything about mountains realized how unpredictable the weather could be any time of year.

Zeb had told her there couldn't be more than forty miles to go, but those forty miles seemed like four hundred. At times a wagon wheel would slip off the side of a narrow road that seemed to hang in the sky. Each time it happened, men would gather to ease the wagon back into position. In this treacherous area Lilly clung to Joseph, afraid to let go of him for an instant. Sometimes the wagons traveled lopsided —two wheels in a creek bed, the other two on land.

They climbed for miles over what Zeb said they had named Hogsback Summit. Then it was down for miles, through a hollow so steep Zeb was constantly applying the brakes. People led their wagons and animals at a snail's pace so as not to get up too much speed. Some men even cut down pine trees and stripped off the branches, then tied them under the wagons so they would drag and help slow the descent.

Then they climbed again for miles and came out on a rise

that overlooked a magnificent canyon, surrounded on every side by snow-covered, granite mountains, their lower elevations covered with pine and aspen. Far in the distance Lilly could see a broad golden plain, beyond which lay a dark mountain, standing like a sentinel of the West. Another mountain range rose in the hazy distance beyond the dark mountain.

The view was awesome even to those who had already been this way.

"The land out here changes all the time, Lilly," Zeb told her as they stood looking out over the spectacular scenery below. Zeb talked almost in a whisper, as though they were in some huge sanctuary of God, where it was not polite to raise their voices.

The group had become so quiet, Lilly felt as though she were in church. The only sound she heard was a moaning wind through the mountains—an eerie, lonely sound that made her shiver.

Was she really here? Was this really happening to little Lilly Brannigan from Scotland? Such drastic changes had taken place in her life in just three years.

"Brother Young says the other end of that canyon is so narrow, not even one wagon could get through," Zeb told her. "We have to take that northern ridge. It won't be easy, but we'll make it."

The journey became even rougher. Lilly wondered how much longer the animals would hold out, constantly pulling up and up and up around dangerous switchbacks, then straining to hold back heavy wagons as they went down again.

"We'll stay a little more toward the north," Zeb explained. "That big valley to the south and west is occupied by Ute Indians. We haven't had a lot of trouble with them, but there's no sense horning in on what they consider their territory."

After several more days of slow, dangerous hauling, they came to what Zeb called Donner Hill. He pointed to an impossibly steep slope. "The Donner party thought going over that canyon wall would be the quickest way into the valley beyond. Folks say if they had dug around it some, like the

Mormon men who came through here last year did, they wouldn't have worn out their animals so bad. I hear they yoked up to fifty oxen and mules to just one wagon to get it over that ridge. We've got an easier road—not the best, mind you, but a lot better than climbing that thing."

Lilly walked beside the wagon, holding Joseph, staring at gouges left by the wagons of the Donner party. She found it hard to believe that any wagon could be taken up such a steep wall. Their own wagon followed a rugged, man-made road around the obstacle, breaking out onto a gentle slope. Zeb halted the oxen and nodded toward a vast valley below. "There it is: Salt Lake—home," he said.

Lilly walked up next to him and looked out over a valley that seemed to go on forever. A huge lake lay shimmering in the center of it. It seemed to take up more room than the land around it. The water was deep, deep blue, but in some places it looked gold, or brown. Little golden islands jutted up in various spots. Not far from the lake, near the north rim of the valley, lay a tiny settlement. Mountain ranges ran to the south from both east and west, coming together in the far, far distance.

"The lake will provide salt—there are hot springs on the north end—and there are plenty of fresh-water streams coming down from the mountains that we can use for irrigation. Before long that entire valley will be green, Lilly— you'll see. Look over there, near the settlement. See the green there? That's where they're already growing crops. I can't wait to start our own."

"Oh, Zeb, it's so beautiful it gives me the shivers."

He put an arm around her shoulders. "This is it, Lilly. This is Zion."

As more wagons came through the road that opened into "home," someone in the crowd started to sing a hymn. Lilly and Zeb joined in. It had been such a long, torturous journey. Nauvoo was behind them now—forever.

Lilly clung to Joseph, thinking about Laura, little Marian, and all the others who had been lost. Catheryn was clinging to Henry, weeping into his arms. But Mary Williams stood rigid, with a stone face, forcing herself to be strong and brave for Hiram. Lilly's heart went out to the woman.

"Hosannah!" Hiram shouted, throwing up his arms. "We are home at last!"

"Hosannah!" others shouted in reply. "Praise be to God!"

Zeb looked down at Lilly, and pulled her close. "I hope you will like it here, Lilly. I'll do all I can on my part to make you happy."

She looked out over the glorious valley again. "I'll be happy, Zeb." But already she wondered what it was going to be like to be in a real house, sleeping in the same bed with him every night. He would want her more often then, and she would have to oblige.

Zeb left her and walked over to the oxen. Lilly looked down to see a black cricket—bigger than any insect she had ever seen in her life. She jumped back, staring at it as it half flew and half hopped into a scraggly bush. Moments later she heard a gunshot. Someone had shot a rattler.

Chapter Eighteen

October 1848

Chase rode along the ridge above Nauvoo, his heart crushed at the sight below. He could not believe this was the place he had visited two and a half years ago, and he was ashamed to be a part of the "Gentile" people who had so outrageously scorned and destroyed what was once a beautiful city and its people. He knew from a glance that Lilly could not possibly still be living below, but he had to make sure. Perhaps, out of fear that he would never find her, she had stayed behind, although he prayed she had not, for surely these people would not have been kind to her. All he could think of was the day the border ruffians had tried to ride off with her, and he prayed that nothing so horrible had happened to her since he had left.

He headed his horse down a hill, angry with himself for leaving her at all. As far as he was concerned, the Mexican War had been a waste of lives. He would never believe it was right for the United States to invade Mexico, and to claim so much Mexican land. But it was done now, and he had been a part of it. He had kept his promise to his father. He would never rejoin the army. He wanted only one thing —to find Lilly.

He winced with a gnawing pain that still plagued his left side when he moved a certain way or his horse's gait faltered. He realized he was lucky to be alive. Sometimes he felt almost guilty for living, when so many others had died. He reasoned there had to be a specific purpose for that life, and Lilly was the only one he could think of. The closer he came to finding her, the more he was sure he still loved and wanted her. With the back pay he had received, and money he had collected from the rental of his mother's house, he was well set to marry.

He rode through the deserted main street of Nauvoo. Some buildings were burned, some were boarded up. His heart tightened with memories as he passed Williams Bootery. The building was a shambles, and the windows that had once displayed Hiram's fine shoes were now shattered. He rode at a slightly faster gallop toward the temple, which no longer seemed to gleam in the sun. It sat abandoned, deserted. But Chase was sure he could hear singing, for the memory of that first day he had come here and had heard Lilly's beautiful voice floating out of the temple was so clear.

He did not bother to dismount. He knew there would be no one inside. He rode toward Hiram Williams's old house —one of the few homes that still stood and was occupied. It angered him that outsiders had moved in and taken over the homes and farms the Mormons had worked so hard to build and develop. As he rode up to the gate, a woman walked around from behind the house.

"What do you want, mister?"

Chase removed his hat, thinking to himself how homely and dirty she looked. "Just looking for someone. Any Mormons left here?"

The woman frowned, walking through the overgrown front lawn to the gate. "Well, I'll be. You, too?"

"What do you mean?"

"Some young man come through here a few months ago looking for Mormons. I'll tell you the same as I told him— ain't no Mormon in his right mind would be caught living around here now. Can't you tell? We got rid of them varmints."

Chase checked his temper. "I was looking for one in particular—a Lilly Brannigan. Ever hear of her?"

The woman let out an astonished laugh. "That young man asked for the same girl! She must be right popular! But then, them Mormon women must be a little bit wild—more than one living with the same man and all."

Chase's heart swelled with hope. Billy *had* brought the letter!

"The other young man—what did you tell him?"

"That the Mormons are all gone—have been for a couple years now. They all went west. God only knows where they ended up."

"The young man—did he say anything about a letter? Did he mention he would look for them to deliver a letter to Lilly Brannigan?"

"Oh, he mentioned a letter, all right, but he wasn't about to go wanderin' all the way out west into hostile land just to chase down a Mormon woman. Far as I know he headed on back to wherever he came from."

Chase's hope quickly faded. He tried to remember how long it had been since his last posted letter. What was Lilly thinking now? Did she wonder if he was dead? Maybe she had even married someone else! But surely she would wait until she knew for certain what had happened to him.

"You gonna go out to that Godforsaken land?" the woman at the gate asked him.

Chase looked to the west. "Yes, ma'am," he answered, more to himself than to her.

"Well, if you don't find her, you can always go looking for gold. You hear about the gold strike out in California?"

He looked back at her. "I heard," he answered. But he didn't care. He only cared about finding Lilly.

"Well, mister, my advice is, if you want to head west, wait till next spring. For one thing, they say nobody can go this time of year and hope to get over the mountains. With this gold strike, I expect there will be thousands going west come spring. You'd have lots of company—lots of help. My own husband is going, and my oldest son. They say the gold is just layin' out there in them California hills, waitin' to be picked up. Hope my man gets a share of it. If you was smart, you'd forget that Mormon girl and go on to California—get you some of that gold for yourself. No Mormon will do you any good, son, but gold will."

The woman cackled. She sounded to Chase like an old crow.

He turned his horse and headed out of Nauvoo, wanting only to remember it the way it once was. He was glad Hiram and Lilly and the others could not see it now.

Chase decided he would buy a pack horse and some supplies and travel as far west as he could before winter set in. That would save him a little time next spring. Surely the farther west he went, the more people along the way would know about the Mormons and where they might be. He wondered as he rode out of Nauvoo if the stories of gold in California were true.

As the wagons poured into the valley, those who had wintered there cheered. But already everyone could see what a strain the newcomers would be on the food supply, for the first year's crops had been small. With thousands more to come, Lilly knew herself that winter was going to be a hungry one. But at least they were here, home at last.

Within one month Zeb had built an adobe home for the three of them. It was small—only one room—but it was cool, and he assured Lilly that it would be very warm in winter.

"Next spring I'll start building you a real house," he promised. "We expect more lumber to come in from the mill. In no time, Salt Lake City will be as beautiful as Nauvoo was. And we'll have a temple bigger and grander than the one back in Illinois."

Lilly knew the Mormons well enough by now that she did

not doubt Zeb's promises. But this first winter would be another test of strength and determination. She was grateful their cow had survived the journey. Joseph would have milk for winter. But until bigger crops could be planted in the spring, people would have to share.

Lilly tried to be as responsive a wife as she could be for Zeb. She quickly learned that the mere words "not tonight" were enough to thwart his advances, and she tried not to use them too often, for fear of hurting him. She prayed constantly that she would get pregnant. It frustrated her that she had so easily gotten pregnant by Chase, and could not seem to conceive by Zeb. She wondered if desire and willingness had anything to do with it.

But in spite of her wish to give Zeb the child he deserved, Lilly found herself turning away her husband more often than she received him. She wished she could abandon her modesty and release her pent-up needs, the way she had been able to with Chase. She had seen Chase completely naked, had gloried in his body and in letting him look upon her own. But she had never seen Zeb that way, nor had he seen her in the light of day. Lovemaking was always at night, under covers. Zeb simply pushed her gown up, and fumbled at the buttons of his longjohns.

Except for hands and feet and Lilly's bare legs, they had never touched skin to skin. Zeb had touched her breasts through her gown, but had never opened it or put his lips to that part of her. Chase had drawn from her wild desires she didn't even know had existed within her; Zeb seemed to have no idea how to draw anything from a woman.

She told herself it didn't matter, that there were other things more important—like Joey, and just being alive. Zeb was a good man. Every day she could stand and look at the mountains and gather new strength from them. And the affection she could not truly give to Zeb she would give to Joey.

By the time Chase arrived at Winter Quarters, it was already cold. A stinging late-November sleet whipped at his face like tiny rocks as he rode in, and he pulled his hat down on his forehead. He hadn't really minded the miserable trip, which he had undertaken almost entirely alone. The thought that Lilly could be at this Mormon settlement was all the incentive Chase needed to brave the elements and whatever enemies might be lurking in the night shadows.

His chest tightened with excitement as he tried to imagine what it would be like to see her again. Surely she was more beautiful than ever. He rode down a gently sloping hill, leading his pack horse. He hoped he looked all right. He had shaved carefully that morning—not an easy job in cold weather.

Chase asked the Mormon men who ran the ferry across the Missouri if they knew Lilly. None of them did, but one man explained to Chase that so many of the people now at Winter Quarters were new arrivals that it was impossible to know everyone. After all, thousands of Mormons had gathered here over the past two years. And many of those who had come here from Nauvoo had already gone on to Utah.

"Next spring we will go, too," the man added with a wide smile, his words carrying a choppy German accent. "It is our Zion. We are very excited to go. Big country! Such big country!"

Chase nodded, caring little about what the Mormons were doing or how big the country was. He just wanted to find Lilly. He studied Winter Quarters as the ferry landed, and it pained his heart to see the crude sod homes, tents, wagons, and few cabins. These people were living a life far removed from the one they had led at Nauvoo. Life was hard for them, and apparently still dangerous. Another man on the ferry had told him they had lately been experiencing outlaw raids. Thieves and murderers lurked around their camp and hounded newcomers. Those left at Winter Quarters were anxious to leave for Utah.

Chase noticed several two-wheeled carts, and asked what they were used for.

"We brought them here, with our belongings in them," the German answered.

Chase frowned. "But, they don't look properly rigged to be pulled by an animal."

The German laughed. "A *human* animal pulled them," he

answered. "*We* pulled them. My wife and I, we each pulled one—one for our belongings, one for the children!"

Chase stared at the man in amazement. "You pulled them by hand?"

"All the way from your city called St. Louis. It is Brother Young's idea—a way to help us afford to come here. We do not all have the money, you know, for good wagons and animals. Brother Young and his people build the carts for us and see that we get as many as we need. For all who arrive here from their mother countries, Brother Young has Mormons waiting for them with carts, ready to lead them here. Next spring we will go all the way to Utah with them."

Chase shook his head at the determination these people had. He mounted his horse, and led it into Winter Quarters. Although there were few buildings, and most of those were sod, the Mormons still had laid out streets. Everything was orderly and clean. In the distance, he saw a graveyard. Considering how new the settlement was, he realized the graves had to hold nearly all Mormons, and he prayed Lilly was not lying in one of them.

The sleet had ended, but a cold wind endured. Chase kept his poncho wrapped tightly around his shoulders as he stopped to ask people about Lilly, but most of them were too new to know her. Finally, he found a man who at least knew a woman named Lilly. The man mumbled her name as he nailed a shoe on a horse. He paused, then looked up at Chase.

"Yes, sir, I remember someone called Lilly. But I don't believe it was Lilly Brannigan." He called over another man —one who had originally come from Nauvoo the year before. "David, did you know a Lilly Brannigan among those who went on to Utah?" the man asked. "Or perhaps she is still among us."

The one called David rubbed his chin. He looked up at Chase. "Only Lilly I knew was Lilly Adams. I think, though, that her name was Brannigan before that. A little Scottish girl—prettiest thing in the whole settlement—and a voice that outshone even her looks."

"That's her," Chase said, a mixture of joy and dread moving through him. "You say her last name is Adams?"

"Yes, sir. She married Zeb Adams—oh, a couple years ago already. They have a little boy—real good-looking kid. Of course, with a mother like her, how could a kid turn out ugly?" The man frowned. "What's your interest, anyway?"

It was all Chase could do to keep his composure. Lilly—married? How could that be? Why?

"I . . . we used to be friends," he answered. He looked away for a moment, trying to act casual, but he wanted to scream, to hit someone, to cry, to ride hard for Utah and grab Lilly and ask her why she had not waited for him. "You sure she was Scottish—had a beautiful voice?"

"Yes, sir. Who could forget that face or that voice? She was an inspiration to all of us—her singing, you know. That young Zeb Adams has got himself the prettiest wife of any man here or in Utah."

Chase felt numb with rage and jealousy, disappointment and terrible hurt. "She's not here at Winter Quarters, then?"

"No, sir. She and her husband went on to Utah."

"Thank you," Chase answered. He turned his horse.

"Where are you going, mister?" David asked him. "It's a miserable day to be out riding, and you must have come a long way already. We'd be glad to give you something hot to eat and drink, shelter for the night."

"No, thank you," Chase answered, looking back. "It's light enough that I can cover some ground yet today."

"Where you headed?"

"Fort Laramie, if I can get there before the snows gets too bad."

"Laramie! Mister, that's a long way. You could get caught in a blizzard and buried alive before you get there. Don't try that trip this time of year."

"I've got no choice. I've got to get as far west as I can this year. That will save me time getting to Utah."

"I wouldn't try it if I was you, mister."

Chase just kept riding. The two men watched after him, shaking their heads. "The man's crazy," one of them muttered. "Must be something mighty important for him over there."

Chapter Nineteen

In the spring of 1849, Brigham Young and his followers realized their settlement was about to become a gold mine. Scouts informed the inhabitants of Salt Lake that thousands of gold-seekers were headed west, many of them bound to come through Salt Lake. The experienced Mormon travelers realized how badly the newcomers would need supplies, and how willing they would be to trade items the Mormons might need in return for the fresh produce they could grow in their fields.

Zeb planned to grow as big a crop as possible so he would have plenty to provide the expected surge of travelers. He broke open more land, and Lilly helped. Lilly shared Zeb's enthusiasm, until the day he was called to a meeting of the elders.

She gave little thought to the meeting, for Brigham Young seemed to always be calling meetings, especially lately. But when Zeb returned, she noticed a strange, almost disappointed look on his face. Lilly rose from a freshly dug trench in which she had been planting corn. Joseph toddled beside her, dropping in some of the kernels himself, the way his mother had shown him. As soon as Lilly stopped planting, the boy ran off to chase a butterfly.

"Zeb, what is it? You look upset."

He watched her closely. "Lilly, you know how important it is to the Mormons to do missionary work. We've got missionaries all over the world."

"Of course I know that. That's what brought me here from Scotland. Are they sending you away, Zeb?" Her heart tightened.

"Not exactly." He sighed. "Lilly, Brother Young thinks

it's important to expand our territory as fast as possible—before this land becomes too settled by Gentiles. With this gold discovery and all—and with thousands of people expected to come west now—well, it's likely that if we don't expand our borders to protect ourselves, we'll end up just like we did at Nauvoo—a little town surrounded by people who hate us."

Lilly felt an odd dread come into her heart. "What are you trying to tell me, Zeb?"

He looked past her, at Joseph. "We have to leave Salt Lake, Lilly. The house will have to wait a while longer." He met her eyes again.

"But, I've just grown used to it here. It's so beautiful, Zeb."

"I know. I like it, too, but it's pretty where we're going, too. I've seen it, Lilly. I came through there when we came back from California. It's called Carson Valley—in Nevada. It's . . . even farther west."

She turned away, blinking back tears, and stared out at the western mountains. Another journey! Again, their lives would be endangered. How she hated the thought of living in a wagon again, submitting Joseph to disease and hardship, heading into even wilder country. What if she *did* get pregnant, and gave birth way out there in that hostile land? Was it even drier there, even hotter?

"Is anyone else close to us going? Catheryn? Hiram and Mary?"

He put his hands on her shoulders. "No. I think maybe Frieda Dutch will go. You like Frieda, don't you?"

"Yes," she answered quietly. "I came all the way across the ocean with her." She remembered singing the hymn on the ship when it was landing at New Orleans. How long ago had that been? And how long ago had she sung it for Chase? Her heart had not been that gloriously happy since. "When do we leave?" she asked.

"As soon as possible. I'm sorry, Lilly. I didn't want to make you have to travel again. But Brother Young asked, and I—"

"And you're a Mormon," she answered for him. "The

faith comes first. Brigham Young comes first—before family, before everything." Her voice sounded suddenly cold.

"I'm sorry, Lilly. It isn't really like that—the way you put it. It's *God* that comes first. And if you were Mormon—"

"I'm not Mormon, Zeb!"

"But you *could* be. You might as well be. 'Blessed are the Gentiles,' it reads in the Book of Mormon. 'If it be so that they shall fight not against Zion, they shall be saved.'"

Lilly turned and looked up at him. "I don't *want* to be Mormon, Zeb, but I won't fight against your Zion. I'll go to Nevada. But I'm making a demand of my own, Zeb."

He frowned. "Demand?"

"Once we get settled in Nevada, I intend to stay there. I'll never get into another covered wagon—either to go farther west, or to come back to Salt Lake. Do you understand? I won't do that to Joseph. I'm tired, Zeb." Tears welled up in her eyes. "I'm so tired. I want my own house—and before Joseph gets any older, I want him settled in one place. I never want him to know the loneliness and agony of never having a place to call home—of never really belonging anywhere. Promise me, Zeb, that we'll stay in Nevada, and you won't go running off and leaving us—not for any reason."

He nodded, knowing her well enough by now to realize she meant every word. "All right. I promise. This will be our last journey."

She handed him the sack of corn. "Save it for Nevada." She walked over to Joseph and picked him up. "Come on, Joey. We have to pack the wagon again."

Zeb watched her with a heavy heart. He knew her disappointment ran deep, and that she was not really happy with him. Everything his wife had done since she had married him had only been for Joseph. But he loved her, and he was sure she loved him, in her own way. Lilly's independent streak had just shown itself. It was part of what he loved about her. He let her have the last word. They would settle in Nevada.

Lilly realized it was possible she would never again see any of these people she had loved and called family. After traveling the trail of sorrow and hope, sharing with them the agony of death and the celebration of life, leaving them now tore at her heart so much that she felt physical pain.

Hiram and Mary, Henry and Catheryn, and all the children . . . how could she leave them?

"'Behold, God is my salvation,'" Hiram read from 2 Nephi in the Book of Mormon. "'I will trust, and not be afraid.'"

Lilly caught the slight tremble in his voice. She knew how hard this was for him and Mary, too. Leaving Mary hurt most of all.

"'For the Lord Jehovah is my strength and my song; he also has become my salvation. Therefore, with joy shall ye draw water out of the wells of salvation. And in that day shall ye say: Praise the Lord, call upon his name, declare his doings among the people, make mention that his name is exalted. Sing unto the Lord; for he hath done excellent things; this is known in all the earth.'"

Hiram lowered the book and looked at Lilly and Joey, while Brigham Young, who stood in the circle of people gathered to bid farewell to those heading for Nevada, continued.

"'And now, behold thy brothers murmur, saying it is a hard thing which I have required of them,'" Young spoke in his gentle but commanding manner. Lilly watched the Mormon leader with resentment. He was a big man, with a commanding appearance. "'Behold I have not required it of them, but it is a commandment of the Lord. Therefore, go, my son, and thou shalt be favored of the Lord, because thou hast not murmured. Wherefore, let us be faithful in keeping the commandments of the Lord.'" Young halted for a moment, looking up into the sky. "'And I also spake unto him, saying: Surely the Lord hath commanded us to do this thing; and shall we not be diligent in keeping the commandments of the Lord? Therefore, if thou wilt go down into the wilderness to my Father, thou shalt have a place with us.'"

The little service ended. Then came the hugs and the goodbyes. Mary Williams clung to Lilly. "Oh, how we'll miss you, child. How we'll miss you and your singing."

Lilly could not control her own tears as Mary finally pulled away. "God be with you, Lilly."

"And with you, Mary."

Mary turned to Joey and picked him up, while Catheryn embraced Lilly. "God be with you, Lilly." She kissed Lilly's cheek. "And please take good care of my brother. We've always... been so close. And now, after losing my Marian..."

Lilly squeezed her hands. "We'll always be together, Catheryn, in spirit. And we can write."

"Oh, yes, do write, Lilly. Tell me everything about Nevada, and I'll keep you informed of what is happening here."

The hugging and crying continued. How could anyone put into words what they felt? Lilly supposed it could never be done, whether they spent an hour or a week. It was time to leave, and that was that. Joey was passed around like a little prize, and the boy began to cry out of simple confusion. After all, everyone else was crying. He sensed something terrible was about to happen, but he wasn't sure just what it was going to be, and it frightened him.

Hiram handed the boy to Lilly, studying her lovingly as he did so. It had taken time, but Lilly had finally managed to understand Hiram's ways; and that he had truly cared for her. She was grateful he had never again mentioned Chase.

"It's been a long journey from Scotland, hasn't it, Lilly?" Hiram's eyes were full of tears. He hugged her and Joey together. "Oh, how we'll miss you, and how we'll miss your sweet voice, Lilly. Promise me you'll never stop singing. Wherever you go in Nevada, they'll build a chapel, and you must sing for them—then, and along the way. It will give all of you more faith for the journey."

"I'll keep singing, Hiram," she answered, remembering with a broken heart that she had made that same promise to another man. "I'll keep singing," she repeated. It was all she could think of to say. She didn't want to use the word goodbye. Hiram let go of her, and Lilly turned, handed Joey to Zeb, then climbed into the wagon. Zeb handed the boy up to her.

"You ready?" he asked.

"I will never be ready, so we might as well go," she answered.

People gathered at the back of the wagon—Hiram, Mary, Beth, Gerald, young Henry; Henry Guest, Catheryn, Myra, Jeffrey, Ella, Herbert, and Henry and Catheryn's baby girl, Adrienne—just six months younger than Joey. Others gathered—people Lilly had come to know and love along the way. She heard Zeb saying goodbye to someone, then felt the wagon lurch. Her stomach and heart lurched with it.

She sat back inside the wagon. "Away and away and away—far, far away," she muttered.

"Go 'way, mommy?" Joey asked, crawling onto her lap.

"Yes, Joey. We're going away."

They took what had come to be called the Hastings Cutoff, an extremely dangerous route, but much shorter than trying to get over the Wasatch Mountains farther north. The danger lay not so much in the land, but in lack of water. At first, travel was relatively easy, until they came upon the last fresh spring, where they loaded every barrel and jar and waterbag they had.

Zeb had not taken this route before, but since he had been to Nevada he had been chosen as the leader. Scouts had told him about the many miles the cutoff would save. But it would mean traveling forty or fifty miles without a trace of water, trees, or grass. It would be a trying experience for humans, and even worse for the poor animals that had to do all the work, but they were to try it as an experiment, for any future Mormons who might want to use it.

They traveled with forty wagons, thirty-eight men, twenty women, and nearly fifty children. Some of the wagons carried nothing but tools and equipment, so that the new settlers would have what they needed to set up a new sawmill, build homes, repair wagons, and make their own furniture and necessities. Among the thousands who came from Europe, nearly every trade imaginable was represented, which was one of the reasons the Mormons were able to take care of all their own needs.

Plows and other farm equipment were also carried by wagon, and a small herd of draft horses, milk cows, and bulls were herded along. Cages of chickens were tied to the sides of wagons.

The sun shone down so fiercely that the journey soon became miserable. Comfort could be found neither inside nor outside the wagon. Joey fussed the first few hours, but was soon too hot and upset to make sounds. Lilly's heart ached for him as he lay in the shade of the wagon top. Wagons rolled over hard-packed earth, and in places they passed over what Zeb said were dried-up river- and lakebeds. Lilly wondered how on earth a river or a lake could ever have existed in this horrible place, and she began to worry that where they were going, it would be just like this. Zeb had promised otherwise, but maybe he had just said it to soothe her about the trip.

This was not the cool green of the mountains around Salt Lake. There wasn't even any color here. They had left mountains behind, and more lay ahead, but so far in the distance that it seemed impossible to ever reach them. Between the two ranges was this wide, endless expanse of desertlike land—nature's oven—and she and Joey and everyone else would surely be baked alive. After a day's journey they came upon another spring, but the water was so putrid that even the animals would not try to drink it. Lilly felt sorry for the poor, plodding brutes, their heads hanging, their breathing coming in loud snorts, their mouths frothing from thirst.

In the afternoons they rested, but there was no shade, unless one wanted to sit on the rocky ground under a wagon. The animals were fed bunches of grass brought along in the wagons for this part of the journey, and they were allowed to drink a little water from small pans held under their noses.

Once they got started again, Zeb traveled half the night, for it was much easier to travel when the sun was gone. In fact, the nights were surprisingly cold, and Lilly bundled Joey under several blankets as he slept. She coated Joey's cheeks with a cream she had purchased at Nauvoo. She decided not to put any on her own face, in case Joey's sunburn got worse. But she could hardly sleep for her own sunburn, and the discomfort the dry air brought to her skin and lips. Her lips were badly cracked, and sometimes they bled, and she wondered if she would look like a shriveled-up old lady by the time they reached Carson Valley.

Travel changed back and forth from easy rolling on hard ground to terribly difficult hauling through soft sand. The second night they again kept going after dark, but the animals seemed to be practically crawling. Their water supply was getting low. After several days terror struck Lilly when their own oxen suddenly collapsed, unable to go any farther. The teams of several other wagons did the same, and Lilly could see they still seemed to be in the middle of the horrible desert, with not a shade tree or a stream in sight. She tried to control her terror, not wanting Joey to sense it. Scouts came back to the wagons, saying it was a good twenty-five miles yet to the Humboldt River, the nearest fresh water.

The men held a meeting. Lilly's heart pounded with dread when Zeb announced that the men had decided to unhitch the teams and drive them ahead to fresh water, so they could get their strength back. Then they would be driven back and hitched up again, hopefully rested enough to get the wagons through the desert.

Lilly could not imagine anything worse than being left alone in the middle of the desert, with its raging heat and intense silence. There was nothing here—nothing. And if the men didn't make it back, they would end up pieces of dried, cracked flesh, burning in the desert sun.

Still, she knew their only hope of survival was to do as Zeb suggested. The men unhitched teams and gathered the animals together, and Lilly vowed she would not transmit her terror to Joey. She actually smiled for Zeb.

"We'll be waiting for you, won't we, Joey?" she said, telling the boy to wave goodbye to his father.

Zeb read the fear in her lovely green eyes. "I *will* be back, Lilly. Please trust me. I'm sorry about this."

She nodded, forcing herself not to cry out, not to beg him to stay. If he didn't go, they would all die anyway. The decision had been made for them out of necessity.

"Just get going," she told Zeb. She knew it was with great reluctance that he left with the others. Every man on the train was required, for it would be a difficult job herding the now thirsty and balking animals through another twenty-five miles of desert.

The men were gone only a few hours when one of the

women began to pace, rubbing her hands, working herself
into a frenzy—talking about how they were all going to die,
and that the men would never come back. Children began to
cry, including Joey. The woman kept mumbling, then began
screaming, and crumpled to her knees, sobbing. Lilly
stormed over to her, grasped her by the arms, and jerked her
up.

"Stop it, Sister Manley!" she ordered. "Where is your
faith? The men will be back. They *will*!"

"Oh, Sister Adams, how can you say that?" the woman
wept. "Look out there! We can't even see them anymore!
They're gone! All that's left are those horrible heat waves
...endless desert! We're in hell, Sister Adams! It has already swallowed up our men, and now it will consume
us—like fire!"

Lilly slapped the woman, hard.

"How dare you carry on like this and upset my little boy!"
Lilly told her. "Do you think you're the only one who is
suffering and afraid? We *all* are! Your carrying on isn't helping anything. At least we're *together*! We just have to make
the best of it until the men get back, and I'll not have you
behaving like this in front of my son!"

Joey's tears had subsided to little sniffles, as he stood
clinging to Lilly's skirt. He looked up at her, his little sun-
burned cheeks and nose breaking her heart. She let go of
Sister Manley and picked the boy up.

"Let's join in hymn now—everybody," she urged. She
began singing *All Is Well*, and stared straight at Sister Manley as she did so. Soon Sister Manley wiped her tears and
joined in. Lilly repeated the verse vigorously, as though she
believed every word. Soon all the women were singing, as
though they were standing inside the cool temple sanctuary
at Nauvoo, still full of fire and excitement at finding their
Zion. By the time the hymn was finished, all the women
were smiling.

"Now, let's decide what to prepare for supper," Lilly told
them. "After that we'll stretch blankets and quilts between
wagons so we can sit under them for shade. That will give
us shelter from the sun, but leave openings for air. That's the
trouble with being inside the wagons. There is no air. We

can tell stories." She looked around at the women—some from Germany, some from England, some from Sweden. "Many of us are from other countries. We can sit around and tell each other about the countries we came from. Those of you who speak a different language can give the rest of us lessons."

Lilly walked to her own wagon and took out some blankets, and tied them to the back of her own wagon and the front of the one behind it. "Come on," she told the others.

In moments the rest of them were doing the same, and babbling about things they could prepare to eat without having to make a fire, for they had to be careful not to use too much of the wood they had brought along. Children began to laugh as they walked under the quilts and wagons, peering out from or crawled through wheels.

"Thank you, Lilly," Frieda Dutch said, coming to stand beside her. "What would we do without you?"

"You'd do just fine, Frieda."

"But you're so brave, so strong."

Lilly almost laughed at the words. There they were again. Chase had told her, Hiram had told her, Mary, Catheryn, Zeb. Strange that she still didn't feel that way on the inside.

"I didn't like her upsetting my Joey, that's all."

"Say what you like, Lilly. You're still a godsend, as far as I'm concerned. I was so glad when my husband told me you and Zeb would be a part of this journey. I didn't want to come, but with you along, I knew I could bear it."

Lilly stared across the hazy horizon into which Zeb and the others had disappeared. She just hoped the men would return.

After four days, the women witnessed the blessed sight of men and oxen on the horizon. When they reached camp, Zeb was surprised to see everyone was calm. Blankets were tied between wagons and children played underneath. Barrels and crates were situated under the blankets, and the women sat there together, knitting, laughing, talking. They looked haggard, hot, and dirty.

He hugged Lilly close. "You all right?"

"As good as can be expected. Sister Manley had a bad

time of it at first, but we calmed her down. I just kept telling them you would be back. We figured if we sat under the blankets we could still catch the breeze—what there is of one. It's a lot more comfortable than inside the wagons."

"Was that your idea?"

She shrugged. "I was just trying to think of ways to keep cool and busy." She rested her head against his chest. "Oh, Zeb, I'm as close to a crazy woman as I ever want to get," she admitted, stubbornly fighting tears.

Zeb grinned as Joey ran up to them and hugged him around the leg. "Papa! Papa!" He had finally changed "Poppy" to "Papa," and the sound of his little voice greeting Zeb was the nicest thing Lilly had heard in a long time.

After two weeks, the land finally became mountainous, greener, and more colorful, with huge pines scattered here and there. They traveled through a red, rocky pass into a valley through which a wide creek meandered lazily, fed by mountain streams. Grass grew lush here, and a small lake glittered in the distance. To the west and south, mountains rose in granite splendor, capped with snow, their sides covered with deep-green pines.

Zeb halted the oxen and told Lilly to get out of the wagon. As she climbed down, he came around the back of the wagon and swung Joey up onto his shoulders.

"This is it," he told her. "Southeast of here is Washoe Lake. That little one to the south is Rock Lake—at least, that's what we call it. I'm sorry about the desert, Lilly. We thought it would be a lot shorter route. But, at least—"

He saw tears in her eyes. She walked away from him and stared at the green valley dotted with huge ponderosa pines, the fantastic mountains to the west, and the glimmering lake.

"It's more beautiful than Salt Lake," she said. "Oh, Zeb, I didn't think a place like this existed beyond the Rockies. We don't have to go any farther, do we? We don't have to go over any more mountains, or through any more deserts?"

"No. We're home, Lilly. And I promise, this time we'll stay. But you'll have to live out of the wagon for a while until the other men and I can get some lumber cut."

"I don't mind."

"The mountain men around here call the creek over there Ophir Creek. This place is called Washoe Valley, and there are trading posts north and south of here. Trappers say both places will probably turn into settled towns once the gold-seekers start coming through. But I don't think we have to worry much about settlers. Travelers will be on their way to California. We'll grow crops and make money selling supplies to the miners, like at Salt Lake. The mountains to the west are the Sierras."

"Over there!" she said excitedly. "Let's settle right over there, where that big pine stands on the knoll. It must be the biggest tree in the valley."

She climbed back into the wagon and Zeb headed for the pine. Already Lilly had decided she would never leave this place called Nevada. She drank in the beauty of the Washoe Valley and knew this was where she belonged. This was forever. Nothing and no one would make her go back. The future was all she would think about now—the future, and Joey, and the home they would make here.

Chapter Twenty

June 1849

Chase's chest ached with anticipation and apprehension as he came upon the rise that looked down on Salt Lake City. He wanted to be happy at the sight of frame houses sprouting everywhere, taking the place of the original adobe homes. The Mormons were obviously prospering, as they always had a way of doing.

If not for the news he had heard at Winter Quarters, he would be happier about the progress he saw below. Carefully planned streets were laid out in perfect patterns, and he could see the beginnings of the all-important temple. Crops grew everywhere around the city, and he noticed people working in fields, and on buildings. The air was filled with the sound of hammers pounding and saws slicing through fresh lumber. A school building sat on a rise, and horses and wagons moved about in every direction.

Chase wished he could feel glad for the Mormons. But never had words cut so deeply as when the man back at Winter Quarters had told him Lilly was married. The thought of being with her again was all that had kept him alive through the pain and struggle of the past months. When he first learned that Lilly was married, he felt lost. He blamed Hiram for sending Lilly to live with Zeb Adams; and he blamed Mormons in general, who surely had somehow convinced Lilly she should be married.

He had barely made it through the journey to Fort Laramie, where he had spent the most miserable winter of his life. He had considered writing to Lilly, then decided he could never put into words all that had happened to him, how he felt now, and how much she meant to him. And if she really was married, a letter from him now would only create problems for her.

But, then, maybe I should *make problems for her,* he thought. *Maybe she deserves it.* He decided that if he was going to do that, he would rather do it in person. Surely she had gotten his first letters. Surely she had realized he might be wounded—would have checked government records to see if he had been killed before she committed herself to another man.

Why had she married? His only hope was that he would come here to Salt Lake City and find out none of it was true. He would find Lilly and get some answers. Maybe she would still be single—still be waiting for him. He wanted to hate her, but he had lived with her memory for so long—had dreamed of her, loved her, wanted her, envisioned the day he would come back to her, walking tall and strong again.

"Hope you find your woman."

Chase turned to the scout, Hank Webber, with whom he had shared the long trail from Fort Laramie.

"I'm not so sure I want to."

Webber grinned. "Maybe you'll find she's free as a bird. I wish you luck, Mitchell."

Chase looked out over Salt Lake. "Yeah. Thanks," he answered quietly.

Webber turned to signal the rest of the wagon train to follow.

The gold strike in California was big news. Wherever Chase had traveled, people talked about gold. Most of them were planning to make the treacherous journey west to find it. He had spoken to men who had been doing quite well in their own businesses, or at farming, who were selling everything they owned and uprooting their families, to take the tremendous risk of death on the way, and of finding nothing once they got to California. Some had left whole families behind to struggle on their own until they returned rich men.

Chase thought them fools. The Mormons had been forced to move, but these people were giving up a good life and the comforts of civilization for something they could not even be sure was out there. Chase figured the women along must be furious at their husbands—the journey had been one of hardship and death. One of the women had given birth, only to have the baby die the next day. The woman had not spoken to anyone since. The thought of Lilly going through this miserable trip made him feel sick, and he was torn between anger at her for marrying someone else, and worry that perhaps she had died on the journey and he would never see her again.

Still, when he thought of Lilly's strength, her independence and her youth, he could not imagine anything getting the better of her. The thought of her being in another man's arms tore at his guts like a plow ripping open the earth. A thousand times a day he had argued with himself about whether he should see her at all. To see her and find out she belonged to someone else might only make life even more unbearable. Sometimes he thought about putting his hands around her neck and squeezing. Her promises had been so true, her smile so beautiful, her voice so angelic. He could not believe after all his letters that she had not waited for him.

He headed toward the city, along with the twenty wagons, and thirty men on horses. They had decided to take the route through the Mormon settlement in hopes of finding supplies. But Chase had a very different reason for being here.

Friendly faces greeted them, but Chase did not recognize anyone. Help of all kinds was offered, for these people well knew the hardship of the journey west. The Mormons apparently had set up a regular welcoming committee, since they passed tables where food and clothing were being offered— free for the most destitute, for sale or trade to anyone else.

"We expect several thousand of our own people to arrive this year from Winter Quarters," he heard a Mormon man saying.

Chase drew his horse up next to the man. "Excuse me," he asked. "Do you know a Lilly Brannigan? Her last name might be Adams now."

"Sister Adams?" The man brightened. "We all know Sister Adams. Oh, how we miss her voice at worship."

Chase's heart fell. No one sang like Lilly—it had to be her. Hate and love rushed through him in sickening waves. *Miss her voice? Had she died?*

"Where is she?"

"Oh, she's gone on to Nevada—she and her husband Zeb, and their son. Fine boy they've got."

Chase struggled with a myriad of emotions. "How about Hiram Williams? Is he here at Salt Lake?"

The man nodded. "Brother Williams lives at the north end of town. He built one of the first houses—big white frame, two story. Of course, it's not finished inside yet. We're slow to get—"

Chase started to ride off.

"Wait, mister!" the man shouted. "You won't find Hiram at the house. Up the street there—he's opened a shoe shop."

Chase nodded, tipping his hat. The fringes of his buckskin jacket danced as he headed up the street, his heart pounding. He had to know, for once and for all! It seemed strange to be coming into Salt Lake in much the same way he had come into Nauvoo—alone, dressed in buckskins, seeing a Mormon city for the first time. So many things had happened to him and to the Mormons in the past three years.

Had it really been that long? Yes, even longer than that—three years and three months, to be exact. Lilly had surely been through hell on that journey west, and now—Nevada! Webber had told him the trip through Nevada was the worst part—hot and miserable and waterless. What had Lilly been through? Why would she leave the apparently thriving city of Salt Lake and go on to such a Godforsaken place as Nevada? Had she been forced? There had to be an explanation. He would talk to Hiram first—he could give him some answers.

People and horses and wagons moved up and down the street of shops. There was not a tavern in sight and Chase knew he would not find one, although at this moment, he realized he could use a shot of whiskey.

He spotted the sign then, just like at Nauvoo: WILLIAMS BOOTERY. It was an eerie feeling to be with these people again. They had saved his life once, and had been kind and generous. But it was with mixed emotions that he anticipated seeing Hiram Williams. The man had done everything he could to discourage Lilly from being interested in him.

He halted his horse in front of the store, dismounted, and walked inside to a counter at the back, where a heavyset, white-haired man sat with his head bent over a leather shoe.

"Hello, Hiram."

Hiram looked up from his work. His face literally paled as he removed his spectacles and put down the tool he had been using on the shoe.

"Chase! Chase Mitchell! What on earth—" He looked Chase up and down, then put out his hand, but Chase did not shake it.

"I came to find out if it's true, Hiram—about Lilly being married."

Hiram scrambled to think straight. Seeing Chase Mitchell was the very last thing he would have expected! And the baby! He had promised Lilly never to reveal the real father, and now, here he stood, before his eyes.

"Chase, I thought . . . we were under the impression that

what happened between you and Lilly was...was just a passing thing. You left, and there were no letters—"

"No letters! I wrote constantly!"

Hiram could see the color rising in Chase's cheeks. He stayed behind the counter, thinking at first that Chase might try to hit him.

"There were none that I know of, Chase. Of course, Lilly hardly spoke to us right after you left. But the last few months we became close again—on that terrible journey to Winter Quarters, and here. She became like a daughter to us again. We lost our Laura on the journey from Winter Quarters."

Chase sighed, closing his eyes and turning around for a moment. "I'm sorry to hear that. Did Lilly make it all right?"

"Yes. She's a strong girl—kept all of us going sometimes with her songs."

Chase felt the awful pain. "She kept me going too, Hiram —her memory. The thought of coming back to her was all that kept me alive after I was wounded. I was hospitalized for months. That's why I couldn't get back to her." He faced Hiram again. "I don't understand any of this, Hiram. Lilly *loved* me! I promised her I'd come back, and I meant it. Is it true she's married?"

Hiram's blue eyes showed their despair over Chase's predicament. "I'm sorry, Chase. She married Zeb Adams— Catheryn Jules's brother. It's Catheryn Guest, now. Sister Catheryn got married again. She lost a daughter on the journey. It was terrible, Chase, but we trusted God to—"

"*When*! When did she marry Zeb Adams?" Chase almost shouted the words.

Hiram studied the man's blue eyes. The resemblance to little Joey was uncanny. If he got just one look at the boy, he would know. "About eight months after you left," he lied.

"Why didn't she wait for me?"

"I don't know, Chase. If I did, I would tell you. There were no explanations. She simply married the man, and they had a son. He's a fine boy."

"Well, I intend to find Lilly and ask her myself!" Chase answered, his blue eyes blazing.

Hiram realized the disaster it could bring Lilly and Zeb if Chase Mitchell showed up now.

"Chase, if you truly love her, don't go walking into her life now," Hiram said quietly. "Leave her alone. Lilly is happy."

"Happy? Fine! But what about *me*? What about all the pain I suffered, the hell I lived through, just to come back to her? What about all my letters? What about my hopes and dreams? She *promised* me she would wait." He leaned over the counter, tears in his fiery eyes. "If you hadn't sent her away, it might not have happened! I don't doubt you did everything in your power to convince her I wouldn't come back."

Chase shoved a shoe aside angrily as he spoke. Hiram hung his head and rubbed at his eyes. "Dear God," he muttered. What could he say? How could he explain, without giving away the secret Lilly so dearly wanted to keep?

"Please, Chase, I beg of you," he said quietly, "leave her alone. She has a husband and a son. She could even be expecting another child by now. And she's been through so much."

Well, so have I!" Chase answered. "I wish seeing you again could have been under happier circumstances. I'm sorry about Nauvoo—sorry about your daughter. But I've lost the only thing that has ever meant anything to me, and I'm going to find out *why*."

He turned and stormed out.

Chase rode to the small frame house to find Catheryn planting flowers along the front of the veranda. She looked up at him, shading her eyes and frowning at first. Then a shocked expression came over her face, as Chase dismounted and came through the gate. Catheryn struggled to think quickly, for she was sure it was Chase Mitchell who approached her. He removed his hat.

"Catheryn Guest?"

She lowered her arm, still holding a small spade. "Yes?"

"I'm Chase Mitchell."

"Yes. I saw you once when you were at Nauvoo."

Chase struggled to stay in control. "I've just been to see Hiram Williams. I came from Winter Quarters, where they told me Lilly had married your brother." His jaw flexed with repressed anger. "I checked with Hiram because I couldn't believe it. He, uh, he told me it was true, and I . . . I hoped you could give me some answers."

"Answers?" Catheryn prayed inwardly that her face would not give anything away. She felt sorry for Chase Mitchell, whose blue eyes—eyes that were so much like little Joey's —now were pleading, hurt.

"Why, Mrs. Guest? Why in God's name didn't Lilly wait for me? I wrote her so many times. My God, she must have received most of the letters after she had already married your brother! Did they have a good laugh over them?"

She saw his anger and stepped back a little. "Neither Lilly nor my brother would have laughed over such a thing, Brother Mitchell. But I assure you, as God is my witness, there were no letters. I swear it."

Chase frowned. He knew from her eyes that the woman was not lying. "I don't understand. I wrote her a couple of times a month—from Texas, from Mexico."

"Perhaps someone intercepted the letters for some reason. But I assure you, it would not have been any of us. You should know us better, Brother Mitchell."

Chase scrambled to think why none of the letters had reached Lilly. He studied Catheryn's eyes, wishing she were lying. "But . . . even if she didn't get any letters, the fact remains she married your brother only eight months after I left. That doesn't make any sense, Mrs. Guest. She loved me. I know she loved me."

Catheryn quickly realized why Hiram had told him eight months instead of only barely four. She put a hand on his arm. "I'm sorry, Brother Mitchell. I'm sure she thought she loved you and that you loved her. But perhaps, knowing we were going on such a difficult journey into the wilderness, and not hearing from you at all . . . I don't know. Perhaps it all just frightened her. Maybe she thought you would never find her. My brother is a good, good man, Brother Mitchell. He loves her very much and is good to her, I assure you. He won't take any other wives, like some of the others. He wants only Lilly. Who can tell what goes through a young girl's mind? Lilly was very confused and lonely, you know, after you left. She was in a new country, and maybe circumstances convinced her you were just being fanciful with her and that she could not really depend on you. I wish I could give you a better answer, but I can't, except that she never received any letters."

Chase turned around, but Catheryn had already caught the tears in his eyes. "Then, I'll get an answer from the horse's mouth," he told her. "I already know she's somewhere in Nevada. It probably won't be hard to find her. You Mormons have a way of standing out wherever you go."

Catheryn's heart quickened with dread. "No! You mustn't go to her!" she told him.

"I have a right!" he told her, turning back to face her. "I suffered some terrible wounds in Mexico, and the thought of coming back to Lilly was all that kept me alive—the only reason I learned to walk and talk again. You have no idea what I suffered, Mrs. Guest—no idea!"

She studied him with kind eyes. "There are all kinds of suffering, Brother Mitchell. You lost something you only hoped to have." Her eyes teared. "I lost a child coming here. I'll never even be able to visit her grave. I probably wouldn't even be able to find it again. I understand suffering, Brother Mitchell."

Chase's anger subsided at the stricken look on Catheryn's face. He turned away, running a hand through his hair. "I'm sorry. Hiram told me."

"And I'm sorry for you, Brother Mitchell. I truly am. But you have to remember how young Lilly was. So much time has passed now—she's nearly twenty. Little Joey is—" She hesitated, realizing she must be careful about Joey's age. "Let me see. He must be about eighteen months now. For all any of us knows, Lilly could be with child again. Please, Brother Mitchell, don't interfere in her life now. What you and Lilly had was such a long time ago—and so short-lived."

"It's because your brother is a Mormon, isn't it? Lilly took the Mormon faith and felt she had to marry a Mormon man, rather than a Gentile."

Catheryn was grasping for any excuse she could find.

Chase had just provided her with one. "Yes," she answered, hoping God wouldn't be too angry with her for the lie, for trying to save Lilly's marriage. She didn't want Zeb to be hurt—or poor little Joey. He thought of Zeb as his father. She realized she must do whatever she could to protect him. "That's part of it. She's happy with us, Chase. If the two of you had known each other longer, perhaps it would have meant more—"

"Meant more?" He spoke the words sadly. "It couldn't have meant more to me, Mrs. Guest. You have no idea. You don't know what we had together in that short time. And I find it hard to believe a woman like Lilly would have taken it so lightly."

"Not lightly, Brother Mitchell. Lilly is a good woman. But she was hardly more than a girl when you knew her. After you left, I think something just broke inside of her. When you didn't write. . . . Too many things happened to her at once, I suppose. I'm so terribly sorry. Please don't destroy her life now—her marriage, her peace of mind. She's been through so much."

"So have I, Mrs. Guest." He put on his hat. "Thank you for your time."

"What will you do, Brother Mitchell?"

He mounted his horse. "I don't know," he answered.

"You won't go and see her, will you? Please don't, Brother Mitchell."

"I'll decide on my way to Nevada," he answered, turning his horse. He rode away, and Catheryn put a hand to her chest. "Dear Lord," she said quietly, trembling with dread, "please don't let him see the boy. Don't let him destroy my brother's marriage." If only she could have explained to Brother Mitchell the real reason for the marriage, he wouldn't be so terribly hurt. She pitied him, but she pitied Lilly and Zeb more.

The work never ended. Sometimes Lilly thought she could not possibly lift another rock, or carry another bucket of water, or churn another ounce of butter. She picked up a sack of lima beans, which she had spent two hours collecting. Now she would have to go back to the house and open each pod to get out the beans. That would take until well past dark. It had been an especially hard day, but she knew her aching tiredness was not just from the hard work. She suspected she was pregnant again.

Finally. She had wanted so much to give Zeb a child of his own. Now, maybe, it would happen. Perhaps after this she could use the excuse of the new baby, and later, the excuse that she was afraid of another pregnancy, to limit Zeb's advances even more. She had never really enjoyed her sexual encounters with Zeb, no matter how hard she tried, and she was too afraid of hurting him to tell him what he was doing wrong—or not doing at all. She was simply re-signed to what must be, and when she saw her Joey so happy, felt his love when he put his little arms around her, it was all worth it.

The boy ran up to her then, grinning, his dark curls bouncing. "What this, mommy?" he asked, poking at the cloth sack.

"Lima beans," she answered. "You can help mommy pick them out of the pods."

Joey jumped up and down with joy as they headed toward the temporary log cabin Zeb had built for them. Lilly had almost reached the door when she turned and noticed a rider, sitting alone on top of a distant hill. She stopped to stare at him, a small shadow on the horizon. A strange chill moved through her as she shaded her eyes.

"Who that, mommy?" Joey asked.

For some reason Lilly couldn't speak.

The rider then turned his horse and disappeared down the other side of the foothill. Lilly waited, but he did not return. Just another man who sat on his horse like Chase Mitchell once did. She'd noticed a few over the years. A sudden, unexplainable heaviness filled her. She set the beans down and pulled Joey close. She burst into tears thinking it was only because she was so tired, and probably pregnant.

On the far side of the hill Chase Mitchell rode on. He had come so close to riding into the valley below and searching for Lilly. But if she was there, she was not the same Lilly

Brannigan he had known back in Illinois. There was nothing
here for him now. No matter how much he thought he hated
her, he could not bring himself to interrupt her life; nor
could he bear the thought of seeing her again and not being
able to have her. The memory was dimming. He might as
well leave it that way. He headed for California.

Chapter Twenty-one

1850

A cold, saturating November rain fell, which poured off
the pine and tar roof of the little one-room cabin that sat in
the distance, and turned the little stream that flowed through
the valley into a near river. Lilly felt it penetrating her
woolen coat—one that had belonged to Laura.

This time of year the land was dead. And now, so was
Lilly's heart—just like her stillborn baby. She stood alone at
the little grave, already ten days old. She had been too sick
to attend her little daughter's funeral. The baby had come
early—far too early to have any hope of surviving. Lilly
wondered how miscarrying could be so much more physically painful than having a full-term baby. She had lost so
much blood that Zeb had thought she would die, and this
was the first day she had felt strong enough to go outside.
She had done so against Zeb's pleas that she not go out in
the rain after being so sick. But she could not bear to go
another day without visiting the grave.

She pulled up the collar of her coat and stood close beside
the huge pine that guarded little Laura, the name she had
chosen for the tiny daughter she would never see now. The
baby had lived only twenty minutes.

Zeb had chosen the knoll under the giant ponderosa pine
for burying their baby girl because it was Lilly's favorite
spot.

The agony of her loss moved through Lilly in great waves of horror. There were moments when she felt she could live as normally as she always had; and then the terrible grief would hit her again. Now she knew how it felt to lose a child. And she knew that if it was this painful to lose a baby she had never even held, it must be worse to lose a child a woman has already held to her breast, nurtured, cared for, loved.

Now she wondered more than ever how Catheryn had managed to stay sane after burying baby Marian, and she knew the woman's only consolation must have been that she had other children. At this moment, Lilly could not have loved Joey more. Thank God she still had her precious son. The little boy had seemed to sense his mother's loss and sorrow, for he had been especially good and quiet the last few days, often climbing onto his mother's bed and lying down beside her, cuddling up against her shoulder.

Joey was more important now than ever. He would be three years old in two months. No sweeter, more obedient, more beautiful child existed, as far as his mother was concerned. More and more, he was becoming the center of her world. For a while, when she had been carrying baby Laura, she had seen a chance for real happiness. She had felt new life in her belly—Zeb's life. She had been so excited about having a child for him. And she was sure that it would give her something that would help her love him the way she should—something that would bring them physically closer.

Now, that hope was gone. She had been so sick and delirious after the child had been born that she had not even set eyes on her. Never seeing her, never holding her, had left the most horrible emptiness she had ever experienced. Never had she known this kind of grief, this kind of physical pain from loss. If only she could see her face—just for a moment—even though the baby was dead. It seemed so important to see her. What color was her hair? What color would her eyes have been?

Tears engulfed her. She knelt beside the grave, hardly aware of the big, cold raindrops that pelted her like stones. It didn't seem right that such a tiny piece of life should be buried under the earth, never having known its mother. She began to dig at the little grave, furious with God for always taking things away from her. This wasn't fair to poor Zeb. She loved Joey more than her own life, but why had her child by a man who had deserted her lived to be so healthy and strong, while the child she had conceived legally, by a man who was so devoted to her, died? Life's twisted realities seemed so unfair.

She dug wildly into the fresh dirt, her nails quickly blackening and her tears running freely. She wished she could dig them all up—her mother, Laura, little Marian, the little baby girl she had never seen. If only she had a little face to remember, a little snip of hair. . . .

Suddenly, strong hands grasped her wrists. "Stop it, Lilly!" Zeb pulled her away, but Lilly fought him. Zeb kept hold of her, pinning her arms down as he held her from behind. "Don't do this to yourself, Lilly!"

"It's not fair! It's not fair!" she screamed. "I have to see her face! Why didn't you . . . wait!"

"My God, Lilly, you know she had to be buried." He held her tightly, his own voice shaking. "There will be more, Lilly. We'll have more. It's hard for me, too. I had to bury her alone—my first child." His voice broke. She stopped fighting him. In the next moment she heard his sobs. She closed her eyes and leaned her head against his chest.

"Oh, Zeb," she groaned. "I have failed you in all the worst ways. I'm so sorry."

It was several minutes before he could speak. "You haven't failed me, Lilly," he said wearily. "You've been a good wife to me. You tried to give me a child. For some reason, God saw fit to take our daughter. You can't be blamed for that. Something must have been wrong. Come on, now. Come inside. You aren't even well yet."

Lilly stared at the grave a moment longer. "Don't let anything happen to Joey, Zeb," she sobbed. "If I lost Joey . . ."

"Joey will be fine. And in no time at all, he'll have lots of brothers and sisters. You'll see. But, not for a while—not after what you've been through. You need a good, long rest. With winter coming on, there won't be so much work." He kept a tight hold on her. "If this is anybody's fault, Lilly, it's mine—for bringing you here. You worked so hard all summer. We should have stayed in Salt Lake."

"Who can say?" she almost groaned. "When I was pregnant with Joey, I walked halfway across the country, but he was born healthy." She breathed deeply, her body shaking from sobs. "I just wanted to see her face, Zeb."

He slowly let go of her, but kept his arm around her as they stood looking at the grave. "Just picture the prettiest baby girl you can imagine. Her hair was fuzzy, kind of red. I don't know about her eyes—they never opened. She was so . . . so little, Lilly. I've never seen anything like that. She was all formed—just too little for her lungs to work right, I guess. She must have had something wrong with her that you couldn't see, because she looked perfect. Someday, when you and I go to the Lord ourselves, we'll finally get to see her. You'll know her right away—I promise you that."

He reached into his pants pocket and pulled out a piece of cloth tied with ribbon. "Here." He took hold of her hand and put it into her palm. "Don't try to look at it until we get to the house, or it will get wet."

Lilly looked up at him. He had already lost weight from a long summer of hard work. She suddenly felt selfish for thinking she was the only one grieving. "What is it?" she asked.

"It's some of her hair. I . . . wasn't sure when or if it would be right to give it to you, but I think this is a good time. Maybe it will help—for not being able to see her."

Lilly closed her fist around the piece of cloth, then placed her face against his chest and hugged him. "Oh, Zeb, thank you."

He sighed deeply, and ran his hand over her back. "Please come back to the house now, Lilly. Joey was sleeping when I left, but he might be awake now."

He led her away from the little grave. Lilly's legs felt like rubber as she walked with him, clinging to the tuft of hair—her only link to the daughter she would never see or know. Her vow to stay here in Nevada was even more important to her now. She would never go away and leave behind her baby's grave, the way other Mormon women had been forced to do. She thought of all those little graves out there somewhere, alone. Some of the markers were probably gone now. It brought new tears as Zeb led her inside the cabin, where Joey still lay asleep on his little straw bed.

Lilly removed her wet coat and hat and sat down beside her son, smiling through tears at how sweet he looked when he was sleeping. Zeb came and put a robe around her shoulders.

"You had better go back to bed, Lilly."

She nodded, looking down at the piece of cloth in her palm. She opened it with a shaking hand. She gently touched the thin, fluffy red hairs inside the cloth, and suddenly she could imagine her baby's tiny face—somehow knew that her daughter's eyes had been gray, like Zeb's. She carefully retied the cloth and walked over to a small trunk in the corner of the room—one given to her by Catheryn. She opened it and placed the cloth into a leather bag, which also held the Indian bear-claw necklace. They were now her two most prized possessions. Someday, when he was older, she would show them to Joey. She would tell him about their journey west, and about his little sister, but not that little Laura would have been his half-sister, if she had lived.

That first winter passed in lonely quietude. Joey brought the only joy and activity inside the Adams house. His zestful youth was unaffected by family loss or weather or loneliness. It took only a tin cup and a spoon, or a fluffy snowfall, or a handful of squishy bread dough to keep the boy occupied. He tried to help his mother pat out pie crusts and worked as hard as his little arms and legs could to help his father feed the animals and clean out the stalls of the shed Zeb had built for his horses and milk cows. Lilly wondered sometimes how she would stand the long winters, if not for her son.

Frieda Dutch visited as often as possible. When she did, she and Lilly would sew and bake and gossip. But Frieda had her own family and chores, and sometimes the snow fell so deep that it was impossible to travel. The Dutches lived in the Sierra foothills, where they helped two other families run a sawmill. The rest of the Mormons were scattered to the south, all the way into the Carson Valley, where a small town called Carson City was developing as a supply post for easterners who still poured through Nevada on their way to California.

Few people came through the Washoe Valley, and the empty feeling Lilly had was growing worse. She often wondered what was happening in the rest of the world, and if the story Zeb had heard from a man at the sawmill was true—that thousands of men, and even women and families, had poured into California looking for gold. She could not help wondering if Chase Mitchell might have been one of them. Did he ever think about her? Had he ever tried to find her? Apparently not. All he would have had to do was visit Salt Lake, and he would have found out where she was.

Still, she was often strangely haunted by the memory of the lone rider she had seen on the distant foothill the year before. Maybe it had been Chase. Something about that brief sighting had stayed with her, and had strangely affected her mood. Sometimes she wondered if losing her baby had been punishment for her continued thoughts of him, when it was Zeb to whom she should have been giving all her attention.

Lilly had continued to abstain from lovemaking with Zeb ever since the baby had died. It seemed to her that what little desire she had managed to arouse within herself to be intimate with him had left her completely, as though she had no strength left to face the truth of her loveless half of the marriage. To lie with Zeb again meant facing her awful unhappiness at being married to a man she had never wanted that way. And it could mean getting pregnant again—something that terrified her now. What if she lost another baby? She could not bear the thought of another little grave. She realized that Zeb felt the loss, too, and feared the same consequences—or perhaps simply sensed he was not wanted. Zeb had not asked her to come to their own bed since Lilly had begun sleeping with Joey, and she did not offer.

Lilly put all her energy into helping with chores the following spring. Warm sunshine seemed to strengthen her physically, and Zeb's spirits improved. He loved to farm and was always happiest when he could get out and work with the soil again. Lilly worked by his side—plowing, planting, and feeding the animals. She was almost glad for the endless work. It helped distract her from their lack of intimacy, and kept them both too tired to care.

Lilly's most enjoyable diversion from the hard work and inner loneliness was going to the sawmill, where she could visit with Frieda Dutch. Lilly looked forward to the rare opportunity of being around other women. In late summer, when Zeb decided to build a frame house for his family, the trips became more frequent. On one occasion, they held their own worship service with Frieda and the other families, and followed it with a picnic. As three-year-old Joey ran and played with the other children, Frieda talked to Lilly.

"He is so beautiful, Lilly. Such eyes! I try to decide who he looks like, but he doesn't take after either one of you."

The old pain moved through Lilly's heart, along with the tiny panic she always felt when she feared someone would learn the truth about her son.

"That's the way it is sometimes," she answered, trying to sound casual. "My father had dark hair and blue eyes."

"Oh, I see. I know what you mean. My Martha doesn't look like me or my husband either." She touched Lilly's arm. "Is Zeb teaching Joey about our faith?"

"He reads to him from the Book of Mormon, but he's promised to wait until Joey is twelve before pressing him to decide about his religious life."

"I don't understand, Lilly. After marrying Zeb, why haven't you embraced our faith?"

Lilly stiffened. How could she explain the lingering resentment she had for the Mormons, after so many of them had been so good to her? How could she explain the trapped feeling she had always had—the odd fear of somehow losing herself and what little independence she possessed—when she thought about becoming a Saint? Women like Frieda didn't seem to understand.

"I'm not sure," she answered. "It's just that I have my own faith, Frieda, and I think Joey should have a right to choose *his* own faith."

Frieda shook her head. "You have always been so determined to do things your way, haven't you? I remember when that young Gentile man got hurt after you went walking with him, against Brother Hiram's wishes." She laughed lightly. "Poor Hiram had a time with you, didn't he?"

Lilly's heart pounded harder. "Yes, I . . . I suppose he did." She faced Frieda, eager to change the subject. "Frieda, Zeb read to us from the Book of Mormon, and we had a prayer, but there was no singing. Why don't we sing a few hymns?"

"Oh, yes, that would be wonderful! Zeb is so lucky having your voice all to himself. I hope we can start building a chapel somewhere closer soon. We got a visit a few days ago from some men from Salt Lake City, and they tell us it might not be long before they send us a preacher." Frieda called over her husband, who had been standing near the water wheel with Zeb. "Jake, tell Lilly and Zeb what those men told us the other day about Salt Lake."

The man grinned. "I was just telling Brother Zeb," he said, walking closer. "Oh, how I'd love to see it. They say Salt Lake is growing very fast. Thousands more come every year, and the temple they are building is grander than any we have built yet." The man's eyes actually teared. "We'll go back someday, Frieda—I promise you that. New people will be sent to replace us, and we will go back to Zion."

Lilly glanced at Zeb. She could see the longing in his eyes to return to the city of Saints, and it pained her heart to feel as though she was denying him happiness.

"Lilly has promised to lead us in some hymns," Frieda told her husband.

"Ah, it will be a joy to our ears to hear your voice, Sister Lilly," Jake Dutch said. "Come! Come! I will call everyone together."

Zeb smiled faintly. Lilly thought she saw something more than a longing to return to Salt Lake in his eyes. He seemed disturbed, and showed a lack of enthusiasm as he joined the others in the hymn singing. After a few songs, everyone wanted to hear Lilly. It had been a long time since she had sung for others; she had lost her desire, grieving over Laura. She began to sing softly.

We'll find the place which God for us prepared,
Far away in the west.
Where none shall come to hurt or make afraid;
There the Saints will be blessed.
We'll make the air with music ring.
Shout praises to our God and King;
Above the rest these words we'll tell
All is well! All is well!

But all was not well in her soul, and Lilly knew it never would be. Her voice choked, and she suddenly could not go on.

"Oh, Lilly, we didn't mean for you to get upset," Frieda said soothingly, putting her arm around her.

"It's just . . . losing the baby . . . everything," Lilly answered. She wondered how much more loneliness she would be able to bear—how long she could keep going without baring her soul to someone. Zeb was the only one who knew, who truly understood, but she seldom shared any of her sorrow with him openly. How could she tell him he was part of the reason for her unhappiness—that Chase Mitchell was still first in her heart, in spite of what he had done to her?

"Maybe we had better head home," Zeb spoke up.

"No! No, I don't want to spoil things," Lilly told him, taking a handkerchief from the waist of her skirt and wiping at her eyes. "I'll be all right in a moment." She took a deep breath and held up her chin. "Let's finish the song together."

She soon had all of them singing again, except Zeb, who had walked several feet away and stood watching from under a ponderosa pine. After the songs were finished, he insisted they leave before it got too dark. Lilly reluctantly said goodbye to Frieda and they headed back to the lonely farm in the vast Washoe Valley.

After little Joey had fallen asleep in his mother's lap, Lilly looked over at Zeb.

"What's wrong? Is it all the talk about Salt Lake?"

He stared straight ahead as he slowed the team and halted the wagon. He finally met her eyes; his own were filled with some kind of terrible hurt. "That's just part of it. I made you a promise not to leave here, and we won't. I'm building you a house, Lilly. That should tell you I mean to stay."

She studied the gray eyes that never had held anything but love for her before. Now, she wasn't sure what she saw there. She looked down at Joey. "You resent me for keeping you here, don't you?" She looked back up at him. "I don't care, Zeb. I'm not leaving."

"It isn't that." He sighed deeply, turning to stare out at the valley again. "Jake gave me a message from those Mormon visitors. He didn't understand it, but I did."

Lilly frowned. "What was it?"

He met her eyes again. "They said to ask us if we had had any unusual visitors last year. Hiram wanted to know. Hiram didn't explain—he just said we'd understand if this visitor had come. He wants us to write and let him know how things are with us."

Lilly held Joey closer. Zeb removed his hat and ran a hand through his hair. "He must have gone to Salt Lake, Lilly. He must have come back asking about you."

Lilly's heart pounded with a mixture of dread and joy. Had Chase truly come looking for her? Was there an explanation, after all? She looked down at Joey, her eyes tearing.

"I'm telling you right now, Lilly—that man had better not come here and try to take my wife or my son away from me. I love Joey like he was my own, and I love you. I know things aren't the best between us, but I love you as much as any man can love a woman."

Lilly looked at him, overwhelmed by his devotion, and by the tears in his eyes.

"I expect if he meant to come here and make trouble, he would have done it by now," he told her. "But he doesn't deserve his son, after what he did. And if he comes here, I'd soon forget my Mormon teachings to be forgiving of Gentiles. I can't forgive what he did to you, and I couldn't forgive him if he came here thinking he could just pick up where he had left off with my wife."

"You wouldn't have to worry about it, Zeb. I'm your wife. That's all that matters now."

"Is it? If he came here, what would you do?"

She straightened more, fire coming into her eyes. "I would be true to my wedding vows," she told him. "We made an agreement when we first married, Zeb. You know how I felt then, but things are different now. I've given myself to you physically, and Joey thinks of you as his father. I would never, never take Joey away from you, and you know how I feel about him finding out the truth. It will never happen as long as I'm alive, and I will never leave you!"

His eyes seemed to soften. "You really mean that?"

"You know how I am once I make up my mind. I didn't love you when I married you, Zeb, but I have learned to—more than I ever thought I could." She turned away. "Now, let's go home. And when you build our house, finish the bedroom first, and put a door on it so we can close it off. Joey is getting too big to be in the same room with us."

Zeb frowned at first, then suddenly grinned. "So *that's* the reason you've been staying away from me," he said then. "I was afraid you had decided you didn't want any more babies, or you didn't want me anymore."

She drew on all her reserve of strength to keep from showing the intense agony she felt.

"It wasn't that I didn't want you," she told him. "At first, it was my grief over losing the baby. But now Joey is getting so big." She put a hand on his arm. "I do love you, Zeb."

He put a big hand over her own. "I didn't mean to be so angry. I just got scared, I guess, thinking he might come for you."

"He has no right coming for me. And if he meant to, he would have by now. I'm sure Hiram came up with some kind of explanation to keep him from finding out about Joey."

He squeezed her hand, his eyes lighting up like a little boy. "You really want me to finish the bedroom first?"

Lilly reddened and looked away. He was so easy to please. "Yes," she lied.

He whipped the team into motion. "I'd better get started, then."

The wagon bounced over the rough terrain, and Lilly's

heart felt as heavy as the rocks below. Chase! How could she still love a man who had treated her so cruelly? Why had he come, after all this time? Had he been the man who had watched her from the ridge? She leaned down and kissed Joey's dark hair.

Chapter Twenty-two

The years flowed by with monotonous regularity—plant in the spring; pull weeds and keep working up the soil all summer; harvest in autumn; and spend winter enclosed like bears in hibernation. Zeb tried several different crops—corn, wheat, potatoes, beans. At times he met with success, but just barely enough to make a decent living. There seemed to be more bad years than good. There was either not enough water or too much. The soil was never cooperative, and grasshoppers feasted on the crops two summers in a row, reducing them beyond profitable measure. Harvest time meant drying and preserving, disking up fields, and long absences for Zeb, who had to take his produce to market either in Carson City to the south, or Washoe City to the north.

Lilly enjoyed her small frame house, which Zeb had slowly furnished with items he bought in Carson City or ordered from Mormon visitors, who would bring them to him the next year. Nothing in the house was fancy, but it was the nicest home Lilly had ever had, and she made the best of it. In spite of the hard work she put in helping Zeb with the farm, she managed to keep her home immaculate. A constant nervous energy inside her made her want to occupy every waking moment. She knew deep down it was simply her way of living with her unhappiness, of keeping so busy that there was no time to think about how empty her life was, in spite of her lovely home and her devoted husband.

Joey remained her only real joy. A school was built in Carson City, but Lilly refused to allow Joey to attend because he would have had to stay with another family part of the year. Instead, she and Zeb taught him themselves. Zeb collected books from Carson City, and from the Mormons who came from Salt Lake, so Lilly did not doubt that her son was as well or even better educated than children who were attending school.

Joey was still all they had. Years of forcing herself to be a wife to Zeb had produced no more children. It was a source of great sorrow for Lilly, and she knew it was a terrible disappointment for Zeb, but he never said a word. He kept a joyful attitude, and was a good father to Joey.

As the years went by, Lilly began to wonder if maybe Zeb didn't even desire her anymore. She sometimes studied her plain, tired face in the old mirror over the large oak dresser Zeb had bought for her in Carson City, and wondered what had happened to the young Lilly Brannigan who had come to America from Scotland with so many dreams.

After eight years of working hard under the harsh Nevada sun, and living a lie, it seemed that none of the old Lilly remained. She had long ago stopped singing, and realized one day with an almost shocking sadness that she could not remember the last time she had sung. The Mormons in Carson Valley had built a lovely church, but it was too far for them to go more than once a month to a service, and even then they could only go in good weather. When they did attend, Lilly sang only halfheartedly. All the old dreams of being a famous singer were gone; and there was not enough happiness in her heart for her to sing with the zest and beauty that had once graced her voice.

There were still times, deep in the night, when Lilly thought about Chase Mitchell. Neither she nor Zeb had ever brought up his name again after discussing the possibility that he had visited Hiram. He had never shown up in the Washoe Valley. Their love affair seemed almost unreal now, like a distant dream—something that had happened to someone else in another time.

Joey, now ten-and-a-half years old, was a hard-working young man. It was obvious he would have his real father's tall, strong build. He was bright and devoted to his parents. But already Lilly could see he was beginning to stretch his wings, to feel manhood moving in on him. And the older he got, the more Lilly could see Chase, in his dark, wavy hair, his handsome face, and his intense blue eyes. It was a constant source of pain for Lilly. She was glad now that they had come to Nevada. Anyone back in Salt Lake who had known Chase would surely suspect Joey's parentage.

Lilly corresponded regularly with Hiram and Mary. There were times when she thought how nice it would be to see them all again—the Williams family, Catheryn and Henry, and all the children. Catheryn had given birth to three more children, whom Lilly and Zeb had never seen. Lilly knew how badly Zeb wanted to go back himself and see his sister.

But both Lilly and Zeb knew that the older Joey got, the more important it was to stay away from Salt Lake. What Lilly feared most was not that people would find out Joey's real heritage, but that Joey might discover that Zeb was not his father. He would ask questions. He would not understand, and might grow to hate her or look upon her with scorn. He might not love Zeb the same as he did now, and he would ask questions about his real father, and feel unloved and unwanted because Chase had never come back. She could not let anything like that happen to her Joey, nor could she let anything come between them.

The news came by way of messengers in the summer of 1857. Brigham Young was ordering all Mormons back to Salt Lake. Lilly stood kneading bread while Zeb sat at the table listening to Hubert Rotter and James English explaining the alarming situation.

"The President has declared the government of Utah Territory to be in rebellion against the United States," Hubert explained. "Apostates have been feeding lies to people in Washington, telling them we don't allow federal representatives to perform their duties in Salt Lake, that we have destroyed federal records."

"They say we're fanatics," James put in, a sad note to his voice. "They say we keep harems, and that we're planning to establish our own country here—to claim the entire western half of America for ourselves."

"Brother Young set up a very efficient mail delivery business all across the plains," Hubert added. "We had high hopes of getting federal aid. Brother Young expected we could contract with the government to carry mail from St. Louis all the way to California, but all of that came to naught."

"What does that have to do with our going back to Salt Lake?" Zeb asked, glancing at Lilly. He knew his wife would never go. "Why should we have to leave everything we have built here? I promised my wife she would never have to make that trip. We have a daughter buried on this land, and this is home to us now."

Hubert glanced at Lilly, and saw her lingering beauty, in spite of her years of hard work in the Nevada sun. He looked back at Zeb. "I understand how you feel, Brother Adams, but we are in great danger, and Brother Young needs every man who can bear arms. We have learned that President Buchanan plans to send a whole army against us. The government intends to seize Salt Lake and all of Utah and put down our supposed revolt."

Zeb frowned in dismay. Seize Salt Lake! The Mormons had done absolutely nothing wrong, and they were as patriotic as any other Americans. Hadn't they proven that when they had sent their best young men to march to California with Kearny?

"That's ridiculous!" Zeb exclaimed.

"Of course it's ridiculous," James answered. "But it's the truth, Zeb. You can understand Brother Young's concern. He doesn't want us to be too scattered right now. This venture here in Nevada hasn't really worked out all that well, anyway. You have to admit there has been little success or profit here. Our settlements in California have done better. I'm not saying you would never be able to come back here, but you might discover—"

"I'm not leaving Nevada!" Lilly spoke up then, surprising them with the determination and defiance in her voice. Hubert and James looked at her, with total astonishment on their faces. If not for the seriousness of their request, Lilly would have laughed at their wide eyes and open mouths. "I will not leave my baby's grave, or the only real home I have ever had," she added firmly, looking straight at Zeb. "I am sorry for what is happening to the Mormons, but I am not a Mormon myself, and I hardly think the presence or absence of one man is going to make a difference in any war the Mormon community might have with the federal government."

Joey sat at the table with the men, listening excitedly, ready to go and fight with his father, unsure whether or not he was to consider himself a Mormon. He believed in God and said prayers at the table every night with his mother and father, but he did not attend the Mormon church regularly, and had not yet been baptized into the Mormon faith, although Zeb had taught him faithfully from the Book of Mormon. Joey wondered now at the strange, almost frightened look he saw on his mother's face. Leaving Nevada wasn't the end of the world—they could always come back. And Joey liked the sound of the adventure of such a journey, and of seeing Salt Lake City.

Zeb gave Lilly a chastising look, more because of the presense of the two Mormon men than because he was truly angry with her. He looked at Hubert. "I'll discuss this with my wife after you're gone," he told him. "You can see she is obviously upset. Our journey here was difficult. You can understand why she never wants to climb into a wagon again and disrupt a solid home life."

"Of course." Hubert looked suddenly nervous and upset. He was not accustomed to hearing a woman speak up so boldly, and he was embarrassed for Zeb. "We'll leave it up to you. But we have been told you are a devoted Mormon, Brother Adams. That is why you came out here in the first place. You know how important it is to put the faith above all things."

Zeb nodded. "I know. Thank you for coming. Whatever happens, I pray all will go well for our brothers and sisters

in Salt Lake. And please give our love to my sister, Catheryn Guest, and her family, and to Hiram and Mary Williams."

"We most certainly will."

The two men rose and walked to the door. James turned
and looked at Zeb before leaving. "We'll be forming a
wagon train at Carson City in one week. So far, everyone
has agreed to go back. We hope you will be among us,
Brother Adams." The man glanced at Lilly disparagingly,
then walked out.

Zeb closed the door gently and turned to face Lilly. She
knew that look—the one that had been on his face when he
told her he had to join the volunteers for the Mexican War;
and when he told her they would have to move to Nevada.

"You made me a promise," she told him, holding his eyes
squarely. "I won't leave, Zeb. If you want to go to Salt
Lake, you'll have to go alone."

"No!" Joey spoke up. He got up from his chair. "I want to
go with Pa."

Lilly looked at his impassioned face, then turned to Zeb.
"Please, Zeb! You know why we can't go back there!"

"How come?" Joey asked, pouting. "I want to see it. I
don't remember what it looks like. I was too little when we
came here."

"Joey, go outside," Zeb ordered the boy. "This is between
your mother and me."

After the boy sighed impatiently and walked out, Zeb
stared at Lilly. "They need our help, Lilly."

"You've done all you need to do. Thousands of new converts flow into Salt Lake every year. One man isn't going to
make any difference. And you know good and well that the
moment Mary sets eyes on Joey, she'll know the truth."

"I don't doubt she already knows, Lilly."

"I don't care. I do not intend to take the chance that my
son will find out the truth, and I will not leave Laura's
grave." Her eyes teared. "You promised, Zeb. I stayed with
you. I learned to love you, partly because you're a man of
your word. I know I've failed you by not giving you a child
of your own, but don't punish me by making me leave
here."

Zeb frowned, walking closer. "Punish you? Is that what you think this is—a punishment?"

A tear slipped down her cheek. "You could have chosen a better wife—one who could have made you much happier, given you children. I swear, I wanted that as much as you."

He shook his head. "I know that, Lilly. I don't blame you for it. I've been happy with you—proud to call you my wife. And you know how I feel about Joey."

"Then, keep your promise not to go back to Salt Lake. It's for Joey, as much as it is for me. I know how much your faith means to you, but you've proven your loyalty enough. You don't need to go back. The Mormons are a forgiving people. They'll understand."

He sighed, then leaned forward to kiss her forehead. "You're probably right. One man won't make much difference."

She rested her head against his chest, and hugged him around the middle. "Thank you, Zeb. I get so scared that he'll find out."

He held her, wondering what his life might have been like if he had not chosen Lilly Brannigan to love. But he did love her, even though he had known all these years that she didn't really love him the same. That made no difference to him. She was his wife, and that was all that mattered. She had followed him out here, had given herself to him in the night, had nearly died trying to give him a child.

"I know," he answered. "We'll stay, Lilly. We'll stay."

For three nights Lilly lay sleepless, wondering if she was being unfair to insist that Zeb stay in Nevada. Perhaps Joey would be better off back in Salt Lake. Farming here was difficult, sometimes impossible, and usually not profitable. There was really nothing else here for anyone except wilderness. The only people who came here besides to visit Mormons were people passing through on their way to California or, now and again, a trapper or a trader.

Still, this past summer, a few men had filtered into the Washoe and Carson Valley area, mostly in the Virginia Mountains to the east of Washoe Lake, where they hoped to find gold. The California gold hills were already so saturated with miners that there was hardly a place left for anyone new to stake a claim and dig. Now men were hoping gold could be found in the Sierras and surrounding mountain ranges. Lilly and Zeb both thought them crazy, but the miners stayed in the mountains and bothered no one, and they had become a new source of income, often stopping by the Mormon farms in the valley to buy food. It helped keep Zeb from having to go all the way to Washoe City or Carson City to sell his produce, which was good, since there usually was hardly enough to bother making the trip.

Lilly lay staring into the darkness, weighing the advantages and disadvantages of staying in Nevada. If she had been able to give Zeb a child, she would have felt less guilty for refusing to go back to Salt Lake.

A wolf howled somewhere in the distant hills. Lilly often found the sound soothing, for the wolves' wails seemed to echo her own need to cry out in her unhappiness. She realized that whether she was in Nevada or in Utah, she still would not be happy. She turned toward Zeb, touching his arm, and he drew her close.

"You can't sleep, either?" he asked.

"No. I keep thinking about Salt Lake."

"Don't worry about it. I said we'll stay. Washoe City and Carson City are both building up with Gentiles. They won't fold when the Mormons leave. With more and more men coming into the area to look for gold, we'll do okay, Lilly." He sat up. "Actually, it wasn't the thought of Salt Lake that was keeping me awake. It was those wolves," he told her. "I found the ripped-up carcass of a deer this morning along the north fence. I'm worried about the stock—especially that pig we're counting on to keep us in pork this winter. Jake Dutch lost a horse to wolves last week."

Lilly frowned with concern. "You should have told me."

"I didn't want to worry you."

Zeb started to lie back down, then heard barking and howling closer to the house. He sat up again. "I think we've got a problem."

He had barely gotten the words out before a horse whinnied and pigs began to snort and squeal. Zeb jumped up and quickly felt for his pants that hung over the bed rail. Lilly lit a lamp.

"Zeb, what are you going to do?"

"I'm going to teach those wolves a lesson," he answered, buttoning his pants. He walked to the corner of the room and pulled on his boots. The summer night was warm, and Zeb hitched his suspenders up over his bare shoulders. "No time to bother with a shirt," he added, grabbing his rifle.

"Zeb, don't go out there!"

"Got no choice. Don't worry, Lilly. I've got this new repeating rifle. If the first shot doesn't get what I'm after, the second one will. You stay inside and keep Joey in here."

He hurried out, and Lilly followed. They both practically tripped over Joey, who had heard the ruckus and was already out of his room, his blue eyes wide with excitement.

"What is it, Pa?"

"A wolf, I think. You stay inside, Joey."

"Let me go with you and see, Pa!"

"No. Do like I say and stay in here with your mother."

Joey frowned with discontent while his father hurried out the door. Lilly went to a window and looked at the full moon. After a moment of letting his eyes adjust, she figured, Zeb would be able to see well enough to tell a wolf from the other animals. She waited, her heart pounding. Joey started to talk, but she told him to be still. The boy ran to one window and Lilly stood at another.

"Will Pa be okay?" the boy asked in a near whisper.

"I'm sure he will, Joey. He has that new repeating rifle."

Lilly prayed she was right. The ruckus outside continued. Lilly heard a gunshot, then a squeal. Zeb must have gotten one of the wolves. She could hear him yelling then, trying to scare off more. She peered through the window to see him running about in the moonlight, shooting the gun to scare away the rest of the pack. Then she saw him fall.

She waited for him to get up, but he did not. Everything outside quieted, and still Zeb did not rise. A cold horror began to creep through Lilly's blood.

Lilly rushed to the door with the lantern. "Stay here, Joey."

"But, I want—"

"Stay inside!" Lilly told him frantically. "Do as I say!" She rushed out, grabbing a pitchfork that stood against the side of the house, afraid wolves might still be lurking about. She hurried toward the place where she had seen Zeb fall. "Zeb!" she cried. "Zeb, answer me!"

She reached him and held the lamp closer, then froze in horror. Her husband's hand still gripped his rifle. His head was turned sideways, his gray eyes open in a stare that could only mean death. His body lay across a low stump over which he had fallen after tripping. Lilly saw an axe handle sticking out from the stump, and remembered that just that morning, Zeb had left a double-edged axe wedged in the stump. He had worked hard the day before sharpening it so he could split wood more easily.

"Zeb," she squeaked in a near whisper. She set the lamp down near him, and with shaking hands tried to move him, but his body would not budge. It was stuck fast on the axe.

PART III

Chapter Twenty-three

July 1857

Lilly stood rigid under the big pine tree, staring at the fresh grave, but hearing none of what Jake Dutch was saying over her husband's grave. The memory of the last two days was one black sweep of horror—having to go back inside the house that awful night and try to stay calm for Joey's sake, explaining to him that his father was dead, like the baby calf that had died that spring, like his little half sister. She had had to struggle with Joey to keep him from running outside to see the terrible sight; and as she was trying to determine what to do with Zeb's body the next morning, God had at least seen fit to send over Jake and Hubert Rotter to try to talk Zeb and Lilly into going back to Utah.

The two men immediately took care of Zeb's body for Lilly; then, Brother Dutch rode for help. By the second day after Zeb's death all Mormons within a ten-mile radius had temporarily set aside their travel plans and had come to Lilly's home. They tried to console her, did her chores for her, told her that now she must go back to Utah, since she was alone. All of them thought they understood her sorrow —a husband and father lost to death.

But they didn't understand at all. She shuddered. Why had it taken death to make her realize she really had loved Zeb, to make her see how much she had needed him? Now she longed to have him hold her, to press his big hands against her back; to hear him tell her that everything would be all right; to see that half smile on his homely but lovable face. She had failed her husband—miserably, totally. Now he was gone, and she couldn't make up for it.

She wanted to cry, but all she could muster was a hard stare—a solid wall of defense against feelings. It was Joey who cried, and she had to be strong for him now—he had lost his father. She could not help wondering how he would feel if she told him he actually still had a father. But she would not spoil Joey's memory of Zeb, and she certainly would not confuse his young mind. She pulled him against her bosom and let the boy cry against her black mourning dress.

"'Therefore, if thou wilt go down into the wilderness to my father, thou shalt have place with us,'" Brother Dutch read from the Book of Mormon. "Brother Adams died far away from his brothers and sisters in Salt Lake, but he was an obedient brother, who came into this wilderness to expand the kingdom."

I should have let him go back, Lilly thought. She didn't stop to think that what had happened had been an accident. To her it seemed a fitting punishment—not for Zeb, but for her. She hugged Joey closer, realizing even more clearly how unbearable it would be to lose him, her only son—now, surely, the only child she would ever have. How ironic that he was fathered by a man who didn't deserve to live, while the man who had been such a good father to him was dead. Life seemed full of cruel twists.

"'But behold, the bands of death shall be broken, and the Son reigneth, and hath power over the dead; therefore, he bringeth to pass the resurrection of the dead.'"

Where had she heard those words before? At Laura Williams's grave? Marian's? Or had Zeb spoken them over little baby Laura's grave? The grass had grown over that grave now, and the name Zeb had cut into the little stone over it was beginning to fade. It was nearly eight years old now.

Everyone sang their favorite hymn. Lilly wondered how many times she had sung the hymn, trying to believe the words. And she realized her voice must surely be gone. She felt old today, and her heart was totally absent of joy. She had no desire to sing, and wondered if she ever would again. For an instant she remembered another day—when she lay in the grass with Chase Mitchell, and he told her maybe someday she would be a famous singer. Chase had made her want to sing. And there was a time when she believed he might be right.

And should we die before our journey's through,
Happy day! All is well!
We then are free from toil and sorrow, too;
With the just we shall dwell!

Goodbye, Zeb. Lilly felt the words but did not speak them. *I hope all is well with you now. Thank God you're free from toil and sorrow.*

"Someday you and Joey will be with Zeb again," Frieda told Lilly as she came over and put an arm around Lilly's shoulders. "In death a man is always joined with his first wife and with his children. It's only a matter of time, Lilly."

Lilly just stared at the grave, almost wanting to laugh. She had a sudden urge to ask Frieda if that meant she and Joey would be united with Chase Mitchell in death, rather than poor Zeb.

The singing was finished. The prayers ended. It was done. A sobbing Joey walked off to pick some wild flowers to put on his father's grave.

"You have no choice now, Lilly," Frieda told her then. "You must come back to Utah with us. You can't stay here alone—a widow with a son."

Lilly faced her, her green eyes void of the joy and curiosity and zest for life they had once held. Her normally beautiful face looked haggard, and her lovely thick, red-gold hair was beginning to fall out of the bun she had tied it in. Frieda realized this was a far cry from the young Lilly Brannigan who had gotten off the boat with her twelve years ago at New Orleans. But behind the tired lines, the circles under her eyes, there still lay a certain beauty that could probably be reawakened, once time had healed her loss.

"I'm not going back," Lilly told her, a strange lack of emotion in her voice.

Frieda's eyes widened. "Lilly, surely you realize you can't stay here. There is no way you could run this farm alone. And once we're gone, the only people left will be those worthless Gentile men who have been going up into the Virginia Mountains to look for gold! Most of them are homeless drifters. You would be in terrible danger."

"Joey and I will be fine. Zeb brought me out here, Frieda,

and I made him promise we would stay so I would never
have to make another long journey like the one that brought
us here. Now, my baby and my husband are buried here.
Zeb wanted to go back to Utah, but I wouldn't let him. Now,
Zeb is dead. I'll not go back and enjoy the luxuries of Salt
Lake after making him stay here. If we had prepared to go
back, the accident might not even have happened."

"Lilly, it was just an accident—"

"It was partly my fault. Now, Zeb *is* here to stay. I won't
leave him, Frieda. I won't leave these graves, and I won't
leave Nevada."

Nothing anyone did or said could convince Lilly to go.
And none of them realized just how determined she was
until later in the day when Lilly threatened them with Zeb's
repeating rifle when she heard some of the men mention that
perhaps they should take her against her will. After all, they
reasoned, it was for her protection and Joey's well-being.

Joey stood staunchly beside his mother as she held the
rifle on her Mormon friends, for Joey was just as determined
to stay now as his mother was. Everyone stared at Lilly and
the gun in disbelief.

"I'm sorry," Lilly told them. "You have all been good to
me. I owe much to you, and to my friends back in Salt Lake.
But I am not leaving Nevada, and you can't make me. I'm a
Gentile. I have never been a Mormon, and I am not going
back to Salt Lake. Joey and I are staying right here!"

"Lilly, put down that rifle," Jake Dutch told her. "Did you
think we would beat you or tie you or something?"

She watched them all carefully, and they wondered if perhaps she was a little bit crazy from too many years in the
wilderness, too much loss. Perhaps the horror of the way
Zeb had died had made her lose her mind.

"I don't know," Lilly answered. "I just want all of you to
go on to Utah and leave me here."

"But, what will you do, Lilly?" Frieda asked. "You and
Zeb could hardly keep this place going together. How will
you do it alone?"

"I don't know that, either," Lilly answered, her voice on
the verge of hysteria. "Joey is getting big now. He can help.
We'll . . . we'll survive."

They frowned and shook their heads, pitying the poor, deranged widow.

"We have no choice but to leave as soon as possible, Sister Adams," James English told her. "There isn't much time. We've got to get across the desert and back to Salt Lake before the government sends its soldiers. Brother Young is already thinking about vacating Salt Lake and moving us farther south until the trouble is over."

Lilly lowered the rifle. "Then, go. I wish all of you a safe trip." She looked at Frieda, and saw tears in the woman's eyes. "I'll be all right, Frieda. I always find a way to survive. You know that."

Frieda nodded. "God be with you, Lilly. We all love you. You say you aren't Mormon, but we all think of you as one of us. You know that."

Lilly struggled against tears. "I do. And I thank you for it."

"We'll send someone back in a few months to see if you're all right," Jake told Lilly. "Perhaps you will change your mind then, and come back with us."

"I won't," Lilly answered. "But you are welcome to come back and visit any time. Give my love to Hiram and Mary, and to Catheryn." She forced back the tears that wanted to come and turned to Joey. "Go and get the crate with your father's things in it for your Aunt Catheryn," she told the boy.

Joey ran into the house, and came back out with fresh tears on his face. He carried a crate that held small items of Zeb's—his razor, a small pocket knife, his Book of Mormon, a few clothes. Jake took the crate from Joey.

"Tell Catheryn I appreciate everything she has done for me," Lilly told the man. "Emphasize the *everything*. She will know what I mean."

Jake found the remark confusing, but he nodded. "I'll do that."

"Tell her how sorry I am about Zeb, but that he died a . . . a happy man."

The man nodded again and turned to load the crate into his wagon. He and Frieda would go on to Carson City, as would most of the others present. They had arrived at her

house already packed for their journey. Lilly admired the
Mormons' amazing ability to pick up and move on a moment's notice, their willingness to sacrifice everything for
the "cause." Now they would move out of her life forever.
For the first time since her arrival in America, she would try
to survive in this land without the shelter of the Mormon
community. That thought had always frightened her. But
now, strangely, it did not, for she realized that deep inside, it
was something she had always wanted.

She held Joey's hand as everyone climbed into wagons.
How vividly she remembered the journey west, as men
whipped oxen into motion and wagon wheels began to turn.
They left amid tears and goodbyes. Lilly felt as though an
entire chapter in her life had just been closed; as though
another Lilly Brannigan walked beside those wagons as they
headed back to Utah. Hiram and Mary and Catheryn would
surely be upset when they arrived without Lilly. For a moment, she wondered herself if she was crazy.

She turned to Joey. "It's just you and me now, Joey. We'll
be all right."

Joey nodded. "I'm glad you stayed, Mother. I didn't want
to leave Pa."

"I know. Neither did I." She leaned down and kissed his
cheek. "And right now, your pa would want you to do your
chores. He's gone now, Joey, but the cows still need milk-
ing, and the chickens still need feeding, and soon we'll have
corn to pick. Life goes on, Joey, and we're going to be all
right."

The boy hugged her. She hoped she had done the right
thing. This was all she had left now. Just Joey—the only
person she had truly loved with all her energy and devotion
and passion since Chase Mitchell had walked out of her life.

At night the wolves continued to howl. For the first few
nights after Zeb's burial and the departure of the Mormons, a
woman's mournful weeping could be heard carrying over the
night wind in haunting unison with them. For the next several nights, after Joey was asleep, Lilly took Zeb's rifle and
walked out to his grave, determined to keep the wolves from
digging it up. She cried, venting tears that had built up for

years—for Zeb, and the fact that she had never loved him the way he deserved to be loved; for Scotland and home; for her mother, her friends back in Salt Lake. She let all the fear that she dared not show in front of Joey, the loneliness, and the longing for the love she had wanted to share with Chase Mitchell, flow out of her.

She wondered where Chase was now.

Over the next two months, Lilly and Joey struggled to pick all the corn and dig all the potatoes. Lilly wondered sometimes if her muscles could possibly keep working another day, another hour, another second. Everything ached, but she wanted to hurt. The busy days and aching muscles helped keep her from thinking about Zeb, and the fact that all her friends were gone. Sometimes she wondered how she and Joey were going to get through the winter alone, but she told herself they would manage.

In September, after setting aside a food supply of their own, mother and son loaded their wagon with corn and potatoes and headed for Washoe City with a milk cow tied to the back of the wagon, which Lilly hoped to sell, along with the produce. They had always had two cows, because Zeb drank a lot of milk. But with him gone, Lilly decided they could try to get by with one and sell the other to buy supplies she and Joey would need for the winter.

It felt good to get away from the farm. Lilly breathed the cool autumn air and drank in the glorious beauty of the Sierras. She realized that in spite of her painful guilt over Zeb's death, and the intense ache of missing him, she was also beginning to feel the pleasant joy of being truly independent, for the first time in her twenty-eight years of life. She was free of the Mormon community, and there was no man standing behind her. There was only Joey, and she had made up her mind that she would find a way to make a good life for him. She would never marry again to appease others, and she was sure she would never love again the way she had loved Joey's father. That meant she would have to survive on her own for now, and the thought was both terrifying and exciting. She was meeting a new and daring challenge —a woman alone in a land where such a thing was almost unheard of.

"How much money do you think we'll get for Dumpling?" Joey asked.

"I don't know, Joey. Enough at least to buy some things we'll need for the winter. I'm sorry to have to sell her."

The boy shrugged. He had to be a man now, even though he was only going on eleven. Someone had to help protect and provide for his mother.

They slept under the stars that night, each refusing to show any fear in front of the other, in spite of howling wolves and barking coyotes in the distant hills. Once, Lilly was sure she had heard the growl of a bear. But she knew she had to be strong and not alarm Joey, little realizing that Joey was thinking the same about her.

The next morning found them on the road again. The sun warmed their backs with its rays, and Lilly began to hum, then sing aloud, hardly aware of the fact that she had not sung in full voice in years. She sang softly at first, until Joey encouraged her to sing more and began to join in.

But both their voices faded when they saw a long train of mules approaching, led by five men on horses. Lilly slowed the wagon, watching them carefully, aware of the danger such Gentile men could pose.

"Hand me the rifle, Joey," she said quietly.

The boy obeyed. "Who are they, Mother?"

"Some of those miners, I expect. I remember some of the Mormons talking about a whole town springing up in the Virginia Mountains because of men going there to look for gold." She laid the rifle across her lap. "Some men can't be trusted, Joey—especially the ones who travel alone like these. We have to be very careful."

The men came closer, slowing their train when they saw Lilly. There was no mistaking the fact that a very beautiful woman lurked just beneath the plain dress and unpainted face. She wore her long, auburn hair pulled straight back and fastened behind her neck, but any man could see how lovely that hair would be worn loose around her face and shoulders. Such a beautiful woman was a rare sight in this land. The men thought her prettier than any of the painted prostitutes in Virginia City.

The man in the lead halted his horse and touched his hat.

"Mornin', ma'am. We heard some awful pretty singin' comin' up this trail. That you?"

Lilly moved her hand to the trigger of the rifle, but kept a pleasant look on her face. "Yes. My son and I are on our way to Washoe City."

The man frowned, looking past her, then back at his fellow travelers, who stared at Lilly as though she were some kind of treasure. Lilly noticed they all looked as though they could use a bath. They were dressed in a variety of buckskins and wool pants and jackets, and most of them were wearing guns.

"Just you and your son?" the man who had spoken to her asked. "Where's your man?"

Lilly stiffened, facing the man squarely. "My man is dead. Now, if you'll ride around us, we can be on our way. We have to get back to the farm as soon as we can."

To Lilly's surprise he removed his hat, genuine sympathy in his eyes. "Sorry about your man." He squinted, as though trying to believe what he saw. "You really stayin' on out here alone?"

The old defenses began to rise in Lilly. "I am perfectly capable of running a farm alone, sir. And I do wish you would ride on."

"Only folks that live in this here valley is Mormons," one of the others spoke up. "I heard they all left for Salt Lake. You a Mormon, ma'am?"

"I hardly think it's any of your business," Lilly answered, her voice firm and determined. All she could think of was how "outsiders" had treated the Mormons during the years she had been with them, and the day Chase had been attacked.

"Hold on there, lady," the first man spoke up, beginning to smile. Lilly noticed he had one tooth missing in front. "Don't make much difference to us if you're Mormon or not. I got nothin' but admiration for a woman stayin' on alone out here." He glanced at Joey, still grinning, then back at Lilly. "My name is Whiskey Stokes. Me and these men are just on our way back from Washoe City, headin' back up to Virginia City with some supplies. Is there anything you need? Better yet, you got anything to sell? I see you're haulin' corn and potatoes."

Lilly blinked, unsure whether to trust a man named Whiskey. "As a matter of fact, I *was* on my way to sell my produce at Washoe City." She frowned. "Is Virginia City that town up in the Virginia Mountains where men are looking for gold?"

"Yes, ma'am. Most gold has been found up around Gold Hill—enough that me and a lot of others are stayin' to see if we can find more." He glanced at the corn and potatoes again. "Ma'am, you'd get a lot more money for them supplies up at Virginia City than you will at Washoe. Men in a gold town will pay top dollar."

Lilly glanced at the Virginia Mountains, which rose on the eastern side of the valley. "I don't think I'd want to drive a wagon all the way up there alone. The road up can't be very good, and I can't be away from my farm for that long."

"You're right on that one. But me and these men here, we'll buy some of the corn and potatoes off you—the milk cow, too, if she's for sale. We'll take it all on up to Virginia City—make ourselves a profit and pay you good to boot."

"How much?"

Stokes studied the cow and the produce again, while the rest of the men stared at Lilly. "You can get fifty dollars for that there cow—ten cents for every ear of corn and every potato. I'll pay you in real gold."

Lilly's eyes widened at the exorbitant prices. Apparently, such items would sell for even more in Virginia City, since Whiskey Stokes intended to make a profit. She only wished she could take it all up to Virginia City herself, but there was no one to watch the farm.

"All right, Mr. Stokes. Count out however much you can pack and carry."

Stokes grinned and signaled the others to come to the wagon. "Bring some of them gunnysacks, Keats," he yelled to one of them. "And you boys be honest about your count, you hear me? Ain't nobody here gonna cheat the nice lady." He looked at Lilly again. "By the way, ma'am, what's your name?"

Lilly watched the others closely, but she felt an air of

respect as they gathered around the wagon, and her apprehension began to fade. "Lilly," she answered, looking at Whiskey Stokes again. "Lilly Adams."

Stokes put out his hand. "Glad to meet you, Mrs. Adams."

Lilly hesitated, then let go of the rifle and reached out to shake his rough, sun-wrinkled hand. She found a certain excitement in coming into contact with a world that had been denied to her since her arrival in America. "And I'm glad to meet you, Mr. Stokes," she answered.

When she smiled, Whiskey Stokes's eyes lit up. "Ma'am, I got to tell you, that singin' we heard made our hearts all warm and sentimental. It was like a mountain spirit. We couldn't imagine what it was, so we halted and just listened for a spell. And when you sang *Home, Sweet Home*, we just got goose bumps. I ain't got no family, but a lot of these men do—families left behind. And considerin' the kind of women that's up at Virginia City—well, ma'am, lookin' at a fine woman like you is a sight, I'll say, let alone hearin' that pretty singin'. I ain't never heard a voice like yours."

Lilly reddened, and moved her hand back to the rifle. "Joey, please go back there and keep an eye on those men."

"Yes, ma'am," he said, and hopped down.

"Thank you, Mr. Stokes," she replied.

"I'll tell you one thing. Up at Virginia City a lady like you wouldn't need no corn or potatoes or anything else to sell to get rich. All she'd have to do is sing. Men would throw gold dust at your feet to hear that, let alone just to be able to set eyes on a proper woman. Oh, there's a few wives up there, but none that looks like you."

Lilly glanced behind her and saw that nearly two-thirds of her load of corn and potatoes had disappeared.

"Thank you again, Mr. Stokes," she answered. "But I have no intention of leaving my husband's grave or his farm. Perhaps we can work something out, though. If you could send someone back next fall, I will have plenty of food to sell."

The man nodded. "That I'll do. But it ain't good, you tryin' to stay here alone through the winter."

"I've spent many winters in this valley, Mr. Stokes."

The man put his hat back on. "Suit yourself."

Keats came around the wagon and handed a leather pouch to Lilly. "There's two hundred dollars' worth of gold in here, ma'am. The men are roundin' up the rest. We owe you three hundred fifty dollars."

Lilly looked down in shock at the leather pouch, and slowly drew it open. She had never had two hundred dollars in her hands at once in her whole life, let alone in real gold. She stared at the nuggets inside—some large, some tiny. Joey suddenly appeared at her side. "How do we know this is real?" he asked. "My Pa used to talk about something called fool's gold."

Stokes grinned, and dismounted from his horse. "I'll show you. Hand me one of the bigger nuggets."

Lilly took one out and gave it to the man. Joey watched in fascination as Stokes stooped down to pick up a rock, then laid the gold nugget on the edge of the wagon bed. He pounded it with the rock, flattening it, then held it up to Joey.

"Your first lesson in mining, son. If I had done this to pyrite—that's what fool's gold is—it would have busted into little pieces. Gold ain't brittle—it's soft. You can even bite into it with your teeth." He put the flattened nugget into the palm of Joey's hand. "That's the real stuff, all right."

Lilly and Joey just stared at the gold piece while the men got together the rest of what they owed her.

"Here you go, Mother," Joey said, handing over the piece to her. "Real gold! I bet Pa never saw anything like this!"

Lilly thought sadly about Zeb—how hard he had always worked. If he had lived to see this, he could have gotten rich selling his produce at Virginia City. "No, Joey, I don't think he did." She looked into the pouch, her mind racing with new ideas, and with curiosity over what life must be like in a place like Virginia City.

She carefully closed the bag, deciding she had much to think about. If she was to survive this new independence, she had to learn to socialize with these Gentiles. After all, she was one of them. She had lived among Mormons so long that she felt almost a foreigner again. It had always been Zeb who went to Carson City or Washoe City to sell his goods.

Lilly's socializing had always been with Frieda and the other Mormons. Now, here were these men, "outsiders" she was supposed to fear, handing her more money than she had seen all at once in her whole life.

"Here's the rest," Stokes told her, interrupting her thoughts.

Lilly accepted another pouch, her hand actually shaking. Gold! She had heard so many stories from Zeb about the gold rush in California—tales of great riches. Some men had attained great wealth only to lose it just as fast. It was easy now to understand why some men gave up so much to come and find the precious metal, for her own heart pounded with excitement.

She set the gold in her lap, already thinking about how carefully she would spend it, how much of it she would save.

"You're welcome to take it on in to Washoe City to make sure of its worth," Stokes told her. "There's a sheriff there who can come after our hides if we've cheated you."

Lilly reached into the second pouch and took out a nugget, put it between her teeth, and bit down on it. Her teeth left an impression. The other men grinned at her cautious distrust and her almost childlike curiosity over the gold.

"I don't think that will be necessary, Mr. Stokes." She looked at the rest of the men. "Thank you for taking these things off my hands. If you come through the valley again, you're welcome to stop by my home. It's a white frame house with a red barn in back. There's a huge old Ponderosa pine on a hill not far from the barn—the only one in a mile radius. It's bigger than any others in the area—kind of a landmark. You can't miss it. I could cook you a meal if you're hungry."

They all grinned. "A good, home-cooked meal is worth a fortune," one of them spoke up. "Between your cookin' and your singin', you could be a rich lady, ma'am."

They carried their sacks of food back to the mules. Each man took another look at Lilly before mounting up.

"Best of luck to you, Mrs. Adams," Stokes told her.

Lilly nodded to him and the others as they got into motion.

"Git up there!" one man shouted to a balking mule. The animal squealed and snorted. Each man grinned and nodded to Lilly as he passed. Joey stared after them almost longingly.

"I wonder what it's like up in the mountains, Mother? There must be some real gold mines up there."

Lilly looked down at the sacks of nuggets. "It looks that way." She lifted the sacks in her hands again, her childhood daydreams of being rich returning. Her mind raced with ideas of how she could make a good life for Joey.

"We'll go on to Washoe City, Joey, and buy the supplies we'll need. Now we don't have to worry about having enough to get through the winter. And I can afford to hire some men to cut wood for us, so we'll have enough to keep warm."

Joey sat down and took one of the sacks of gold. "Pa would be happy for us, wouldn't he?"

Lilly smiled. "Yes. I think he would." She rose and climbed into the back of the wagon. "Let's find a good hiding place for the gold, Joey. We don't want anyone to know we're carrying it. Gold can make some men do wicked things, and we still can't be sure who we can trust. But I think Whiskey Stokes and his friends are good men." She wrinkled her nose. "They don't smell the best, but that isn't how we judge people." She opened a sack of oats she had brought along for the draft horse. "Let's put it in this."

"They're heavy for such little pouches," Joey told her, climbing into the back of the wagon with her.

"They are, aren't they? I never knew gold was this heavy."

She shoved the pouches in among the oats and tied the sack closed, pushed it into a corner of the wagon, and climbed back onto the seat to pick up the reins. Then she snapped the horse into motion, while Joey sat down beside her again.

"We have a lot of money, don't we, Mother?" the boy asked.

"Yes, we do, Joey."

"Are you happy now?"

Lilly looked at him, studying the intensely blue eyes, the

dark, curly hair, the winning smile. He was a walking replica of his father. *I would be happier if I could have been married to your real father all these years*, she wanted to tell him.

"Gold doesn't buy happiness, Joey," she said aloud. "It's loving and caring that mean the most in life. But we needed this very much to get through the winter. I think maybe your father is looking down on us, watching over us. This is like a miracle, and we should thank God for it."

"Pa would have, wouldn't he?"

She looked ahead, her eyes tearing.

"Yes, he would have, Joey."

She headed for Washoe City, deciding she must forget about the past now and think about what the future might hold for her and her son. They had learned a great deal about the Gentile world in the last few minutes. She had some planning to do.

Chapter Twenty-four

January 1858

Lilly put some wood on the fire, listening to the wind howl outside. A sudden storm had just blown in from the Sierras, rattling the windows with relentless force.

She walked back to the kitchen to finish Joey's birthday cake. It was January 5, and he was eleven today. It was his first birthday since Zeb had died six months ago. January in the wilds of Nevada was always a lonely time, but this particular day Lilly knew things would seem even lonelier. She was determined to make it as cheerful as possible. She had used precious sugar to make a thick frosting for the cake, and had colored some of the frosting with homemade blueberry jam so she could make flowers on the top and write Joey's name on it.

It was a good day to bake—so cold that the heat from the wood-burning kitchen stove was welcome. She decided they might as well spend all their waking time in the kitchen, since it was turning out to be the warmest room in the house. She smiled at the finished cake, proud of her decorating job, then went to the kitchen window to look out at the barn, where her son had disappeared earlier to feed the cow and plow horses and clean out their stalls.

The wind whipped so hard that the snow blew sideways past the window. She sighed, walking back to study the cake once more, anxious for Joey to see it. She had knitted him a sweater as a gift, sitting up late every night after he fell asleep in order to finish it for today.

Things were going to go well now, Lilly was sure. She had spent most of her gold on extra seed corn for next spring, as well as a strong, young pair of draft horses. The two old mares they had used for years were getting tired and slow, and with all the extra planting Lilly wanted to do in the spring, she knew she would need stronger horses. But she hadn't been able to bring herself to sell the older mares. They were a part of the world left by Zeb Adams.

It seemed as if more and more men were headed for Virginia City. Whiskey Stokes and Daryl Keats had stopped to visit her twice, both full of stories. Lilly had gladly cooked meals for them, while Joey listened excitedly to lessons about mining.

Whiskey had played a few tunes on his harmonica for Joey, and Lilly had ended up singing for the men. The visits were a blessing for both mother and son.

Now, she could hardly wait for next year's harvest. She would hire men to help get in the crops and to take her produce to the mining town. Stokes and Keats had assured her a tidy profit in Virginia City. Lilly had spent a good deal of time during the last several weeks thinking about ways she could make money—not for herself, but for Joey. Ever since meeting Whiskey and his men, her mind had whirled with ideas. To Lilly, the most practical one was to increase production and make money selling food to the miners. That way they could stay on the farm, near Zeb and Laura's graves. Hiring men to help would be good for Joey, who was reaching a restless age, most noticeable in the winter when they were forced to practically hibernate in the house. Watching his eagerness over Stokes and Keats's visits, she realized the boy needed the companionship and guidance of a man, as well as to be kept busy, and she was anxious for spring planting.

She returned to the window to see if Joey was coming yet, but all her happy plans vanished when she noticed smoke billowing out the upper storage door of the barn. "Joey!" she gasped.

She grabbed her coat from a hook by the door and tore out the back of the house, clumsily running through the deep snow. The wind stung one side of her face, but she barely felt it. The barn was on fire!

"Joey!" she screamed as she came closer. "Joey! Joey!"

She couldn't see him anywhere. Lungs hurting with pain from the cold, she made it to the open barn door. Flames seemed to be everywhere, and she could hear the new horses whinnying in terror. "Joey!" she screamed again.

"They won't come out! They won't come out!" her son yelled back from somewhere behind the smoke and flames. "The horses! The horses!"

"Joey, get out of there!" Lilly screamed. "Let the horses go!"

"I can't! I don't want 'em to die!"

In desperate fear for his life Lilly darted inside, through a narrow opening between flames. She put her coat collar over her mouth against the smoke and squinted to try to see Joey. She screamed his name again and he called back: "Over here!"

Lilly knelt lower, where the air was fresher, and felt her way through smoke. She finally spotted Joey, tugging on a rope tied around the neck of one of the draft horses. His face was stained with smoke and tears as he gritted his teeth and begged the horse to follow him out, but the animal was too terrified and too big for him to budge.

"Joey, let him go or we'll be killed! Get out of this barn!" Lilly told him, hurrying up to him and yanking the rope from his hands.

"The horses! The horses!" the boy cried. "It's my fault!"

His chest jerked in a sob. "I set the lantern down and Eliza kicked it over!"

Lilly looked around for the troublesome cow, but Eliza was nowhere to be seen. There was no time to be concerned for her. She grabbed Joey's arm. "Get out of here! Now!"

He reluctantly followed her, sobbing with guilt. A burning beam fell from above and Lilly grabbed Joey close, ducking over him to protect him. The hot wood struck her on the back and rested just long enough against the skirt of her dress to set it aflame. She ran with Joey, who saw the flames and stopped her to beat them out with his hands.

Mother and son ran then through a literal wall of flame toward the exit, immediately rolling in the snow to douse more flames that licked at their clothing. The flames were quickly snuffed, leaving both of them with only a few minor burns that neither of them even felt right away. Once clear of the building, they stood together in stunned horror, watching flames break out of every corner and open seam of the barn. The wind blew with such force that in just moments the entire barn was engulfed beyond hope.

Joey sobbed uncontrollably, muttering about the horses. He heard one last whinny and clung to Lilly. She held him close to her breast, trying to soothe him, telling herself to be calm for his sake.

"My poor Joey," she whispered, kissing his thick, dark hair and realizing what a sad birthday this would be for him now. The barn glowed red, and she remembered with an aching heart how hard Zeb and Jake Dutch and other Mormon men had worked to build it.

"Come on, Joey. Let's go to the house. There's nothing more we can do."

Lilly wiped a cool rag over Joey's face as he held his burned hands in a bucket of cool water. The boy was still shaking and crying, blaming himself for the fire, and Lilly was too concerned about him to care about her own shattered nerves and bruised back.

"It was an accident, Joey," Lilly kept telling him, realizing the horror it would have been if he had been killed himself. "At least you're all right. You never should have stayed inside that long."

"But, the horses!" he kept repeating. "I tried to save them, Mother. All that money you spent on them!"

"We'll get more money. We'll be all right."

"But how? Without the horses, we can't plow next spring. And all the seed corn was in there, too. Even if we do get more horses, all the feed is burned up, the harnesses are gone, and the equipment—"

"Hush, Joey. I said we would manage, and we will. I have a little money left."

"I tried to put it out. It happened so fast, Mother. All that hay—when the wind blew through the door, it just caught fire so fast."

She rewet the rag and held it to his neck. Joey jerked in another sob when they heard a crashing sound in the wind. The barn had fallen in, burying the precious new horses under the debris, and probably Eliza, too. Lilly wondered about their other two horses. She had not seen old Randy and Butternut.

She dressed the burns on Joey's hands and pushed their old, stuffed sofa in front of the fireplace in the main room of the house. She made Joey lie down and covered him with several quilts.

"You try to sleep, now, and stop blaming yourself. Who can tell why these things happen? They just do."

"It isn't fair—Pa dead, and now the barn burned, the horses gone. All that money you spent on them—"

"I told you to stop worrying over it. I want you to rest or you'll be sick. When you wake up I want you to eat, and we'll still have some birthday cake." She sat down on the edge of the sofa, stroking his hair. "And I have a present for you."

"I don't want one," he answered. "I don't deserve it."

Her eyes teared. "Oh, yes, you do, Joey. You have no idea what you mean to me. I'm so proud of you, and I need you so much. What happened today was just an accident. It could have happened to me or anybody else. Things often happen to us in life, Joey, that force us to start all over again."

She sat beside him until his eyes began to droop from weariness, then slowly rose and went into the kitchen to cry. Lilly realized only then how much her back hurt. She knew that she also could have been killed. What would happen to Joey out here in the middle of winter if she were to die? She had seen plenty of death over the years, knew how easily it could come. And she realized with sudden clarity that it was dangerous for both of them to try to struggle alone here on the farm without help. She had some money left—enough to hire the men she had planned to hire in the spring—but now there were no plow horses and no equipment, nor was there any corn to plant. She would never have enough for everything they would now need, and she and Joey couldn't possibly do the extra planting and harvesting alone.

Lilly held her head in her hands, letting the tears flow until anger and determination took their place. Life seemed to keep handing her challenges she didn't want. So far, the only good thing it had brought her was Joey, and she had to be careful or she would lose him, too. For now, she could only be grateful he was alive. She felt suddenly aching tired, and wondered how Chase would feel if he knew he had a son in this predicament.

Lilly rose and walked wearily back to the window. The barn lay in smoldering ruins, flames still licking at the fallen timbers. The wind had calmed somewhat, and clouds above broke open slightly to allow a few dwindling rays from the setting sun to light up the Virginia Mountains to the east.

"I'm keeping this land for you, Joey," she said softly. "I don't know yet how we're going to survive, but Zeb would want you to have this. It's all we have that's our own."

Suddenly, her heart took new hope. She spotted Butternut, who wandered from the side of the house and into view, pawing at snow to look for grass, obviously unconcerned over the fire. Lilly's eyes teared with joy that at least one of the horses had escaped the fire, even if it was one of the old mares.

She closed her eyes and said a prayer of thanks, then walked back to where Joey slept. She leaned down to kiss his hair, then went to her bedroom to wash the soot from her face and change her clothes. She couldn't reach the burns on her back to put salve on them, and she squinted with pain from them as she pulled on her clean dress.

By the time Joey awoke nearly two hours later, Lilly was sitting near him in a rocker, holding his new knitted sweater in her lap. He sat up and looked at her through swollen, bloodshot eyes, ready to cry again.

"Happy birthday, Joey," Lilly told him. She handed him the sweater, and he took it, holding it gingerly with the parts of his fingers that were not burned.

"You shouldn't give it to me," he muttered.

"Why not? You're my son, and I love you more than anything on this earth. We're going to eat some supper and some birthday cake, and then we'll talk about what we should do next. We'll decide together. We still have a wagon, and there's an old harness in the tool shed. Butternut is out there wandering around, unhurt, so we aren't stranded; and there is still food in the house and wood for heating."

"Butternut is okay?"

Lilly smiled at him. "She's out there rambling around like nothing happened. You know Butternut. All she cares about is where her next meal is coming from. That's why she's so fat."

Joey smiled a little, but his eyes were still sad. "What are we going to do, Mother?"

"I told you. We're going to celebrate your birthday and thank God you're alive. After that, we'll think of something, but today we're not going to worry about it."

Joey leaned forward to hug her. "Thank you for the sweater. I'm sorry about the barn and the horses, Mother."

"It was an accident. We have each other. That's all that matters."

The boy's tears came again. "I miss Pa," he sobbed. Lilly hugged him tightly.

"I miss him, too, Joey. But it's just the two of us now, and somehow we're going to hold on to this land, because Zeb loved it and he'd want you to have it. So, that's what we'll do. We'll find a way."

* * *

"Haalloo, Mrs. Adams!"

Lilly heard the shout from outside and recognized the familiar greeting. It was Whiskey Stokes and Daryl Keats. Their visit couldn't have been more welcome, as it had been only a few days since the barn had burned, and her heart was still heavy with grief and worry. She wrapped a shawl around her shoulders and stepped out onto the porch. Joey was already running to greet the men.

"Hello, there, Joey," Whiskey said with a laugh. "Brung you some pyrite. Ain't worth much, but it's perty."

Lilly waved at the men. She could recognize them from a distance now—Whiskey, with his weathered, drooping leather hat and stained buckskins, the gap in his mouth left by the missing front tooth evident even from a distance; Daryl Keats, in the balding bearskin coat, his heavy black beard making it difficult to see anything but hair unless the man was close.

Whiskey handed a small leather bag to Joey, then rode with Daryl up to the house. He tipped his hat to Lilly.

"We wasn't gonna stop till we seen that barn. What happened, ma'am? Everybody all right?"

"I'm afraid we had an accident. The cow kicked over a lantern, and it was so windy the fire spread faster than we could stop it. I've lost everything—the horses, all my feed. One old mare survived."

Both men frowned, shaking their heads. "That's mighty bad luck," Keats told her. "But at least you and the boy are all right."

"Yes. That's what I told myself. I'm not sure what I'm going to do yet. I can't afford another pair of draft horses and more seed. And if I don't get a crop planted in the spring, I'll have no income." She wrapped her shawl closer. "Oh, I shouldn't be standing here telling you my problems. Please come inside, both of you. I was just getting ready to call Joey in for lunch. You'll join us, won't you?"

Whiskey grinned. "Yes, ma'am. Sounds real good."

The two men dismounted and followed Lilly inside.

"I'm awful sorry about your misfortune, Mrs. Adams," Whiskey told her, hanging his hat on a peg on the wall.

Daryl did the same, and both men took chairs at the table. "You need anything—anything at all, you let us know."

"I'll do that. And I appreciate your offer of help, Mr. Stokes." She set some coffee in front of both of them. Since Zeb's death, she had decided to start using coffee more. She enjoyed the hot brew, and couldn't quite understand why the Mormons were against it. "And please call me Lilly," she told both men.

Whiskey reddened a little. "Well, Miss, uh, Miss Lilly, it feels kind of strange, but if you say it's okay. And you call us Whiskey and Daryl. Both of us always did feel kind of out of place bein' called mister. Back in town it's just Whiskey and Blackbeard."

"Blackbeard!" Lilly laughed lightly. "Doesn't anyone in Virginia City use formal names?"

"Not many. It's mostly Duke and Dogface and Pancake and Sourpuss and the like."

Lilly shook her head as Joey came inside, dumping the leather bag of pyrite out onto the table. "Look at this, Mother. It's fool's gold."

Lilly eyed it wryly. "Something tells me even the ones looking for real gold are rather foolish," she answered. She eyed Whiskey. "How many men up there really find gold, Mr.—I mean, Whiskey?"

Whiskey and Daryl both laughed. "Right now, most are still lookin'. There's been a few small strikes, but the big one is there, Miss Lilly. Men like me and Daryl, we can smell it. It's a feelin' you get. Somebody is gonna hit the big one, and Virginia City will explode with people. You'll get all kinds of business."

Lilly sighed as she filled tin plates with stew. "Not if I don't have anything to sell." She set plates in front of the men and sent Joey to wash his hands. While the boy ran off to the washbasin, she filled a plate for him and herself, then sat down across from her guests. "Do you really think that will happen—hundreds more coming to Virginia City?"

"Hundreds? More like thousands, ma'am," Daryl answered.

Lilly frowned, thinking. She told herself there had to be a way such growth could benefit her and Joey. Supplying them with food would be the best way, but first she had to buy more draft horses and seed, hire men to help. That would take money—a lot of money—and she had no idea where she was going to get it.

Whiskey and Daryl carried on about new strikes being found nearly every day, more outsiders coming in—developers, realtors, surveyors, bankers, suppliers.

"So far, our biggest business is the saloon," Whiskey added with a laugh. "All them poor men discouraged over findin' no gold have to go someplace to drown their sorrows."

"Yeah, and Whiskey does his share," Daryl put in. "That's how he got his nickname."

Joey came back to the table and began to eat his stew while he watched Whiskey and Daryl, and took in everything they said.

"Searching for gold must be very lonely," Lilly said when they were all nearly finished.

"Yes, ma'am, it can be," Daryl answered.

"There's men up there from all over the country," Whiskey added. "Lots of 'em left whole families behind. They get mighty lonesome for home, but there's somethin' about findin' gold—*gold fever*, most call it. It hits a man like a disease—like alcohol or gamblin'. He always means to go back, but he keeps tellin' himself, one more day—just one more day. There's a song about men who work in the mines. Let's see—"

He scratched his chin and leaned back, pulling out his harmonica and playing a tune. Daryl hummed a few bars he couldn't remember, inserting words here and there that he knew:

For the mine is a tragic house,
It is the worst of prisons—

He hummed a few more bars.

With a machine they give you air.
By you always burns a lamp,
And your body struggles with the stone.

Hands work, never do they stop.
Hmmm, Hmmmmm, Hmmm . . ."

Joey listened, totally entranced by the words. Lilly tried to pick up the tune, and the sound of her lilting voice made Whiskey stop playing long enough to ask her to sing something for them.

"Will you sing *Home, Sweet Home*, like you did that first day we met you?" Daryl asked her. Whiskey played the tune on his harmonica, and Lilly sang.

Mid pleasures and palaces though we may roam,
Be it ever so humble, there's no place like home!

The song always made her miss Scotland.

A charm from the skies seems to hallow us there,
Which, seek through the world, is ne'er met with
  elsewhere.
Home, home! Sweet, sweet home!
There's no place like home! There's no place like home!

She finished, and to her dismay, noticed tears in Daryl Keats's eyes. "Ma'am, the way you sing that, you'd have half of Virginia City cryin'—all them hard-nosed, foul-mouthed men would be like babies in your hand."

Whiskey sighed deeply. "It's like I told you that first day we met you, Miss Lilly," he said. "The men up there in the mountains would throw gold at your feet to hear you sing, let alone to set eyes on a beautiful, proper woman."

Lilly smiled nervously. "I'm not so sure Virginia City is the *place* for a proper woman."

"Oh, ma'am, those men wouldn't lay a finger on a lady like you," Daryl put in.

Joey's eyes lit up. "Mother, you could go to Virginia City and sing! I'll bet you'd make a *lot* of money! Heck, Daryl and Whiskey like to listen. If they do, so would the other men!"

"Oh, I don't know, Joey." Lilly rose and took her plate from the table. The memory of Chase's words came to her suddenly, like a sword in her heart. *Remember, your voice is something that belongs to just you,* he had told her. *It can help you through bad times. Don't let our parting take the music from your heart.* She thought of her old dream of being a singer, and Chase's comment that Lilly Brannigan sounded like a famous name one would see on a theater bill. She remembered the little girl back in Scotland who used to go out into the foothills and sing to a pretend audience. She turned back to Whiskey Stokes.

"Do you really believe men would pay to hear me sing?"

Whiskey grinned. "Sure they would."

Daryl was wiping at his eyes. "You'd be a rich woman in no time. You'd be surprised how easy it is to get rich in a gold town, ma'am, if you've got the right merchandise."

Lilly smiled self-consciously, folding her arms and pacing. Suddenly, it all seemed to fall into place.

"Are we going to Virginia City, Mother?"

Lilly turned to look at her son. "I'm not so sure it's a good place for a growing boy."

"Why, heck, it's the *best* place for young Joey," Whiskey told her. "He needs to be around men, ma'am. And we'd see to it he was looked after."

Lilly saw the eager grins on the faces of the men, the shining excitement in Joey's eyes. "I suppose perhaps we could go, for a while—just long enough to make enough money to buy more horses and seed."

"Wouldn't take you long to do that," Daryl told her.

"We could keep the farm, couldn't we, Mother? If you could earn money singing, we wouldn't have to sell it. We could come back and have an even bigger farm, I'll bet. Maybe we'd get real rich, and I could have horses. I could *raise* horses—sell them to the miners."

Lilly walked back to her chair. "Don't go making big plans, Joey. I'm not sure how it would all work out." She faced Daryl and Whiskey. "The fact remains that I have to make some money if I'm going to survive here and keep the farm," she told the men. "My husband loved this place. He died here. I refuse to sell this land, but I have no money now. Do you think I could make enough money over the winter to buy some horses?"

"I've got no doubt about it," Whiskey told her. "Fact is, I'd wager you'll make a lot more singing than you'd ever make workin' this farm."

Lilly sat back down, leaning closer. "Would the two of you help me? I wouldn't want to go to a place like that all alone. I need friends with me—men who know the others and can help bring me some business."

"Ma'am, you know all you have to do is say the word," Daryl told her. "Me and Whiskey will wait right here, if you want. You can pack what you need and go back with us tomorrow."

"The sooner the better, if you want to start makin' money," Whiskey added.

Lilly looked at Joey. "I don't suppose I have to ask if it's all right with you."

The boy grinned.

She looked back at Whiskey. "All right. If you'll wait for us, Joey and I will go back with you to Virginia City."

Whiskey laughed and slapped his knee. "You made the right choice, ma'am—the right choice. Ain't a woman from here to California got a voice like yours!"

Lilly shook her head. "Maybe you're right," she answered, rising to pick up their plates. "I just hope you're right about the money." She turned away. "May the Lord be with us," she muttered.

Chapter Twenty-five

A myriad of signs for businesses cluttered the busy, disorganized main street of Virginia City. Lilly gazed at the conglomeration of hastily built stores and hotels, as well as several hundred tents that advertised a variety of services— wheelwrights, supplies, stables, blacksmiths, realtors, banks, and assay offices. But it seemed that every other sign spelled SALOON.

The bald mountains that surrounded the city were dotted with tents and more buildings. The town swarmed with men of every shape and character, most of them looking as though they hadn't bathed in a considerable length of time, a few in fancy suits. Lilly suddenly felt as though she was stark naked, as men gathered around the wagon and walked with it, staring at her.

"Whooeee!" one of them shouted. He removed his hat and bowed, and Lilly reddened.

"You no-goods listen up!" Stokes shouted to the men who had gathered. "This here is Lilly Adams—a respectable lady from the valley who's fallen on hard times. Any of you willin' to pay for it can come to my camp and listen to her sing for you. And if your hides are worth two cents, you'll help me build a place for her and her boy to live."

Joey grinned excitedly as the crowd grew. He was proud of how pretty his mother was. A variety of painted women in gawdy dresses came out of tents and doors. Some glared at her as though she were some kind of challenge; others smiled and waved. Lilly smiled faintly at them, unsure what the men would think if she was too friendly. This was a world so foreign to her that she felt as though she had again landed in a new country. Rowdy piano music and raucous laughter filled the air, along with the constant sound of hammers and saws, and an occasional explosion in the distant hills.

"Where'd you find her, Whiskey, you ole devil, you!" one man shouted. He was drunk and walked beside Whiskey's horse, hanging onto the saddle. "You gonna keep her all to yourself?"

Whiskey gave the man a swift kick, knocking him into a half-frozen watering trough. Men and women alike screamed and laughed.

"I told you, she's a proper lady!" Whiskey again shouted, his voice barely discernible above the shouts and laughter.

Men followed the wagon to a camp several hundred yards beyond what appeared to be the end of the town. Many of them circled the wagon and stared at Lilly, and she moved an arm around Joey, wondering now if she had made a good decision after all.

"You men listen up, for once and for all," Whiskey Stokes told them, turning his horse to face them. "This here is Mrs. Lilly Adams, a widow woman from the valley."

"She a Mormon?"

"What difference does it make?"

"I'll talk to them," Lilly told Whiskey, swallowing her own fear and apprehension. She had come to Virginia City, and she was determined to succeed here. She stood up in the seat box, and a few of the men removed their hats.

"Jesus, would you look at that!" one of them muttered.

Lilly took a deep breath for courage. "My husband was Zeb Adams, and he was a Mormon. I lived with him and with the Mormons for the past thirteen years, since I came here from Scotland, but I am not myself a Mormon. However, I will not tolerate any insults of the fine people I know the Mormons to be." They all listened in fascination to her lilting accent. "My husband was killed in a farm accident several months ago, and I recently lost my barn and draft horses to a fire. I have come here in hopes of earning the money I need to keep my husband's farm going. I can cook for you, and I would be glad to entertain you with song."

"Just song?" one man yelled out. Another turned around and landed a fist in the man's face.

"Whiskey done told you she's a proper lady," the man grumbled.

Lilly felt her cheeks going crimson, but she kept her composure and refused to crumble under their stares and remarks.

"Yes, just song," she answered. "Give me a chance, and I think you will get your money's worth." She turned to Joey. "This is my son, Joseph. He is eleven." She made a point to directly meet the eyes of nearly every man watching her. "Now, if you will give me a couple of days to get settled, I will be glad to cook for as many of you as I possibly can. And you may come here evenings for some singing."

"Some of you go gather up some lumber and let's get a cabin built," Daryl Keats said. "The lady will pay for it as soon as she earns out the money, and I guarantee that will be quick. I've heard her sing, and it will be worth your gold nuggets to listen."

He rode through the crowd, and most followed, though a few remained to watch Lilly unpack her belongings. She had brought along most of her dishes and pans, her clothing, and some furniture. Her heart still ached at leaving behind the little house Zeb had built for her, but right now she had to think about survival. As she began to unload the wagon, she felt a thousand eyes on her. She told herself she had to get used to the stares, but for the moment, she could not abide them. She ducked inside Whiskey Stokes's tent and sat down on a cot, needing a moment alone.

The inside of the tent was warm from an old cast-iron stove Whiskey used for heating. Its chimney stuck out the back of the tent. The interior smelled of unwashed men, and of whiskey and smoke. Lilly curled her nose, but being inside was still better than feeling the relentless stares.

She had sat there only a moment when she heard someone scream, "Look out!"

"Catch that goddamn team!" someone else yelled.

"Is the boy all right?"

Lilly's heart immediately tightened at the last statement, and she dashed outside to see a crowd of people gathered around someone. She dashed to the scene to see Joey getting up and helping up a beautiful but heavily painted woman with bright red hair.

"There you go, Nettie," one of them said, brushing mud off the woman's purple taffeta dress with more vigor and familiarity than necessary.

The woman called Nettie hit at his arm. "You go any further and I'll have to charge you," she chastised him.

The others laughed raucously. Lilly watched the woman tuck some hair up into her fancy curls. Farther up the street men were chasing a team of horses that seemed to be running wild, pulling an empty wagon. Again Lilly wondered what kind of place she had brought Joey to, but the boy seemed excited.

"Thank you, ma'am," he was telling the redheaded woman. "I'm sorry about what happened."

Lilly noticed how Joey stared at the woman. She wondered what boys his age thought about the female gender, and suddenly realized that in a place like this her son might learn more than he needed to know.

"Well, I don't mind risking life and limb for a fine little gentleman like you," the woman answered.

Lilly noticed her limp as Joey led her over. "Mother, this lady saved me from getting run over by a runaway team of horses. What's your name, ma'am?" he asked.

The woman winced with pain and held onto his shoulder for support. "Nettie." She looked at Lilly. "Nettie Abler, ma'am. I was just . . . well, I came up here to be nosy, I guess. I heard all the commotion about some proper lady coming here to sing."

Men gathered around, staring at Nettie with almost as much awe as they had stared at Lilly, but Lilly could guess the reason was much different. She held out her hand.

"Thank you for saving my son," Lilly told her. "I'm Lilly Adams, and this is my son, Joey."

Nettie just stared at Lilly's hand for a moment, then glanced around at the men, then held her chin proudly and shook it. "Well, I'm glad to meet you, Mrs. Adams, but I'm not real happy about the circumstances."

Lilly frowned. "Are you hurt bad?"

The woman looked down. "Not sure. A wagon wheel ran over my foot just as I got Joey out of the way."

"Come inside Whiskey's tent and we'll look at it."

Nettie met Lilly's gaze, her blue eyes showing astonishment. She smiled nervously. "I . . . I don't think you want me to do that, ma'am."

Lilly looked around at the staring men, and realized that proper women were probably not expected to associate with women like Nettie Abler. She looked back at Nettie. "Nonsense. You just saved my son's life. Joey is all I have in this world. You must be a very fine woman to do what you just did. Now, come inside. I'm sure Whiskey must have some coffee or something. We'll see if you need a doctor." She moved to put an arm around Nettie's waist, and helped her walk inside Whiskey's tent.

"Can you beat that?" one of the men muttered.

Whiskey Stokes ordered them all back to what they were doing. "Let's get that lumber up here," he shouted.

Nettie sat down on a cot while Lilly unbuttoned her shoe. Nettie pulled up a mound of petticoats, revealing a long, slender leg and a fancy garter that held up her stockings. Joey stared with pleasure. Nettie hesitated a moment, realizing how brazen her move must look to these people.

Lilly sent Joey outside to help Whiskey, telling him to watch where he was going this time. Nettie laughed nervously. "Sorry about that, Mrs. Adams. Women like me, we get to where we forget how to act around decent people." She pulled off her stocking and wiggled her toes.

Lilly examined her foot. "It's bruised, but I don't think anything is broken. Can you move it in all directions?"

Nettie wiggled the foot more. "So far. I think it's going to swell, though." She shrugged. "Oh, well, a swollen foot can't stop a woman of my profession. Our feet are our last worry."

Lilly felt her cheeks go crimson as she rose. "Would you like some coffee, Nettie?"

"Sure. Why not?" The woman pulled her stocking back on. "I'm sorry about my crude remarks. Comes from being around these wild men too long." She replaced her garter and pulled down her petticoats. "You shouldn't have invited me in here, you know. I'm the kind of woman—well, every man in Virginia City knows who Nettie Abler is, if you get my meaning."

Lilly handed her some coffee and sat down beside her. She guessed Nettie was about the same age as she, but Nettie had a hard, used look to her. "I lived with the Mormons too long to go judging others," she told the woman. "The Mormons believe in forgiveness and in looking to the future. Everyone makes his or her own mistakes, and decides whether to learn by them." She thought about her own situation. "Besides," she added, "we all have reasons for what we choose to do in life. And we all have to learn how to survive."

Nettie sipped some coffee and studied Lilly. She was beautiful—she could make a lot of money as a paid prostitute. But she knew instinctively that Lilly Adams was the kind of woman who could never turn to such a profession, even if she was destitute.

"Well, thank you for publicly befriending me," she told Lilly. "I know it wasn't easy for you. You seem like a nice lady, Mrs. Adams. What are you doing in Virginia City?"

Lilly explained her situation to her and Nettie set aside her coffee cup. "Well, I will personally make sure you get plenty of business, Mrs. Adams. Whiskey is right, you know. Men will give you a day's diggings to listen to you sing and to set eyes on a proper woman as beautiful as you are."

Lilly reddened, feeling overly complimented. "You're a very beautiful woman yourself."

"Yeah, well, maybe," Nettie answered. "But I'm not so much under all this paint." She pulled on her shoe. "Listen, if I were you, I'd forget about going to all the work of cooking for these no-goods. Make life easy on yourself and just sing for them. I guarantee you'll make plenty, and you won't have to wear yourself out trying to fill men's bellies. There are plenty of places for them to eat around here."

"I'll remember that."

Nettie buttoned her shoe and stood up. She put out her hand. "Thank you again, Mrs. Adams." She smiled, her teeth even and white.

"Call me Lilly. And you're the one to be thanked. You come and visit whenever you want, Nettie. I'll need friends in this town, and it would be nice to have a woman to visit with."

Nettie frowned. "You serious?"

"Of course I am!"

Nettie studied her closely, then smiled. "I just might do that, but I'll be discreet. You have to be a little bit careful, Mrs. Adams—I mean, Lilly. You talk to me too much, and any decent women who come to this town won't have anything to do with you. More women will come, you know. If they hit the big one, men will bring out their families."

"I've been pretty much alone most of my life, Nettie, and I make my own decisions."

Nettie frowned and nodded. "You're a strong woman, Lilly. I can see that. And you know, in some ways, we aren't so different." Nettie reached over to hug her, then ducked out of the tent. Lilly stood at the entrance of the tent as several men gathered around Nettie. "Say, boys, I've got a lame foot. How about carrying me back to the Nugget Saloon. I could use a little whiskey to kill the pain."

Two men lifted her onto their shoulders and carried her off, as several others followed, laughing and making remarks. Lilly watched, amazed at the wild freedom of Virginia City. She felt a strange kinship with Nettie. Whiskey approached her.

"What do you know about Nettie Abler, Whiskey?"

The man laughed. "Nettie's the most notorious woman in Virginia City, Miss Lillie—highest paid, too. Why, the men hold her almost in as much honor as a woman like you, only in a different way, if you get my meanin'."

Lilly shook her head. "I get your meaning."

Joey came running up. "Come on, Mother. We have to decide where to put our house."

"I'm coming. You go on ahead."

The minute Lilly stepped outside, she could feel men staring at her. She could not imagine she was anything special to gaze upon—her hands were work-worn, she wore no rouge, no fancy dress, no pretty hairdo. Lilly underestimated her own natural beauty. But she did not underestimate the money-making advantages in Virginia City. Surely, if these men liked looking at her as she was now, she could charge a fortune to allow them to listen to her sing if she could get her skin back in shape with some creams, get herself some prettier clothes, and maybe wear just a little rouge.

"Is there some way to get hold of a piano and someone who knows how to play it decently?" she asked Whiskey.

"Oh, there's lots of peeaners in Virginia City, ma'am. And plenty that knows how to play them. We'll have you in business in no time."

Lilly walked over to where Joey was standing, and Whiskey hurried away to help some men who had begun clearing away a spot for her first crude cabin. Lilly was amazed at the eagerness of the men. A big, burly man in a top hat and black wool coat walked up and asked her if she wanted a sign painted to put up and advertise where people could come and listen to her sing.

"But . . . are you sure you want to go to all this trouble? You haven't even heard me yet."

The man shook his head. "Ma'am, all we had to do was hear you talk and see your pretty face. If Whiskey Stokes and Daryl Keats say you got a voice worth all this, then we believe 'em. Now, what do you want me to put on the sign?"

"Brannigan," she answered. "It's my maiden name. Lilly Brannigan."

Chapter Twenty-six

As soon as Lilly stepped out of her cabin, she lost some of her courage. From the porch of the little house, perched on a hill not far from Whiskey's tent home, Lilly could see the entire main street of Virginia City in the distance. What she saw now caused her heart to beat faster, and she wondered for the first time if she really could do this.

At least a hundred men had gathered on the hillside in front of the small platform of crates where Lilly had planned to sing for them. Hundreds more were coming down the street toward the site. Those standing just in front of the crude stage were already passing a hat, and she hadn't even opened her mouth yet. All she had done was practice quietly with two men who were to accompany her with a piano and a fiddle. Over the past few days, Lilly had discovered that whatever was needed in Virginia City, there was someone who could do it. There were carpenters, doctors, smithies, and even a few musicians, although none excelled in his field.

Lilly would be accompanied by Harry "Hands" McClannahan, who ordinarily used his talent on the piano at the Nugget Saloon. A man named Chester Heath would play the fiddle, and both men were waiting for her now, smiling. Joey tugged at his mother's hand.

"Come on, Mother. They're all waiting. I bet they've collected a hundred dollars already, and you haven't even sung yet!"

Lilly forced her legs to move, but they felt numb. This was much more difficult than the first time she had sung, back in Nauvoo. There her audience was made up of kind, Christian men and women who expected only hymns. This audience was ninety-five percent men—most of them rugged, bearded, hard-nosed prospectors and miners who expected entertainment. Suddenly, she was not so sure she could provide what they wanted, until Whiskey walked toward her on his bowed legs, all grins.

"Miss Lilly, you look worried. Don't be. You just think about how you sang for me and Daryl back in the valley. This ain't no different, I promise. You start out with that there *Home, Sweet Home,* and you'll have all of them wrapped around your little finger."

"I hope you're right, Whiskey," she answered, swallowing. She noticed Nettie Abler sitting not far from the stage. The woman smiled and winked at her. Lilly suspected Nettie was partly responsible for the big crowd. She smiled back, deciding she would invite Nettie to eat with her soon. She hadn't visited with her since the day Nettie had saved Joey from the runaway horses.

As Lilly walked with Joey toward the stage, the men began to clap and whistle. Joey ran to sit beside Nettie. Whiskey climbed up on the crates, and held up his hands. Men were still arriving. Someone walked up with a hatful of money, and handed it to Lilly.

"This one's full," he told her. "We've got to find another one to pass."

Lilly took it, thanking the man quietly and staring dumbfounded at the mound of gold, paper money, and coins. Whiskey was announcing her name and suddenly the crowd of men cheered and clapped. He came down and took the hat from Lilly, telling her he would watch it for her. Lilly wasn't sure how she managed to climb up on the crates, or how long her legs would hold out, and she wondered with sudden amusement what Hiram Williams would think of all this. It made her relax. She glanced at Joey, and he smiled back.

Hands McClannahan began to play the piano, and the crowd quieted. All eyes were on Lilly Brannigan. She closed her eyes and drew a deep breath, pretending she was in the foothills of Scotland again.

In moments she had captured the crowd with her strong soprano voice, which carried over the hills around Virginia City like magic. When she finished *Home, Sweet Home,* she thought at first they were not pleased, for there was hardly a sound, and no applause. Then she noticed that a man in the front row had tears in his eyes. He started clapping, then rose as others followed, whistling, shouting for more.

Lilly realized then that her voice could make her rich. And more important, she had discovered what truly made her happy—singing for a huge audience, just like she had once imagined as a little girl. When everyone had sat down again, Lilly went into another song. As she glanced at Nettie, she noticed the woman was crying softly. She wondered about Nettie's background. But for now there was only the singing. She sang Scottish folk songs and ballads, American songs she had learned over the years, and a few hymns. She sang encore after encore, until she finally had to stop, afraid that she would ruin her voice for the next concert. When the crowd had finally disbursed and Joey had finished collecting the money, a total of six hundred dollars in paper money and coins lay on the table in Lilly's house, along with a hatful of gold nuggets whose value Lilly couldn't even guess.

She felt faint. Lilly sat down in a chair, staring at the money, while Joey kept exclaiming over it, counting it again and again.

"Dear God," Lilly muttered, amazed. "Joey, go and get Whiskey. We have to get this into a bank, where it will be safe."

"I'll get him right now!" the boy said eagerly, rushing out the door. Lilly just sat staring at the money. "Dear God," she whispered again.

Within one year Lilly's earnings had far surpassed anything she and Zeb together had ever earned. Business was so good that there was no time to go back to the farm. The area's big gold strike finally came when Henry T.P. Comstock, called Old Pancake by most, struck gold on land he owned that stretched from Gold Hill on the south end of town, to Six-Mile Canyon on the north end. He shared the claim with two Irishmen—Patrick McLaughlin and Peter O'Riley—as well as with another of the original prospectors at Gold Hill, James Fennimore, rumored to have committed a murder in California and fled to Washoe to avoid the law. Fennimore changed his name to Finney and since he was from Virginia originally, came to be called Virginny Finney.

It seemed to Lilly that everyone in town had a nickname. She had even heard a few refer to her as the "widow woman." Men seemed to hold her in some kind of reverence, which was fine with her, for she had no personal interest in them. Her all-consuming interests were Joey, and making enough money to give him the best of everything, and she was aided by the discovery of something even better than gold—silver.

The heavy, bluish sand that was being thrown aside in search of gold was thought to be useless. The bothersome sludge clogged rockers and gave men aching muscles from shoveling it out of the way. But one curious prospector decided to have the odd sand assayed, only to discover that one two-and-a half-foot cube of Comstock ore yielded $3,000 in silver and only $876 in gold. Virginia City became a silver town overnight, with a new rush of miners flooding in. The highest-yielding mine came to be called the Ophir. Old Pancake sold his share and vanished, as did so many prospectors—men who slaved away to discover the gold or silver, but had no real understanding of how to actually mine it. They sold their discoveries for far less than their worth and left to go prospecting someplace new, and were often never heard from again.

Wealthier developers moved into town, and Virginia City grew. To Lilly's relief, a school was built. She continued to sing, and in spite of often being snubbed by other "respectable" women who had come to town, Lilly insisted on continuing her friendship with Nettie Abler. After learning about Nettie's unfortunate background, Lilly could only love and sympathize with her, even if she could never approve of the life Nettie led now.

Nettie's family had been killed in a fire back in Pennsylvania—parents, two sisters, and a brother. Nettie, only eight, had been left homeless and penniless. An uncle had taken her in—a man who turned out to be cruel and sadistic. He accepted money from friends to visit poor Nettie at night in her bed. Lilly could not imagine a more horrifying childhood, nor could she condemn the woman now. She was not sure how her life might have ended up if such a thing had happened to her. She would never forget the way Nettie wept when she told her story, and Lilly determined nothing would end their friendship.

Lilly fiercely protected her earnings. Joey was doing just fine, and the more money she could make, Lilly figured, the more wonderful a ranch Joey could have someday in the valley, when he was old enough to run it himself. He talked incessantly about raising horses.

There had been a time when she had wanted more than anything to see Chase Mitchell again. Now she prayed that he would never show up, for Joey was getting bigger, and it would be harder than ever to tell him the truth—to see the shame that would surely be in his eyes.

Before long, Lilly decided that what she earned through singing was not enough. She needed to invest in something more dependable—something that could continue to earn money for Joey if something should happen to her. And she could think of no more practical way to earn money in a place like Virginia City than to buy shares in whatever mine was earning the most at the time—the Ophir.

Lilly announced to Whiskey, who now worked in the Ophir, that she wanted to visit the mine and see how it was operated. "I intend to make an investment, Whiskey, but I want to know how my money will be used and how it will grow."

Whiskey shook his head. He had gotten over being surprised at Lilly Brannigan's independence—the way she deliberately defied the eyes and gossip of other women by visiting often with Nettie Abler; the way she so carefully guarded her money, spending it wisely and with great frugality; and the way in which she remained moral and respectable in spite of being a woman alone in a place like Virginia

City. He had no doubt that she was a rich woman already.
She gave three concerts a week, and men gathered by the
hundreds each time to listen. Lilly was ever kind and open to
them, graciously singing special requests, always ready with
a smile.

"Ma'am, it's a smart thing to invest in the Ophir," he told
Lilly. "I'll take you there tomorrow. The men will be glad to
show you around."

The next day, Lilly followed Whiskey and others up the
steep mountain, to a building where ore was dropped into
bins after being brought by wheelbarrows from the mine.

The noise inside the processing mill was painfully loud.
The sound of metal scraping against metal in the crushers
and stamps, as well as the steam engines turning the whir-
ring, oscillating belts, left Lilly close to deaf. For hours afterward, her ears rang so loud she could barely hear other
noises around her, and she wondered how the men could
bear working there, let alone in the sweltering heat of the
mine shafts hundreds of feet below the streets of the city.

When she returned to town, Lilly met with the mine's
owners to discuss buying shares in the Ophir and another,
smaller mine that had good potential. The men watched and
listened to her skeptically. They were not accustomed to
dealing with single women. But when Lilly plunked several
thousand dollars on the table in stacks of bills, their attitude
changed. The power of money gave her satisfaction. At last
she was in control of her own life—she felt as though she
actually belonged. And what she belonged to now was Virginia City.

Another year passed, and by 1860 Lilly's holdings and
investments had grown. She built a bigger home, farther
removed from town, and a small theater where people could
come and hear her sing for a price, but where no alcoholic
beverages were allowed. None of the men seemed to mind.
Lilly's Little Theater, as it came to be called, was a star
attraction, as was the beautiful, auburn-haired woman who
operated it.

Men came to gaze at her creamy skin, her provocative
green eyes, the way she filled out her beautiful gowns. She

was somewhat of a mystery to most of them—a woman who was seldom seen socially and who no man was brave enough to try to court. She had an untouchable quality about her, and held an almost revered position in the hearts of many of the men.

A few of the more respectable women in town, impressed by Lilly's wealth, began to overlook her strange association with Nettie Abler. She became somewhat popular among them. But Lilly was not fooled by what seemed to her empty gestures. Nettie remained her truest friend.

Virginia City grew to a population of several thousand. It filled up with more prospectors, developers, realtors, and all the suppliers needed to support so many citizens. Beneath the town lay a honeycomb of mines—the Yellow Jacket, the Knickerbocker, the Caledonia, the Dayton, the California, the Crown Point, and many more. The hills were covered with mills.

To reach Virginia City, people struggled over mountainous roads, in spite of the danger of pathways that snaked through canyons and over chilling precipices, hauling more machinery. Hundreds of thousands of acres of pine forests on nearby mountains were stripped clean for a stretch of nearly a hundred miles in order to find enough timber to shore up mines, build more buildings, and feed the large steam engines.

It wasn't until the summer of 1861 that Lilly and fourteen-year-old Joey had a chance to visit the farm again. They took Whiskey and Daryl along for protection, and Nettie so that she could see the place she had heard so much about.

For Lilly, however, the trip was for more than just nostalgia. Back East there was a war going on over slavery. She was not completely surprised that the issue had finally come to war, but she was worried about how long it would last, afraid that once Joey was old enough, he would go marching off to join the Union Army—something he thought sounded terribly exciting. Lilly had lain awake nights imagining with terror her son going off to war, never to come back, just like his real father had done. She hoped that visiting the farm would keep the boy's mind on staying put in Nevada.

It was a sad sight. The farmhouse was dilapidated, and

everything was overgrown. Lilly and Joey walked up to Zeb and Laura's graves and pulled weeds away from the head-stones.

"We'll live here again someday, won't we, Mother?" Joey asked, gently touching Zeb's headstone.

"Yes, Joey, we will. I promise. But I want to build us the finest home anyone ever had. I've invested in the Ophir and the Yellow Jacket both, and we're making a lot of money. It's all going to be yours someday. You've always wanted to raise horses. You can do that here, if you want. But we have to make even more money, first. And I want you to get your schooling."

She put a gloved hand on his shoulder. She wore beautiful clothes now—feathered hats and comfortable buttoned shoes. It felt good to be wealthy on her own—to be singing for audiences, earning money with her voice—and yet strangely sad. She stared at Zeb's headstone, remembering another life—a time when she sang hymns for people who had become like family to her. It had been so many years since she had seen any of her Mormon friends that it seemed like another life—something she had only thought about, but had never participated in . . . that terrible ocean voyage; watching her mother's coffin sink into the sea; her life at Nauvoo; the agonizing, death-filled journey west. And Chase. He remained the most stinging memory, perhaps be-cause she saw him every day in Joey.

"Will you sing for Pa, Mother?" Joey asked. "You know —that hymn he always liked?"

A lump rose in her throat. Poor Zeb. He had been so good to her, so patient. "Yes, Joey, I'll sing for him."

Joey stood back and looked at her expectantly, and she sang softly for him, her heart aching at the tears that came into his eyes. He turned then to face Zeb's grave. She felt again the terrible guilt of knowing the boy's real father was actually still alive. She knew she was somehow cheating her son, but she would rather see him grow up without a father than to know the truth.

She struggled not to cry in front of Joey, but inside, she wanted to fall to her knees and weep bitterly. She wished so many things in her life could have been different—that she had been a better wife to Zeb; that she had never had to marry him at all and ruin his chances for true happiness. She realized the only time she had been truly happy was when she had been with Chase. Her independence and wealth did not give her the warm, beautiful feeling she had once had when she was near him.

"We'll start the house this summer, Joey," she told him aloud. "I think I can take the risk. I promise you that by the time you're eighteen, you can start a ranch here in the valley. It will be our little retreat."

"You won't ever sell it?"

"No, Joey—never. This is Zeb Adams's land, and soon, you'll be running it yourself. But I want to do it right."

"Do you think Pa would want me to go to Utah and be a Mormon?"

No! No, don't go there! she wanted to shout. "I think Zeb would have wanted you to do whatever you feel is right, Joey."

He looked around at the farm—the only boyhood memory that was truly vivid for him. "I want to stay right here in Nevada—have a ranch here, like you talked about."

"Then, that's what we'll do." She breathed a sigh of relief, praying the war would end soon. She and Joey walked back down the hill to where Nettie waited. She watch Lilly closely. Nettie was wise in reading people's eyes, at seeing distant loneliness and fear. She had seen that look often in Lilly Brannigan's eyes. She stepped closer to her as Joey ran off to investigate old, familiar places.

"What is it, Lilly?" Nettie asked.

"What?"

"What is it you aren't telling me? I've spilled my guts out to you about my past, and my guess is you've got one of your own—one you've never told anyone about."

The fear came back into Lilly's eyes. "I've told you everything," Lilly answered, turning away.

Nettie grasped her arm. "Lilly, you can't hold things in forever. Sometimes it helps to talk—to share the burden you're carrying with just one person. Otherwise, the weight just gets heavier and heavier."

Lilly's eyes filled with tears. "I can carry it, Nettie—I

have to, for Joey's sake. And if you're really my friend, you'll respect my wish that you never bring this up again."

Nettie sighed, folding her arms. "I *am* your friend, Lilly. And someday you're going to have to unload. Just remember, you can trust me. I'm here when you need me."

Lilly smiled through tears. "I know. And I thank you for that." She turned away again. Joey was running back toward her, a smile on his face. She put a hand to her heart. That was what hurt the most—Joey's beautiful, provocative, winning smile. He was beginning to mirror the handsome young soldier she had once known and loved.

Chapter Twenty-seven

1861

Hiram stared at the poster, which said: COME TO LILLY'S LITTLE THEATER AND HEAR THE VOICE OF MISS LILLY BRANNIGAN, OUR SONGBIRD FROM SCOTLAND. EIGHT O'CLOCK TO TEN O'CLOCK P.M. TUESDAY, THURSDAY, AND SATURDAY.

He was not totally surprised that she had ended up running her life in a place like Virginia City. He had to smile at the memory of her stubborn, independent streak. He hoped she had not sold out her morals for this new life.

He headed his horse up the street after inquiring where he might find Lilly's Little Theater. He found the neat, freshly whitewashed building in a quiet section of the town—if one could call any part of Virginia City quiet. Potted flowers decorated the boardwalk in front of the building, and a young man was sweeping sand from in front of the door.

Hiram dismounted and tied his horse, his heart aching at the thought of Lilly being here, instead of at Salt Lake, where he had always thought she belonged. If she had never had to leave with Zeb, she wouldn't be here now. Still, she was apparently doing well. The building projected an air of quiet respectability.

As he approached the steps, the young man with the broom looked up at him. Hiram's heart nearly stopped.

"Can I help you?" the boy asked Hiram. "My mother doesn't sing until later tonight."

Hiram's eyes teared as he nodded. Could this really be the same little boy who had been only two years old when Lilly had left Salt Lake?

"Joey?"

The boy frowned in surprise. "You know me?"

Hiram nodded, suddenly realizing he had better explain. He couldn't tell the lad he looked like his real father. "I . . . when you mentioned your mother singing, I realized who you had to be. I knew her well, and I knew you when you were just a tot. I'm Hiram Williams."

Joey's eyes lit up. "Really? I was so little I don't remember you, but Mother and Pa used to talk about you all the time—you and your wife and kids and all." He put out his hand. "Yeah, I'm Joey. I feel like I already know you real good, Mr. Williams."

Hiram gripped his hand firmly. "Hello, Joey. My, what a fine, handsome lad you turned out to be. How old are you now?"

"I'm fourteen, sir—be fifteen come January."

Hiram smiled. It appeared as though Lilly had done a good job of raising him. "Is your mother around? I'd like very much to see her again."

"Sure!" Joey set the broom inside. "Come on in. She'll be real excited about this."

The boy led Hiram inside the building and headed to the back. Hiram looked around the big room, which was clean, but smelled of smoke. Everything was tidy. There was a stage, decorated with a backdrop depicting a valley with trees and flowers. A piano sat near it. He walked toward the door where Joey had gone, then stopped as it flew open and a beautiful woman appeared, her face alive with a smile of joy.

"Hiram! Hiram Williams!"

He was stunned. She was much more beautiful than he remembered her. The passing years, and the hardship and loss, had somehow enhanced her beauty, rather than destroying it. Her dress was a cream-colored satin, gracing the milky skin of her bare shoulders in gentle gathers. Her red-gold hair was swept up at the sides and fell in a cascade of curls at the back, and her smile was warm and genuine as she rushed up to him to greet him with a hug.

"Oh, Hiram, what brings you here? I can't believe my eyes! Is Mary with you, or anyone else I know?"

She pulled back. They both had tears in their eyes. "No, I'm afraid no one you know is with me. I came with a group of Mormon men who are looking into reestablishing a settlement near Carson City. I decided I couldn't come this far without finding you. I came across a man in the valley who said there was a Lilly Brannigan in Virginia City who sang prettier than anything anybody ever heard, so I knew it had to be you."

Lilly blushed a little and led him into her office. "I'm so glad you looked me up, Hiram. It's good to see an old friend."

Hiram felt strange at being called an old friend, after the hard feelings there had once been between them. But time had a way of healing things. He wondered if it had healed her hurt over Chase Mitchell.

"I'll go finish sweeping, Mother," Joey told her. "Maybe you want to talk alone with Mr. Williams for a while."

Lilly gave him a quick hug. "You're too understanding for someone so young, Joey Adams," she told him. "Go ahead and finish. We'll all do something together a little later."

Joey nodded to Hiram and left. Lilly's smile momentarily faded as she watched him go. She glanced at Hiram.

"He seems like a fine boy, Lilly. You've done well with him."

Each knew what the other was thinking. Lilly turned away quickly. She walked over to a polished mahogany desk and sat down behind it. "Have a seat, Hiram," she told him, her enthusiasm beginning to return.

Hiram studied the obviously expensive desk, which displayed a neat array of books and ledgers, as he sat down across from her in a leather chair.

"Oh, Hiram, it must have been such a difficult trip for you. Are you all right? Would you like something to drink? Apple juice? Lemonade?"

"No, thank you, Lilly. I can only stay the night, and then I'm heading back. Everyone is waiting for me at Carson City." He studied her lovingly. "Of course, I could stay longer if you wanted to consider coming back to Salt Lake with us. People still talk about you and miss you—especially Mary. Catheryn and Henry are still there, and Mary and the children."

She lost her smile. "No, Hiram. I miss them all so much, but this is home now. I can't go back to that life. And Joey likes it here, too. He doesn't want to leave the farm. Someday he's going to have his own ranch there, and we're even building a new home on that land. I've already hired men to start." She sighed longingly. "How is Mary?"

"Oh, she's got the usual old-age complaints, but she's doing all right. You should see Salt Lake, Lilly. It's a big, beautiful city now, and the temple is rising—it's much more magnificent than any we have ever built."

Her smile returned, only softer. There was a hint of sorrow in it. "I have no doubt it's more beautiful than any building in this whole country. I'm so glad for all of you. We heard that the trouble with the government turned out to be nothing."

He grinned and nodded. "Thanks to the diplomacy of Brigham Young. Oh, what a home he has built for himself —and his many wives, I might add. It's two stories, with white pillars. My own home is quite fine. I always wanted to make up to Mary for taking her from our home in Nauvoo. This one is even better."

"I have no doubt about that, either."

Hiram frowned. "Lilly, I do wish you would think about coming back. This place—"

"I'm fine here, Hiram. This is a very respectable theater, and we allow no gambling or drinking or roughhousing. I have made a great deal of money, and have invested in a mine that is doing quite well. My home in the valley will rival anything anyone has built yet out here. We're placing it not far from the old house, a little closer to Zeb and Laura's graves. You remember, I wrote to tell you I lost a baby girl."

"Yes. I'm sorry about that, Lilly."

"I won't leave the graves, Hiram."

He sighed deeply. "There were no other children?"

She reddened slightly and looked away. "No. I just . . . couldn't seem to conceive."

Hiram sighed. "Well, at least Zeb had Joey. He loved him like—" He hesitated.

"Like he was his own?" Lilly finished for him. The joy left her eyes again, and she looked down at a ledger sheet on her desk. "Zeb was a wonderful father to Joey."

"And you're a wonderful mother. I have no doubts about that." He sighed again and cleared his throat. "Lilly . . . did you get my inquiry a few years ago—about someone coming to see you?"

She felt her cheeks go crimson. Her blood warmed at the thought of Chase. Hiram noticed her visibly stiffen. "Yes. We realized what you must have meant."

"He came to Nauvoo, Lilly. I couldn't bring myself to tell you in a letter. I never even told Mary about it. He went to see Catheryn, too."

She flashed him a look of fear. Catheryn! Had she told Chase about the boy? Surely not! Surely, if he knew . . .

"He was a little late!" she said aloud, turning away.

"Lilly, he claimed he wrote you—many times. I don't know if it's true or not, but I thought you should know." He saw her tremble. "My God," he said, "does it still upset you that much to talk about him after all these years?" She kept her face turned away from him. Hiram frowned. "I'm sorry to bring it up, Lilly. I just thought you had a right to know."

Lilly struggled to stay in control. "Did he tell you about the only letter I *did* receive?" she asked, her voice shaking, the words bitter.

"What do you mean?"

She faced him, a tear making its way out of one eye and down her cheek. "The letter he sent me telling me he was wro g to want to get married. He said that what we had was just infatuation, and that he intended to make the army his life! He said he was never coming back!"

She angrily wiped at tears while Hiram listened in surprise. "He never mentioned anything like that, Lilly. He seemed sincere when he told me he had written you several times, and seemed surprised that you had never received the letters. He said he had been wounded in Mexico and hadn't been able to get back right away. He was extremely upset to hear you had married. He ... couldn't understand why you didn't wait longer."

She sat up straighter, looking him squarely in the eyes. "You didn't say anything? You didn't tell him? I don't want him to ever know, Hiram, and I don't want Joey to know!"

He shook his head, feeling sorry for her. "No, I didn't tell him. I made a promise, remember? I wouldn't have wanted him to come here and make trouble for you and Zeb."

Lilly reached for her handbag and took a handkerchief from it. "Thank you," she muttered. "I'm sure ... Catheryn didn't say anything either."

She broke down into tears. Hiram rose and put his hand on her shoulder. "It's all in the past now, Lilly."

"I wish it could be for me," she wept. "It wouldn't be so bad, if not for poor Zeb. He was so good to me, and I was such a terrible wife. I never loved him the way I should have."

"Zeb was a patient, understanding man. I'm sure you weren't nearly as terrible as you think you were. He always seemed happy."

"If only I had a chance to make up for it—to tell him I loved him. My whole life has been a lie, Hiram, for Joey's sake. He must never know. He thinks of Zeb as his father." She looked up at him with tear-filled eyes. "What would he think of me, Hiram? I would die if I ever saw shame in his eyes. He's my whole life! He's all I have—the only honest love I've ever known."

Hiram knelt in front of her. "Lilly, the boy seems happy and well adjusted. If you told him, I hardly think he would be ashamed of you or hate you—at least, not for long. The bond you share with your son can't really be broken. He seems to have a warm, forgiving personality. Why, I've only talked to him for a moment, and I can see that. A lot of Zeb's gentle nature rubbed off on him. You have to have more faith in him, Lilly."

She shook her head. "I'll never tell him. Never!"

"That's your choice, and I won't interfere with it. I never even told Mary my suspicions."

She tried to smile through her tears. "Thank you, Hiram." She studied his eyes. "Do you really think Chase Mitchell was serious about the letters?"

"He certainly seemed to be. He was so upset when he left I was sure he would come out here. That was why I asked then if you had had any unusual visitors."

Lilly closed her eyes, remembering the man on the rise. It gave her shivers to think it might have been Chase. She rose and walked away from Hiram to look out a window into an alley. "I had no visitors. Apparently Chase Mitchell wasn't all that upset." She faced Hiram. "And I never got any letters. Maybe he was lying. Maybe he had changed his mind again and thought he could just walk back into my life after telling me he didn't want me." She drew in her breath. A hardness came into her green eyes. "It's a good thing he didn't try. I'd shoot him before I would let him come between me and Joey. I'm glad he never came to see me— glad he doesn't know about Joey. It serves him right, not even knowing he has a son!"

Hiram watched her a moment, seeing through the firm defiance in her eyes. "You never really stopped loving him, did you, Lilly?"

Her determined hatred vanished. She turned to watch a wagon rattle through the alley. "No," she answered in a near whisper. 'But if it's possible to love and hate a man with equal passion, then that is how I feel about Chase Mitchell. I've never been truly happy for one moment since the day he left Nauvoo. Joey is my only joy. My biggest regret is never having loved Zeb like I should have. I will never forgive myself for that—or forgive Chase Mitchell."

"It isn't good to hold too much hatred in your heart, Lilly. We learn from our mistakes and we move on."

Lilly smiled bitterly. "Thank you for keeping the secret. I'm sorry for all the hurt I caused you and Mary."

"We're old and tough. We can take it."

Lilly thought about the night Mary had wept against her shoulder. "Yes, I suppose." She wiped her eyes and blew her nose. "Let's not talk about it anymore. You will come to our house and I'll cook you a fine lunch." She took Hiram's arm and led him to the door. "Joey, we're going to the house. Please get the buggy," she told her son.

Hiram watched the boy, realizing how painful it must be for Lilly to have to look at him every day and see Chase Mitchell in that handsome smile and those blue eyes.

For a few short hours Lilly was with the Mormons again, through Hiram. To see him again hurt in many ways, for it brought back all the old memories, yet she cherished every moment, for she knew this would truly be the last time she would ever see him. He was getting too old to make another trip, and she was determined she would never go back across the desert, no matter how much safer the trail might be now.

As they shared a meal, Joey got to know Hiram better. Hiram told them about the thousands of emigrants who inhabited Salt Lake now and the talk of bringing railroads west. Lilly thought sadly how wonderful it would have been to be able to come west by train instead of by wagon. She had never seen a train herself, but she had heard about the wood-eating monsters that could pull hundreds of people and their belongings all at once. People around Virginia City talked about building one into Gold Hill someday to bring supplies and haul the ore back out, but Lilly could not imagine how men could construct a track through the maze of mountains and canyons that led to the gold fields. For now, everything came and went by wagon. Most of the refined gold and silver was taken over the mountains to San Francisco, or south to Reno and Carson City, by an express company called Wells Fargo.

"Someday the West will be as populated as the East," Hiram told them. "We can see it happening. More and more people come out every year—to settle, not to look for gold. But then, gold remains the biggest draw."

Lilly thought about her own first journey west with Hiram and Zeb. She wondered how many Gentiles had come here without realizing or appreciating that the Mormons had paved the way for them—had cut many of the first roads.

Hiram and Lilly talked late into the night—about Salt Lake, about Mary and the family, about the home Lilly planned to build in the valley, about Joey—but there was no more mention of Chase Mitchell. Lilly sang Hiram's favorite Mormon hymn for him once more, and in the morning he left.

Chapter Twenty-eight

1863

Chase threw down his cards, then shoved his money toward Garth Wheeler. "Garth, with your reputation, I should have known better than to get involved in a card game with you."

Wheeler grinned. He was a handsome man for his age, which Chase guessed to be perhaps fifty—ten years older than he was. But Garth Wheeler was a man who took care of himself and lived a good life, mostly off other people. He was probably the most notorious gambler in San Francisco —a man who had had two wives and had left them both, after bleeding them of their fortunes. There was a careless charm about him that made him likeable in spite of his questionable character, and he had never been accused of cheating. Chase figured he was very lucky, as well.

"Chase, you're a fine opponent. It was neck and neck there for a while," Garth answered, chewing on a thin, expensive cigar. "I do hope you have some money left."

Chase grinned. "If I did, I would never tell you."

Garth laughed. "You don't fool me, Mitchell. You raked it in good on that gold claim you sold, and you're a smart man. You shouldn't go spending it all in one place, like a lot of those fool prospectors. I heard about the Lilly Branni-gan."

"I sold that mine six years ago."

"Ah, but everybody still talks about it." Garth removed the cigar from his mouth. "Dammit, Chase, you know everybody wonders about the name of that mine. Satisfy my curiosity—who is Lilly Brannigan?"

Chase's smile faded into a kind of sad resignation. "A woman I knew once, that's all."

Garth's eyebrows arched. "You never married her?"

Now the smile was completely gone as Chase gathered up what was left of his money and dropped it into his pockets. "No."

"Oh, do I detect some bitterness?"

A piano player began to pound out a lively tune in the smoky saloon. "It was a long time ago. I met her back in Illinois. She was living with Mormons—came over here with them from Scotland—but she wasn't Mormon herself." Chase picked up his drink and studied it. "She was the pret-tiest woman I had ever set eyes on." He swallowed his drink, then gave Garth a warning look. "I would just as soon change the subject."

"All right," Garth answered, waving him off. "Sorry I asked. But don't tell me you've never been married—a handsome young man like you."

"I'm not so young. In these parts, forty can be pretty old."

"Why, hell, I'm forty-nine and feeling just fine. And you look as strong as a man half your age."

Chase shrugged. "I've been in my share of brawls over the years—never lost one yet."

Garth laughed, his dark eyes sparkling. He wore only the finest silk suits and satin vests. His dark hair was still thick and neatly cut. A thin mustache sat perfectly over his upper lip.

"At any rate, I've never been married. Never found a woman I wanted that bad," Chase added.

"Except Lilly Brannigan," Garth said slyly. Chase gave him an almost threatening look. Wheeler quickly changed the subject. "I've been married twice, and it's hard to say which woman was more beautiful. It didn't matter much. They were both rich. I did quite well."

Chase grinned and shook his head. "You're a bastard, Wheeler."

Garth frowned. "You know, both of them told me that, too." They laughed. "But then, I've been on my own ever since I was ten, and my mother deserted me on the streets of Philadelphia," Garth added. "I've been practicing survival ever since."

"Getting back at your mother by using women to get what you need?" Chase suggested.

Wheeler shrugged. "By God, you might be right. I never thought of it that way." He laughed lightly. "I didn't know I was gambling with some kind of philosopher."

Chase shook his head and chuckled. "I haven't done so well with my own life, so I don't think I fit that title."

The men had met only two weeks earlier, when they had attended a meeting of Wells Fargo shareholders in San Francisco. Both had money to invest—most of Garth Wheeler's from gambling and con schemes; Chase's from selling the Lilly Brannigan. It was not the biggest yielding mine among those of the original gold rush of 1849, but it had done well.

Never able to really settle down after learning of Lilly's marriage, Chase had invested his money and spent many years drifting from one job to another. He had not really needed the work, but he had wanted to stay busy. There had been women in his life—one he had even come close to marrying—but he had never quite forgotten Lilly. He had been tempted many times to look her up again, but had decided it was no use now. Too many years had gone by. The hurt had run too deep. And, after all, Lilly was married. He figured she probably had six or seven children by now, and after living on a Nevada farm all these years, she probably didn't even resemble the Lilly he had known. He wondered if she could still sing the way she used to. Maybe she wasn't even in the Washoe Valley anymore. Maybe she had gone back to Utah.

Chase and Garth had struck up a kind of temporary friendship, but only because each was drifting and happened to be in San Francisco at the same time. They had hit every fancy club and saloon in the city, gambling well into the night, often spending the rest of those nights with the prettiest, highest-paid prostitutes they could find. In many ways the two were alike—drifters with money. But Garth Wheeler's money was ill-gotten, and he had no scruples. Chase didn't trust him for a second. But there was something about Wheeler's total lack of morals and his open honesty about his *dis*honesty that made him entertaining.

"Well, Chase, I guess this is goodbye, unless you want to come with me. I'm leaving San Francisco for a time to try my luck in new places."

"Where are you headed?"

Garth relit his cigar. "Virginia City. They say it's a hell of a wild town, full of prospectors just waiting to get taken. Sounds like the prospects of making a little money there are very good."

Chase laughed. "I expect they are. But no, thanks, Garth. I, uh, don't have much use for Nevada." Why did the thought of Lilly still cause such an ache in his heart? It made him angry. "I was thinking about driving for Wells Fargo."

Surprise showed on the other man's face. "For God's sake, why? That's a dangerous job, Chase. You don't need it."

Chase shrugged. "It's something to do. Besides, if I'm going to invest in the company, I might as well get a first-hand look at how it operates. Kind of like protecting my own investment."

"Well, then, I might see you after all. They make a lot of runs to Virginia City."

Chase nodded. "I don't mind driving wagons full of gold and silver back and forth, as long as I don't have to stay there."

"What on earth do you have against Nevada?"

Chase rose and put on his Stetson. "I don't know. There's just . . . nothing there, that's all. California is prettier."

"Well, Garth Wheeler goes where the money is. Makes no difference to me how pretty a place is."

Chase shook his head and put out his hand. "Good luck, Garth. Don't break too many hearts or cheat too many people."

Garth shook his hand. "I'll do my best. Nice knowing you, Mitchell. We'll probably meet again sometime, unless you do something even more foolish, like get yourself involved in the War between the States back east."

"No, thanks. I've had my fill of war. I did my bit down in Mexico, and I'm still carrying the scars. I'll stay this side of the Sierras. You can look me up when you come back this way if you want—as long as it's not for a business deal. I don't trust you any farther than I could throw you."

Garth laughed, taking the remark as a compliment. "I'm off to Nevada, then. I want to get started right away in the morning. There is a wagon train of supplies going to Virginia City. If I don't head out soon, I'll find myself buried in some damned snow drift on top of the Sierras. Good luck to you, too, Mitchell."

He left, walking in the straight, cocky manner akin only to men like Garth Wheeler. Chase smiled sadly. He had been tempted to go with him, but there was nothing in Nevada for Chase—at least, not anything he wanted anymore.

By 1863 the name Lilly Brannigan was familiar to every man, woman, and child of Virginia City. Her rich voice had a way of bringing back old memories. She could make a person feel more in love, or homesick for wherever he or she had come from. There were no "original citizens" of Virginia City, except for the few babies who were born now and then. Not only were many states represented in that wild mountain town, but other countries as well, and all shared the same occasional nostalgia for home.

Lilly fed that nostalgia through her songs. But when a miner asked her once to sing *My Bonnie Lies Over the Ocean*, Lilly's beautiful smile faded, and she seemed to temporarily lose her composure. She had to force herself to keep smiling.

"I . . . I don't think I know that song," she lied, remembering the day Chase Mitchell had sung it to her, using her name instead of Bonnie.

"Oh, everybody knows that one," the man answered. He stood up and started singing it, and others joined in, the men giving Lilly a rousing rendition of the song in unison. They motioned for Lilly to join in, and she had no choice but to do so. She wondered suddenly how she could feel so alone with so many people around her.

Bring back, bring back,
Oh, bring back my Bonnie to me . . . to me.

She could see Chase's face, leaning over her, his blue eyes alive with love. Was it true about the letters? If it was, then why had he sent that awful letter of rejection? If only Joey didn't look so much like his father. Maybe then it would be easier to forget his face, his eyes, his unnerving smile. But the older Joey got. . . .

Oh, bring back my Lilly to me.

She could hear Chase singing the words as clearly as if it were yesterday. But yesterday had been seventeen years ago.

Garth Wheeler watched her closely, totally enraptured by the fact that she was single and rich and surely very lonely. Her songs moved from gentle melodies to hand-clapping tunes accompanied by a banjo—songs of mining and the west that were so lively the audience joined in the singing. He could see there was not a man watching who was not spellbound by Lilly Brannigan—her beauty, her charm, her voice, the innocent, sometimes sorrowful look in her captivating green eyes.

Could this be the Lilly Brannigan Chase Mitchell had named his mine after? He had conned enough information about her in Virginia City to reckon she was. An old geezer named Whiskey Stokes had been the most helpful. The old man seemed proud of his friendship with her, and had bragged about being the one to bring her to Virginia City. "Her and the boy," the old man had said. "Fine son she's got."

Garth wondered if Chase knew the woman he once loved had a child. This had to be her. How many beautiful Lilly Brannigans could there be who had once lived among Mormons? Yes, this was surely Chase Mitchell's Lilly. And being a woman, there had to be a way not only to get under her dress, but to get hold of her money. She definitely had money. She apparently owned her theater, and he had learned she was building a mansion of a home in the Washoe Valley.

Obviously, the best way to get to her money was to marry her, and that, indeed, would not be an unpleasant situation. She stirred desires in him that the best whores had not, for she was almost pristine—a woman of flawless virtue, or so everyone told him. Garth had yet to meet a woman of "flawless" virtue, and he wondered if this one might have some stain on her past that would be useful to him. After all, Chase Mitchell still carried a flaming torch for her. He had surely been involved in her life before she had married her Mormon husband. What had gone wrong? He didn't really much care. Even though the men of Virginia City said Lilly Brannigan was not interested in being courted, Garth Wheeler knew she most certainly had some passion and womanly needs buried under all that perfection, or Chase Mitchell would not still be so affected by the mention of her name.

He watched the flow of her satin gown, studied her milky skin, tried to envision how her long hair might look over her shoulders, her bare, ample breasts, if it were let down. Every man in the room was in love with her. That presented the kind of challenge Garth Wheeler liked. He felt a surging desire to be the one to break her down, to win her affection and her money. He would have to be careful with this one— she was a smart woman. And he did not doubt that any man who did her wrong would be tarred and feathered by the citizens of Virginia City.

The one-woman concert finished, and the whole room stood up and applauded. Garth was amazed at how well-mannered they were, considering the wild atmosphere of most of the saloons in town. But here they sat, at tables with no liquor, making hardly a sound. Garth watched her bow, and wondered if she was the reason Chase Mitchell wanted nothing to do with Nevada.

If Chase doesn't want her, he thought, *he surely won't mind if I have a turn at her. It will be quite a topic for discussion if I ever run into him again.*

He made a swift exit. He didn't want to meet Miss Brannigan yet. He had some planning to do.

Lilly studied a bill she had received from one of the carpenters she had hired. The house was coming along nicely. By next summer it would be finished, after nearly three years of construction. It was going to be as grand a home as any in the West—two stories, with eight large rooms. There were two bathing rooms downstairs, plus one for each bedroom upstairs and a large, bright kitchen. Men were already busily landscaping the grounds, including installing a fountain on the front lawn from a natural spring Zeb had once used to bring water to the house. She had already ordered fine furnishings and velvet draperies from San Francisco, and she had promised Joey they would spend a lot of time there next summer.

How she wished Zeb could see the home she was building on the site of the old farm. The fields were gone, replaced by broad, green lawns. A curved brick drive lined with shrubs led to the gracious double-door entranceway. The sprawling ponderosa pines would remain—their cool, green shade would be welcome in the summer. The fields would be turned into pasture and fenced corrals for Joey's horses. Already he had picked out an expensive palomino mare and her chestnut-colored foal. He had wanted to buy a stallion and start raising horses right away, but Lilly had insisted he wait until he was eighteen. The horses Joey had already purchased were boarded in Virginia City, waiting to go to their new home in the valley, and Joey visited them every day. He curried them himself. He was learning all he needed to learn about horses from an old stable man, who was happy to teach the boy.

Lilly put down her pen, picturing her new home, wishing Hiram and Mary and the others could see it. She wondered what they would think of her now—what Laura would have thought. How she wished she could bring her friend to her estate. Oh, how Laura would have carried on! The thought brought tears to her eyes but a smile to her lips.

It had been so long since she had stood by Laura's grave, somewhere out on that long, lonesome prairie! How fast the years went by. How she wished she could see the half smile on Zeb's face when he looked at her grand house.

She hoped the huge gravestones she had ordered for Zeb and little Laura's graves were fitting enough. She was determined they would not be lost to the elements. She didn't doubt that the graves of many of those who had died on that terrible journey west were already lost forever—dug up by wolves, trampled over by wagons and animals, their pitiful wooden markers destroyed by the elements.

Joey suddenly barged into her office, his face glowing with excitement. "Mother, come and listen! They're going to build an opera house—just for you!"

Lilly frowned. "What?"

"Half the men in town—they're gathered out in front of the theater. Some man called Garth Wheeler is getting them all together, asking them to donate money to build an opera house for Virginia City. He's talking about bringing in actors and dancers, too!"

Lilly smiled in amusement, rising slowly.

"Hurry up!" Joey urged. "Come and listen!"

Lilly was doubtful as she followed Joey to the front of the building and opened the door to look out. A well-dressed man with a fine build and pleasant voice was standing on the boardwalk in front of the theater, rallying a crowd of men who watched and listened.

'What do you say, men? Is Virginia City just as good as San Francisco?"

There was a barrage of shouts and whistles.

"Don't we deserve our own fine opera house?"

Everyone cheered, and the man who led them removed a silk top hat and handed it to a ragged-looking prospector standing at the front of the crowd. "Pass it around, sir. Everyone put in what you can and spread the word. In one week we will start construction, right over there." He pointed to a steep foothill just east of town. "This is mostly for Miss Lilly Brannigan, men. She deserves a proper setting for such a fabulous voice."

They shouted their agreement.

"It will be our gift to her for all the joy she has given us. I will be collecting donations for the next two weeks. All the money will go into a special fund at the Nevada Bank. You have my word. We'll show everyone how civilized and modern Virginia City has become. Whatever is needed after all of you have donated, I will contribute myself so that we can get the building underway immediately. Remember, this is for Miss Brannigan, so don't be stingy!"

Lilly stayed just inside the doorway, hardly able to believe what she was hearing. Sixteen-year-old Joey went up to the man on the boardwalk. "Hey, mister, you want to meet my mother in person?"

Garth turned. The young man looked familiar, but Garth couldn't quite figure out why. "Yes, of course."

"I'm Joey Adams—Lilly Brannigan's son. Her real name is Mrs. Adams. She just uses her maiden name when she sings."

Garth nodded. "So, you're the son! Well, Joey, I'm glad to meet you. A lot of these men have told me about you." He shook Joey's hand. "You say I can meet your mother?"

"Yes, sir, she's right inside. It sure is nice of you to get everybody started on building an opera house. My mother has said a lot of times she used to dream about singing in one."

Garth smiled, secretly feeling a small victory had been won. He could think of no better way to win Lilly Brannigan's heart than by acting on what she loved most—her son and her singing. Winning her trust meant everything. He followed Joey through the doorway of the theater to meet Lilly face to face, and in spite of his scheming, and the fact that he had had plenty of women, he could not help the slight flutter of his heart at the sight of her. He bowed slightly, removing his hat.

"I am honored to meet you, Miss Brannigan," he told her. "I have heard you sing several times, but you never noticed me in the audience. I am Garth Wheeler, come here from San Francisco to look into mining investments."

Lilly felt a slight flush rise to her cheeks. She didn't know this man, and any man she didn't know, she also didn't trust. But this was certainly the most handsome and charming man who had ever graced Virginia City. His clothes were immaculate, and his manners seemed impeccable.

"Hello, Mr. Wheeler," she said softly. "I . . . heard your little speech out there. I don't know what to say."

"There is nothing to say. All you have to do is sing—in the finest opera house in the Sierras." Garth turned to Joey. "Young man, would you please go out there and keep an eye on that hat? Needless to say, not every man out there can be trusted. Bring it to me after it has been passed around."

"Yes, sir!" Joey ran out to the crowd, feeling suddenly important. He liked Garth Wheeler. The man was doing something wonderful for his mother. Inside, Lilly frowned slightly as she studied Garth Wheeler's dark eyes. "I don't quite understand, Mr. Wheeler. You don't even know me."

"Oh, but I don't need to. I only need to hear you sing, Miss Brannigan. The very first time I heard you, I knew you deserved more than this little building in the middle of this wicked town. A voice like yours—beauty like yours—belongs in a place more fitting. The proper acoustics will enhance your voice, and you need more space. I've seen the lines of men waiting outside this building every night, glad for the chance to just hear you through the windows. I am a man of means, with no family to concern me. I have been a lot of places and have earned my fortune. I like to find worthy subjects to spend my money on."

Lilly felt slightly unnerved by his handsome face, the way his eyes moved over her. "I'm no pauper, Mr. Wheeler. I don't need your charity."

He looked hurt. "Oh, Miss Brannigan, I hardly call it charity. I am perfectly aware that you are quite well set. I am doing this simply because I want to—because this town owes you a proper setting for your talent. Besides, don't you agree it's time Virginia City moved up in standing with the other great cities of the West? Why, I hear they'll be taking nearly eleven million dollars' worth of ore out of Gold Hill this year, and even more next year. Look how the town has grown. It's time we brought some class and refinement to Virginia City, don't you think?"

Lilly crossed her arms self-consciously. "I suppose. But you haven't been a citizen of Virginia City for long—I never heard of you until today. What difference does it make to you how refined we are?"

Garth laughed. "My, you're a skeptic, aren't you?"

"I've learned to be one. Someone I knew once taught me."

"Hmmm." Garth wondered if she meant Chase Mitchell. "Well, to answer your question, I've done these things before. As I said, I have no family, no particular responsibilities, but I do have money. I've spent most of my time in California—I decided to come to Virginia City because I've heard so much about this booming gold town."

"More silver than gold."

"Oh, yes! Isn't it amazing that the gold miners were throwing away all that silver without even knowing it? At any rate, here I am. I came to visit, heard you sing, and immediately I realized what a necessity it was that Virginia City have an opera house. Surely, you agree with that."

Lilly felt a stab of pain at the words. Singing in an opera house was her dream. Now, here was this stranger talking of building one in Virginia City. At last, she could sing in the surroundings she had always dreamed about. How ironic that it was a total stranger who was going to make that dream come true. "I don't know what to say, Mr. Wheeler."

"Please—call me Garth. And since it looks like the opera house will be built, I hope you will work with me on the plans. I really don't know much about how a voice carries, what a singer wants to see in the way of staging and seating. Perhaps you can help me with such things. As soon as the money is raised, I'll hire carpenters who know what they're doing." He was pleased at the look on her face. He could see she was touched. In fact, she looked nearly ready to cry.

"I would be pleased to help you," Lilly told him. "But next spring I will be going into the Washoe Valley often. I'm building a summer home there."

"Then, we'll get most of the opera house done over the winter, even if we have to haul lumber and equipment over the Sierras in a snowstorm."

Joey came running in then with a hat so full of money the boy had to press his hand over the top to keep it from falling out. "Look at this!" the boy exclaimed. "You want me to count it, Mr. Wheeler?"

Joey looked up at Garth with wide, blue eyes and a

charming smile. Suddenly even Garth, who was accustomed to faking everything, had to struggle not to show his surprise. Chase Mitchell! *That* was why the boy looked familiar! He looked just like a young Chase! Garth could not help but stare at the boy for a moment.

"Mr. Wheeler? You want me to count it?" Joey repeated.

Garth blinked and swallowed. "Oh! Yes, of course. You look like a fine, honest young man. Dump it out on that table over there and count it for me." Garth watched the young man walk over to the table. Joey was sixteen, he had been told, but the boy was tall and broad. He looked more like eighteen or nineteen. He dumped out the money and turned to look once more at Garth. His profile, the smile—there was no doubt in Garth's mind. Now he wondered not only if Chase knew Lilly Brannigan had a son, but that he was surely the boy's father. Garth was aware that the boy's Mormon father had died—but perhaps his *real* father was not dead at all!

"He's a handsome boy, with fine manners, Miss Brannigan."

Lilly was watching Joey, and Garth could see the love and devotion in her eyes. "Yes, he is," she answered. "I'm very proud of him. His father would be, too, if he could have lived to see what a good young man he's become."

Garth watched her carefully. "Yes, I'm sure he would. I'm told he's dead."

Lilly met his eyes, her own showing such great sorrow that Garth actually felt sorry for her for a moment. "Yes. He died in a freak accident, six years ago. The home I'm building is on the site of our old farm in the valley."

"Oh, I would love to see it."

She smiled, reddening slightly. "Maybe in the spring. I feel I owe you something for instigating the construction of an opera house, Mr. Wheeler—I mean, Garth."

He gave her his most charming smile. "Letting me take you to dinner would be payment enough. I would be honored."

Lilly smiled nervously. "I don't know. I . . . rarely see men."

Garth frowned. "A beautiful young woman like you? Pardon me, Miss Brannigan, but you can't mourn your dead husband forever. You said yourself it has been six years." He wondered if she had actually gone six years without taking a man to her bed! To a man like Garth, that seemed incredible. How interesting that this woman, who had surely borne an illegitimate son, was so chaste now. The challenge was growing more interesting. He saw the color come to her cheeks, saw her defenses rising.

"Don't take offense, Miss Brannigan. I am not talking lightly. I am just concerned. You're certainly the most beautiful woman in Virginia City, and you shouldn't be living your life alone. Surely, you would at least like to do something besides sing every night and retire to a lonely room afterward."

She moved away from him slightly. "I'm not lonely, Mr. Wheeler."

He noticed she was not using his first name now. He had overstepped his bounds. He put on his serious look.

"Forgive me, Miss Brannigan. Please don't take everything I say so seriously. I'm simply a man who enjoys life and likes to see others enjoy it. I beg you to allow me to come calling tonight and take you to eat—to the fanciest restaurant in Virginia City. Besides, it will be mostly business. I want to talk about the opera house."

He saw her struggling with her emotions. She sighed deeply before answering, watching him carefully.

"All right. I suppose I owe you that much."

Garth smiled, his eyes moving her, awakening needs that had been buried inside her so long that she hardly recognized them.

"Thank you, Miss Brannigan. You have made me a very happy man." He glanced at Joey again as the boy carefully counted the money. Yes—Joey Adams was every bit Chase Mitchell. This would be his most interesting conquest—pleasant in every aspect, and profitable. He felt almost guilty for plotting to take advantage of such a beautiful woman—a devoted mother, no less. But then, a man had to look out for himself.

Chapter Twenty-nine

1864

Lilly walked into the supply store with a basket on her arm. She had invited Nettie for supper, much to the chagrin of Garth Wheeler, who seemed to have a way of occupying nearly all of her spare time. In the several months they had worked together on the opera house, he had become an almost constant companion. Lilly's feelings for him were mixed.

There was something about the man that made her wary —a distant sense of danger that made it difficult to feel real affection for him. He seemed too possessive for a relationship that was, in her mind, far from serious. She had seen too little of her old friends, like Whiskey, and Garth had a special aversion to Nettie. He found it impossible to understand why a proper woman like herself would want to be friends with a prostitute. Everyone in town had more or less accepted the friendship, except Garth.

Lilly walked to a barrel of onions and began to sort through them.

"Anything I can help you with, Miss Lilly?" the storekeeper asked.

"No, Lenny, I just need a few things. I know where they are."

The man grinned. "Won't be long now, will it?" Lilly met his eyes. "Before you'll be singing in the opera house," he finished.

Lilly smiled, excited about the near completion of the huge structure, which had been planned in detail by Lilly and Garth. It had taken only the winter to complete the Virginia City Opera House—complete with built-in seats, a balcony, a large stage, and several scenic backdrops.

"No, it won't be long. I'm looking forward to it. But I will only be able to sing there from April until July. I promised Joey we'd go to our new home in the valley in August and spend a month or two there."

"Well, you'll be sorely missed," the man answered.

"Thank you, Lenny."

"You won't leave us for good, will you? I mean, we all helped build the opera house just for you."

Lilly put two onions in her basket and walked to the potato bin. "I'll never leave Virginia City for good, Lenny," she answered. "I plan to live here part of the year, and in the valley the rest of the time. I think it's best for Joey to go to the valley, where it's quieter, and where he can think about being on his own and raising horses. He's always loved them. He's seventeen, and he's got to start thinking about what he wants to do with his life."

"Well, he surely is a fine young man—handsome, too. 'Course, with you for a mother, how could he be anything *but* handsome."

Lenny studied her curved figure. Her slender waist was accented by the fitted bodice of her blue taffeta dress. Lilly Brannigan was all beauty and poise and perfection, and he hated to see her marry up with the gambler Garth Wheeler.

"Miss Lilly?" he said as he stepped closer, lowering his voice.

Lilly turned to look at him expectantly.

"Reason I asked about you leaving Virginia City—well, folks around here think you might up and marry that Garth Wheeler, and go to the valley to settle."

Lilly's eyebrows arched. "Marry?" Her cheeks colored slightly. "We're just good friends, Lenny. We've been together a lot over the past few months because of the opera house."

The man nodded, frowning. "Well, ma'am, the way Garth talks around, he seems to have the impression you two might be getting married."

Lilly turned back to the potatoes. "I'm aware of Garth's feelings, Lenny, but marriage is something I—" She stopped, looking back at him. "I would really prefer people didn't go around talking about what I am going to do with my personal life, Lenny. If we ever decide to get married, you'll know it from me, not from some rumor."

The man reddened slightly and nodded. "Yes, ma'am. I just thought—well, I was talking to Whiskey in the saloon the other night, and he doesn't like Wheeler too much. I don't either. I just thought I'd tell you that. We'd hate to see you marry a man who—well, who might not be fitting for a lady like you."

Lilly turned to start putting potatoes into her basket. "Mr. Wheeler is a good businessman, and he's responsible for the opera house," she answered. "That is my only concern right now. I believe I can make my own decisions when it comes to marriage, Lenny, but I appreciate your concern. I know you mean well."

She heard him walk away, and her heart pounded with the thought of being with a man again, making love again. She was well aware of Garth Wheeler's feelings for her. He made them very obvious. He took her to dances and to restaurants, and came often to visit, long after their need to collaborate on the opera house was through.

She stared absently at a potato. Garth was handsome, charming. He had kissed her for the first time a few days ago, and she had no doubt he knew how to handle a woman sexually. But caring about a man again terrified her, and no one she had met in the ensuing years aroused her the way Chase Mitchell had—the way his mere memory still did.

That was not all of it, though. Garth gambled and drank. A lot of men in gold towns did—men she knew were good-hearted and respectable—but to Garth such things seemed a passion, and there was an air of mystery to his background that made her wonder about him. When she asked about his past, he was always evasive, and sometimes he contradicted himself.

Still, those problems were not as acute as the simple fact that he often made her feel uneasy. Occasionally she would notice a cold, almost cruel look in his dark eyes, or an insincerity when he expressed his affection for her. He was handsome, charming, and apparently he had money. Yet Lilly was unsure of just what the investments were from which he claimed to have gotten his wealth. And she could not forget another handsome, charming man who had deserted her many years ago.

Now she realized she had come to love her freedom and independence.

Lilly moved to a barrel of withering carrots, anxious for the fresh produce that would be arriving in another couple of months from California's first harvest of the year. She hungered for fresh beans and other vegetables, and hoped the drying carrots she picked through would be good enough for her stew. She paid for her items and carried them outside to where Joey waited to drive her back to the house in their buggy. Lilly had just placed the basket inside when she heard Garth call out her name. She turned, little noticing the scowl on Joey's face when the man approached her.

Garth came close and kissed Lilly's cheek. "Are you sure you won't change your mind about letting me take you to dinner tonight, instead of cooking for that woman, Lilly?"

"That woman has a name, Garth. It's Nettie Abler."

"A name every man in town knows, and not for her virtues."

"Garth, we have been over this before. I haven't visited with Nettie in ages, and I'm looking forward to this evening."

"Well, at least let me come, too, then."

Lilly rolled her eyes. "I'd like some plain woman talk for a change."

"*Woman* talk! With Nettie? What can you possibly have in common to talk about?"

Lilly smiled in amusement and climbed into the carriage. "That's my business. If you want to do something tomorrow evening, I'll be available." She turned to her son "Let's go, Joey." She looked back at Garth and waved, blowing him a kiss.

He watched her drive off, wishing he could find a way to strangle Nettie Abler. Women like that could be dangerous to his plans. He decided he had better move in fast now, before Lilly Brannigan slipped through his fingers.

"I don't much like him, Mother," Joey was telling Lilly as they headed toward home. "You aren't going to marry him, are you? Everybody in town thinks you are."

Lilly touched his arm. "Well, everybody in town doesn't know a thing about my personal business. I have no plans right now to marry Garth Wheeler, Joey. If and when I do, I would talk to you about it first."

Joey scowled. "I liked him at first, but he tries to control all your time now. Everything is different. We never see our old friends anymore."

"Well, we will tonight. Nettie is coming for dinner, and I plan to have Whiskey and Daryl over sometime soon. Now that the opera house is about finished, I'll have more time to spend with you. Just remember that in August, we're going to the valley."

Joey grinned then. "I can't wait. We'll go alone, won't we? I mean, Whiskey or Nettie could come, but I'd rather Garth didn't."

"Of course he won't come. It wouldn't look proper. It will be just you and me, Joey, and maybe Whiskey and Daryl for a little protection."

Joey shrugged. "You don't need them. I can protect you."

Lilly smiled proudly, her heart feeling almost sad at how much he had grown. "Of course you can," she told him aloud. *Oh, Joey,* she thought. *You're so much a man already. Where have all the years gone?* She suspected her son had visited the prostitutes a time or two, but she had said nothing to him about it. How could a young man not take advantage of that part of manhood in a town like Virginia City? And how could she stop him, without unfairly embarrassing him? These were times when she wished she had a man to guide him, a father to direct him. But then, he did have a father—one who had deserted him. It seemed so unfair to Joey. She had considered Garth being a father to him, but that seemed unlikely now. It was becoming more and more difficult to decide what to do about Garth Wheeler —and about her own emotions.

Lilly welcomed Nettie with open arms, bringing her into the gracious dining room, where the table was elegantly set. "I was going to make stew, but decided to use the vegetables around a roast and potatoes. I hope you're good and hungry, Nettie."

"Oh, it smells wonderful. I'm so glad you asked me, Lilly. I never get to see you anymore. I'll be glad when the opera house is ready. I miss talking to you."

Lilly served wine and a meal grand enough for a governor. Nettie had to laugh at such treatment, and as always, Lilly was warmly entertained just by watching and listening to this woman, whose life was so drastically different from her own. She had grown accustomed to Nettie's flagrant way of dressing and her loose talk. If nothing else, Nettie Abler was honest in expressing her opinion, which was part of the reason Lilly had invited her. They shared a glass of wine after dinner, and Lilly took Nettie to the parlor, where they could talk alone. They sat beside a fire. The wine had increased Lilly's confusion about Garth Wheeler, and she felt she had to discuss her doubts with someone. She could not imagine anyone better suited to share such intimate emotions with than Nettie.

She set her glass aside and leaned back in her chair. "I want to talk to you about something in particular, Nettie."

Nettie's eyebrows arched in expectation, and her eyes filled with a kind of disgust. "Garth Wheeler?"

Lilly frowned. "Yes. How did you know?"

Nettie laughed wryly. "Hell, Lilly, everybody in town is making bets on when you two will tie the knot."

Lilly looked at the fire. "I didn't know it seemed that serious to everyone else."

"Well, *is* it serious?"

She looked at Nettie. "I have a feeling Garth takes it more seriously than I do." She sighed deeply. "I don't know, Nettie. I've worked so hard for what I have. I'm not sure I'm ready to share it with someone else. And there's something about Garth—I don't know. It's hard to put a finger on it. Sometimes he almost frightens me, and yet he's been nothing but charming and attentive and affectionate. Never once has he said or done an unkind thing. I just wondered if you had any kind of opinion about him."

Nettie set her glass aside. "I've got an opinion, all right, and if you hadn't asked me for it, I would have come here and given it to you, eventually, whether you wanted it or not."

Lilly watched her eyes. "You don't like him."

"Lilly, there aren't many women who know men better than I do—especially men like him. I've seen lots of Garth Wheelers in my time. That man is up to something, and he knows I see right through him. Why do you think he doesn't want you talking with me?"

Lilly frowned. "I never thought about it that way."

Nettie leaned forward, resting her elbows on her knees. "Lilly, he came to see me once. Why do you think we haven't seen much of each other? The few times you did have a chance to visit with me, I always made sure I was too busy. Garth Wheeler told me to stay away from you. He told me my kind could only damage your future—especially if you should get a big name once you start singing in the opera house."

Lilly felt anger growing in her heart. "Oh, Nettie, you should have told me! You know I would never stop seeing you, for any reason."

Nettie shrugged. "I thought for a while that maybe Wheeler was right. But then I wondered if he could have some ulterior motive. I know he's possessive, and he's been going around town talking like he's going to pop the question any time, and that he expects you to say yes. I watched his eyes while he was talking to me, Lilly. He's no good. I can smell that part of him right through those fancy-smelling men's perfumes he wears. He's hustling you."

"Hustling?"

Nettie rolled her eyes "He has some ulterior motive for building that opera house. Personally, I think he's after your money."

Lilly leaned forward, putting her head in her hand. "I've already thought of that. But sometimes he seems so sincere, and I have to admit, I'm lonely. I haven't . . ." Her cheeks reddened. "It's been a long time for me, if you know what I mean. Garth can be so . . . gentle and sweet. He kissed me the other night, and it felt good."

Nettie grinned a little. "Sure it did! Hell, every woman needs a man somewhere in her life. But, Lilly, you could have your pick. There are a lot of men around more decent than Garth Wheeler who would give their right arm to court you."

Lilly smiled bashfully at the compliment. "Maybe." She looked at the fire. "But Garth is the first man I've come across who even came close to making me feel like . . ." *Like Chase Mitchell once made me feel,* she longed to say. "Like a woman should feel about the man she's going to take to her bed. And God knows, my bed has been empty for a lot of years."

Nettie closed her eyes and sighed, leaning forward and taking Lilly's hand. "Honey, don't let that loneliness make you act irrationally. You've worked too hard to build what you have, and you have a son who should inherit all of this someday. Just be damned careful, and think of Joey. There are plenty of men who would marry you just for you, without expecting to claim all that's yours for themselves. I just don't think Garth Wheeler is one of them. I'm telling you, Lilly—on top of his gambling and drinking, that man is some kind of con artist."

Lilly met her eyes. "But, why would he have started that opera house, when he didn't even know me at first? I mean, he couldn't have known clear back then that he might marry me. What other way would there be for him to get his hands on my money? I don't have a dime in that opera house, Nettie. It's all contributed money, and Garth put in a lot of his own."

Nettie frowned. "I'm not sure what his original plan was. I only sense that he's up to something. Maybe you'll find out if you hang on long enough. Do you have plans to marry him?"

Lilly sighed and leaned back again. "No. Something just isn't right about the whole thing. You know me better than that, Nettie."

"I know how lonely you are. Men like Garth Wheeler pick up on that mighty quick. You remember that." Nettie smiled then, raising her wine glass. "Hey, let's talk about something more uplifting, like the fact that the opera house is opening soon. I've already bought my tickets. Here's to the Virginia City Opera House."

Lilly looked at her and smiled, picking up her own glass.

"Yes. Bad or good, Garth *is* responsible for the opera house. I can't wait until opening night. It's like a dream come true for me, Nettie. I used to imagine such things when I was a little girl back in Scotland, singing alone in the foothills, pretending a great audience sat before me."

"Well, now there *will* be a great audience, and you'll have a proper stage and backdrops and lighting. Why, I don't doubt you could end up singing in an even bigger opera house in San Francisco!"

Lilly laughed lightly. "I would never take Joey out of the valley. I have no desire to go anyplace else."

"Well, we'll see. Anyway, here's to the opera house."

They touched glasses and sipped some wine, and Lilly's thoughts turned again to Garth Wheeler. Her mind and intuition, her heart and womanly needs, all ran in circles, clashing into each other. She knew the situation was going to come to a head, and soon. She had to make up her mind how she felt about the man. She had to place common sense and practicality above her deeper needs. She sipped some more wine, aching at the thought of again going to an empty bed, wondering if that was how it would be for the rest of her life.

Chapter Thirty

Lilly's first performance in the new opera house was set for April 15, 1864. Garth had also arranged for actors to come in from San Francisco to put on a musical, but Miss Lilly Brannigan received top billing and was the biggest draw. He had a grand piano shipped all the way from San Francisco, along with an excellent pianist who, according to their arrangement, would be well paid to stay in Virginia City to provide the music for upcoming plays and concerts.

Lilly insisted Chester Heath accompany her with his fiddle. Garth, who planned to eventually build an entire orchestra, also shipped in a trumpet player and a French horn player.

Lilly was as excited as a little girl. She would not allow her qualms about Garth to spoil her first performance. She was doing this for the men and women of Virginia City who had given her such a faithful following, who had literally been responsible for her fortune, and who had contributed from their own purses to build the opera house.

Still, her butterflies were almost worse than they had been that first day she had performed in Virginia City. Garth had told her there would be people in the audience from as far away as Reno, Carson City, and Washoe City, and even a few from San Francisco.

Garth showed up at Lilly's dressing room with a bouquet of roses minutes before she was to go on stage. "Joey has a front-row seat," he told her. "So do some of our more prominent visitors from San Francisco and other towns." His eyes were alive with excitement. "You look sensational, Lilly!"

She reddened as his dark eyes drank in her creamy skin and the soft, green taffeta gown she wore that enhanced her sea-green eyes. Her hair was swept up in a bundle of red-gold curls and decorated with tiny fresh flowers. Garth shook his head, his eyes moving over her in just the right way to make a woman give thought to romance.

"You're the picture of the perfect woman, Lilly. Every man in that audience tonight is going to fall in love." He handed her the roses. "And I'm already in love." He came closer, moving a hand behind her back and pulling her close. "You must know that by now, Lilly. We've been together so much. We know each other so well. I can't hold back my feelings any longer. I love you, and I want you to marry me."

He watched her beautiful eyes light up from the compliment, then take on a look of apprehension. Garth had hoped she would finally give in, for he was anxious to get into her bed and find out what Chase Mitchell had thought was so wonderful about her that he had never forgotten her. More than that, he knew now just how extensive her holdings were. He had gone on his own to check out the home she was building in the valley. It was a literal mansion.

"Garth, I can't think about something so serious right now—" ·

"Surely you've already been thinking about it. You know how I feel about you, Lilly, and I know you can sense my desire when I'm near you. I want you to be my wife. I would be the proudest man in Virginia City with you on my arm."

She swallowed, hardly knowing what to say. Intuition told her not to let Garth Wheeler down suddenly or cruelly. He was not a man to be scorned or insulted.

"You must realize you've taken me by surprise, Garth. I . . . I appreciate all the things you've done to make the opera house a reality—and your generosity and attention all these months. In fact, I feel I should contribute something myself."

"Lilly, quit beating around the bush. You're a beautiful woman, and you have much left in you to give a man. You can't deny yourself the rest of your life. Your husband has been dead nearly seven years now."

She pulled away slightly. "You don't understand." She walked over and put the roses in a vase. "Please don't press me, tonight of all nights, Garth. All I want to think about is my performance."

He sighed and walked up behind her, then took hold of her arms and bent down to kiss her shoulder. The touch of his lips to her skin sent a momentary wave of terrible need through her blood. "Please give me some time to think about this, Garth."

He turned her, and leaned down to kiss her mouth lightly. "Lilly, I've been patient and attentive for months; I've respected the kind of woman you are. I've loved you secretly and passionately for a long time—I think maybe from the first day I met you. I've even ordered a pair of palomino horses for Joey for the ranch—"

She closed her eyes and turned away. "Garth, you shouldn't have done that."

"I like doing things for the boy," Garth told her.

He came closer and put on a look of deep disappointment

and despair. "Lilly, if you don't marry me in the not-too-distant future, I'll have to leave Virginia City. I can't go on forever like this—wanting you as I do, but not being able to have you. The opera house is finished now. I wanted that— for you. At first it was just because of your beautiful voice, and because I thought Virginia City needed some culture. But as I got to know you, I fell in love with you. It was quite unintended, I assure you. I've never been married before," he lied, "never met a woman I felt I wanted to spend the rest of my life with. I have been all over the country, made my own fortune, and now I want to share it with someone."

She stepped back. "I'll think very hard about it, Garth," she told him.

He looked relieved. "That's all I need to hear." He stepped away. "Go out there now and knock them dead, Lilly."

She forced a smile for him, telling herself she would not let anyone or anything cause her to give less than her best this night. "Thank you, Garth. And I do appreciate and respect your proposal. I've been through so much in my life that it takes a lot of consideration. Surely, you can understand that."

She turned and took one last look in the mirror, failing to notice the dark rage that had begun to appear in Garth Wheeler's eyes. By the time she turned he was smiling. She took his arm, and he led her through a hallway toward the stage. The dance troupe from San Francisco had just finished its act, and someone from the crowd shouted, "We want Miss Lilly!"

Lilly looked at Garth and smiled. More men began shouting, then clapping their hands rhythmically. Lilly set aside her anxiety over Garth. She mounted the steps to the stage and was greeted by resounding cheers and applause. Gaslights lit up the stage, but she could see beyond them to a packed house. She searched the front row then for Joey, and he smiled at her, his pride evident.

The small orchestra began to play and the crowd quieted. Lilly breathed deeply to calm her nerves. She raised her eyes to the balcony seats, and caught sight of Nettie, sitting in a curtained-off section of the balcony, with three other color-fully dressed women.

She opened her mouth and filled the rafters with her voice, as the audience sat spellbound. Garth watched from the wings.

Each of the four nights a week the opera house was open it was packed. Tickets had to be bought days ahead of time. As visitors to Virginia City left to go back home, and businessmen traveled to other cities, the name Lilly Brannigan quickly spread to San Francisco and Reno. Lilly seldom arrived now at her dressing room without finding a multitude of cards and flowers.

Still, as thrilled as she was with the audience response and with the success of her singing career, she had not forgotten her plan to spend part of the summer in the valley on the old farm—more for Joey's sake than her own. Just before her fiftieth appearance on the stage, Lilly bowed to her audience and announced that Saturday night would be her last appearance until October. "I am going to spend some time with my son in the Washoe Valley," she told her audience.

There came a wave of sighs and groans.

"We'll miss you, Miss Lilly," one man shouted.

"And I'll miss you," she replied. "Mr. Wheeler and the others who share an interest in the opera house will see that other entertainment is provided. An acting company has been hired from Reno. I hear it is very good."

"T'won't be the same, Miss Lilly."

"I'll be back, I promise." She bowed again, then glided off the stage. There was an immediate surge to the ticket booth to purchase any tickets that might still be available for her Saturday-night performance.

Lilly headed for her dressing room, wondering, as she often did, how she could still be so lonely. Thank God she had Joey—or Joe, as he preferred to be called now. It had been over six years since they had left the valley to come to Virginia City. Joe was seventeen but looked like a man in his early twenties, and he was anxious to build the ranch now. For the past three years he had worked hard at a variety of jobs around to earn his own money to buy some horses. He didn't want his ranch to be something that was just inherited from his father and financed by his mother—he wanted to do his own part. Lilly was proud of his efforts, and the fact that he had his own personal pride.

In fact, Joe was so excited about going to the valley that Lilly wondered if she would be able to get him to come back to Virginia City with her. It seemed incredible that he was getting old enough to live on his own. It was something she had failed to consider all these years. Lately, he talked about "his" ranch and "his" horses, and had been shyly hinting that he was very interested in a certain pretty young lady who had come to town with her banker father. He was becoming his own person, considering a life without his mother, and for Lilly, the word *loneliness* took on a new meaning at the thought.

But she realized she had to accept it somehow. She told herself not to let the thought of being alone make her do something foolish, such as marrying Garth Wheeler. Garth had acted colder, more remote, since the night he had proposed and she had put him off. Instinct kept telling her to give him a final no and get it over with.

Tonight, when she walked into her dressing room, she realized that time would come sooner than she had thought. Garth was waiting for her. She hesitated, and their eyes held for a moment. Lilly knew why he was there, and she shivered a little at the strange look in his eyes, as though he had already won some kind of victory. As Lilly walked past him then to take the flowers out of her hair, she said, "I thought you were going to talk to some men from San Francisco after I finished."

"I was. But I decided something else was more important."

"Garth—"

"I thought you would give me some kind of answer before going off to the valley," he interrupted, rising from his chair and coming to stand behind her. "It's been nearly four months since I proposed to you, Lilly, and you've been avoiding me ever since. I feel like a fool telling you how much I love you, baring my soul to you. Tonight I was even prepared to give you a ring. I spent a hell of a lot of money on it, Lilly."

She closed her eyes and sighed, then sat down in front of her makeup mirror. "I'm sorry, Garth. I just didn't know how to go about—"

She looked up at him in the mirror, saw the anger in his dark eyes. She met his look challengingly. "I really do appreciate the opera house, Garth, but if you thought it would buy my love, it can't. If I thought you truly loved me, I would consider your proposal. But . . . people talk . . . and you're so evasive about your past. There is just too much about you I don't know. I'm sorry. I've realized lately that there is only one man I have ever loved, and he's gone."

She took the pins from her hair and began to brush it. Her heart began to race when she saw the almost evil look in his eyes then.

"What do you mean . . . people talk?" he asked her.

Lilly was determined not to mention Nettie. "Friends— like Whiskey and Daryl. They see you out at night, know more about you—"

"They don't know *anything* about me!" His answer was so quick it startled her. She slowly put down her brush as he continued. "It's that damned Nettie, isn't it? Are you really putting that whore's opinion over your own good judgment?"

Lilly rose, facing him. "Don't call her a whore."

"A whore is a whore! What's she been telling you—that I have some ulterior motive for wanting to marry you?" He was both frustrated and furious. A desperate feeling of failure was beginning to consume him. No wonder Chase Mitchell didn't want anything to do with Lilly Brannigan anymore. *Bitch!* he thought. He had met his biggest challenge, but he still hadn't pulled his last ace.

"I don't know what to think, Garth. I only know I have a strong desire to protect what I've worked so hard to build. You're a gambling man. I don't care to have my fortune gambled away by my husband."

"Good God, Lilly, I don't intend to do any such thing. I have my *own* money."

"And if I marry you, everything I own will *also* become yours."

His dark eyes drilled into hers. "My, you can be blunt, can't you? I never thought you to be such a selfish, ungrateful woman, the way you put on all those kind, generous airs around others! You're more money hungry than I realized!"

"I'm not money-hungry. I'm a mother protecting her son's inheritance."

He sniffed at her haughty glare, stepping closer, a threatening look in his eyes. Garth Wheeler was not about to be outsmarted by a woman! He had tried using charm. Now it was time to play a rougher game.

"So," he said slowly, "you say there is only one man you ever truly loved, and that he's gone. I suppose you're referring to Joey's father—the man who is buried down in the valley?"

She felt sudden alarm as his eyes began to sparkle with hideous victory. "Of course," she answered cautiously.

He nodded, clutching his hands behind his back. He strutted away, then turned to face her. "I see. I thought maybe you meant the boy's . . . *real* father."

With great joy he watched her pale. He also laughed out loud.

"What are you talking about?" she asked with a shaking voice.

He snickered. "This could have been a lot easier, Lilly. All you had to do was marry me. We could have shared the money and had quite a good time doing it. But now you will have to sign it all over to me—deeds to land, shares in the mine, savings accounts." He shrugged. "Unless, of course, you prefer that I tell Joey the truth about his father—let him know what kind of slut his mother was before she married her Mormon husband."

She looked ready to faint as he stepped closer. "Tell me, Lilly, why *did* you marry that Mormon man? Was it to give your illegitimate son a name? I wonder what the rest of the men in this town would think if they knew the truth about their precious, angelic Lilly? Of course, they don't really matter. What really matters is Joey—what *he* would think, the names others would call him."

Never in her life had Lilly had the desire to kill someone
—until now. If she had a gun in her hand, she would gladly
have used it at that moment on Garth Wheeler. She struggled
to keep her composure.

Her green eyes cooled to ice, and she stood rigid and
determined. "How did you know?"

His eyes moved over her. "Before I came to Virginia City,
I met a man by the name of Chase Mitchell back in San
Francisco." He saw her eyes widen. "One night, after a few
drinks—well, you know how a man loosens up when he's
been drinking. He told me about a woman he once knew by
the name of Lilly Brannigan. I must say his eyes showed a
great deal of sentiment." He smiled haughtily. "Mitchell has
done well for himself—made a gold strike, some good investments. Bought some stock in Wells Fargo, too, I believe. Why, he might even decide to make a run with them
between San Francisco and Virginia City. Yes, ma'am, he
just might show up here." His eyes fell to her full bosom,
and Lilly felt naked. "The man named his mine after you,
Lilly. Isn't that interesting? You must have left quite an impression on him."

Lilly turned away, her heart beating wildly, her mind racing with indecision. Chase! He was alive, and only as far
away as San Francisco!

"Of course, Mitchell left more than an impression on
you," Garth was saying. "He left you a son. I knew that the
minute I laid eyes on Joey. I learned a few things about you,
put two and two together, and I figured out that Chase
Mitchell probably doesn't know anything about his son—
and, more important, I don't think Joey knows about his
father. You haven't been keeping any secrets from your boy,
now, have you, Lilly? It isn't very fair of you."

Lilly clung to the back of a chair. Chase! What if he found
out? What if Joey found out? Oh, how she hated Garth
Wheeler! She grabbed a vase of flowers and threw it at him.
Garth put up an arm and deflected the blow, shattering the
vase. Water spilled over the floor and flowers flew in every
direction. "Get out of here!" Lilly screamed at him.

Garth just grinned, brushing off the sleeve of his silk
jacket. "My, my, the gentle lady does have a temper, doesn't

she? I knew there was some heated emotion buried somewhere under that cold exterior. I just wish it had come out in
some other form. I did so want to marry you and enjoy
whatever it is that left such an impression on Chase Mitchell."

"What do you want!" Lilly almost snarled, visibly shaken.

Garth's smile faded. "Just your money and stocks, things
like that."

"They aren't mine to give. What I have belongs to Joe,
too. I have put his name on everything. He would have to
sign."

Garth snickered. "He's only seventeen. You can sign for
him. Face it, Lilly. You have no choice, unless you want me
to tell Joe the truth. Believe me, I'll do it. I am a man who
gets what he wants. My first two marriages paid off hand-
somely. But those women weren't as difficult and stubborn
as you, so I have had to resort to other methods. And I'm
telling you now, if I can't get what I want from you, you'll
dearly regret it."

Lilly felt her old stubborn defenses rising. Now she understood where his money had come from. She couldn't
stand there and let him steal everything she had worked so
hard for. She could lose her Joey, she knew, but his future
was more important than her own hurt and sorrow. She had
lived with those things all her life. And, if keeping all that
she had built for Joe meant losing his love, she would have
to live with that, too. She would not give in to a man like
Garth Wheeler. She held his eyes defiantly.

"Perhaps I *will* regret it," she told the man. "But if it
means keeping all that Joe and I have struggled to build
together, then I will have to take my chances. I'll not turn
over one cent to you, Garth Wheeler." Disbelief, anger,
frustration passed through his dark eyes. Now Lilly felt the
victor, even though she realized she would surely lose her
son's love and respect.

"What do you mean, you'll not turn over one cent to me?"
Garth growled. "I'll march right over to your house and tell
Joe everything!"

"Then, do it! Joe's as big and strong as a man now. He's

in his prime. Do you think he's going to believe the story—coming from you? Even if he does, he'll be sure to show you just what he thinks of what you're doing. I don't really think you want any damage done to that handsome face. It might prevent you from romancing some other woman next year."

His face reddened with rage and he held up his fist. "I'd like to—"

"Please do," she told him, her voice cool and calm now. "If you hit me, it will make my own story even more valid. And I wouldn't want to be in your shoes then. The men around here can be pretty rough and unforgiving."

He threw his arm out and knocked more flowers to the floor. "Who do you think you are?" he snarled.

"I'm calling your bluff, Garth. Isn't that what you call it at the card table? I have the best hand, because I'm the only one who knows the real truth. And right now, I'm going to go home and tell Joe." She walked past him.

"I'll go back to San Francisco and tell Chase Mitchell!" he threatened.

Lilly stopped, wondering what Chase would do. Would he come to Virginia City? Maybe he should. Maybe it was best to get it all over with and risk the consequences. The lie she had been living was like a constant heavy weight around her shoulders. Now, just the thought of telling Joe the truth made her feel lighter. And she *would* have to tell him. Chase might come, and she couldn't just suddenly spring the truth on Joe.

She turned to face Garth once more, amazed at how he seemed to almost wither in front of her. "You do whatever you want, Garth."

Chapter Thirty-one

The ticking clock on the fireplace mantel was the only sound in the suddenly silent parlor. Joe stared at his mother in disbelief, trying to digest everything she had just told him.

Lilly twisted a handkerchief nervously in her hands. The ticking of the clock seemed to grow louder with every passing moment that Joe said nothing. "I . . . loved him very much," she said then, finishing her story, her stomach churning. "I would have waited forever for him, if not for that . . . that awful letter. I couldn't let you be born without a father, Joe." She stared at the clock. "Zeb offered to marry me. But even after I married him, I kept hoping Chase would come. Zeb never . . . touched me . . . for many months after our marriage. But I learned to love him . . . for the good man that he was." She faced her son. "And Zeb loved you like his own." Her eyes teared. "I was so young then, Joe. I didn't know anything about men or . . . or that it could be so easy to conceive."

Tears slipped out of her eyes at the hurt in her son's eyes. "Why didn't you ever tell me?" he asked, rising from the sofa.

She choked in a sob. Joey! *He's all I have!* "Because I never wanted you to feel the shame of it." She wiped at tears with the handkerchief. "I wanted you to be happy and secure. Zeb made life that way for you. And . . . the more the years went by, the older you got, the more afraid I became that you would find out. I didn't want you to hate me, Joe . . . to lose your respect for me. I was just trying to protect you."

The young man turned away, running a hand through his hair. "I feel . . . so cheated."

"I'm sorry, Joe. I didn't mean it to be that way. I thought I was doing the right thing by you. I didn't think this day would ever come." She breathed deeply for control. "But now, I'm almost glad. Living with all of this has been so hard. All these years, I've been so lonely."

Joe walked to a window, and looked down on Virginia City in the distance. He thought about how hard he, and especially his mother, had worked to get what they had. His mind raced back to his youth on the old farm, and he tried to imagine what it must be like to live with someone you don't love—to live with a secret all your life.

"What about Pa? I mean . . . he was happy, wasn't he? He must have known you didn't really love him . . . not the right way. But he always seemed happy to me."

"Joe, I *did* love him, in a very special way. I tried so hard. I appreciated the good man that he was. But I'll always wonder if I should have done more, knowing just how lonely he really must have been deep inside." She swallowed before continuing, her throat hurting so badly she wondered if she could keep talking. "It was you who kept us together— kept us both as happy as we could have expected to be. You had a father in Zeb, and he genuinely loved you as much as any man could love his own son. And for that reason, more than any other, I loved Zeb Adams. It just wasn't the same deep, passionate love I had felt for Chase."

"Tell me again about Chase Mitchell," he asked, still staring out the window.

Lilly went through the story again, told him how much like his father he looked. "I was so sure he loved me as much as I loved him," she finished. "I know now that something went wrong that had nothing to do with our love for each other, Joe. I don't know just what it was, because I've heard conflicting stories since then. It has something to do with whatever happened once Chase reached Texas and his father. Like I told you, he came looking for me once at Salt Lake. All I got was that one terrible letter telling me he wasn't coming back. But Chase claimed he never wrote a letter like that. And according to Garth, he even named a mine after me out in California."

She blew her nose and leaned against the fireplace, feeling suddenly very tired and old. "I don't know what to believe anymore. I only know that after finding out I was married, Chase apparently decided to stay out of my life. No one has heard from him since. I had no idea if he was dead or alive until Garth told me he had met him in San Francisco. There were times when I thought about trying to find him, just to get some answers that might help me get over the hurt. But there was always you to consider. I was terrified of you finding out the truth."

The boy turned to look at her, an older, more mature look about him then. "Did you think about him a lot while Pa—I mean, Zeb—was still alive?"

Lilly dropped her eyes. "Of course I did. How could I help but think of him? I loved him and there was always you to remind me of the past. You're a replica of your father, Joe."

He searched her eyes. "Did you ever hate me for it?"

Her eyes widened. "*Hate* you! I never once hated you or blamed you. It was all *my* doing. You were an innocent party, and you were my son! We've always been so close. Surely you know how much I love you!"

"What about Chase Mitchell? Do you love him? Hate him?"

She felt the little rush of long-buried emotions. She shook her head. "I don't know how I feel anymore. For a long time I *did* hate him. Then the years took away some of the hate. Only the hurt remained. And there were moments when, if I allowed myself to think about him too much, I . . . I knew a part of me still loved him, in spite of what he had done. The last few years, after seeing Hiram, I have wondered what the truth really is."

Joe watched her, trying to envision her as the beautiful young woman Chase Mitchell must have fallen for. It was not difficult to picture. She was still beautiful—something he knew because of the way all the men in Virginia City talked about her, but something he had never really taken time to study and consider himself because she was his mother. A son didn't see his mother the way other men saw her.

"What did you mean earlier," he asked, "when you said

something happened with Garth, and that was why you had something to tell me? What does Garth have to do with this? Just because he met my father in San Francisco doesn't mean you had to tell me all of this now."

Lilly wiped at her eyes again. "Garth . . . tried to blackmail me. He told me I either had to marry him or sign over all my assets to him in order for him to keep quiet about what he knew." She faced her son squarely. "I refused to do either one. You can hate me, Joe, shun me—whatever you want to do now. I'll even leave Virginia City and get out of your life if you want it that way. But I would rather you knew the truth than to give up everything I've worked so hard to build up for you. Whatever you think of me, all I have is yours. You can still have that ranch in the valley—all of it. My past mistakes shouldn't cost you a fortune."

Joe sighed. This woman he called Mother suddenly seemed like a stranger to him. She had lived all her life with a lonely secret that must have been hell for her. It seemed incredible that she had loved another man, apparently with much more passion than she had ever loved Zeb Adams. He couldn't quite picture it, but it was obviously true.

"I would never stop loving you, Mother," he told her. "And I . . . well, hell, anybody knows the kind of woman you are. All these years you've never been around men, except for Garth lately. I didn't like him, but I tried to understand maybe you'd want a man in your life again. I mean, the way you've lived, everybody respects you. And what happened with my real father—I know it must have meant very much to you. I mean, you must have loved him a lot." He ran a hand through his thick, dark hair. "If you thought I'd think less of you or something, I don't. I just feel . . . I don't know, kind of disappointed, I guess—cheated, like I said. You should have said something a long time ago."

"I know." She hung her head. "You don't know how I wish I had."

Joe sighed and walked toward the parlor exit. "I'm going to pack a few things and get a horse ready."

Lilly's heart pounded with alarm. "Why? Where are you going? It's late, Joe."

His blue eyes turned icy with anger, reminding her of how Chase looked the day they were attacked along the creek. "I'm going to find Garth Wheeler and tell him . . . no, *show* him what I think of his little scheme! And then Garth and I are going to San Francisco to find my father."

"Joe, just let it go. I don't want you to get hurt!"

"*I'm* not the one who will be hurting!" he told her. He stormed out into the hallway and toward the stairs that led to his room. "It's Garth Wheeler who will be hurting, Mother, when I'm through with him! And I have to find my father. You didn't think I'd listen to all of this without wanting to find him and meet him, did you?"

Their eyes held. "I . . . I didn't know what you would do."

"Well, I *am* going to find him, and I'm going to learn the truth about this whole mess! You never should have had to go through this all alone, Mother—never! Chase Mitchell has some explaining to do!"

He started up the stairs, and she grabbed his arm. "Joe!"

He turned to see the terror in her eyes.

"You'll come back, won't you? Promise me you'll come back. I love you, Joe, more than my own life."

He closed his eyes and sighed, putting a hand over hers. "I can't say yet what I'll do. It depends on what happens when I find my father." He couldn't bear her tears. He stepped down a couple of steps and hugged her. "Don't cry, Mother. It will all work out. Isn't that what you told me after the fire, when I thought it was all my fault? Mother, if I don't come back right away, don't worry about it. I have a lot of things to think about." He pushed her away slightly. "And I have to get going right away. This is the best time of year to cross over the Sierras."

Chase! Her heart raced with the thought of his existence. Now he would meet his own son! What would he think? She hoped he would suffer some of the terrible guilt she had been forced to live with all these years.

"Be careful, Joe." She wiped at her eyes again. "I love you. I hope you understand . . . why I did what I did."

He turned to finish climbing the stairs. "I think I understand," he said on the way up. "But I won't understand everything until I hear my father's side of the story."

Lilly slowly sat down on the bottom steps. It was done now. After all these years, the secret was out. She felt drained, weak. Whatever happened from now on was out of her hands.

"Oh, Chase," she muttered, her whole body jerking in a silent sob. "Why? Why?"

Garth removed everything but his underwear, deciding it might be best to get to bed early so he could get the hell out of Virginia City in the morning. He could hardly believe Lilly would go through with her threat to tell Joe the truth herself, but if she did, he couldn't be sure how the boy would react, or what the two of them might tell others in town. He was a man who knew when it was wise to move on.

He contemplated making good on his promise to find Chase Mitchell and tell him what he knew, but he was worried that the man would realize he had tried to pull something on Lilly and their son. Chase could be dangerous if crossed. Considering the way he had talked about Lilly Brannigan, he apparently still loved her. Once he found out he had a son, things could get uncomfortable for Garth Wheeler.

Garth stretched and pulled back the covers of his bed, shaking his head at how the evening had gone. Lilly Brannigan had much more backbone than he had given her credit for, and he decided he had better find himself another victim soon. His funds were getting low. The past year in Virginia City had been a waste. He took one last puff on his cigar and put it out, then sat down on the edge of the bed and reached over to turn down his lamp. But before it was out, the door to his room suddenly burst open. Joe Adams stood in the doorway, a look of fury in his deep blue eyes. The young man kicked the door shut and came toward him, fists clenched.

"Now listen, Joe—"

Garth didn't get a chance to finish. Joe charged at him and Garth kicked out, catching Joe in the chest and knocking him backward into a table. The young man shook off an array of cigars and jars of men's scented oils, leaping back to his feet and grabbing Garth away from the door before the man could run out. He threw the man over the end of his bed, then reached over the bed and jerked him up by his undershirt, landing a heavy fist into Garth's left cheek. The skin on his nose split and began to bleed on impact. Garth fell back again and rolled off the bed.

"Joe, let me explain—"

Joe jerked him up by the hair and punched him hard in the midsection, enjoying Garth's grunt of pain. He landed another fist against the side of his head, sending Garth against a wall.

Garth's heart pounded with fear. He had been so surprised by the attack that he hadn't had a chance to get in a good punch himself. He was sure he could lick the daylights out of the younger, inexperienced Joe Adams, but Joe had youth and quickness on his side. Garth's head reeled with desperate indecision, and his body screamed with pain as he felt himself being jerked up again.

"You dirty, thieving sonofabitch!" Joe growled. "We're going to San Francisco, you bastard! We're going to find my *father*!"

Garth felt another punch, this time to the ribs. He doubled over, wondering if the boy might beat him to death before they had a chance to go anywhere.

There came another punch to the back of his head. Garth landed near a chair where he had hung the little revolver he always wore under his coat. Desperate confusion consumed him. All he could think of to make Joe stop was to hold a gun on him. He scrambled for it but Joe was on him again, grabbing his arm just as Garth managed to get the gun out.

Garth managed to knee the young man in the loins, making him hesitate enough that he was able to land a hard left hook into Joe's face. Joe tumbled sideways and Garth started to rise, but Joe hit him again. Garth heard the shot but didn't even realize it was his finger that had pulled the trigger. Joe's body jerked, then he stumbled backward, blood quickly staining his shirt.

"Joe!" Garth choked.

The young man just stared at him a moment, then fell forward. Blood poured from under his body. Garth looked down at his pistol, then tossed it aside. "My God!" he muttered.

"What's going on in there?" someone shouted from outside the door.

Panic immediately swept through Garth Wheeler. He had shot Lilly Brannigan's son! There wasn't a man in Virginia City who was going to wait around for answers. He grabbed his pants and jacket and scrambled through the window, running along the rooftop of the porch below his second-story room. He climbed down some vines at the side of the building, but before he reached bottom, more men had gathered in the street below.

"Hey! Look there!" someone shouted. It sounded like Whiskey Stokes. "Somebody is tryin' to run!"

"Grab him!" came another voice.

Garth ran down the alley, but in moments, several men had hold of him.

"Hey!" he heard someone shout from the upstairs window. "He shot Joe Adams!"

"Joe Adams! Miss Lilly's boy?"

"I can explain!" Garth yelled, his voice giving away his desperate fear. He felt himself being dragged somewhere, but there were so many men around him that he didn't even know where he was. There was so much shouting that no one could hear him, and no one seemed to care, anyway.

"Somebody get the doc!" people were shouting.

"And Miss Lilly! Somebody better get Miss Lilly!"

"Get a rope while you're at it!" another shouted.

"No! No, wait!" Garth begged, but a shower of fists silenced him.

Nettie came out of the Nugget Saloon to see what all the yelling was about. "What's going on?" she asked a man running by her with a rope in his hand.

"Garth Wheeler just shot Joe Adams. He's gonna hang!" the man told her, heading toward the crowd.

"Joe Adams! Is he dead?"

The man was lost to her. Nettie ran into the crowd of

men, finding Whiskey Stokes. "Whiskey! Whiskey, what happened?"

The man had tears in his eyes. "I don't rightly know for sure, Miss Abler. All I know is somebody says Wheeler shot Joey."

"Dear God! Come up to the hotel room with me, Whiskey!"

Other men were bringing a wagon for Joe. Nettie saw the town doctor run into the hotel and upstairs. She and Whiskey followed. Nettie grasped her stomach when she saw young Joe lying on the floor of Garth's room, covered with blood. The doctor stooped down and rolled him over.

"This looks pretty bad," he said after examining the ugly wound in the boy's middle. "Get him into the wagon and take him up to Miss Brannigan's. I'll work on him there."

"I'll ride with him," Nettie told the doctor.

The man scowled at her, but remembered she was a good friend to Lilly. "All right."

"I'll come, too," Whiskey told Nettie. "I'll get my horse."

Nettie fought tears when she heard Joe groan as men picked him up. They carried him as carefully as they could down the stairs and out to the wagon. Up the street a crowd of men was already throwing a rope over a signpost and making a noose to put around Garth Wheeler's neck. There would be no trial for him. Nettie knew it was wrong, but she didn't care any more than the others.

"So," she muttered, watching the crowd. "You finally played your hand, didn't you, Garth?" She climbed into the wagon, looking down at Joe. Whatever Garth had done, it surely had something to do with young Joe, and with the strange secret Lilly had refused to share with Nettie. Somehow, Garth must have discovered it. She leaned over Joe, smoothing back his hair and talking to him soothingly as the wagon lurched away. "You'll be all right, Joe," she told the boy, praying she was right. If Lilly lost her son, she would want to die herself.

By the time the wagon reached the other end of the street, Nettie could see the dark outline of Garth Wheeler's body, dangling hauntingly against the gaslights.

Chapter Thirty-two

Lilly sat beside Joe's bed in stony silence. She had been there for three nights and three days, leaving only to relieve herself, sleeping rarely, and then by resting her head on the side of the bed. Not only did she have the weight of Garth's death on her shoulders, but her son's pain and suffering as well. Joe could die now. And as far as she was concerned, all of it was her fault. If she had told Joe a long time ago about Chase, none of this would have happened.

The sin Lilly had committed had come around to punish her in the worst way possible. She had already decided that if she had to add another headstone to the two graves on the hill under the pine tree, then she would make it four. She would join Zeb and baby Laura and Joe on that hill.

The doctor came in again. "We've wired for the surgeon from San Francisco," he told her quietly. "I've done all I can, Mrs. Adams. I don't dare try to remove that bullet myself. He could be paralyzed for life if I make one wrong move. But I have to warn you, he could die before the surgeon gets here. We just have to pray. It's all we can do."

Lilly couldn't remember the last time she had prayed. Zeb used to always pray at the table, and before going to bed. She could use Zeb's quiet strength at the moment. She had wanted this independence, but now she reasoned that if she and Zeb had told Joe the truth—if they had gone back to Salt Lake in the first place—Zeb would still be alive, and Joe wouldn't be lying here with his life in danger.

The doctor left. Lilly sensed someone else come into the room. "Lilly?" She recognized Nettie's voice. "You really ought to get some rest."

"I'm all right," Lilly answered. Her voice sounded far away to her, as though it was coming from someone else.

Nettie sighed, coming to stand at the foot of the bed. "When are you going to tell me what happened, Lilly? I know it has something to do with Joe and your past. Garth found out, didn't he?"

Lilly seemed to wither. She covered her face and wept. "Lilly, you've got to share the burden, or you'll go crazy. You need to be strong, for Joey's sake, but right now you're a mess. You've *got* to get some rest. But you aren't going to rest until you get rid of whatever it is that's eating at you. You're blaming yourself for this. Why?"

"Oh, God, Nettie, it's all my fault. Joe could die, all because of my own past!"

Nettie walked over and patted her back, then pulled a chair up next to Lilly's. "Come on now, Lilly. Nobody, including Joey, would blame you for what happened."

Lilly blew her nose and wiped at her eyes. "But it *is* my fault." She looked at Nettie. "Nettie, Zeb Adams—the man buried in the valley—he isn't Joe's real father. His father is still alive, and living in San Francisco. Garth met him."

Nettie stared at her a moment, then closed her eyes and sighed. She pulled her chair closer and put an arm around Lilly's shoulders. "For some reason, I'm not surprised. There was always something about your attitude toward Joe —the way you acted the day we visited your husband's grave in the valley." She gave Lilly a light squeeze. "All right. What's the whole story?"

Lilly sobbed out the truth and Nettie listened with an aching heart, finding it amazing that Lilly thought what she had done was so sinful.

"For God's sake, at least you loved the man," she told her in the end. "You're only human, Lilly. Do you think you're the only woman in the whole world something like this has happened to?"

Lilly rested her head against Nettie's shoulder. "I suppose not. But when it does happen . . . you *feel* so alone, Nettie."

"Oh, honey, I know that feeling. How do you think I felt when I was going through all that hell as a little girl? All the shame and horror—I didn't have anybody to turn to either. The only trouble is, I let it ruin my life. What happened to you isn't so terrible, Lilly, you can't let it ruin *your* life, or

Joey's. And if this boy's real father is still alive, he has a
right to know about Joe, Lilly, and what has happened here."

Lilly wiped her eyes, then rose and bent over Joe. She
leaned down to kiss his cheek, then turned to look at Nettie,
feeling suddenly stronger, more determined. "Nettie! You're
absolutely right. Maybe if Joe met his real father, it would
give him some incentive to live."

Nettie smiled. "Sure. If nothing else, he'd want to live
just to give Chase Mitchell a good licking for leaving you."

Lilly wanted to smile in return, but there were none left in
her. "It might not be just his father he'll be angry with. If I
don't lose Joe to death, I might have lost him anyway."

The tears wanted to come again, and Nettie grasped
Lilly's arms. "Lilly, how could you think you would ever
lose Joey's love? Didn't he tell you before he left that he
loved you and would try to understand? Joey's the most
open, caring young man I've ever known."

Lilly wiped at her nose with a shaking hand. "He's a lot
like Zeb that way, even though Zeb's blood doesn't run in
his veins."

"You raised a damn good kid, Lilly. And didn't he say
when he left that he was going to find his father? It must be
very important to him. Don't you think you should try to
find the man yourself and bring him here?"

Lilly's heart pounded at the very thought of it. Chase!
What would it be like to see him again? What would he
think of all of this? Would he come?

"Garth mentioned something about Chase working for
Wells Fargo. Maybe we could contact him by wiring their
office in San Francisco."

"Fine. I'll go tell Whiskey to do that right now."

Lilly grasped her arm. "Nettie, will you . . . will you explain to Whiskey? I hope I won't lose his friendship."

"You won't. And nobody else in town will turn on you,
either. Don't you worry about it for one minute."

They walked to the door. "Thank you, Nettie. You're a
good friend."

Nettie smiled for her once more and went out. Lilly
leaned over Joe and gently stroked his hair out of his face.
"I'm right here, Joe. I hope you can hear me. Mother is

here, and I've sent for Chase Mitchell. I've sent for your father, Joe."

She listened to his shallow breathing, and the horror of what life would be like without him swept through her with shuddering force. To lose him would be bad enough, but knowing it was her fault for keeping the truth from him made it worse. Haunting memories of other deaths, other graves, tortured her mind. Her mother, lying at the bottom of the sea; poor Laura, buried somewhere far, far away on the lonely prairie; all the Mormons who had died on the way west; Zeb, lying with little Laura under the big pine tree.

"Would you sing that hymn for him, Mother?" Joe had asked the day they had visited Zeb's grave. *"That Mormon hymn he liked so much?"*

How many times had she sung it for others? Joe liked it, too. She sat down beside, him, took his hand, and began to sing softly.

She was surprised at how comforting the old hymn was to her now. Joe stirred slightly as she sang, and her hymn became a prayer that her son's life would be spared.

For nearly three weeks Lilly helped Joe cling to life. She stayed constantly at his side, reading to him, singing for him, encouraging him when he wanted to give up. After the first week he was conscious more often, but his pain was close to unbearable, and Lilly wished there was some way she could take his suffering upon herself and free him of it.

She hoped the surgeon from San Francisco would arrive soon. Joe had to be kept as still as possible because of the dangerous location of the bullet. It had torn through his insides and lodged near his spine. The doctor claimed the inner damage would heal, but Joe would never rise and walk again if the bullet was not removed. He was kept sedated with laudanum, the only thing that helped the pain, and he had to be diapered because he could not get out of bed.

Lilly could see him getting thinner, paler. Whiskey and Nettie visited every day, sitting with Joe while Lilly took time to wash and change her clothes. Whiskey and others were so understanding about the truth that Lilly wondered why she hadn't told people a long time ago.

The doctor from San Francisco finally arrived. It took him
two days to determine just how he would go about operating
on Joe. He insisted, against Lilly's strong protests, that he
could not operate with her present. Joe was carefully carried
downstairs to the kitchen table by six men, screaming with
pain all the way. His cries tore at Lilly's heart. He was laid
face down, and the men held several oil lamps overhead so
the doctor would have plenty of light. Joe's screaming finally stopped when the doctor held a heavy dose of ether
over his nose and mouth. Lilly withered into a love seat in
the parlor to wait.

Hours slipped by. Finally, Joe was carried back upstairs,
looking pale as death, his eyes closed, his voice silent.

"The bullet is out," the surgeon told her. "Now, all we can
do is wait. It might be several more hours before he comes
out of the sedative. I'll watch over him with you."

Lilly followed them upstairs. She felt as though she were
in a daze. She helped Joe into bed, remembering the days
when she had tucked him in, told him stories, and sung to
him. If only she could get back those years, do everything
over again, avoid all this pain.

She sat down to wait. The mantel clock downstairs
chimed ten o'clock. So far, her only consolation was that Joe
was at least still alive. The surgeon left for a while, and she
remained, holding Joe's hand. She heard the front door open
and close, but paid little attention to the muffled voices
downstairs. All her senses were zeroed in on Joe. At least
the life-threatening bullet was gone, but whether he would
ever walk again was yet to be seen.

She heard footsteps coming upstairs. The doctor must be
coming back to check on Joe. She rose to greet him, full of
more questions. The door opened. It was not the doctor who
stood there; it was Chase Mitchell.

Lilly just stared. He looked hardly any different from the
way he had looked the day he had left Nauvoo. He was
older, just slightly heavier, but in a manly, muscular way.
There were the same blue eyes, the same handsome face.
His hair was still thick and wavy. His skin was suntanned,
his features still sharp and virile. And she was sure she detected tears in his eyes.

"Hello, Lilly," he said softly.

She closed her eyes, trembling. "My God," she whispered. She should hate him with as much passion as she had once loved him, but in this hour of need, with their son lying between life and death right beside them, she could feel nothing but a strange relief. She felt suddenly dizzy, but just as suddenly, strong hands grasped her arms.

"Some man named Whiskey told me all of it, Lilly, on the way over here. My God, woman, someone should have told me years ago!"

"I . . . I didn't want Joe to know," she squeaked. Chase! He was standing right before her, and all the lost years seemed to vanish. He was here! He had come!

"As God is my witness, Lilly, if I had known, I would have come for you and Joe. I *did* come, but nobody told me about Joe. All they told me was you had married and had a son. I never knew he was *my* son!"

She finally found her voice and some strength, and pulled away from him, afraid to touch him—afraid all the old feelings would come back full force. "Why, Chase? Why did you send me that letter telling me you were never coming back?"

He frowned. "Lilly, I never sent any such letter. And I remember Hiram and Catheryn Guest both telling me you never got any of *my* letters. All I can think of is that maybe my father had something to do with it. He wanted me to stay in the army. He considered you a Mormon, and he hated the Mormons. He must have stopped all my letters. Maybe *he* sent you that letter you got. I don't know of any other explanation. But I swear to you, I never sent any such letter."

She couldn't help the sob that tore through her then. She put her hands over her face, and let out a pitiful groan. "All those wasted years," she said, awful agony evident in her voice. "I loved you so much. I never got over the hurt, and I lived with this awful secret eating at me."

He came closer. "I loved you, too, Lilly. I never once stopped loving you. It was hard for me, too, because I thought you had somehow betrayed my love for you. I've been a lonely man, Lilly. But maybe, somehow, we can pick up the pieces. Joe is our son."

She turned away and he reluctantly let go of her, to look at the young man lying in the bed. Even in his sick, thinning condition, Chase could see the resemblance. "My God," he muttered, moving around to the other side of the bed. He leaned over the boy. "I couldn't quite fully believe it until now, seeing him." He knelt near Joe's head. "Joe?" he spoke up.

Lilly took a handkerchief from her pocket and wiped her eyes, turning to watch father and son with mixed emotions. "He hasn't come out of sedation yet," she told Chase. "We don't know if he'll be able to walk."

Chase shook his head, then put his face down as though praying. "My God, Lilly—he's already grown!" The words came out with such pitiful remorse that Lilly began to believe he really was telling the truth about the past. "What if he dies before I ever even get to know him!"

Lilly realized he was crying. Suddenly, her own worry didn't seem so terrible. At least she had had Joe all these years. Chase Mitchell had had nothing, or so it seemed. She sat down in a chair beside the bed, watching him for several minutes, waiting for him to get control of himself. He rose then, and turned away for a moment.

"You never married?" she asked.

He shook his head. "I, uh, never found a woman I cared that much about." He cleared his throat. "Not like I cared for you." He sighed deeply. "I feel like this thing with Joe and Garth Wheeler is partly my fault. I met Garth in San Francisco. I only casually mentioned you one night. I had no idea that scheming bastard had found you and figured it all out. I'm sorry, Lilly. If I had known, I would have come here and gotten rid of him."

Lilly took hold of Joe's hand. "It isn't your fault—it's mine. If I had told Joe the truth a long time ago, the situation would never have arisen."

He pulled a handkerchief from his vest pocket and wiped his eyes. "That war cost us dearly, Lilly. I never should have left Nauvoo. Never."

"All we can do is what we think is right. We can never be sure where our decisions will lead. I probably should have done more to find out what had happened to you, but I was young and scared and ashamed. I was carrying a baby who needed a father, and I had gotten that letter."

He turned, and she was again struck by how little he had changed. Here he was, Chase Mitchell, the man she had loved with such intense passion, such trust—the first man to make a woman of her, the only man to draw true passion from her soul. She reddened slightly as his blue eyes moved over her, and she suddenly wondered how she looked. She had been through hell, and she was sure it showed.

But to Chase she was as beautiful as ever—more mature, a prettier roundness to her. The captivating eyes were still there. She looked so tired, and circles showed under her eyes, but the old Lilly was still there, and he could see how beautiful she still was. He had seen drawings of her on posters in town, even a few pictures. It seemed everywhere he looked he saw a poster advertising Miss Lilly Brannigan, songbird of Virginia City. He and Whiskey had passed the opera house on their way to Lilly's home, and Whiskey had told him about the huge audiences she drew.

What a long way she had come from the Lilly he had known at Nauvoo. "You've done well, Lilly," he said aloud. "Not just financially, but with the boy, so I'm told. Everybody carries on about what a fine young man he is—how he was going to start a ranch in the valley."

Lilly nodded, turning her eyes back to Joe. "Yes. He worked hard so he could buy the best palominos he could get his hands on. He loves horses. We were going to go to our new home there to spend the rest of the summer. Now..." Her voice broke. He came around to stand behind her, putting big, strong hands on her shoulders.

"He's going to be all right, Lilly. I feel it. Now that we've all found each other, God will make sure this works out right."

Wild emotions rushed through her at the feel of his hands on her. It seemed strange to think this man, who was almost like a stranger to her now, had once been intimate with her, had made her give herself to him in wanton abandon, had drawn such ecstasy from deep inside.

"Let me hold you, Lilly."

She shook her head. "It's too late. Everything has changed."

"Has it? The only thing different is that we're older. None of this was our fault. We loved each other, honestly, completely, with as much passion as we possessed. We have a son who needs us now. I intend to stay and be with him, get to know him, help him recover." He sighed and knelt in front of her to take her hands.

So close! She turned her face away. She was amazed at the emotions he could draw from her after all this time.

"I was wounded, Lilly," he told her, "so badly that it took me months to recover. I lost my hearing, my equilibrium, my ability to walk."

She looked at him in sympathy. "Hiram mentioned you were wounded. I didn't know it was that bad."

"It was very bad. The only thing that kept me going, made me want to live, was the thought of coming back for you."

She closed her eyes. "Oh, Chase," she whispered.

"It's over now. The point is, I know pain and suffering. I want to help Joe through this, if you'll let me."

She nodded. "Of course." She met his eyes then, and in the next moment, her head was on his shoulder and his strong arms were around her. He stood, pulling her up with him, holding her tight against him.

How long had it been since a man had held her this way? How long since she had let someone else be strong? All the pent-up tears and agony vented itself as she wept against his chest.

"I'm here, Lilly," he said softly, "this time forever. We'll help Joe through this together, and then we'll decide about you and me. We'll just have to take one day at a time and not worry about tomorrow." He kissed her hair, remembered the ecstasy of the two days he had spent with her so long ago. "Maybe, after a while, we can find what has been lost all these years," he told her. "I'm willing to try if you are. It might be way too late for me and Joe, but we can try. I have a small fortune of my own. I want to share it with Joe, help him get the ranch started, like any father would do."

"Chase, I don't know if we can just . . . pick up where we left off."

"I'm not talking about picking up where we left off. I'm talking about starting over. We've both had plenty of experience at that, haven't we?"

She wiped her eyes and looked up at him. "Yes . . . I suppose we have."

Their eyes held, and she knew that if it were not for Joe and her worried, tired state, she could fall back into his arms as though she were seventeen again.

Chapter Thirty-three

Joe opened his eyes to see a man with his same blue eyes —a man whose smile was like a reflection of his own.

"Hello, Joe." The man quickly pulled up a chair and leaned closer. "I'm Chase Mitchell."

Joe blinked and stared. "My . . . father?"

The man nodded. "You don't know how happy I am to see you open your eyes. Your mother is sleeping—her first good sleep in a long time. I think I'll just let her, while we get to know each other a little." The man put a hand on his arm. "How do you feel?"

"I don't know. I—" His eyes suddenly widened, and he rolled to his side and vomited. Chase hurried out to get the doctor, then came running back into the room on his heels.

"My God," Joe groaned.

"It's all right, son, it's just the sedative," the doctor told him. He looked at Chase. "It's the ether."

Chase got a pan and some towels and came back to Joe's bedside. "I'm sorry," Joe muttered.

"You don't need to be," Chase told him. "I've been through all of this myself, Joe." He cleaned up the mess while the doctor tended to Joe.

"There's still no fever. That's good," the man told Chase. "You just relax. You're going to be all right. Are you in a lot of pain?"

"Not like before," he answered. "Did you get the bullet out?"

The doctor grinned. "I did." He looked at Chase. "Did you notice that when he leaned over, he bent his legs for support?"

Chase's heart swelled with joy. "I didn't even think about it!"

"Joe, try moving your legs," the doctor told the boy.

Joe wiped at tears of shame for being sick in front of the new father he had just met. He breathed deeply against the pain and managed to wiggle his feet and move his legs slightly.

"Damn, that's a pretty sight!" Chase exclaimed. He helped the doctor roll Joe onto his stomach to examine the incision and change the dressing.

"Everything looks good," the doctor told Chase.

"Does this mean I'll be able to walk?" Joe asked, his voice weak.

The two men carefully turned the boy back over. "It looks that way, son," the doctor answered. "But it will take time. You don't want to do too much at once. There is probably a little nerve damage around the area of the spine where I took out the bullet, but nerves can heal just like muscle. If you take things slowly, you'll be all right." He looked at Chase. "I'll leave you two alone for a while."

The man carried out the soiled towels, and Chase followed him to take a peppermint stick from a stand in the hall. He came back inside and sat down near Joe again. "This should taste good to you. Just suck on it, don't chew it. It will help get rid of that bad taste in your mouth."

Joe took the candy and sucked for several seconds until the bitterness in his mouth went away. He watched Chase the whole time, wondering if this was real, or if he was just dreaming it.

"How did you find us? I was going to come and find you until this happened."

"Your mother sent for me."

"She did? I didn't think she would. She was afraid it would just mean more trouble."

Chase sighed, studying the boy lovingly. "I think maybe your mother has always tried too hard to protect you. She was just afraid of losing you."

"I don't know why. She's still my mother." He grimaced slightly.

"Pain?"

"Some, but it's nothing like before. I'm sorry for getting sick," Joe told Chase.

"I told you, it's all right. I've been through worse, Joe." He stood up and pulled out his shirt. "I want to show you something." He lifted the shirt and pulled down the waist of his pants slightly, showing only part of the scar from his wounds. Joe frowned at the sight. "It looks worse down along my hip and leg," Chase told the boy. He tucked in the shirt. "This wound is the reason I didn't make it back to your mother when I promised, Joe. It happened down in Mexico. I was laid up for months. I think you know the rest. As far as the letter your mother claims she got, she and I have talked about it. My father had a lot of power among the troops I was with, and he didn't want me marrying, especially not what he considered a Mormon woman. The only thing I can figure is that he made sure none of my letters reached Lilly. And the one she did get, he must have written himself."

Joe rubbed at his forehead. "I can't believe a man would do that to his own son."

"If you knew my father, you'd understand." Chase sat back down and took hold of Joe's hand. The boy did not resist the gesture, and as much as Chase grieved for his son's suffering, he realized it at least put the boy in a weakened state that left him more vulnerable, which made the job of winning him over a little easier.

"What upsets me the most, Joe, is I had always promised myself that if I ever had a child of my own, I'd be with him as much as possible, and not neglect him the way I was neglected. Now I find out I have a seventeen-year-old son who's grown up without ever knowing me." His eyes teared. "I'm sorry. It never would have been that way if I had known. I'd like to be as much a part of your life as I can be—help you get your ranch started, at least be a friend. Apparently, your mother did one hell of a job raising you."

Joe felt comforted by the strong hand that held his. He didn't know this man, but he liked him already. "Mother is a strong woman—real determined. She's a real good businesswoman, too. We didn't have anything when we came here. I love her. Would you tell her that?" His eyes began to droop a little. "Tell her it doesn't matter what happened. She just did what she thought was right."

Chase squeezed his hand. "I'll tell her. And you and I have a lot of getting acquainted to do."

Their eyes held, but Joe was struggling to stay awake. "I'm glad you came," he told Chase. "Real glad. I was going to come and find you," he told him again. His eyes closed. "Will you stay and kind of help my mother? She doesn't know it yet, but she needs you. Do you still love her?"

Chase's smile faded, and his chest felt tight. "I think I probably do, Joe," he answered. "But we have a lot of getting acquainted to do, too. We'll all spend some time getting to know each other. The important thing is you—getting you back on your feet."

Chase leaned closer, realizing the boy had fallen back to sleep. He sat there watching him then, holding his hand, which he realized was nearly as big as his own. He closed his eyes against the tears that wanted to come and told himself it was at least better to find him now than never to have known him at all. He reached over and took the peppermint stick from the boy's hand. "I don't really know you yet, but I love you, Joe," he said then, wishing he had thought to say it while the boy was awake.

His eyes teared as he set the candy aside and rose. He tucked the blankets around Joe, then quietly left the room. When he stepped outside the door, he noticed Nettie Abler standing in the hall. He had met the woman when he had first arrived. Her friendship with Lilly surprised him. The woman looked him over as she stepped closer.

"I might have known from Joey's looks that his father would be the handsomest man who ever walked into Virginia City," she told him with a sly grin. "It's really too bad you belong to Lilly."

Chase quickly wiped at his eyes with his fingers. "I'm not so sure that I do."

"Of course you do. And she belongs to you. When you came here, and I saw the look on your face, I knew you weren't the bastard Lilly thought you were. You already love that boy in there as much as if you'd been with him all these years, don't you?"

Chase sniffed, clearing his throat and putting on a smile. "You're right there. He's awake. At least I got to talk to him. He seems like a great kid."

"He is. Lilly did a good job with him. And part of her love for him comes from her love for you. When she told me about you, I could see she hadn't stopped loving you for one second."

Chase ran a hand through his hair. "Well, I wish I could be as sure of that as you are."

"You can be. She's been through a lot, but she's a strong woman."

Chase nodded, looking Nettie over. "Pardon my asking, but how did you and Lilly . . . I mean, you don't seem to have much in common."

Nettie laughed lightly. "You mean how did a prostitute get to be such good friends with a proper woman like Lilly?"

Chase shrugged. "Those are your words, not mine."

Nettie just grinned and shook her head. "Well, I met Lilly the first day she came here. Joey went and stepped in front of a runaway team of horses and I yanked him out of the way—came close to breaking my damned foot in the process. That crazy Lilly went and accused me of saving the boy's life. She's been determined to call me friend ever since. I tried to get away from her, but she just wouldn't leave me alone. She insisted it didn't matter what I did for a living."

Chase read the affection beneath the words, and Nettie's eyes seemed to tear.

"She's one nice lady, Mr. Mitchell." She stepped closer and touched his arm. "Don't you let her slip away from you again. If you do, I'll sic the whole town of Virginia City on you, and you wouldn't like that."

"From what I hear happened to Garth Wheeler, I suppose you're right." He looked somberly at her.

"You say the boy is awake? Talked?"

Chase nodded.

"Good." Nettie turned away, trying to hide more tears. "I need some brandy or something. I'm going downstairs."

She quickly hurried down the stairs, and Chase watched after her a moment before walking to the doorway of Lilly's room. He opened the door and peeked inside, watching her sleep. *I still love you, Lilly Brannigan*, he thought. He wanted to grab her up and shout it to her, but she seemed so delicate now, still so afraid and unsure. It was too soon. First, they had to get Joe well.

Joe took his first few weak steps after five days, and every day thereafter he walked a little more. When he was in bed his mother or his father was at his side every waking moment. Lilly read and sang to him. Chase told him war stories, as well as stories about the gold rush in California, and what it was like when he discovered gold himself for the first time.

In the evenings after Joe fell asleep, Chase and Lilly sat up late talking, each of them feeling the old attraction, the powerful urges that had once made them forbidden lovers. But Lilly was afraid to care that much again, and Chase was afraid to move too quickly. She was a different woman from the Lilly he had known back in Nauvoo. She was more independent, more determined. She didn't need him in the same way she had needed him then. Now, she needed the love and support of the man she had gone so long without—needed to be a woman in the fullest sense.

It wasn't until six weeks after Chase's arrival that Lilly really felt like her old self again. With her confidence that Joe would get well came the ability to give more thought to Chase and the reality of his presence—the reality of the love she still held in her heart for him. But even then she was desperately afraid to make the first move. Deeper passions were stirred to life when one night, as they sat in front of the fireplace talking again, Chase joked about Nettie—how much he liked her, in spite of what she was. Lilly wondered how many women like Nettie Chase had been with during their years apart. It only then occurred to her that a man had needs, and there were always women willing to fill those needs, especially when the man looked like Chase Mitchell. It stirred a surprising jealousy in Lilly's soul, and she actually reddened as she looked back down at her knitting.

"Nettie always knows just the right things to say around men," she said almost sarcastically. "I'm sure you find her most amusing."

The moment she said the words, she regretted them. She realized that she not only had allowed ill feelings toward Nettie because of Chase, but had given away her jealousy.

Chase lit a pipe and grinned after puffing it a moment. He picked up on Lilly's words, seeing a pathway to what he really wanted to discuss.

"Lilly, I said I never found love again," he told her. "But a man has needs that can't go neglected forever."

She kept knitting nervously. "Well, I—it's really none of my business, is it? It really doesn't matter now, one way or another. I'm sorry I said anything at all. I feel like a fool and a traitor. Nettie is my best friend. She wouldn't touch you with a ten-foot pole as long as she knew I didn't want her to."

Chase leaned forward. "Is that what you're saying—that you don't want her to?"

Lilly stiffened, sitting up straighter. "No. I mean I . . . I don't know. Please don't do this, Chase."

She kept her eyes averted as Chase puffed the pipe again. "Why not? It's time to talk about it, don't you think? Nettie said that for a time you were actually considering marrying Garth Wheeler. You want to tell me why? You surely couldn't have loved a man like that."

She kept looking at her lap. "I don't know. I just . . . the thought crossed my mind, that's all. But there was something about him I didn't like. I don't think I ever would have gone through with it. I've learned to like my independence. I've done just fine on my own. I don't really need a man to survive."

"No. You probably never have. But there are other needs, Lilly—needs that money can't fulfill. I tried buying it with prostitutes, but it didn't work. I had one specific need that no woman could do anything about."

She stared at her knitting needles, afraid to look into those blue eyes. He had avoided the subject so far, and she almost dreaded this moment. Yet, she realized, she had also wanted it.

"I needed that special kind of love you and I had, Lilly. I needed to be with a woman who could feed every emotion, not just the physical need. A woman who really cared, who loved me totally, the way I loved her."

"Chase, don't."

"Why not? Joe's getting better, Lilly. In a few more weeks we can go to the valley. You and I can't keep living together like this without making some decisions. I want to be near Joe, and we both know what Joe would like to see happen. I want to see it happen, too."

Her cheeks felt hot, and she trembled with indecision. The old hurt had never really left her. She rose and walked away from him.

Chase studied her beautiful form beneath the soft brown taffeta dress she wore. She was even more enticing than she had been at seventeen. He set the pipe aside and stood up. "I want to get married, Lilly. I want to do what we should have done all those years ago. Maybe you think it's too late, but I don't. You're still young enough to have at least one more child—a child I could know and be with from birth."

She shook her head. "It isn't fair to Zeb. I was such a poor wife to him."

"Zeb! The man has been dead for seven years! Even so, do you think he would want you to be as lonely and unhappy as I know you've been all these years? He would *want* you to be a real woman again. He would want you to be with the man you've always loved."

She turned to face him. "Loved? For a long time I hated you. You can't just . . . just come back and pick up where we left off."

"I told you, we aren't doing that. We're just starting over. I've seen you again, and I've fallen in love all over again. I don't need your money, Lilly. I have plenty of my own. And we could always make an arrangement where I could work at the ranch, be with Joe all I wanted. So I have absolutely no other reason for wanting to marry you except that I love you and want to be with you—the way it should have been in the first place. I still want you the same way I did back in Nauvoo. And don't tell me there was a time when you truly hated me. You never stopped loving me any more than I stopped loving you. Keep looking me straight in the eyes and tell me I'm wrong."

She stared at him, suddenly feeling awkward. She wanted desperately to tell him she never wanted to love that way again, but in the next moment he had hold of her arms. He was so close now, so virile, so much the Chase she had loved with such passion.

"Go ahead, Lilly. Tell me you don't love me anymore— that you don't think you could ever love me that way again."

Suddenly the tears came. "I'm . . . afraid," she managed to say.

"There is nothing to be afraid of anymore. I'm here to stay, and this time, nothing can make me leave you, Lilly."

How she wanted to believe him! He came closer, and in the next moment his mouth covered hers. A flood of pent-up needs surged through her like mighty ocean waves as her salty tears mixed with their kiss, and his strong arms came around her in the embrace she remembered so well. Her sobs turned to whimpers of need as his tongue found its way between her lips and his own soft groans of desire told her nothing had changed. Nothing!

She felt herself being lifted, and she knew that no matter what else happened, both of them needed this moment. This desire had hung there between them since the day he had arrived. It was unspoken, yet each had seen it in the other's eyes.

She hugged him around the neck, breathing in his manly scent as he carried her up the stairs to her room. Desperate fear mixed with desperate need. From that moment on she was hardly aware of the time or the room or all her reasons for not caring again. There was only Chase Mitchell, laying her back on the bed, invading her mouth, his strong hands touching her body in ways she had not been touched in years. As much as she loved and respected Zeb's memory, he had never made her feel the way she felt at this moment —totally wanton, her needs almost desperate.

"God, I love you, Lilly," Chase groaned. "I never, never stopped loving you."

Her clothes were coming off as if by magic, and somewhere between kisses and tears and whispered words of love and apology his did, too. A lamp by the bed remained lit, and she saw the ugly scars at his side and on his leg. He had told her the truth about his injuries. Poor Chase—lying near death and thinking he would one day come back and marry her. Fate could be so cruel.

His lips moved to her neck, and she cried out when they trailed farther down and found her taut nipple. This was the only man who had ever made love to her entire body. This was the man to whom she had always belonged. This man had been her first.

Both were too eager, too full of old memories and old needs to prolong the inevitable. In moments he was pushing himself inside of her, making her gasp with ecstasy and near pain. It had been a long time since she had experienced anything like this, and even longer since she had done this with as much desire as her partner. He groaned her name over and over as his lips found her mouth, her cheek, her neck, her eyes. The feel of his damp skin against her own, of her bare breasts rubbing against his chest, was ecstasy. She was not the young, inexperienced girl he had taken in that old cabin along the river. She was a woman, and she understood so much better now the real meaning of love and sacrifice, of sexual fulfillment.

They moved in a gentle rhythm, their fiery needs voiced in groans and gasps and exchanged words of love. He moved his hands down under her hips and pushed deep, surging into her in wavelike motions that made her arch up to him with equal need. It seemed as though a fire burned deep in her belly that only Chase Mitchell could quench. She neither understood nor condoned falling under his spell again. She only knew she had been too long denied, and that she could no more control this feeling than she could control her heartbeats.

His body shuddered as his life poured into her. After a moment he groaned her name, pulling her close, kissing her hair. "I love you, Lilly Brannigan. Nothing you tell me can change that, and nothing will ever make me leave you again."

"Oh, God, Chase, I love you, too. I always loved you."

He kept kissing her eyes. He was still inside of her, and already he was moving again, his desire returning almost instantly, just as it had that first time he took her.

"I don't think I'll ever be able to get enough of you," he moaned. He smothered her with hot kisses, and she lay in glorious abandon, wanting to enjoy him again. She reached up and grasped the bedrails as the sweet, rhythmic intercourse started all over again. This time he moved more slowly, more deliberately, stretching out the ecstasy for her. She knew his blue eyes were drinking in the sight of her full breasts, her flat belly, her slender thighs, parted for him. She gave herself with the same sweet abandon she had felt eighteen years ago, and suddenly, it seemed it had been only yesterday.

She arched up to him, feeling the beautiful climax building. She cried out with the glory of it, then reached up and kissed him wildly, feeling totally out of control of her emotions.

His powerful arms came around her, and he pushed deep and hard.

"Lilly, my poor Lilly," he whispered.

She was lost beneath him. He moved in circular motions that made her cry out with the terrible ecstasy of it. Chase! He was here, making love to her! It was like some kind of dream. But it was not. No dream was this real, this wonderful.

He buried his face into the pillow beside her and groaning her name as again his life spilled into her, and already Lilly found herself hoping he was right—that it was not too late to have one more child, one they could share.

For several minutes they both lay there, spent, wilted,

their love as strong and demanding as it had been all those years ago.

He finally pulled himself away from her, and Lilly nestled against him, feeling as though someone had just lifted a huge weight off her shoulders. The final fear had been conquered. She could love again, and it felt wonderful.

He kissed her hair. "You can do whatever you want, Lilly. I'll not take away that independence. We'll work together building the ranch, and you can sing at the opera house all you want, whenever you're ready."

She kissed his chest. "It doesn't seem so important anymore. I always thought if I could sing for an audience like that, I would be happy. But I've never been truly happy since the day I watched you go down the river on that boat. A part of me died then. You just brought me fully to life again." She moved back a little to look him in the eyes. "Don't ever leave, Chase—not for anything."

"I won't." His eyes glittered with love. "I have some things to take care of in San Francisco, but I'll take you with me when I go. You should see it, Lilly—you'll love it. As soon as Joe is well enough to be on his own, we'll go there. We'll take Joe to the valley first, and go on from there."

Her eyes teared. "I would like to see it, very much."

"They have a grand opera house. I'll take you there."

"Oh, I'd love that!"

He kissed her lightly. "Who knows? Maybe, in a couple of years, we can get you a singing engagement there. I wasn't surprised to find that your voice was famous in Virginia City."

She smiled through tears. "It's not so important anymore. And whether or not I sing here again, or in San Francisco, depends on . . . on whether or not I'm taking care of a new baby by then."

He grinned. "That's entirely possible."

He moved on top of her again, and the talking ceased.

The huge, two-story mansion in the wild valley waited for its new owners to come and fill it with warmth and love. On the front lawn, a fountain flowed with foaming white water that bubbled cheerfully, and fenced green pastures waited to be filled with palominos. All around, the land spread out in greens and browns and yellows, and the horizon was graced with mountains in every direction, their granite peaks sheltering the valley like great watchdogs.

Chase drove the buggy a little farther down the foothill that overlooked the ranch. "It's beautiful, Lilly, just like it was the day I came here to see you," Chase told her. "Did I ever tell you that? I came close to riding down here and finding out the truth right then and there."

Lilly thought about the lone rider on the distant hill, and it gave her chills to think how close he had been.

"I'm going on ahead," Joe told them. He rode off on his own palomino while Chase and Lilly watched from the buggy. Lilly's heart ached for her son when she watched him ride straight to the old house, more interested in his place of childhood than in the new mansion. He headed then for the hill under the ponderosa pine and dismounted. Lilly watched him stand beside Zeb's grave.

"He still misses Zeb terribly," she told Chase.

"I understand." Chase drove the buggy closer to the new house, amazed at what Lilly had accomplished on her own. "It's beautiful, Lilly."

She sighed. "Yes. But it wouldn't have meant nearly as much if I had come here without you. And if I had come without Joe—"

A lump rose in her throat, and he moved an arm around her shoulders. "He's going to be all right, Lilly. Look at him—riding a horse. I admit he still walks a little crooked, but he'll improve in time. He gets better every day. Let's go have a look at our new home."

Lilly looked down at the ring on her hand as he drove the buggy to the front steps. She was really his wife—really Mrs. Charles Mitchell—the way it should have been all those years ago.

"Do you think someday we could visit Salt Lake, Chase?" she asked. "I want to see the look on Hiram's face when he sees us together."

He grinned. "Sure—maybe we can go next spring. I wouldn't mind seeing old Hiram myself. And I hear Salt Lake is quite a city now."

"The whole West is growing. When Zeb and I got to Utah, Salt Lake was nothing but a few adobe houses. Virginia City didn't even exist."

"And just think—the little girl from Scotland has been a part of settling the West. You're one hell of a woman, Lilly."

She thought about poor Zeb. "I'm not so sure of that. I've just done the best I knew how." She blinked back tears. "I wish Laura Williams had lived to see all this—and to see us together again. I still miss her sometimes."

He took her hand. "You've got to concentrate on the future, Lilly. You've lived with the past for too many years. Let go of it."

She leaned against him, relishing the feel of his strong arm around her. He had come back, this time forever. Nothing would ever take him from her again, and Joe was alive and getting better. Chase was right. It was time to put the past behind her.

She turned and drank in the sight of her new home, built with money she had earned on her own. She had chosen to stay here, and she had survived. She could hear the words echoing through the valley:

We'll find the place which God for us prepared,
Far away in the West . . .

I sincerely hope you have enjoyed my story. For information about other books I have written, and publication dates for future books, feel free to write me at 6013-A North Road, Coloma, MI 49038. I will send you a newsletter and a bookmark. *Be sure to include a self-addressed, stamped envelope.* Thank you.

GET LOVESTRUCK!

AND GET STRIKING ROMANCES FROM POPULAR LIBRARY'S BELOVED AUTHORS

Watch for these exciting romances in the months to come:

May 1989
THIS TIME FOREVER by F. Rosanne Bittner
LOVE'S MIRACLES by Sandra Lee Smith

June 1989
LOVE'S OWN CROWN by Laurie Grant
FAIR GAME by Doreen Owens Malek

July 1989
SHIELD'S LADY by Amanda Glass
BLAZE OF PASSION by Lisa Ann Verge

August 1989
BODY AND SOUL by Sherryl Woods
PROMISE OF SUMMER by Louisa Rawlings

September 1989
STAR STRUCK by Ann Miller
HIDDEN FIRE by Phyllis Herrm

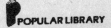